PRISONER OF MIDNIGHT

A Selection of Recent Titles by Barbara Hambly
from Severn House

The James Asher Vampire Novels

BLOOD MAIDENS
THE MAGISTRATES OF HELL
THE KINDRED OF DARKNESS
DARKNESS ON HIS BONES
PALE GUARDIAN
PRISONER OF MIDNIGHT

The Benjamin January Series

DEAD AND BURIED
THE SHIRT ON HIS BACK
RAN AWAY
GOOD MAN FRIDAY
CRIMSON ANGEL
DRINKING GOURD
MURDER IN JULY
COLD BAYOU

PRISONER OF MIDNIGHT

Barbara Hambly

This first world edition published 2019
in Great Britain and the USA by
SEVERN HOUSE PUBLISHERS LTD of
Eardley House, 4 Uxbridge Street, London W8 7SY.
Trade paperback edition first published
in Great Britain and the USA 2019 by
SEVERN HOUSE PUBLISHERS LTD.

British Library Cataloguing in Publication Data
A CIP catalogue record for this title is available from the British Library.

ISBN-13: 978-0-7278-8860-0 (cased)
ISBN-13: 978-1-84751-986-3 (trade paper)
ISBN-13: 978-1-4483-0198-0 (e-book)

All Severn House titles are printed on acid-free paper.

Severn House Publishers support the Forest Stewardship Council™ [FSC™],
the leading international forest certification organisation.
All our titles that are printed on FSC certified paper carry the FSC logo.

Typeset by Palimpsest Book Production Ltd.,
Falkirk, Stirlingshire, Scotland.
Printed and bound in Great Britain by
TJ International, Padstow, Cornwall.

For Laurel

ONE

'**A** letter for M'sieu.' The elderly clerk at the front desk of the Hotel St-Seurin looked up from James Asher's signature in the register; Asher felt a sinking in his heart. Had he been a man inclined to panic, he would have done so. But he only thought, *Something's happened.*
Damn it.

> March 12, 1917
> Mountjoy House
> Grosvenor Street
> London
>
> Jamie,
> Forgive me. I do not know what is best to do. If the course I have taken – choosing not to meet you in Paris Wednesday – means that our parting a year ago was to be our last meeting, our last parting . . . I truly do not know what to do. Or what you would have me do.
> I cannot turn away from this. Not because of the War, but because of the greater shadow of the Undead, an unspeakable shadow that could cover the earth.
> When we parted from Don Simon Ysidro nearly two years ago, I told him never to come near me again, a request which I believe he has honorably respected. When I have dreamed of him since then – as you know I have – it has always felt NORMAL: the way I dream sometimes about Mother, or about Aunt Faith's horrid cats, or about you. Just a dream about a person who is (or was) a part of my life.
> On the three occasions, prior to my parting from him, on which Don Simon has entered – or manipulated – my dreams, I've been clearly aware of the difference. I think you once mentioned that you also know when

your dreams are being tampered with by the Undead. Sunday's dream was like neither of those.

Don Simon is a prisoner, somewhere. The dreams that I have had were unclear – uncharacteristically unclear – but I sense, I KNOW, that he is being held captive, in terrible and continuous pain. If he were not, he would not have asked for my help – as he did, as he is. His voice, crying out of darkness, was broken up, like fragments of a torn manuscript. The only words that were clear were, 'City of Gold'.

The American liner SS *City of Gold* leaves Southampton on Wednesday, for New York.

Jamie, I don't know what's going on. But at the shipping office today (you can see that I'm at Aunt Louise's town house) I encountered Captain John Palfrey, whom (if you remember) Don Simon manipulated into being his dogsbody at the Front in the first year of the War (and apparently ever since). Captain Palfrey – still unshakably convinced that Don Simon is a top-secret British agent rather than a vampire – says that he had the same 'psychical' (as he terms them) dreams last night: dreams of captivity, of desperation, of unbearable pain . . . and of the name City of Gold. He believes that 'Colonel Simon' has been taken prisoner by German agents and is for some reason being transported to the United States.

You know more about German agents than I do, but it sounded like a very inefficient procedure to me. Yet I remember how representatives of the British government have tried to get hold of a vampire to use for their own purposes of warfare. Now that people are saying that America is going to enter the War, I wouldn't put it past the Americans to attempt the same sort of thing, if they could but find some means of force or coercion.

Maybe I would have hesitated, or thought about it longer, had not my Aunt Louise been also preparing to sail on the *City of Gold*. She contends that German submarines would never DARE attack an American ship

'Oh, wouldn't they just?' Asher muttered through his teeth, and wondered what newspapers Aunt Louise had or hadn't been reading lately.

and has repeatedly asked me to join her. Conditions here in Britain are very bad, as I'm sure you know, shocking prices and queues going down the street and around the corner, and food crops being grown in all the public parks and allotments. Aunt Louise says that the government will soon be rationing food

Asher reflected that if Aunt Louise thought pleas to voluntarily cut down consumption of meat and sugar were bad in Britain, she should visit Germany, where bread was being made up from sawdust and sausage meat from rat carcasses and worse. In the cold pine forests of East Prussia, where for nearly a year he had been impersonating a German officer named von Rabewasser, he had seen men cook and eat the leather of their boots . . . and the bodies of the dead.

and that this is no place for a civilized person to live, and certainly no place to condemn a small child to grow up. She is urging me ('commanding' is probably a better word) that I sail with her and bring Miranda, 'To get her out of this dreadful War.' She has, as you doubtless recall, always been against my going off to the Front or in fact becoming a medical doctor at all. (She still blames you for that.)

Dread smote Asher like an arrow beneath the breastbone at that, and his hand shook as he turned the paper over. He was well aware that U-boat captains were rewarded according to the tonnage of Allied shipping destroyed, not by what direction those ships were headed in. Every German Asher had talked to, from private soldiers to General von Falkenhayn himself, spoke as if the US were already officially one of the Allies. This wasn't surprising, since over the course of the war the United States had loaned Britain (and France and Belgium)

billions of dollars and was selling far more foodstuffs and
weapons to Britain than it was to Germany. *If she convinces
Lydia to take Miranda with them . . .*

His eye fleeted down his wife's spidery scrawl . . .

> She may in fact be right – one doesn't know what's
> going to happen here – and I have no idea what to do for
> the best. I took the train down from Oxford this morning
> and left Miranda at Peasehall Manor with Aunt Lavinnia
> (for which Aunt Louise has been berating me as a 'bad
> mother' ever since I arrived at her door – not that she has
> ever been a mother herself). Poor Miranda will miss me
> terribly, but I WILL NOT put her in even the smallest
> possibility of danger from submarines, even imaginary
> ones, as Aunt Louise insists that they are.

Asher gritted his teeth again, conscious of a strong desire to
slap Lydia's aunt.

> I confess this is one reason I'm going down to
> Southampton tomorrow – to escape her constant harping
> on the subject of Lavinnia's unfitness to look after a child.
> I'm also going to see if I can get a look at the baggage
> before it's loaded, though I don't hold much hope that the
> kidnappers would be that careless with their prisoner.
> Captain Palfrey goes with me. I have lent him the money
> to purchase a First Class berth (he was going to travel
> Second, all he could afford). I may need to call on his help
> and I don't think Second Class passengers are permitted
> in the First Class areas of the ship. (The *City of Gold* is
> horrifyingly luxurious in an American fashion, all frosted-
> glass and black lacquer.) It is a great comfort to me to
> know that I'm not entirely without help in this awful matter.
> I don't know what else to say. We sail on Wednesday
> at two. Jamie, I am sorry – I am so very sorry. I cared for
> Don Simon. I am ashamed to say that I care for him still,
> though I know what he is. Although he cannot help what
> he is, I pity him (affronted as he would be to hear me say
> so!). But I swear to you, to keep him from becoming a

slave or a tool of whoever it is who has taken him prisoner – whoever it is who has found a way of coercing the obedience of vampires – I will kill him. As I know you would – as I know I must. I have packed the appropriate impedimenta: garlic blossoms, aconite, silver bullets, a hawthorn stake, and surgical knives. (I read up in your notes, as to what I should need.) I am still trying to devise a convincing explanation to the ship's authorities (and to Aunt Louise) should it be discovered that I have murdered a fellow passenger. (If he is a prisoner I am not sure that he would qualify as a stowaway.)

I wanted so much to see you – to see for myself that you are well. After a year of letters I would give anything to be able to talk to you, even for five minutes, even about nothing, about the weather or the food here . . . Anything, just to hear your voice. You'll be back in the War before I return from America. I feel as if I'm cutting myself adrift from all that I know and care for, walking alone into the dark. I don't even know where I'll be able to write to you now. If you can, wire me at General Delivery in New York City, to at least tell me that you got this. To at least tell me that you forgive me.

Please forgive me.

I love you to the end of my days.

L

He felt cold to the heart, as if he were sickening for fever, as he folded the paper. *Today.* His eyes went to the clock above the desk.

An hour from now, she would be gone.

Maybe forever.

He became aware of the clerk regarding him worriedly. Asher had heard himself described by Americans as possessing a 'poker face', but guessed that in the past three years, that white-haired old man on the other side of the counter had seen thousands of men read letters, their expressions unchanging as their worlds collapsed into irretrievable ruin around their ears. God knew, he'd seen it enough times himself.

He took a deep breath and tucked the letter into the pocket of his uniform greatcoat. 'Thank you, M'sieu.'

The old man handed him his key. 'Is there anything I can do for M'sieu?' A requisite query about extra towels and hot water, always supposing the hotel's coal ration were not already spent. But the clerk spoke so quietly Asher knew that wasn't what he was asking.

'Thank you, no, M'sieu.'

As he climbed the stairs – the St-Seurin had a lift of sorts, but it was shut up and Asher guessed its operator was either at the Front or long dead in Flanders mud – Asher was aware of the man's pitying glance upon his back.

Part of him was cursing by every god of the ancient underworld, shouting impotently that after a year of bone-breaking cold and abyssal loneliness – of watching men he knew die (he had long since ceased to think of the troops among whom he operated as 'the enemy', though he knew they'd kill him if they learned who he really was) in some of the most senseless military actions he had ever heard of – he wouldn't see Lydia after all. Wouldn't touch her hand, hear her voice, lie in her arms for the six nights permitted him before he had to return to Hell.

Part of him stood aghast at the thought of what she was walking into (*Damn you to Hell, Don Simon! Damn you to Hell, Aunt Louise . . .*). Adrift, as she said, from everything she knew and cared for; setting forth to kill a man whom Asher knew quite well that she loved.

Part of him knew she was probably right.

And if any person had come up with a way of enslaving and reliably controlling a vampire, that person could peddle the method – and the luckless vampire himself – for whatever figure he cared to name. Any government in the world – not to speak of a hundred private buyers, the owners of mines and factories eager to murder strikers and socialists with impunity – would fall over itself to acquire an unseen assassin, who could tamper with the perceptions of victims or witnesses, then vanish in a mist of illusion. He thought of American businessmen he'd met. Most of them made Attila the Hun look like a Methodist missionary.

The result, to the people of the world, to every one of their descendants, would be, as Lydia had said, unspeakable.

He unlocked the door of his allotted room, stepped in swiftly and shut it behind him. With pistol in hand (*no sense taking chances . . .*) he made a quick inspection of the tiny chamber, the armoire, and under the bed. For seventeen years – he had been recruited while still up at Oxford – he had served the Queen in the endless shadow war of poking into secrets, lining up local chiefs and villages in support of Britain's goals, making maps, reading correspondence that the *Abwehr* and the Austrian *Evidenzbureau* would really rather he didn't . . .

And for another ten, he had worked with, against, and among the vampires, in shadows deeper still. His throat and forearms were tracked with bite-scars, and even among the cold pine forests of the Eastern Front he wore silver chains wrapped around his neck and wrists. He never entered a room without ascertaining who else, if anyone, was in it, and identifying immediately at least two ways out.

He turned the key, put the threadbare rag of the bedside rug on the end of the bed – the room was freezing cold and he had no intention of taking off his boots – and lay down, still wrapped in his greatcoat, to consider the ceiling in the gray chill of the afternoon light.

Should I feel horrified that it's true, or relieved that I'm not going mad?

For he had not been in the least surprised by Lydia's letter.

The dream had been three nights ago. That last night that he'd spent in the frozen darkness of those endless forests, before setting forth, ostensibly for Berlin, but actually for the point at which he would slip across the lines. Dreams of suffocation and pain. Of agony as if the skin were being eaten from his living bones. Dreams of having been buried alive, with the gnawing ghosts of every person whose life he had taken sealed with him in the tomb. Exhaustion that broke the mind almost to the point of madness, coupled with utter, naked terror. The knowledge that whatever was coming, it was going to be worse than this present hell.

A part of him knew the dream concerned Don Simon Ysidro. The pale-haired Spanish vampire who had saved his life – who had saved Lydia's life, and Miranda's. The vampire he had sworn to kill. (*Of course you have*, Ysidro had replied calmly to Asher's declaration of this intention. *And I will endeavor not to cross your path . . .*)

It was Ysidro's whispery voice – shattered with screaming – that he'd heard say the words, 'City of Gold'.

He'd waked to bone-breaking cold, for the snow still lay over the Pripet Marshlands, and the stink of latrines and corpses. To the shuffling of Dissel – his orderly – carrying wood to the little tin stove in his hut. He'd told himself, *Only a dream.* A dream born of living eye-deep in this place that was devouring him. A dream of Hell, well-deserved by a man whose machinations would very likely condemn to hideous death the men he'd been living near for months, brave men fighting in a pointless, senseless war. Men who trusted him . . .

Once before, he'd quit the Foreign Office, sickened by the man he had to be in order to serve Queen and Country. In the hour of his country's need he'd committed himself to such service again, and had found the task not one whit less dirty, ruthless, and cold than it had been back in 1901. His parson father would have assured him that he was doing the Lord's work at the Front, but enough remained of his rectory upbringing to make him ask himself if that dream – that abyss of pain and hopelessness, that sense of being shut away utterly from even the off-chance that God would hear his screams – was himself crying out.

Good to know that it wasn't. The thought brought no comfort. He listened to the grumble of military transports in the Rue St. Martin, far below his windows, and the curious silence of this gray wartime Paris. His eyes traced the cracks in the plaster ceiling, as if planning a route along them.

A route that he knew he'd have to follow, once full darkness fell. Though no German bombs had dropped for a year and a half and blackout was no longer in force, electricity was in such short supply that the whole district (including the hotel) would be black as pitch. *At least nobody's going to stop me for walking around with a lantern . . .*

He stopped that thought, chilled. Knowing where his mind was going.

His own fear surprised him, after what he'd been through in the past two years.

The *City of Gold* sailed at two. By Lydia's description it was grand enough to possess a fairly powerful wireless – strong enough to receive signals from a military base like the one at Brest, even when hundreds of miles out to sea. He wondered if the military credentials with which the Foreign Office had so obligingly supplied him would serve to get him on one of the overcrowded military trains.

To hold a vampire prisoner on shipboard means a coffin lined with enough silver to keep him powerless. That means serious amounts of money. Either a government, or some extremely wealthy man. In either case, they'll have hired help.

In either case, they'd have the resources to outflank and overpower Lydia the moment they became aware that she was asking questions. Captain Palfrey, whom Asher had met at the Front two years previously, was a well-meaning head-breaker who would be lucky if he lasted twenty-four hours.

Her only defense will be to not ask questions. The spy he had been knew this instinctively. *She cannot afford to be perceived as a threat. She has to know beforehand where to look, and who to watch out for while she does it.*

Damn it. Asher felt almost physically sick with weariness at what he knew he had to do that night. It would be a long way to Rue de Passy in the bitter cold of the unlit streets, for the Metro had long ago ceased to run.

To say nothing of those he would be seeking.

The Undead. Those who hunted the night.

Damn it, damn it, damn it.

TWO

I will never forgive myself.

Dr Lydia Asher craned her head over the general level of the crowd in the ticketing salon, to view the gangplank, and the towering black wall of steel, in the chilly gray of the spring afternoon.

She wouldn't let herself finish the thought, but only whispered in her heart, 'Oh, Jamie . . .'

How could I do this to him?

How could I do this to poor Miranda?

And she told herself – in the voice of the long-departed Nanna who had ruled the nursery at Willoughby Close with a rod of ice and steel – *Don't cry.*

Crying wouldn't do any good anyway.

Jamie in the harsh lights and freezing cold of the Gare de l'Est, just after Christmas of 1915. Wrapped in his military greatcoat and a couple of scarves, shivering in spite of it. After nine months of Listening Post work – sitting in a German uniform in the holding areas with prisoners of war, piecing together information about the High Command's plans and conditions in Germany itself – he was going behind enemy lines on the Eastern Front. They'd had three days together in Paris. He'd said, *There won't be a day that you won't be in my thoughts.*

Miranda on the front steps of Peasehall Manor the day before yesterday, with Aunt Lavinnia's ancient chauffeur waiting in the car to take Lydia to catch the train for London. A thin, little, red-haired, marsh-fairy, who looked as if the first wind would carry her away, her golden-haired doll in her arms. *Will you be fighting the Germans again?* she'd asked. Not blood-thirstiness in her eye, but craving for adventure and daring deeds. And Lydia, aware that knowledge of her mother's heroism was what made these partings bearable to the little girl, had replied, *I will . . .*

To Aunt Lavinnia's affronted shock.

I can't let Don Simon be enslaved. Whoever has taken him must *be stopped.*

The corollary to that – *and Simon must be killed* – was almost more than she could bear.

She looked around her at the well-dressed, well-mannered, yammering crowd.

Some of her fellow passengers she'd observed at three o'clock that morning – not of course the respectable ones – when she and Captain Palfrey had sneaked to the pier to watch the loading of the heavy luggage. She hadn't had much hope that she'd glimpse a trunk being carried aboard that was large enough to contain the body of a small, slender man. (*Lined with silver mesh*? she'd thought. *To weaken him and keep him helpless*?) But she couldn't not look.

They'd stationed themselves between two warehouses, across the pier from what was politely referred to as the Third Class terminal – a long shed where the emigrants waited all night to go aboard.

She'd had no luck with suspicious luggage, though there'd been some hefty impedimenta on the little electric trolleys which had passed them. Those wealthy enough to be traveling First Class on the *City of Gold* saw no reason not to take along different frocks for each dinner in the First Class dining salon, for each evening of dancing in the First Class lounge, and a wide variety of walking suits for leisurely strolls along the First Class Promenade. Not to mention shoes to match, and hats, and coats of fur or camel hair; their own pillows (though the literature provided by the American Shipping Line assured its passengers that everything was new, immaculate, and of the finest materials – 'Of course that's what they'd *tell* us,' had sniffed Aunt Louise); their own tea- and coffee-sets for entertaining in their cabins; their own books, game-counters, musical instruments, ornaments. Aunt Louise certainly had – and, Lydia had to admit shame-facedly, she herself was guilty as well. (Not stationery, of course. 'What's the point of traveling on a first-class liner,' said Aunt Louise, 'if one can't send out notes on its letterhead?')

Through the windows of the Third Class terminal she had seen them by the harsh glare of bare electric bulbs: those who had crossed half of Europe to achieve passage on an American ship, bound for America. When the door opened to admit more travelers (or, despite the cold of the night, fresh air) she had heard their voices: Italian and Belgian French, Russian and Yiddish and several of those incomprehensible Middle European languages that were Jamie's specialty, Czech or Polish or Slovene. German, too – families in flight from areas where the borders of the Austrian Empire, Romania, and Russia ran together in a linguistic hodge-podge now soaked in blood. Families in flight from the devastation of the War.

Their thin, frightened faces, their shabby odds and ends of luggage, were as different as possible from those around her now. Even without her glasses ('Take those things off at once!' had commanded Aunt Louise. 'You know better than that!'), Lydia, from long practice and a London 'season' when she had come 'out', could price their clothing at three or four times the cost of the farms out of which those poor people had been shelled by the advancing armies. The sum paid for the hat worn by the woman in front of Aunt Louise – an astonishing confection of dark-green velvet, huge black silk roses, and a stiffened black silk bow easily the size of a Christmas turkey – had probably been more than any of the Third Class women had ever seen. Almost certainly, the woman's two little black French bulldogs, held on leashes by a uniformed maid, had eaten better than any Third Class passenger for every meal of their pampered lives (and would continue to do so on the *City of Gold*).

Lydia now winced inwardly, recollecting how, every time the door of the Third Class waiting shed had opened, she had heard the crying of children. *Hunger*, she'd thought. Thirst, exhaustion, and cold.

The memory took her farther back. Miranda on the steps of Peasehall Manor ('Mrs Marigold cries sometimes,' had said Miranda, of her doll, 'but I don't'). Aunt Louise had raked her over the coals yesterday morning at breakfast, when she'd informed her that she wasn't bringing her daughter to America with her. 'Really, Lydia, you talk all the time of how much you care for the child but I do not consider your actions those of a responsible mother! Leaving her with *Lavinnia*, of all people, who hasn't the strength of character herself to keep her nursery staff up to their work! You've seen how those daughters of hers turned out, slouching like a couple of unstrung bean-plants. I swear they don't even wear corsets!' She'd shaken her head, a tall, commanding woman whose dark-red hair had just begun to fade at the temples. 'In America, the child can be given a decent upbringing, until it's time for her to be sent away to school . . .'

To Lydia's mention of the danger from submarines, Louise had retorted, 'There is no such danger. None at all. It's all been invented by the newspapers. I daresay your poor little girl stands in more danger at Lavinnia's – God knows what farmers are putting in their milk these days! I'm sorry to say that England is *not* the place I would wish to see any child grow up nowadays. Irish Republic indeed! Nothing short of treason. Why, I hear they're even discussing universal suffrage! Slack! Undisciplined!' The middle sister of Lydia's tribe of aunts, and the widow of a diplomat, Louise, Lady Mountjoy had made her home in Paris up until the start of the War and had firm opinions concerning how children should be raised, despite (or because of, Lydia reflected) having none herself.

Finding England, too, unsatisfactory under wartime conditions ('The War *overhangs* everything so! *Nothing* else is talked of and I for one am quite sick of hearing about it . . .') she had taken one of the four Promenade Suites on the *City of Gold*: Ultra-First Class, Lydia mentally termed them. Each suite consisted of two bedrooms, a parlor, a dressing-room, a private bathroom, a tiny kitchen, and two windowless, closet-like inner cells for servants: one's *other* servants had accommodation suitable for their status down on C Deck immediately below. (This, Lydia gathered, in addition to a personal cabin steward at one's beck and call.)

Perusal of the American Shipping Line's illustrated literature on the subject of these Promenade Suites had convinced Lydia that whoever had kidnapped Don Simon Ysidro – if her dreams, and Captain Palfrey's dreams, had not been entirely hallucinatory – they were most likely to be traveling in another of these extremely expensive Promenade Suites.

The reflection comforted her, as it reduced the scope of her search to manageable proportions.

It would simply be that much more difficult to conceal the coffin – or trunk, probably – of an imprisoned vampire, even in one of the lesser, two-room First Class suites.

For that reason she had tasked Captain Palfrey – who had military credentials – with getting her a list of the other Promenade Suite passengers, and he had come through handsomely. Surreptitiously consulting the paper he had slipped her last night outside the Third Class terminal, she could now, standing meekly among Aunt Louise's immediate entourage, make an educated guess as to who had the other three Promenade Suites.

The diminutive woman in the green velvet hat with the huge black roses, almost certainly. Lydia heard her speak in French to the woman who held the leashes of the little bulldogs, and guessed that this was the Russian Princess Gromyko. (A glance at the womenfolk attached to the other two Ultra-First Class groups convinced Lydia, even without her glasses, that these were Americans.) That being the case, the woman holding the dogs must, by the probable cost of her frock (dark-blue wool challis modestly accented with machine-made lace – *two pounds six at most* . . .) be her secretary-companion Mademoiselle Ossolinska, and the white-bearded, cadaverous gentleman hovering beside her would be her personal physician, Dr Boris Yakunin. Other members of the Gromyko entourage not present included two maids, two footmen, a Persian butler, and a chef.

Those would – like Aunt Louise's butler and maid, and Lydia's own maid Ellen – already be aboard, laying out hairbrushes, nightgowns, negligees, personal tea-urns, dresses and shoes for dinner tonight, plus books and magazines and sheet music, and arranging personal knick-knacks on the sleek black tables.

The two American parties in the other Promenade Suites, according to Palfrey's list, were both millionaires. (*At eight hundred and fifty pounds for the crossing, they would have to be!*) Spenser Cochran, Lydia guessed, was the trim, elderly gentleman looking on with cold disinterest as a sleek-haired young secretary (his nephew, said the list) dealt with the red-blazered representative of the American Shipping Line in charge of paperwork. An angular woman in an expensive (but obviously *not* Parisian) silk gown of rather too emphatic a shade of petunia stood beside him, complaining in a grating drawl about the delay. Her audience was not Cochran, but a handsome, dark-haired man in the modest garb of a professional, streaks of silver at his temples and a medical bag in hand. That would be (another quick glance at Palfrey's notes) Dr Louis Barvell, also a 'personal physician'. They were hemmed about by a cluster of the men whom the list described as 'private detectives', large individuals in rough tweeds and bowler hats, smoking cigars.

And well they should stand guard, reflected Lydia, considering the number of diamonds Mrs Cochran was wearing on her hat, brooch, ears, fingers, wrists, and shoe buckles.

The other American party nearby also included a male secretary and what looked like a female 'companion', which would make the tall, stout, extremely well-tailored gentleman Mr Bradwell Tilcott, of Philadelphia, and the stately gray-haired *grande dame* in eggplant faille (*Worth*, Lydia estimated) his mother. Maids, a footman, a chef and a valet (names appended) had undoubtedly already gone aboard.

The ticket agent made his way respectfully toward Aunt Louise, and Aunt Louise's secretary-cum-companion – a sweet-faced, gray-haired and murderously efficient widow named Mrs Honoria Flasket – intercepted him with their travel papers. One could easily, Lydia guessed as they moved off toward the First Class gangway, transport an unconscious and encoffined vampire aboard unnoticed. All the stewards seemed to be concerned about was whether the papers were in order. Nobody searched or even glanced at their trunks.

With her aunt's attention diverted she sneaked her glasses on again, and scanned the 'cabin luggage' as it crossed the gangway lower down. On another gangway, she recognized faces she'd glimpsed last night outside the Third Class terminal. A golden-haired girl of fifteen taking competent charge not only of three younger siblings but of their heavy-muscled, ox-like mother as well. A tall old hook-nosed Jew, exactly like Shylock in a bad production of *Merchant of Venice* in his rusty black coat and pince-nez, clutching a heavy satchel to his breast with both long arms (*must contain his money*) while two little children clung to his coat-tails. A blonde man whose face bore what were clearly shrapnel-scars, helping an elderly Italian woman and her gaggle of black-clothed daughters. A brown-faced woman shepherding six or eight children of various ages. ('Honestly,' sniffed Aunt Louise behind her, 'I don't see how a woman can keep track of that many children! I'll wager she can't remember all their names.')

Pilgrims setting forth on the last leg of their journey to the Promised Land.

In front of them, Lydia heard the gray-haired dowager bray to her son, 'I *do* trust Alvina will have my bath ready when we get to the suite.' Jamie would have identified the origin of her twangy inflection in moments. '*Heaven* only knows who they'll have put at the Captain's table with us, or what kind of wines they have on board . . .'

And at the Front, Lydia found herself remembering, the surgeons she'd worked with for two and a half years would be making tea for themselves with boiling-hot water tapped from the cooling coils of the machine-guns, if they weren't elbow-deep in dying men because there was an enemy 'push' going on. *That's where I should be.* Guilt closed strangling around her throat. *Doing what I can . . .*

Then she stopped, halfway up the gangway, at the sight of a huge box – nearly eight feet in length and close to a yard wide – being maneuvered with care and profanity up the luggage bridge by four struggling porters. She was too far to see details, except for its size, and groped quickly for her glasses.

If I can't slip away from Aunt Louise and follow it to its destination surely *the whole cabin staff will know where it went. There can't be another like it . . .*

I'll have to ask Ellen. Servants always know everything.

'Come along, Lydia,' said her aunt briskly. Lydia hastily removed her glasses. 'Richard and Isobel –' She named her brother and his wife, Lord and Lady Halfdene – 'are probably already in the suite, to see us off . . . if they haven't perished with boredom, waiting for those tedious ticket officers to finish their paperwork with us out here! I saw them on the boat-train coming down this morning . . .'

Lydia cast a last glance at the enormous chest as she was escorted, firmly, off the gangplank and onto the First Class Promenade.

The Promenade Suites had, of course, their own private promenade, facing out over the deck well into which the luggage 'Not For Use On Voyage' had been craned last night. As her aunt led her up the stairs to this exclusive precinct, Lydia could look down and see the stevedores still moving the last of it through the open doors and into the First Class baggage hold. Too few stevedores for the task, she reflected. She could see where some of them moved clumsily, working around maimed or missing hands, crippled or artificial legs. A year ago, or two, in the hammering, rat-ridden, maggot-whispering hell of some clearing station on the Front, she might easily have been the one who'd held the ether-cone over that barrel-chested man's face while one of the surgeons took his leg off. Maybe she'd visited that skinny dark man's bedside when he woke up blind on one side where his eye (and a substantial section of his cheek) used to be.

Entering the parlor of Aunt Louise's suite it felt like it had been someone else who had been there, who had done those things. Gauze curtains veiled the portholes, and the electrical fixtures were wrought like lilies of frosted glass. *Is this the same world? The same era in time?*

Am I the same person?

The parlor of their suite was crowded already. Uncle Richard had brought his daughter Emily, in stylish black mourning (*Poiret . . .*) for her husband, dead in the trenches at the Somme. 'I have *told* her,' observed Aunt Isobel, 'that one isn't supposed to wear mourning anymore, and I can quite see why. It's such a terrible reminder—'

'Not to speak of being *so* depressing.' Aunt Louise scrutinized her sister-in-law through her lorgnette, though whether her expression of disapproval concerned the exiguous traces of black at collar and cuffs – all the recognition Isobel accorded not only her son-in-law's bloody death but that of her son Charlie as well – or simply her accustomed scorn for Isobel's plebeian (though extremely wealthy) ancestry, Lydia could not have said.

But just as Mortling – Aunt Louise's butler, called from retirement at the age of seventy-seven when his successor to the post had joined the Leicester Infantry – tottered unsteadily in with the tea-tray, two more of Aunt Louise's sisters, Aunts Faith and Harriet, knocked at the door, with Harriet's barrister husband and two daughters in tow, and the entire party had to move down to the ship's First Class café. As they emerged onto the private promenade their way was blocked by the four sweating porters and that enormous chest – a cabinet, Lydia now saw, of heavily carved black wood, with locks of silver – which was being maneuvered into the suite next door to Aunt Louise's.

Oh, you're joking. They all backed up to the wall to let the enormous thing pass. *Don't tell me it's going to be this easy . . .*

'I do hope Lavinnia plans to bring Maria to town for the season,' commented Aunt Isobel, as they descended the steps to the regular – as opposed to the private – First Class Promenade on C Deck. 'You were just up at Peasehall, Lydia dear, did she happen to mention it?'

Lydia forced her attention away from the Princess Gromyko's party, entering the Willow Grove Café (as it was called) immediately before them, and blinked at her aunt.

'I certainly hope she plans to,' put in Aunt Louise. 'It's the girl's third season and she's twenty. Lavinnia will never get her off her hands at this rate.' She didn't even bother to sound distressed about this. Demonstrating herself superior to her older sister had been Louise's *raison d'être* since their mutual nursery days.

A black headwaiter in a white linen coat shiny with starch led them to a table among the potted palm trees. (There wasn't a willow in sight.) As the other party were seated just behind them, separated only by the green fronds, Lydia clearly heard the Princess Gromyko whisper to her bearded physician in French: 'Is the room secured, Dr Yakunin?'

Honestly, even in novels *it's not* this *easy . . .*

He held up a key. 'None can enter, Madame,' he whispered. 'And not the smallest shred of light can penetrate.'

THREE

'**A**nd in any case,' trumpeted Aunt Louise, completely drowning out the princess's next quiet words, 'I should say it's Maria's upbringing – or *non*-upbringing – that has more to do with it than the War.'

If I jump up and put my hand over her mouth it will only call attention to myself . . .

'And, I am heartily tired of *every* conversation turning on the War, even on this ship. The girl should have been disciplined from the first and kept to proper behavior, instead of being left to her crochets and fusses. Dresses like flour-sacks – or like pajamas! Cut all the way up to the calf, with her ankles flashing about for all the world to see, not that *Maria's* ankles are anything to look at . . .'

Dr Yakunin murmured – Lydia could only just make out the words – 'The authorities seemed to find your *douceur* . . . acceptable. Not a question was asked.'

'. . . and Peasehall can't be worth more than seven thousand a year these days . . .'

'Well, he could sell off the Gainsboroughs. I'm told Americans will pay practically anything for portraits . . .'

A chime sounded, and a steward's voice called politely, 'This is the last call, ladies and gentlemen. All ashore that are going ashore,' first in English, and then in French. Lydia suspected that a few years ago the announcement would have been made in German as well.

She and Aunt Louise walked their well-wishers to the head of the First Class gangway. The crowd of First Class passengers surged around them, and lined the rail for final goodbyes; Lydia caught a glimpse, through the press, of Captain Palfrey, like Sir Galahad in mufti, staring down into the waving mass of color on the pier. She wondered for a moment if his beloved Miss Aemilia Gillingham was down there somewhere, seeing him off. Or did he look beyond the crowd, to the lines of horses being loaded in the transport for France? Or to the men being taken off the hospital ship in the next berth, carried quietly across to the ambulance-vans, to be taken to the nearby Netley Hospital.

Maybe he was just gazing at England, green beyond the gray buildings of Southampton, under a silver afternoon sky.

The green finality of the Southampton Water widened between them and the dock. Between them – Palfrey, the Princess Gromyko, the commanding Mrs Tilcott and that golden-haired young girl in Third Class with her siblings and their mother – and whatever lives they'd had before the War. Between them and whatever they'd hoped for, or planned for, or thought they'd be doing, prior to the summer of 1914.

Between them and a past that was gone. A world that would never be the same again.

And no guarantee whatsoever, thought Lydia, her heart

thumping hard, *that we're even going to make it to America.*
The night without sleep, the journey yesterday afternoon down
from London, weighted her bones like the leaden apron she'd
insisted on wearing at the casualty clearing station, when
she'd operated the fluoroscope machine. She felt light-headed,
and separate from herself.

Jamie, I'm sorry.

Miranda, I'm so sorry.

Salt wind flicked her face. Gulls cried somewhere above the
piers. The cheering on the docks faded as the great vessel slid
into the main channel. Tug boats whistled, and an answering
blast came from the overcrowded ferry-boat, crossing the
Water far below where Lydia stood.

She thought about the hawthorn stakes, the garlic and wolf-
bane, the silver-bladed surgical knives in her locked satchel
back in her stateroom.

Simon, I'm sorry.

*If I cry Aunt Louise will ask me why, and tell me not to be
silly . . .*

The overpowering scent of frangipani retreated, and she heard
Aunt Louise call out imperiously to the deck steward.

*Now if only Aunt Louise – and Ellen – will let me alone this
evening so that I can see what this cabinet is, that the Princess
Gromyko has hidden in her suite . . .*

She pushed grief aside, focused her mind on the problem at
hand as if she were in a dissecting room.

*I wonder if the princess knew Prince Razumovsky in St
Petersburg?* In spite of herself, Lydia smiled at the recollection
of the big nobleman – one of Jamie's mysterious 'friends' –
who had befriended her in the Russian capital some years ago.
*Surely I can scrape acquaintance somehow. All the Russian
nobles are each other's cousins . . .*

She drew a deep breath, as if steadying herself to walk across
a narrow and railless bridge. *You can do this . . .*

But for a long time she only remained where she was,
watching England slide away. Tugs and pilots steered troop-
transports away from the other piers, guided colliers and small
freighters in. Fishing-smacks and coast-wise sloops dotted the
water, fry too small to interest submarines in the Channel. Isle

of Wight ferries paused to let them pass, and the small freighters that had braved the danger of torpedoes, with their bright flags, Danish and Swedish and the American stars and stripes. Still those gentle green hills were visible beyond, thin trails of smoke from villas and farmsteads. Memories nearly unbearable.

Jamie . . .

Flat American accents approached and faded behind her, as the emerald slopes and chalk cliffs of the Isle of Wight approached and faded: 'Nonsense! Jazz is no more music than it's music when Stella bangs on the kitchen pans . . .' 'Did you see *The Rink*? I thought I'd make myself sick, laughing . . .' 'I like Arbuckle better . . .' 'He absolutely took one look at her on the wedding-night and ran out of the room – *and* went back to his mother's . . .' *Jamie would take such delight in those accents.* '*Pure*-bred Persian, darling, with the cutest little face . . .'

Not a word about the War.

Palfrey had told her last night (*this morning . . .*) that the Germans had a new type of submarine. Long-range subs that could operate mid-ocean . . .

Despite Aunt Louise's blithe reassurances, she'd been looking forward to getting far enough from England's shores to be out of range of German subs.

And now there *was* no 'out of range'.

She shivered, thanking a God she didn't quite believe in that she'd been adamant about leaving Miranda at Aunt Lavinnia's. The little girl's stoic sadness at bidding her mother goodbye once again had torn at her heart. *But at least I won't have to lie awake nights in terror at the thought of seeing that freezing dark water close over her head . . .*

Yarmouth. A huddle of roofs, a smudge of distant smoke. Then, a little while later, the bizarre white shapes of the Needles, and the south coast of England retreating into shimmery haze to the north. The crowd was dispersing. Captain Palfrey strode to her side, hand extended, cerulean eyes anxious. 'Did you see anything?' His voice crackled with suppressed excitement. 'Someone brought in an enormous box . . .'

'I saw.' Lydia took his arm. *Maybe I'll be able to get a nice cup of tea before I have to don my secret disguise as Mrs James*

Asher, Respectable Lady and Vampire Hunter. 'Its owner has the suite next to Aunt Louise.'

'Surely,' argued Palfrey, 'they needn't be so . . . so *draconian* about all this. Might not the Germans have simply drugged Colonel Simon and brought him aboard . . . I don't know, disguised? In a bath-chair and wrapped up in blankets?'

'I doubt they'd have been able to get him past the health inspector.' (*Particularly not if he happened to burst into flames with the first touch of sunlight.*) Resolutely, as he linked his arm through hers, she put the ghosts of Jamie and Miranda aside, and coaxed into her voice the lilt of a humor she didn't feel. She wondered what this staunch young hero was going to do when he learned that her aim was not to rescue 'Colonel Simon', but kill him.

'I can almost certainly get up a conversation with this Princess Gromyko by admiring her dogs,' she went on, when they sat over coffee and biscuits at the Willow Grove. 'We probably have mutual acquaintances in Petersburg – Petrograd,' she corrected herself, the name of the Russian capital having been changed at the start of the war because 'St Petersburg' sounded 'too German'. 'And with the rioting going on there, we certainly won't run out of things to talk about. If worst comes to worst I can corrupt her maid. We have six days,' she pointed out, and cast a quick glance through the ferns to the table where the princess and her somber-eyed physician had earlier sat.

'For six days, we know approximately where Don Simon – *Colonel* Simon – is.' Her voice grew quiet. 'In those six days we have to find him. Once we reach New York, they could take him . . . anywhere.'

And do anything.

The café was quiet. It must, Lydia guessed, be past five o'clock. Behind her, she heard a little girl declare scornfully to her weeping brother, 'Only *babies* are scared of submarines.'

In spite of the coffee her head ached, and she rubbed at her eyes. Meeting Palfrey's troubled expression, she managed a smile. 'Are you prepared to romance the princess's maid if necessary?'

When they emerged from the café, she saw that the Channel had widened around them. Some miles off she descried a destroyer, patrolling for submarines in the relatively confined waters. Something that could have been the troop transport, and the horse-boat, made dark specks in the silvery distance. Something that might have been Guernsey floated still farther away in the green-black sea.

But England was gone.

I'm going to America, she thought, as she parted from Palfrey and turned her steps back toward the stair that led up to the Promenade Suites.

If I get there alive . . .

Her thoughts ducked quickly away from that fear. Like the artillery shells that had burst over the little hospital at the Front, there was nothing she could do about the situation.

I wonder if Ellen is done with unpacking? I can tell Aunt Louise I'm seasick, and need to lie down . . .

Though her aunt's response to that would probably be, 'Don't be silly, girl. It's all in your mind.'

'Lydia, dearest!'

She turned as her aunt came striding along the deck. 'I've been looking all over the ship for you! I must say –' the older woman's pouchy face fairly beamed – 'that this is everything that the advertisement promised. I have had the most interesting conversation with Mrs Cochran – such vulgar jewelry! And that *frightful* accent! And Mrs Tilcott is *very* knowledgeable about New York, though she claims that the society in Philadelphia has much better *ton*. I'm almost sorry now that I signed a lease on that apartment, though Mrs Tilcott assures me that it's in one of the *best* – ah!'

She stopped, fairly glowing with smug pride.

Lydia followed her gaze down the promenade.

And her breath seemed to congeal in her lungs.

Two figures coming toward them.

One of them unmistakable.

No . . .

It couldn't be.

No . . .

She wanted to put her glasses on to be sure but she knew it was true. Instead she turned, trembling, blazing, upon her aunt and whispered, 'How *dare* you? *How* dare *you—*'

'Now, dearest,' admonished Aunt Louise serenely, 'you can't tell me it isn't for the best.'

'Mummy!' cried Miranda, and breaking free of the repressive nanny who followed her, ran down the deck to throw herself into Lydia's arms.

FOUR

James Asher had first come to the house on the Rue de Passy in the autumn of 1907. He still bore the scars of it, on his throat and wrists, but at least he'd got to know by sight most of the vampires of the Paris nest. They'd be at the Front now, he guessed, along with nearly every other vampire in Europe.

For two and a half years, all the vampires in Europe had been in Flanders. Feeding to their hearts' content, three and four and five kills a night. No one had noticed.

Vampires lived, not merely on blood, but on the energies released by the soul at death. Only thus could they maintain their power to deceive, their fearful gift of illusion, their ability to tamper with human thought and perception. That, as much as their terrible strength and preternatural speed, made them deadly.

They walked among the trenches in the darkness. Clustered around the casualty clearing stations just behind the front lines, thick as moths around lamp-chimneys. Flitted in and out of the moribund wards in dead of night, whenever the exhausted orderlies turned their backs. They drifted ahead of the ambulance-wagons into No Man's Land when the artillery fell silent and the machine-gunners dropped asleep on their weapons. To the older ones, the stronger ones, the psychic charge of human death gave the ability to walk in human dreams, to make people think they'd had conversations they'd never had, seen things they'd never seen. Or dismiss things they *had* seen as, *I must have been dreaming* . . .

All these things increased with feeding.

It was a drunkard's dream of the Big Rock Candy Mountain,

he thought. Of wandering through lakes of gin and rivers of booze: all the blood, all the deaths, all the stolen lives and stolen strength they could devour.

And no one was even aware of them. What were a few drops of blood – or a pint, or a gallon – in an ocean?

Looking up at the beautiful seventeenth-century façade before him, Asher didn't know whether Elysée de Montadour would be in Paris now. Some of the masters of some of Europe's nests – London's, he knew, and almost certainly others – stayed closer to home, sensing the danger of being away from their own territory too long. *Those that're masters'll find their error*, the Master of London had said to him once, *when they come back and find some upstart's moved in an' set up housekeepin'.* Though Elysée had never impressed Asher as being particularly intelligent, she might well have developed a concern about being supplanted, as the war progressed.

One thing he had learned of vampires over the past ten years was that most of them were savagely territorial.

The handsome *maison particulière* on the Rue de Passy hadn't changed. In fact its long windows looked cleaner, and the whole building better-maintained, than the dwellings nearby, which for the most part had the decrepit appearance of structures which these days lacked the staff to scrub factory-soot from their doorsteps or mud from their walls. No lights were visible in the windows, but only those on the ground floor were shuttered. The Undead – Asher knew – though they often preferred the illumination they'd known in life, were indifferent to total darkness.

Senses keyed to the pitch that harked back to his years of spying in Russia, in Austria, in Berlin, he crossed in front of the house. Then, after a few moments, crossed back.

Elysée, at least, would know his footsteps. Would recognize the sound of his heart.

Some of her fledglings would as well. The thought frightened him badly. One or more of them might be in residence, and the beautiful Master of Paris might be away. In that case he was a dead man. Fledgling vampires, on the whole, mistrusted it when their masters formed bonds with the living.

Still, there was no other way to learn what he needed to know in time to get the information to Lydia. So he walked back and forth before the house twice more, keeping his distance from anything that looked like cover for an attack. But he was scaldingly aware that a vampire – and particularly one who'd been gorging on four or five kills a night for two and a half years – could be on top of him before he so much as heard the whisper of its passage.

Then he climbed the two shallow steps, and knocked at the door.

She opened it at once. She'd been waiting for him.

'La!' She flung up one hand in a theatrical gesture. The other held aloft an immensely elaborate branch of candles. Their light flashed in her green eyes like mirrors. 'Monsieur le Professeur! I had thought you were gone away to the East – perhaps killed. Please do come in.'

At least, he reflected as she stepped back from the door, *she can't possibly be hungry*. Not that satiation had ever kept any vampire from a promising kill, but Elysée de Montadour was too nosy to do away with a good source of gossip. The luminous glance flicked over his face, taking in what he'd seen on those few occasions that he'd had access to a mirror larger than the broken fragment he shaved in. Since the start of the War he'd lost forty pounds, weight his six-foot frame could ill afford. The silver that had threaded his brown hair and mustache in 1914 had widened to hand-breadth streaks.

She herself still looked exactly like the twenty-year-old courtesan that François de Montadour, then Master of Paris, had killed in 1799. Killed, and absorbed her soul, re-releasing her consciousness back into the body that he'd infected with vampire blood.

'Madame.' He bent over her hand. It was warm. She'd been out already in the early-falling spring night, and had killed. With paint on them, her inch-long claws could pass easily for mere fingernails. 'Is this a convenient time to talk? I would have sent a note,' he added, 'but I reached Paris only this afternoon, and the news awaiting me here was such that I could not wait.'

'About Don Simon?' A mocking smile lilted her voice, and she slipped his greatcoat from his shoulders, her fingernails brushing the nape of his neck. Upstairs, the drawing room, with its gilt-trimmed wall-panels of straw-colored silk, was warm from a large (and in these days, extremely expensive) fire in the marble grate, and from clusters of candles in wall sconces. On the far wall an oil portrait of her – a Corot, Asher thought – smiled the secret smile that flickered even now on the lips of the woman beside him.

She was watching him from beneath those impossibly long lashes. Waiting for him to react to her words.

'Tell me.'

She pouted as if on a stage. Unlike most vampires, Elysée de Montadour was always in motion, always making little *moues* and smiles and theatrical gestures. Asher wondered if she was that way when she hunted.

Probably. Sexuality hung about her like patchouli and almost certainly, he reflected, made concealment unnecessary. The most devoted husband in Paris would follow her down a dark alley without a second thought. It was, as Don Simon Ysidro had told him once, how vampires hunted: through the illusion of desire.

That, too, was something that strengthened with the power they absorbed from their kills.

'That he's been hanging about the clearing stations where your pretty wife works, like a lovesick schoolboy? Oh, without a word of thanks, so far as one can tell. Which makes it all the more hilarious. He writes poems about her, I daresay. You didn't know?'

Her eyebrows quirked and she laughed as she tweaked his mustache. 'Oh, my dear Professor! Don't tell me you didn't know!'

He shook his head. 'It doesn't surprise me, though.'

'And here I thought you were behind it!'

'Behind what?'

She'd settled herself on a loveseat to one side of the fire, and invitingly patted the cushion next to her. He took the chair across the hearth. She made a little face at him – one step short of blowing him a flirtatious kiss. 'Tattling to his bank,' she purred. 'Serves him right, abominable *aristo*. He has about ten of them – different banks, I mean. And Heaven only knows how many apartments and hidey-holes here in Paris, and properties that he rents under a dozen different names. I saw him only Saturday, striding along Rue Notre-Dame des Victoires like an icebox ghost. He said one of his lawyers had wired him that there was some sort of trouble at Barclay's, refusing to transfer funds to the Banque d'Algerie through which he holds his Paris house. Another man – *any* other man – would have been hopping up and down and spitting, he was so angry . . .'

Her eyes twinkled maliciously and her French, in general almost completely modern, slipped for a time back into the slightly trilled r's of that language's eighteenth-century pronunciation. '"*Given my understanding that America is not even involved in the War*",' she mocked, with a good imitation not only of Ysidro's whispering voice and antique Spanish inflection, but of his haughty stance and his way of looking down his nose as well, '"*I fail to see why this stock-holder's conviction that anyone doing business as a corporation must be a German spy warrants investigation*" . . . You know his way! Like a schoolmaster with a frozen poker up his backside.'

She laughed again and leaned back, voluptuous even in the unshaped garments that women considered (for reasons which utterly escaped Asher) the height of fashion these days.

'And was he able to straighten out this contretemps?'

'La, who knows?' She shrugged, regarding him with lazy interest. 'Who cares? I have not seen him since that night, you know.'

'Has anyone?' The dreams of agony had been Sunday night.

'You know the Spaniard.' She waved her hand. 'If you were to offer to bring him ten virgin maids in their nightgowns to kill, he wouldn't give you his address.'

'Is that what you do?' Asher kept only a level curiosity in his voice. 'Bring each other kills?'

Her smile widened. Long lashes veiled the copper hell-mirror of her eyes. 'Would you like to stay and see?'

He thought of the dark mansion above him. Of the black labyrinths of the old gypsum-mines that stretched for miles below Paris. Of the games he'd seen the vampires play when they chased – leisurely as drifting ghosts – some weeping and terrified prey. The recollection turned him sick.

'It is not that I don't trust you, Madame,' he said, rising and again taking her hand. 'I do so, absolutely.' He made the lie obvious in his voice, like a kind of secret jest, and she gleamed a dark amusement back at him. 'But I see that you're expecting company—'

There were two card tables set up in the long room, and he knew that after they hunted, vampires sought one another's company. Music, gaming, and gossip continued to draw, evidently, beyond the frontier of life, and as Ysidro had said to him once, night was no shorter for the Undead than it was for the Living.

'Oh, la, a few friends merely! Xaviero of Venice, and a couple of the St Petersburg boys. And of course my own dear precious Serge . . .'

'—and I fear that in the excitement of the chase one or another of your fledglings might get carried away. But if I might beg of you a favor,' he added, not liking the way she kept hold of his fingers, nor the way she studied him, now that her curiosity about his return to Paris had been satisfied. Vampires, he knew well, liked to toy with their prey: converse with them, flirt with them, go to the opera with them or on moonlight drives in the park. Sometimes they would court a chosen victim for months, satisfying their physical hunger with the blood of the poor while they ripened the piquancy of the eventual 'harvest', as they sometimes called it, with the spice of cat-and-mouse horror and betrayal.

Like Scheherazade, he had learned the value of keeping the game going until he could get out the door.

'And what is that?' Interest brightened her eyes – interest in something other than killing him for the sport of it.

'Could you – or your *beaux garcons* –' he knew the Master of Paris chose her fledglings for their looks – 'make further inquiries about this? About who this American is, and how he managed to light on Don Simon's banking arrangements? There's something very odd going on here,' he went on, holding Elysée's gaze and looking grave. 'And this isn't the first time that I've heard this rumor about German agents routing funds through Paris banks – God knows they've got more money in them than the German ones do right now. It was why I returned to Paris,' he continued, extemporizing freely. 'I had hoped to locate Don Simon here – as Madame Asher returned to England nearly two weeks ago – since I knew he worked with a number of private banks. I should feel better,' he added, 'if I knew that he was all right.'

If I knew that someone wasn't holding him captive in torment – something no one would do, whose goal was not to use the vampire's power for some scheme of their own.

Barclay's Bank. Banque d'Algerie. American stock-holder. Saturday night sometime . . .

Most vampires, he knew, could be lured by two things: blood, or money. A threat to the funds that guarded them would act as infallible bait.

Britten at the embassy would know. He works with the banks.

Asher kept his eyes on hers and didn't dare glance at the clock, but he guessed it was now close to ten at night. In fact, when he did reach the icy pavement of the Rue de Passy again a few minutes later he confirmed it.

Eleven hours until the embassy opened its doors. The *City of Gold* had sailed at two – probably later, given the possibilities of coaling problems. It would take him roughly four hours to get from Paris to Brest. And who knew how long it would take him to actually locate Cyril Britten tomorrow morning and how long it would take Britten to dig out the information about who had set what sounded like a very neat trap for Don Simon Ysidro.

'I shall ask.' Elysée looked pleased at the prospect of a puzzle. 'Of course, Serge will make a mess of it. He can stop your breath with his smile, but my *God*, I have bought clams in the market with more brain than he has! Louis-Claud . . .' A dreamy expression came over her face at the name of another fledgling. 'Well, he had at least the wits not to get himself drafted, for all he was healthy and young . . . Augustin is clever. A lazy beast, and tricky . . . He's still at the Front, though.'

Her green eyes narrowed, as if there were something about her fledgling Augustin that displeased her. Asher knew that at the best of times, the Paris nest was an undisciplined snake pit, filled with faction and intrigue. 'Where do you stay, my sweet Professor?'

'Hotel St-Seurin, in the Rue St-Martin.' He knew she'd follow him if he refused to tell her anything.

'Brr! What a ghastly part of town! Come here.' With abrupt ebullience, she released Asher's hand, caught his face between her palms, and kissed him – hard – on the mouth. He felt a rush of desire for her, the mad impulse to return the kiss, to bear her down on the Turkish rug before the fire. For over a year he had neither seen nor touched a woman and the need, for a dizzying moment, was unbearable.

But completely aside from his love for Lydia – and his knowledge that this woman's flesh was only warm because she had killed earlier in the evening – he knew where that would end.

So he drew back, shivering a little – aware that she could hear the pounding of his heart, and was amused by it – and said, somewhat unsteadily, 'Tomorrow night, then.'

He started to ask her, *And will this beautiful Serge, this handsome Louis-Claud, be here as well?*

But with a sensation like waking up, he saw that she was gone.

He let himself out.

FIVE

I n her bed on the *City of Gold* Wednesday night, Lydia got no sleep.

If Don Simon cried out in his prison in dreams of agony, she lay awake, oblivious and impervious, shaking as if with fever whenever she closed her eyes.

In her mind she saw the red head on the pillow of that pretty two-room suite that Aunt Louise had taken – in secret, gleeful at scoring over Aunt Lavinnia – as a nursery, where cold-faced, efficient Mrs Frush sat waiting for Lydia to depart (''Tis past time for a child to be abed, M'am . . .').

On her fingers she felt again the warm clasp of her daughter's small hand, and saw the joyous sparkle in Miranda's eyes. 'I'm glad Aunt Louise came and got me, Mummy. I'm glad she told me I could come with you after all.' She hugged Mrs Marigold to the stiff folds of her brand-new nightgown. By Miranda's account, Aunt Louise had 'taken her for a walk' from Peasehall Manor Tuesday evening, leaving a letter for Lavinnia – who had been at a Soldiers' Aid Society until late – explaining that Lydia had sanctioned this last-minute change of plan. (*And I'll lay any odds she looked up the times of the Aid Society meeting in advance.*)

On the way back to London, Aunt Louise had purchased everything the little girl had needed for her 'adventure' (including, apparently, Mrs Frush, whom Miranda had never met before in her life, and a downtrodden little nursery maid named Prebble). Mrs Marigold was the only thing Miranda had had with her, when they'd left the manor for their 'walk'.

Aunt Lavinnia would be spitting blood. Lydia was well aware that this had been the true object of Aunt Louise's virtual kidnapping of their mutual grand-niece. To prove that she, not Lavinnia, was the better mother, or would have been, had Louise's marriage to Lord Mountjoy not been childless. (*For which the souls of her unborn children*, Jamie had once said, *offer up thanks every day*.)

Dining at the captain's table, Lydia had barely been able to touch her sôle Colbert and suprême de volaille, or speak to her table-mates, aware though she was that she should have been making inroads of friendship to the sinister Princess Gromyko. All she had been able to think about had been the newspaper photographs she had seen of the bodies of the children recovered from the water after the Germans had sunk the passenger liner *Lusitania*; the lists of names of the dead from the torpedoed *Sussex*; the casualties from the *California* and the *Britannic*. She had learned as a girl – and as a young lady in her London 'season' – how to keep her countenance and appear to be listening, no matter what she felt inside. But anger had turned her nearly sick.

Aunt Louise, of course, hadn't even noticed. 'It's an absolute disgrace!' she had proclaimed to the table at large. 'You wouldn't see the British Army go over to the side of the rioters – not that there has ever been a major riot in London. And as for this talk about calls for abdication—!'

'Only what you could expect from Russkies,' had responded Spenser Cochran, his dark eyes sharp in a seamed, wolfish face. A slim-built, medium-sized man, he had a voice like chains being dragged over broken flint and as far as Lydia was able to tell, ethics to match. He had demanded more speed from the ship ('With what I'm paying I deserve to get to my business in New York on time!') despite warnings of submarines ('All cowardly nonsense!') and warned Captain Winstanley about anarchists, strikers, and socialists sneaking aboard the ship and corrupting the crew. ('Hipray – that's my lawyer – will be glad to check the credentials of your stewards and engineers, and if there's any trouble my boys can give a hand rounding up the ringers. We'll turn 'em over to the authorities the minute we reach the States . . . No, no trouble, glad to do it . . .')

Now he started, as if (Lydia suspected) his diamond-embellished wife had perhaps kicked him under the table, and he made a jerky little bow in the direction of the Princess Gromyko. 'Present company excepted, M'am.'

'I have heard tell,' put in Mrs Cochran, in the treacle drawl of the American South, 'that the peasants in your country, Princess, are as bad as the niggers in mine. Though –' she uttered a tinkling laugh – 'it's actually hard to picture anybody *that* stupid . . .'

One of the black waiters removed her soup-plate impassively and set in its place a dish of oysters. Seeing the glance the man traded with another waiter – also of African descent – Lydia recalled things she had learned from the men she'd cared for at the Front, and earnestly hoped that for the remainder of the voyage the staff would be careful to spit only in the appropriate person's food.

'I can only assume,' returned the princess in her sweet contralto, 'that Madame has not travelled in rural Russia.' Her English bore a trace of a French accent – in Russia, the upper classes used Russian only to address servants.

'Or in rural Yorkshire, for that matter.' Aunt Louise polished off her salmon mousseline in two bites. 'I've encountered tenants on my late husband's lands who will walk half a mile through the fields rather than pass a raven on a stump. You'd think such things would be corrected in schools! What we pay rates for I don't know – and half of them don't attend even if there *are* schools!'

'Exactly, M'am!' Cochran jabbed his asparagus fork in her direction – he, like his physician Dr Barvell on the opposite side of the table, was a vegetarian. Then he hastily corrected the gesture, as if table manners were a branch of learning only lately mastered.

'And what the – what the dickens do miners and mill-girls need book-learning for anyway? Or farmers either? Only stirs 'em up. Every strike at my mills, every walk-out or lock-out at any of my refineries, you trace it back and you find some know-it-all ditch-digger that somebody taught to read, just enough to make him think he's got all the answers—'

The regal Mrs Tilcott had waded into the conversation at that point with corroborative tales from her late husband's experience with his mills, railroads, mines and refineries, while her son – large, meek, and exquisitely dressed at her side – downed a dozen oysters and asked the waiters to bring him another serving of sole. He also made several somewhat fulsome attempts to engage Lydia's attention, until the princess, with a sapient glance at Lydia's pallor and distraction, had stepped in with tactful answers to his chat.

Lydia was grateful. On closer view, (though hazy with myopia), Her Illustrious Highness did not appear in the least sinister, being a tiny, dainty woman in her mid-forties wearing almost as many diamonds (though in far better taste) as Mrs Cochran.

The only conversation that might have interested Lydia at all had been the snatches that had drifted across the white-and-crystal fairyland of the table from the two medical men. 'But can one transform the personality with such injections?' and, 'Nevertheless, six months of a rest cure – without access to the written word, to writing implements, to any form of over-stimulating conversation – will transform even the most stubborn cases of female hysteria . . .'

And at her elbow, Mrs Cochran had regaled the princess with tales of how 'freedom has absolutely *ruined* the darkies!'

Mr Tilcott had pressed Lydia to accompany him to dancing in the First Class lounge after dinner – the *City of Gold* had its own orchestra – but she had excused herself. It had been a long day.

I'll do better tomorrow evening. Lydia turned over in her bed for the hundredth time. The cabin was stuffy, and seemed oddly silent after the noises of the clearing station and the constant thunder of the guns. Nevertheless, she found the movement of the ship soothing rather than otherwise. *The princess's suite is just next door . . .*

What else could be *in a box that large?*

Is the room secured? the Princess had asked. *Not the smallest shred of light can penetrate . . .*

Presumably, the box was stored in one of the 'servant's rooms' on the inside of the Promenade Suite, the equivalent of those which housed Ellen, Louise's maid Malkin, and the faithful butler Mortling. Did that mean that the princess's maids – Palfrey's list had noted two of them, in addition to her secretary Mademoiselle Ossolinska – had quarters down on C Deck like Aunt Louise's companion Mrs Flasket? And how was she to get around the two footmen?

She pushed aside an assortment of books and magazines to rearrange her pillows.

What if I'm wrong? What if Don Simon isn't on the ship after all? Have I – has Aunt Louise! – put Miranda in danger for an illusion?

No, she thought, with a queer, utter certainty. *He's here. I know he's here.*

Vampires were supposed to lose all their powers on running water – hadn't Dracula had to ship himself like a box of potatoes to England in that silly book? But Don Simon, who ought to know, had confirmed this to her, though the business about having to sleep in one's native earth, he had said, was nonsense. In his travels he'd always required a living helper.

Could he even contact me – touch my dreams – once aboard?

Then her mind slipped back to anger at Aunt Louise – whom she knew she couldn't quarrel with, not if she was to continue sharing a suite with the formidable dowager – and the newspaper pictures from the *Lusitania* victims. All the way up here on B Deck, she had little sense of the sea, save a gentle rocking (apparently enough to incapacitate the Princess Gromyko's maid Evgenia, to judge by the conversation at dinner).

But she was aware of the Atlantic, scrimmed with spindrift and bone-breakingly cold, eighty feet below her.

Waiting.

She didn't know if she slept or not. Her one thought, when the first thin lines of gray threaded the edges of the curtain over her room's porthole, was that the thing she *didn't* want that morning was to encounter Aunt Louise at breakfast. Rising silently, she slipped into the dressing room, gathered clothes by the soft glow of the night-light, and moved silently into the bathroom – Aunt Louise had sharp hearing, even sound asleep. Despite her aunt's horrified insistence that *no* lady – even one taking x-ray photographs and assisting surgeons in the midst of German shelling on the Front – was properly dressed without a corset, Lydia had sneaked a number of brassieres into her luggage. Thus she was able to dress herself speedily and discreetly, and to make her way along the promenade in the gray cold of morning, salt spray stinging her cheeks.

The First Class dining room was open, but, to judge by the empty tables, the gleaming ranks of silver warming-trays and chafing-dishes on the sideboards, only just. One of the few other passengers in the room was, a little to Lydia's surprise, the Princess Gromyko, clothed in an elegant walking suit of claret-colored velvet (beautifully corseted beneath the exquisite lines of that Paquin jacket – no brassiere nonsense for *her*!) and another extremely Parisian hat. The two French bulldogs lay politely at her feet, diamonds glittering on their collars in the bright electric radiance of the dining-room lamps. Quickly pocketing her glasses, Lydia made her way among the tables. *After all, it's the Captain's Table and I am entitled to sit there . . .*

Nevertheless she asked, in her fluent French, 'Do you mind if I join you, your Illustrious Highness? I meant to tell you last night how much I love your dogs, but I'm afraid I was a little indisposed and not at my best.'

'Darling!' The princess beamed upon her warmly, and signed for one of the stewards – already on his way from the buffet – to pour Lydia coffee from the Crown Derby pot already upon the table. 'Please forgive me for the way I broke into Mr Tilcott's remarks to you, but you looked so wretched my heart positively *bled* for you. And then everyone was going on and *on* about the poor, and it would look *so* bad if one drowned one's table companions in the soup, *n'est-ce pas*? Much as one might wish to do so. I trust you are recovered?'

'I am, thank you. So silly.' Lydia managed a trusting smile. She judged the diminutive princess to be just the right age to cast as a protective older sister to her own confiding youth. 'I've crossed the Channel half a dozen times and sailed all the way to China five years ago, and I've never been seasick before.'

'*Alors.*' The princess made an airy gesture. 'It is as I suspected: the company, and not *mal de mer*. The ghastly Lady Mountjoy is, I believe the captain said, your aunt? And you are Madame Asher?'

'I am,' said Lydia. 'But I wish you would call me Lydia.'

'And you must call me Natalia Nikolaievna. And this is Monsieur le Duc, and Madame la Duchesse – *very* much set up in their own conceit, as you see.' She slipped the little dogs fragments of buttered toast. 'And the beautiful little fairy I saw you with on the deck yesterday evening – your daughter, yes? In my country red hair is not fashionable – those peasants your aunt discoursed upon at such tiresome length even say that to be born with red hair is a sure sign that one is destined to become *vurdalak*... vampire. Myself, I find red hair enchanting.'

Lydia made herself look disconcerted. 'What a shocking superstition!' she exclaimed, and self-consciously touched the thick knot of cinnabar braid at the nape of her neck. 'What won't people believe? All that silliness—'

The princess raised her manicured brows, and Lydia halted, as if uncertain.

'It *is* silliness, isn't it?' she faltered. 'I mean, like Aunt Louise's tenant-farmers and their stories about ravens and magpies . . . ?'

'Ravens and magpies . . .' The princess shook her head. 'Even of them, I have heard tales that maybe cannot be dismissed. But the *vampir* – the *vurdalak* –' her lovely brows plunged into a frown – 'I do not mean your beautiful daughter, please do not think I subscribe to that peasant stupidity. But as your

Shakespeare says, There are more things in Heaven and Earth than are dreamt of in your philosophy, and it is best to be cautious.'

'Cautious?' Lydia made herself look puzzled – as indeed she was. Would a German spy with a vampire imprisoned in a secret cabinet, in a completely blacked-out cabin, go around bringing up the subject?

'They scoff at it.' The princess leaned closer to Lydia, her expression deadly earnest. A frost-rime of tiny diamonds glittered on the veil of her hat. 'The captain, and that imbecile ship's doctor, and the officers . . . Yet I believe what my maid Tania told me this morning to be true. There is a vampire on board this ship.'

Lydia was so completely nonplussed that her face must have been expressionless. She only stared at the woman before her, and as if she took Lydia's silence for disbelief, the princess went on, 'It is true, Lydia my friend. Believe it. They try to hush it up – you will hear nothing of it, up here among the *gratin*.' She laid her exquisite hands over Lydia's, and sank her voice to a whisper. 'It killed a young girl in Third Class last night.'

SIX

Too shocked to dissemble, Lydia whispered, 'How do you know?'

'I know because it is true.' The princess seemed not at all discomposed. 'Tania, my maid – the one who is *not* seasick – heard it this morning, from the women in Third Class. She took the children candies, you understand, and bits of treats which she put into her pockets from the dinner they serve the maids and valets.' She slipped another fragment of toast to Monsieur le Duc.

'She is absolutely silly on the subject of children, Tania. There was diphtheria in her village, you understand, and her children died, three of them: Vanya, Tasha, and Marya. Every child, she says, could be one of them, re-born in its next life. She went down there this morning and everyone was speaking of it, of the *vampir*, and the girl who was killed.'

Lydia shook her head, groping to fit this information into the dreams she had had, and the conversation she had overheard. 'It's . . . impossible . . .'

Can Don Simon have escaped them?

Simon wouldn't do something so stupid as to kill in a closed area where every person is counted . . .

Her hands trembled as she set down her coffee cup. The princess was regarding her, grave conviction in those luminous dark eyes.

'Truly,' she said. 'Truly, Lydia – truly, it is not.'

This woman can't possibly be the one who kidnapped him.

Then what in Heaven's name has she got in that giant box?

When Lydia didn't reply – she still felt as if she were trying to sort a hand of cards with hypothermia of the extremities and recent head-trauma – the princess went on softly, 'They exist.' Her grip tightened on Lydia's hands. 'The *vampir*. The *vurdalak*. The *upyr*.'

She paused, glancing at the waiter who refreshed their cups, then shot a quick look around them at the near-empty salon.

'The dead that do not lie still in their graves. Walking corpses that prolong their own existence with the blood of the living. The ship's first officer, the stewards, they asked a few questions, they took the girl's lover and locked him up in the brig. The ship's surgeon signed the papers saying the girl's throat was cut, but it wasn't. It was pierced. Two punctures, above the great vein. No blood was found at the scene, nor anywhere else.'

She leaned closer. 'You say, *impossible*, dearest Lydia. But your heart believes. Your heart *knows*. I see it in your eyes.'

My heart knows that a vampire who has been injured – surely one who has been in torment for four days, as Simon has been! – can heal himself with a kill. Even the thought of it turned her sick.

And the pain whose echo she had felt in her dreams may have driven him mad enough to do it.

She drew a shaky breath. 'Might one . . . Do you think it would be possible . . . to . . . to see her? This girl?'

The noblewoman's eyes seemed to darken as her brows knit, and Lydia went on, 'I . . . I'm a physician, you know. And I ask . . .'

What sort of reason is she likely to believe? Lydia felt a wave of vexation that she hadn't read more novels. *Would she recognize bits of* Dracula?

'The thing is, years ago, when . . . when I was still at school in Switzerland, my friend – a very dear friend – was . . . found dead, in just such circumstances.' *She can't possibly check a story like that and she's certainly not going to tell me I'm making things up.* 'Of course we girls weren't told anything, but I . . . I sneaked into the room where her body lay. And I saw . . .'

She flinched in a fashion which she hoped was realistic, and pressed her hand for a moment to her mouth.

'I didn't know what to think . . .' She threw an uncertain stammer into her voice. 'Later, when the school doctor and the headmistresses and everybody kept saying Mollie had fallen and hit her head and wasn't it a terrible shame, I almost convinced myself that they were right. That I'd only dreamed what I saw.'

Sympathy and vindication blazed in her companion's eyes. Lydia thought, *And if you believe* that, *I bet that cabinet of yours has something to do with holding séances.*

Either that, or it's full of the Russian crown jewels.

She lowered her voice like the heroine of a penny dreadful. 'But I know it wasn't.' (*And I* have *to remember that my deceased schoolmate's name was Mollie the next time I tell this story.*)

'No.' The princess's hand crushed tightly on Lydia's fingers. 'No. They tried to tell me the same thing – my parents, and the priest on our estate. And later, all the mistresses at my school. The world of shadows is not invisible, dearest Lydia. It is the eyes of its deniers that are sealed shut.'

'As I said, I'm a physician,' Lydia continued. 'Do you think that would suffice, for me to get a look at this poor girl's body? I don't suppose they'd let me speak to this young man – what's his name?'

'Valentyn. Valentyn Marek.'

'Did the girl have parents on board?'

'We'll ask Tania.' The princess stood up briskly. 'She can go down there with us, to Third Class. She cannot fix hair like my dear Evgenia can, but at least she isn't laid up with *mal de mer*! And the friends she has made in Third Class will show us, also, where the body was found. Monsieur, Madame . . .' She snapped her fingers imperatively for the dogs. '*Allonz-y!*'

Natalia Nikolaievna Gromyko saw no reason why she should change out of her exquisite walking suit and velvet chapeau to visit Third Class, but conceded to Lydia's argument – *if you look too fine they'll shut their mouths and not say a thing* – when she was backed up by both the maidservant Tania and the stout blonde secretary, Mademoiselle Ossolinska. During the protracted changing process in Her Illustrious Highness's suite (again Lydia thanked her earlier trip to Russia for the knowledge that a garden-variety Russian princess like Madame Gromyko was Your Illustrious Highness, as opposed to an Imperial-bloodline princess, who would have been Your Serene Highness), Lydia gathered that the princess's entourage included a spiritual advisor as well, housed separately in the portion of Deck C reserved for the lower tier of First Class. The cabinet, it transpired, was hers.

'Madame Izora is marvelous,' the princess assured Lydia, as Tania buttoned her into one of Marie Ossolinska's frocks and deftly pinned back the considerable slack out of sight. 'Literally so, a marvel upon the earth! One of the ancient souls. I insisted she accompany me to Paris last year, when things became so impossible in Petrograd. Tonight we shall surely form a circle, and perhaps one of those who dwell Beyond can tell us of this thing, this evil that stalks the ship . . .'

'It was generous of you to bring her,' said Lydia, and Her Highness looked startled that the matter needed comment.

'But of course! How not? Even Paris has become gray and grim, since the start of the fighting. How can one attune oneself with the ineffable, in an atmosphere of prying and politics and shocking prices? Now that these dreary republicans are destroying the last of what was spiritual and good in Russia, I daresay many of us – the Obolenskys, the Dologorukys, the Golitsyns, everyone of decent birth – will be going to Switzerland or England or to the United States. Or to Paris when things look better and it is possible to buy decent wine there again. None of those stupid democrats in Moscow can possibly understand or believe the spirits that come to Izora when she sits in her spirit cabinet—'

I knew *it*!

'—and hears the voices from Beyond. I would ask her to come with us now—'

Lydia hastily summoned every argument she could think of to discourage this addition to the investigation . . .

'—only she will be sleeping at this hour.'

Oh, good . . .

Lydia's own garb of shirtwaist and skirt, thick nondescript coat and shapeless hat that she'd worn the night before last (*was it* only *the night before last*?) to watch the luggage being loaded, was sufficiently anonymous so as not to intimidate (or arouse resentment in) anyone below-decks. Thus when the four women – Princess Natalia, Lydia, Tania, and Mademoiselle Ossolinska, who tightened her mouth at the mention of vampires but spoke fluent Slovene – descended the steps to the 'well' of the ship, they were received without hesitation by the troubled and angry crowd in the Third Class dining salon.

This big, stuffy, low-ceilinged hall was situated on F deck, close enough to the engines to be shaken with their constant thrumming, and to smell of coal smoke and oil. It seemed, as well, to double as a 'day room' for the Third Class passengers outside of dinner hours: newspapers in various Central European languages littered the tables nearest the door, clearly brought by the passengers. Urns stood on a buffet, but the coffee and hot water provided by the American Line to its low-paying clients had long ago run out and nobody had collected the soiled cups. In the open spaces among the tables the passengers were clumped in six or seven groups according – as far as Lydia could tell – to nationalities, but people shouted translations from one group to another, German and Slovene seeming to predominate (*if that* is *Slovene they're speaking* . . .).

When they entered the room Tania looked over the heads of the crowd – the maid was taller than many of the men – and thrust her way swiftly through to a thin, sunburned woman in the worn white linen that seemed almost a uniform among the Central European farmers, calling out, '*Pani* Marek!' The woman cried out, and clasped the Russian maid in an embrace, pouring out a flood of words that Lydia didn't understand and quite possibly Tania didn't, either.

A heavy-shouldered old man with a white mustache the size of a small sheep came up beside them, put his hand on '*Pani* Marek's' shoulder and spoke angrily, first to Tania and then to Ossolinska, who translated.

'M'sieu Marek says that they have put the fiancée of his grandson into one of the ship's refrigerators, as if she were but a piece of meat, and will permit no one to view her. Pavlina was her name, Madame, Pavlina Jancu—'

'They are Poles,' explained Tania to Lydia, in halting French. 'East of Bohemia. Village torn to pieces by fighting, and all lands around. Pavlina from next village, betrothed—'

She paused, as *Pani* Marek poured forth a sobbing torrent of expostulation.

Ossolinska said, 'Madame Marek says of course Valentyn was jealous, for what real man is not? And of course Pavlina attracted the attention of men here on the ship, for she was beautiful, and what beautiful girl does not like to flirt a little? And everyone loved her. But Valentyn would never have raised his hand against her.'

She paused again, to listen, and the golden-haired girl whom Lydia recognized from the Third Class gangway broke from the woman with her – raw-boned and powerful as a farm-horse with a face like stone – and squirmed her way to Ossolinska. In German the girl said, 'It is true, Madame. Valentyn is rough in his ways but he loved her dearly. When they brought her body in he wept, as I have never seen a man weep . . .'

'Ariane!' snapped the hard-faced woman, and pushed through to grab the girl's arm. 'Get away from them! Slavs! Heretics!'

Pan Marek flushed – evidently he recognized at least the words for 'Slav' and 'heretic' – and shouted, gesturing toward another group: '*Oni sa heretykami* . . .'

A gray-haired woman in another group thrust forward and yelled, 'Who you call heretic, *Nemecky*?'

'What else do you call those who insult the Mother of God? Whose priests are whoremasters—'

'Please!' An old man whose long white beard nearly hid the Greek cross around his neck limped from among the Russians as more people started to shout. 'This is not the time . . .'

'Indeed is not!' A heavy-shouldered, dark-faced man pushed up beside him. He was missing an eye and several fingers of his right hand: indeed, of the dozen men in the dining salon, few were of military age. Of those few, only a handful were without recent injuries.

In rough German, the one-eyed man went on, 'We know what kill this girl. We all know.' He looked around him fiercely, met old *Pan* Marek's eye, then Ossolinska's, then swept his gaze to all the crowd around.

'It is vampire. There is vampire, hiding somewhere on this ship.'

'*Gospodin* Vodusek,' pleaded the priest.

'We all know signs, Father Kirn,' said the man Vodusek. 'We all know, could be nothing else. Drinker of innocent blood! Murderer of children! Must be found! Must be destroyed.'

The men crowded closer. Lydia heard the word passed back among them: *Upír. Volkodlak* . . . And among the little crowd of Bosnian Muslims, *Ghawl* . . .

'That's cock,' snapped the scar-faced blond man Lydia had glimpsed in the glare of the waiting-room lights the night before last. Hearing him speak to his friends outside the waiting shed in German, she'd thought that he must be one of the Sudetendeutsche from Western Bohemia. 'And you're an imbecile, Vodusek, if you believe it! It is superstition that the bosses have used for centuries, to get us to sit down and shut up and let them do our thinking for us.'

Vodusek shouted *Nemecky* – German – and something else which Lydia guessed wasn't complimentary. The German swung around on him and shouted back – in Slovene – then turned again to the gathering, muttering crowd.

'Are you all children?' he demanded. 'A man doesn't need to drink blood and sleep in a coffin to do evil—'

Someone had translated this to old *Pan* Marek, who seized the German's shoulder and spun him around; only the scar-faced man's lightning reflexes blocked a punch that would have stunned a horse. Lydia backed hastily out of the way of the escalating fight, but the German didn't return the blow. He stepped back, pale eyes blazing as he glared from the furious grandfather to the glowering vampire hunter to the confused, frightened, angry faces of the people now pressing close around them. He looked as if he might shout something else at them, then shook his head like a dog trying to clear nettles from its ears, and pushed away through them and out of the dining room.

Pan Marek growled something, and his daughter-in-law explained – through Ossolinska – to Tania, 'The man is a Communist, an atheist. No one who had seen poor Pavlina's body could believe that it was anything but a vampire who did this terrible thing!'

'But we must not go saying it is one of us.' The old priest addressed Lydia and the princess in halting German. 'That way leads into shadow indeed.'

'But how are we to explain it to an American?' pleaded *Pani* Marek, through the impassive Ossolinska. 'Americans have no belief! No God! They do not see what we see, what we know!'

'Please understand,' went on the priest, drawing closer to Lydia and the princess as the room dissolved into shouting and gesticulation again around them. 'These people are all frightened, terribly frightened. They flee to new land of which they know nothing. All have come through nightmare. None who have not been there can know.'

He turned to the haggard-faced *Pani* Marek and addressed her, haltingly, in Russian. She nodded, and when her gruff old father snapped at him – Lydia caught the words *Chrystus* and *heretykami* – heretic – and guessed the old enmity between Catholic and Orthodox was involved – she shook her head, pleading. When the priest made the sign of blessing – using three fingers in the Orthodox fashion – the old Pole made an insulting flick of his hand with two fingers, for the Catholic custom, and walked away.

The old priest turned back to Lydia and the princess. 'You are here from First Class, maybe? Friends of our good Tania—'

he smiled at the servant – 'who has brought such happiness to our poor little ones here? If you can – if there is any way such can be done – I beg of you, speak to someone of ship's company. Convince them poor Valentyn would not have harm this girl. I think they seek above all to stop panic: they arrest someone, anyone, and say, "So! Problem is solved." But this is unjust. And problem is not solved.'

He sank his voice – mellow, beautiful, and deep despite his years and his emaciated appearance. 'It is *volkodlak* that has done this terrible thing. It is somewhere on this ship. And it will strike again.'

SEVEN

Old Father Kirn and *Pani* Marek showed Lydia and Princess Natalia where Pavlina Jancu's body had been found, at the bottom of a staircase that led up to the Second Class accommodations on D deck. A couple of stewards had found it, the woman told them, around three in the morning. 'She was still warm,' she whispered, words which Ossolinska translated softly, visibly upset now as she had not been in the dining saloon when the whole matter had been one of words only.

Lydia opened her mouth to remark that bodies frequently retained perceptible heat for three or four hours after death – more perceptible, indeed, to men whose hands were cold from the chill of the corridors – but closed it again. It was not something this woman needed to hear. Instead she looked up and down the corridor – evidently the main communications passage for crew and service staff between bow and stern – and closely scrutinized the metal steps, particularly where they met the wall. Like everything else on the *City of Gold*, they'd been thoroughly swabbed down earlier that morning (*including the cranny beside the wall, drat their scrupulous care!*). She stepped aside as three men came down from above. One of them touched his hat to the little group, asked, 'Can I help you?' in flat American English and the tone of one who really means, *Get along, now, nothing to see here . . .*

Lydia propped her glasses more firmly on her nose and replied, 'Maybe. This is the spot where that poor girl was found, wasn't it?'

The crewman – a cabin steward, by the look of his uniform – looked nonplussed, and a little impatient (*damn sensation-seeking women*). 'I don't know much about—' he began, but one of the men with him, with rather more braid on his uniform sleeves, stepped politely forward and bowed to the princess, then to Lydia.

'It is, M'am, yes,' he said to Her Highness. 'But the man who did it's been arrested, and is under restraint. A crime of passion, we understand.'

Natalia opened her mouth to object, and Lydia touched her sleeve warningly. 'Do you happen to know if there was any blood found at the scene? We've had a little discussion among the passengers,' she added, with a deprecating smile, 'about how it could have been done. I mean, this is a rather public place, isn't it? Even at three in the morning? Mightn't she have been killed somewhere else, and brought here?'

The young officer looked vexed at the idea that the crime was a subject for 'discussion among the passengers', and his eyes flickered to the two obvious Third Class peasants included in the group. But he answered politely, 'No, so far as I know, there was no blood anywhere, though of course the whole area was swabbed down immediately, M'am. As for being killed someplace else –' he frowned slightly, looking more human – 'it wouldn't be that hard to bring her here. This whole corridor's pretty quiet at that hour, in the middle of the grave-yard shift. But why would anybody do that? If somebody wants to get rid of somebody on board a ship, you'd dump the body overside, if you were gonna go carrying it around. And the Third Class gangplank door is just down the hall there. It's not that hard to open.'

'You're right.' Lydia widened her eyes as if enlightened by these words. 'You're quite right. Thank you, sir.'

'My pleasure, M'am. Princess,' he added, touching his cap with slight bows to both her and Natalia. The crewmen walked away, and *Pani* Marek, and Father Kirn, looked at Lydia with uncomprehending inquiry in their faces.

'You did not speak to this man of Valentyn?' asked the priest hesitantly.

Lydia shook her head. 'They're going to be like that awful German—'

'Heller,' confirmed Father Kirn, his lined face grim and sad. 'A Communist, here on the ship with false papers. A thug, wanted in his own country for murdering a man.'

'And a man who believes himself to be right,' said Lydia. 'Just as the captain, and the ship's officers, and everyone will believe themselves to be right, if we start pestering about a vampire, without proof in hand. I think we shall be able to get proof – to get evidence – much more easily, if they're not looking at us and thinking, "Hmph. Silly superstitious women".'

Against Ossolinska's soft-voiced translation for the benefit of the woman, the priest nodded and said, 'You are wise, *Gnä' Frau.'*

'Well, I try to be.' Lydia removed her glasses and tucked them out of sight. 'Only sometimes it's not easy, to know what's best to do.'

And if Simon did this, she thought, shivering a little as she and the princess ascended the steps towards the more rarefied regions above, *does that mean he's managed to escape from his prison, wherever it is? That he's wandering at large around the ship? And, why didn't* he *dump that poor girl's body over the side, if the Third Class gangplank door is just down the corridor? At three in the morning it would have been easy.*

She glanced back at the foot of the stair, even now by daylight augmented with the overhead electrical glare.

Has *he gone mad?* She shivered, not only with fear, but with pity. *From pain, from overexposure to silver – I really* must *make more of a study of vampire physiology, though if Simon* has *gone mad how would I get my information? – or from some cause I don't know?*

The princess was saying something to her but Lydia barely heard, struggling with the appalling prospect of hunting for a deranged vampire through the dark bowels of engine-room, bilges, storage-holds where light never came.

Or did his kidnapper bring him the girl and then . . . What?
Dump her where she'd be easily found, advertising to everybody
on board – or everybody in Third Class anyway – that there's
a vampire on the ship?

That made no sense, either.

It made less sense when Lydia, escaping from Her Illustrious
Highness and the disapproving Mademoiselle Ossolinska – who
seemed to share the German thug Heller's opinion about belief
in vampires but had the good sense not to air this opinion to
her employer – obtained permission to see Pavlina Jancu's body.
The ship's surgeon, Dr Liggatt, accompanied her, having (Lydia
was surprised and gratified to learn) read two of her articles on
pituitary gland function, written in those halcyon days before
the War. He didn't seem to find it odd that she would want to
see the victim of an unexplained death.

'For I'm at a loss, M'am,' he said, in his soft Virginia drawl,
'to account for this poor girl's murder – and murder it was. Not
a slash, but two short cuts in the carotid artery below the left
ear, and her body near drained of blood.'

This was true. The cuts were deep and mangled-looking, as
if the flesh had been pinched or squeezed, and her mouth was
open a little: she had died gasping for breath. Her eyes were
shut, her hair, dark maize-gold, was still braided beneath a
headscarf of red and white. Her nails, when Lydia turned her
hands over, were unbroken.

No struggle.

'Where did the blood go?' Lydia pulled her coat more tightly
around her. As *Pan* Marek had said, they had placed Pavlina's
body in one of the refrigerated meat lockers on D deck, deep
in the complex of kitchens, pantries, vegetable rooms and
sculleries that served both First and Second Class. The sides
of beef, gutted carcasses of lambs and pigs, row after row of
suspended chickens, ducks, pheasants, had all been doubled up
into some other of the meat rooms. The empty hooks and vacant
slabs gave the place the look of a torture chamber.

Lydia couldn't keep herself from wondering – though she
knew not to ask – whether the American Shipping Line would
replace the stone slab on which the girl's body lay, before the

next voyage. She herself had never been squeamish, and two and a half years at the Front had cured her of any revulsion at things like picking maggots out of her food, but she suspected that travelers like Mrs Tilcott would object if they knew that the slab on which the roast lamb served up in the First Class dining room had been used as a morgue table.

'Now that's what I can't understand, M'am.' Liggatt scratched his head. 'I've asked just about every member of this crew, and there wasn't a drop found at the scene, bar the little bit you see there, on the collar of her dress. Nor anywhere else on the ship, far as I've heard. For certain she wasn't killed where she was found. There's crew quarters up and down that corridor and she's got to have cried out.'

Not if a vampire killed her. Lydia recalled the warm, soft crush of a hunting vampire's power over the mind of the victim: a delicious sleepiness that, if not fought consciously and desperately, yielded everything.

But she only said, 'It certainly is odd.'

The electrical refrigeration chilled her to the bone, even through her stout (and decidedly Second Class) coat. Emerging from the locker, she rubbed her hands as she climbed to the promenade deck. It was good to be in the fresh air, bitter though it was under a threatening sky. The sight of her fellow passengers, stylish in walking suits and firmly pinned-down hats, taking the air or sitting in their deck chairs (*now where did Aunt Louise say ours were?*) made her realize that it was long past lunchtime.

Miranda would be asking for her.

She was halfway to her cabin when a steward, hurrying along the promenade, stopped and said, 'Mrs Asher! I was just coming from your stateroom. This came for you just now.'

From his pocket he drew a small beige envelope, stamped with a little picture of the *City of Gold*.

'And I must say, I'm a bit surprised we were still in wireless range of Brest.'

Lydia tipped the man, had the envelope open before she even reached her stateroom. (*And thank God he didn't leave it in the stateroom for Aunt Louise to open.*)

It was from Jamie.

Best Beloved nothing to forgive you are always the treasure
of my heart stop the author's name is Aloysius Bibgnum
stop love you always James

It was the code they used for short words and names, and she
carried the rules in her head.

The first name was always window-dressing, and it needed
only moments to decipher the second.

Cochran.

Now what?

James Asher leaned back on the hard bench of what had been
a second-class car of the Chemin de Fer de l'Ouest, and watched
the snaggle of sidings, sheds, allotments and stacks of disused
railway ties peter out as the train steamed out of Rennes. On
either side of him, jammed elbow-to-elbow, Cameron Highlanders
smoked Woodbines until the air was blue, and traded hungover
grumbles as they headed back to the Front. Noon sun glinted
through naked trees, clumps of mistletoe caught in their branches
like immense birds' nests.

Two women in black walked along the road below the
embankment of the tracks.

There were a lot of women in black in France these days. In
England, Asher had heard, as in Germany, women were discour-
aged from mourning the loss of husbands, brothers, sweethearts
and sons, 'lest civilian morale be eroded' by the sheer and
mounting numbers of women wearing black. Meaning, he
guessed, 'lest people start questioning the war'.

If the train wasn't side-tracked in favor of more urgently
required supplies, they should be in Paris by dark.

Spenser Cochran. Asher thumbed mentally through that
morning's conversation – it already felt like days ago – with
Cyril Britten at the embassy. He'd known the deceptively frail-
looking old man back when first he'd worked for the Department,
and knew he would have everything at his fingertips: which
Americans owned sufficient stock in Barclay's Bank and the
Banque d'Algerie – and the half-dozen other financial institu-
tions among which Don Simon Ysidro held funds under his
various names – to make things difficult for the vampire.

'Well, we keep an eye on Cochran, of course,' the elderly clerk had said, sipping the tea (or what was supposed to be tea) that a quiet-footed woman had brought up to his fusty attic cubicle. 'Like all these rich Americans he owns factories in Germany and Russia, so we do like to be sure whose side he's really on.'

'And whose side is he really on?' Asher had inquired, and Britten had emitted a creaky chuckle. Below them, the elegant eighteenth-century *hôtel* had been just stirring to life, colder than ever with the shortages of fuel. Coming up the fourth flight of stairs to these upper offices, Asher had been struck by the silence. Nearly all the younger clerks were gone.

'Mostly his own.' Britten frowned into middle distance, and pushed a plate of stale biscuits in Asher's direction. A large gray cat with white mittens emerged briefly from around a stack of file boxes, hissed gently at Asher, and withdrew. Despite the cold, the whole attic smelled of cats.

'His father made a fortune selling boots to the Federals during their Civil War – cardboard, of course, and fell apart the first time they got wet – and ran things like gunpowder and medicines, of quality similar to the boots, to the Confederates. He invested the proceeds in railroads and mines, so Cochran Junior came into a fair packet when the old boy died and went to Hell. Junior re-invested in so many things – meat-packing, oil wells, banks – that there are few wealthier men in America now, and according to all I've heard, few stingier. He makes Ebenezer Scrooge look like Diamond Jim Brady: saves the buttons off his discarded shirts and charges his house guests for using the telephone. That's to say nothing of demanding kickbacks from his suppliers and making deals with land companies in the Midwest to raise shipping prices on smaller farms and push them out of business . . . after which he buys up their land, of course.'

The old man's mouth set briefly with disapproval, but fifty years of secret service to Queen and Country had inured him to the vagaries of the powerful. He had been the chief clerk of the Paris section when Asher had first entered the service in the eighties, and had retired, Asher recalled, in 1905, at the age of seventy, and retreated to the Dorset coast to raise strawberries.

Like many men, Asher included, he had been recalled to the colors with the outbreak of war.

'Even among American industrialists, his reputation is smelly,' Britten went on. 'He was investigated in 1904 over the deaths of five strikers at one of his factories, and again two years later, but nothing was ever proved. The "private detectives" who supposedly did the actual killing – three men were beaten to death and two others simply disappeared – were released on the grounds of self-defense. Cochran still travels with a small guard of detectives, I understand.'

He had frowned again, and sipped his tea. His sleeves, Asher had noted, were powdered with cat fur; at least four pairs of reflective eyes gleamed in the shadows of the stacked boxes of files with which the cubicle was choked.

'After that, because of the newspaper stories, he appointed his nephew – whom he'd sent to Yale Law School – to act as press secretary. At Nephew Oliver's advice he has begun making substantial – and very public – contributions to various charities, and has hired an English "consultant" – formerly the Duke of Avon's butler, I understand – to instruct him in the social graces. Oliver Cochran has also worked with the press to suppress news of some of his uncle's odder habits—'

'Like superstitiousness?' Asher had inquired, and Britten's sparse brows had lifted.

'Good Lord, yes. Like a savage in the jungle. You wouldn't think a man that crafty in business could be that credulous, but Cochran has personally kept two New York mediums in business for years, as well as a shady "researcher" in Paris who's supposedly able to extract information from the brains of the dead, and enable people to live forever, among other things. His wife's just as bad, and a good deal more gullible.'

'What was he doing in Paris?'

'Supposedly, winding up the affairs of one Titus Armistead, an industrial rival of his who died in rather suspicious circumstances in—'

'Yes,' said Asher softly. 'Yes, I know who Titus Armistead was.'

And he wondered whether it was from Armistead that Cochran had conceived this scheme of trapping and using a vampire in the interests of 'private industry', or vice-versa? The plan had cost Armistead his life – and, if one believed the Church, and the old tales, and the *Book of the Kindred of Darkness*, his soul – and had ultimately failed. Probably Armistead's daughter had been selling up her father's antique books on the subject of the Undead.

Interesting that Cochran would have crossed the Atlantic in the face of U-boat threats, to acquire them – if acquire them he had.

What else had he sought to acquire?

Whoever it is, Lydia had written, *who has found a way of coercing the obedience of vampires . . .*

I will kill him, she had promised.

I have packed all the appropriate impedimenta . . .

He smiled a little now, as the brown fields of the French countryside fleeted by, dusted with the palest ghost of spring's new grass in the long slant of the evening sun. But his smile was grieved, for he knew how much that beautiful, cool-hearted, scholarly girl loved the vampire.

She would do it, he thought. But it would forever darken her heart . . . and his own.

Cochran. He closed his eyes. There had been no train from Paris to Brest until late afternoon, but his military credentials had gotten him a car and a driver within an hour of his conversation with Britten. He had spent five hard, jolting hours on the roads of Brittany, passing lorries, convoys, and brown lines of exhausted men. The first thing he'd ascertained on his arrival at the British military headquarters had been, *Was any liner sunk in the North Atlantic this morning?*

None so far.

He still didn't know whether the wireless message he'd flung out into the ether had reached the *City of Gold* or not.

If it had, this man Cochran – this man whose reputation for ruthless violence was 'smelly' even by the standards of such men as John D. Rockefeller and Henry Frick – would at least not know that Lady Mountjoy's young relative was asking questions about him. What Britten had told him about the man's methods and employees made Asher shiver, even if he hadn't already succeeded in breaking Don Simon's will to his commands. And if he *could* command Don Simon Ysidro's obedience, would that leverage – whatever it was – be sufficient to turn the vampire against Lydia?

'Shove up, y'fookin bampot,' snarled a voice across from him, and there was a general pushing on the opposite bench, like steers in a byre. A smell of wet wool and stale tobacco.

'Bloody numpty . . .'

'Awa' an' boil yer heid, ye stupid rocket . . .'

They settled down. The train jostled around a long curve. Flashed past a village, women working in a field, harrowing the earth with rakes. All the horses had gone to the Front. To die beside the men.

I need to know more.

Like the men bound for the war once more, Asher cringed inside, knowing there was only one place to get the information he needed.

EIGHT

*I*f Simon has managed to escape, he'll be hiding.

Back in her stateroom, Lydia studied the deck plans of the *City of Gold*. The American Line had thoughtfully provided these – printed on high-quality stock with lavish photogravures of the First Class amenities – for its First Class passengers. The engine rooms on G Deck, she reflected, though permanently sheltered from sunlight, would be subject to the constant comings and goings of the crew. The baggage and cargo holds, also on G Deck or down on the Orlop Deck (*why Orlop?* she wondered) would be largely unvisited through the six days of the voyage: luggage 'Not Wanted on Voyage'. Safer even, she thought, than the coal bunkers, which would presumably be tapped for fuel at some point – *is there a way to get at the schedule for their use?* In any case, not anyplace a vampire would wish to fall asleep, to say nothing of the fact that she couldn't imagine the fastidious Don Simon, sane or otherwise, sleeping in coal dust.

She looked at her watch (*three hours until I have to dress for dinner . . .*) and transferred the picklocks she usually carried from the pouch buttoned onto the lower edge of her corset, into her skirt pocket.

How long would it take for pain like that to turn his mind?

Vampires toughened as they aged, and Simon was one of the oldest in Europe. Still . . .

How many kills would he make before he either healed enough to come to his senses, or is caught?

She opened the slick, black-enameled doors of the built-in wardrobe and brought forth her portmanteau. As she did so, Captain Palfrey's list of passengers caught her eye and she wondered, *what if Simon* hasn't *escaped? Is this – whatever this hold is that Mr Cochran has on him – is it sufficient to let him out, then bring him back again, like a dog on a leash?*

The lined, foxy face of the American millionaire returned to her, the dark sharp eyes that were intelligent, but fanatical and cold. Whatever else was going on, she couldn't imagine him being foolish enough to permit his prisoner to kill in a group of people whose comings and goings were all accounted for.

And yet, she thought, *what if Simon is so badly torn apart by the circumstances of his imprisonment – by being locked in a coffin, presumably lined with enough silver to keep him helpless – that he* must *have a kill, or die? In such a case they'd certainly pick on a Third Class passenger to bring to him for a victim.*

At various points during dinner last night, she'd heard both Cochran and Tilcott refer to the population of E Deck and below as 'animals', incapable of reasoned thought – or of any thought at all – and as 'popish imbeciles'. Clearly, contempt for believers in faiths other than one's own were not the exclusive province of Slavic Orthodox or Polish Catholics.

Her hands shook a little as she unwrapped the things she'd brought – three stakes whittled of hawthorn, packets of dried garlic blossom and Christmas rose, a set of surgical knives and a bullseye paraffin lantern (*matches! Don't forget matches . . . Oh, and a hammer . . .*).

But if Cochran sent his detectives to abduct some poor girl from Third Class for Don Simon to kill, why dump her body where it would be found? If they had to carry her down from

B Deck in the dead of night anyway, why not drop her overboard, as Dr Liggatt said?

It doesn't make sense.

She tucked her implements into a satchel – the hammer made it dreadfully heavy – and added a small box containing a hypodermic syringe and four ampoules of silver nitrate. Though the blood in a vampire's veins did not circulate, Lydia knew that an injection of pure silver nitrate would spread rapidly through vampire tissue, from cell to cell of the flesh which had been altered, cell by cell, by the 'corruption' (*possibly a virus?*) that was the physical component of the vampire condition.

Oh, Simon, I'm sorry.

As she fastened extra chains of silver around her throat and wrists, she wondered if he'd be glad to finally die.

Half-past four. She'd promised Miranda a walk along the First Class Promenade before dinner, which would be served at eight (Mrs Frush had frowned at this departure from her schedule). *If the ship is moving west, what time will darkness actually fall?*

If Don Simon *had* escaped, and *was* lying concealed in some corner of the cargo hold – and if he *had* gone mad – she would much rather encounter him while he was still unwakeably asleep.

At least, she reflected, Princess Natalia was too busy arranging a séance for that evening to insist upon accompanying her on a vampire hunt.

'Going to bring in that Madame Izora of hers,' muttered Ellen, when Lydia emerged from her room. The maid had kept watch against an incursion from Aunt Louise ('*She's been looking for you all day, Miss – M'am . . .*'), and had spent an hour earlier, reading to Miranda in the suite booked as the little girl's nursery. '*Getting in touch with the spirits*, that heathen girl of hers calls it. What kind of spirits would be all the way out here in the middle of the ocean, I ask you, Miss? Naught but a lot of drowned sailors, and who'd want to talk to *them?* That's if this Madame Izora isn't a complete fake, which I'll go bail she is.' She preceded her mistress across the parlor to the door that opened onto the suite's private promenade, opened it and looked out.

But the private promenade on this side of the ship served

Suites A and C, and at a guess, Aunt Louise was on the other side of the vessel, '*kissing up*' (as Lydia's erstwhile medical colleagues at the clearing station would have said), to either Mrs Cochran or Mrs Tilcott (who held one another in active contempt). A tall, strongly-built woman, still pretty in her late forties with masses of springy black curls pinned tight under her starched cap, Ellen had been a nursery-maid at Willoughby Close when Lydia was a child, and guarded her unquestioningly.

'That hair of hers is fake, anyway,' the maid went on. 'The half of it bought in Waterloo Road and the other half dyed like a Leicester Square hussy. I daresay that's Her Highness' note to you there on the desk, asking you to be part of it. Looks like it's all clear, Miss. Before you go, what should I lay out for you for dinner?'

'I think the plum Doucet Soeurs.' For all her willingness to work elbow-deep in trench mud or traipse through coal bunkers in search of vampires, Lydia had made sure she'd brought an adequate wardrobe aboard. 'The mint-green shoes and headband – will you much mind switching out the aigrette on the headband? And the amethysts. You're a darling . . .'

'You watch out now, Miss.'

She'd said that, Lydia recalled, smiling, when Lydia had gone downstairs to get into the carriage for her Court presentation – and in precisely the same tone of voice. *You watch out now, Miss . . .*

Decks E and F were a maze of crew quarters and Third Class 'cabins' – actually dormitories of six to ten bunks – smelling of oil, cigarette smoke, and clothing too seldom washed. Discreet 'lockers' were tucked under stairways and in corners, for cleaning supplies and tools. Floor and walls vibrated with the beat of the *City of Gold's* engines, mingled with the constant low echoes of talk, hard to localize in that anonymous labyrinth of steel: men arguing in five different languages, the shriller tones of women. Sometimes someone shouting, or children shrieking with laughter in play.

Dark Greeks pushed past her, and fair Slovenes. A sandy-haired Belgian mother pulled her children away from 'dirty Mahometan' Bosnians. In her shabby coat, nondescript skirt, and spectacles, nobody gave Lydia a glance. Crew members jostled her without an apology, except for a nod sometimes, her surest gauge that she was, in fact, being mistaken for somebody who belonged down there. (*And if anybody catches me with picklocks in my pockets I'll almost certainly end up in the brig with poor Valentyn Marek.*)

The door into First Class Baggage was just down the corridor from the ship's post office. Lydia had to wait for a moment when no one was in the corridor before trying it. It was locked (a Chubb pin-tumbler) but of the sort (*thank goodness!*) whose latch could simply be forced with a slip of thin, stiff metal – a much quicker method which meant, Lydia knew, that the lock would catch again if the door were closed. With another quick glance up and down the corridor, Lydia slipped through into the hold, checked briefly that the inside handle *would* open the door without the necessity of picking the lock, then shut herself in.

And just as she was telling herself, *you idiot, you should have gotten your lantern out of the satchel* before *you shut the door* . . . she thought she saw the flicker of light, somewhere deep in the hold before her.

With the vibration of the engines, she wouldn't have heard the soft scrape of a lantern-slide closing. But she smelled – or thought she smelled – the faint whiff of hot metal and paraffin.

Someone else is here.

Cochran. Her breath caught in her throat.

Or some of his men. Looking for Simon?

She stood without making a sound. Recalled the casual way he'd spoken at dinner of 'getting rid of' the men who'd tried to organize the mine workers to strike for higher wages or safety equipment in the mines. 'They're like cockroaches,' he'd fumed. 'For every one of 'em you squash, there's fifty hiding . . .'

And when Dr Yakunin had responded that in many cases it was poverty which had made such men as they are, Cochran had lashed back, 'Nonsense! Your honest poor don't go around telling a man how to spend his own money! Not in America, they don't!'

The hatred in his voice was up to anything she'd heard at the Front in reference to the Germans. If anything, it was more personal, more venomous. 'Who do they think they are? A real

American – not one of these Bohunk dagos – if he don't like working in a mine, let him go elsewhere – if anybody'll have him.' In his loudly professed view, Eyeties, Krauts, and Kikes deserved what they got.

And presumably – thought Lydia, standing in the darkness convinced the unseen enemy could hear the pounding of her heart – a snooping woman might 'deserve it' as well.

She opened the door, stepped very briefly into the aperture so that her shadow would block the dim light of the corridor, then ducked back inside and closed the door again.

After a long moment of silence, a single light appeared again, deep within the hold.

And if Simon hasn't escaped, are those 'detectives' – 'thugs' would be a better word – *out hunting some other dispensable prey to keep him in good health? Does Cochran really think nobody's going to notice? Or does he simply think no one will care?*

Grateful that the engine noise covered any chance sound she might have made, Lydia began to move – with infinite caution – in the direction of the light. The hold was filled with what felt like grilled racks or cages to the touch of her slow-groping hand. Numbered, undoubtedly, so that any piece of any First Class passenger's luggage could be located instantly, once they reached New York. One didn't pay eight hundred pounds to wait in a shed for one's possessions.

Though the air was still and stuffy, she had a sense around her of enormous space. According to the deck plans, here was another hold below this one, for mail sacks, Second Class baggage (the lowly Third Class passengers presumably didn't have anything besides carpet bags and satchels), and large cargo.

And I'll feel a terrible idiot if all I uncover is some poor burglar trying to pick the locks on Mr Tilcott's steamer trunk . . .

The light in front of her was clearer now. Moving among the racks of baggage, held close to the floor. Stepping slowly, Lydia lost sight of it, groped her way around another rack, saw it again, clear and quite near to her. A man bending over it, studying the floor . . . moving on . . .

Looking for what?

He swiveled on his heels, snatched the lamp-slide off and swung the beam on her. She saw him move for one instant as if he'd have darted into the maze of racks, then stopped as he got a better look at her.

As he identified her, she could see him thinking, *Not a crew member. Not a threat.*

'Frau Doktor.' He stood. But still he was braced to dodge, presumably in case she turned out to be armed after all.

It was the scar-faced German Heller. The 'Communist thug'.

'What are you doing down here?' she asked.

He removed his knitted cap, and bowed ironically. 'The same as yourself, I expect, Madame.' He slipped his German Army revolver into the pocket of his decrepit jacket. An old-style French infantryman's jacket, Lydia identified it, with the insignia torn off. 'I think that you believe as I do, that this talk of vampires was all my hat, meant to frighten farmers and miners who know no better. I heard you asked to see that poor girl's body.'

'I did.'

'Was she indeed drained of blood, as they said?'

Lydia nodded.

'Completely?'

'Almost, yes. There was no *livor mortis* that I could see.'

'Was there any blood in her hair?' He pulled his cap back on. 'Or behind her ears –' he touched the place on himself – 'as would be the case were her throat cut and she was hung like an animal, to drain out?'

Lydia thought about it. 'Not behind her ears, no. I was looking for *livor mortis*; that's one of the places where it sometimes shows up.' She frowned. 'She wore a headscarf – one of those enormous white embroidered ones that some of the Slovenian ladies wear. Her hair was braided under it, I didn't take it off of her.' *And I should have*, she thought. 'There was some blood on the collar of her dress. Her throat had two small incisions, four or five centimeters below the ear-lobe, in the carotid artery.'

The kind a vampire would make with his claws, before drinking from the wound . . .

'And did they look rather like punctures?'

'Yes. Particularly, I suppose, to someone who isn't used to

coming suddenly on a dead body.' She turned the details over in her mind again. 'At the Front we were always dealing with puncture wounds from shrapnel, you know, or from splinters if a section of shoring was blown out. A man could bleed to death in minutes from even a small tear in the throat like that.'

'Yes,' said the German quietly. 'Yes, I know. So where did the blood go?'

Lydia could only shake her head. 'Dr Liggatt asked that, too.'

'It takes only a little more time than that,' he went on, 'for a body to bleed out completely, if it is hung up by its feet, for instance. This has to have been done . . . somewhere.' He gestured: big hands, like a mechanic's or a miner's, callused like pickled leather in the kind of fingerless knit gloves that she'd seen men wear for warmth at the Front. The scars on his face were mostly the kind that a man would get from shrapnel or flying debris, but one on his temple, older than the others, looked like a knife scar. 'And drained into what? A bucket? One of the wash tubs from the kitchen?' He spoke to her without euphemism, as if he did not expect her to be shocked.

Very much, in fact, as Jamie had always spoken to her, even when she was a girl of fourteen. She tried to imagine Mrs Cochran's reaction to such matter-of-fact discussion, or the response of the young ladies she'd come 'out' with during her Season.

'Have you ever tried to carry a gallon or more of liquid in a bucket without splashing so much as a drop? That's what you're looking for here, isn't it?'

Lydia hesitated, then nodded. *Let's not get into the issue of why I'm carrying hawthorn stakes and silver nitrate in my satchel.*

'You could take it and empty it into one of the cleaning drains,' she said. 'They're on every deck. You'd still have to bind up her neck to carry her to where she was left. And leave her someplace while you went and disposed of the blood. Even a drained body will leave a trail of drips.'

His mouth – thin-lipped and curiously sensitive – quirked in wry amusement at this matter-of-fact view of the logistics of the exercise, and he said, 'So I have – I'm sorry to say – seen.' And there was, for a moment, a world of blood-soaked muddy wasteland in his blue eyes.

And for that moment silence lay between them. An under-standing. *I say, didn't I meet you in Hell last year . . .?*

Lydia took a deep breath. 'But *why?*' she asked, and propped her spectacles more firmly onto her nose. 'That's what I don't understand about all this. Why would anyone do a thing like that? I mean, yes, obviously, they want to frighten people . . . Someone clearly wants people to believe there's a vampire aboard the ship . . .'

Anything, she thought, rather than go down the path of truth, or possible truth: *that there* is *a vampire aboard the* City of Gold.

Why not just tell them what you know? Let Simon be dragged from his hiding place and killed?

The thought turned her stomach. Despite herself, a childish illogic in her cried out against the thought of Don Simon, who had saved her life, who had saved Jamie's life, and Miranda's, being butchered by strangers.

You would rather kill him yourself?

She didn't know how to answer that.

'It's why I want to find out where it was done,' said Heller. 'How it was done. It will tell us something – if only that we are up against someone who is smarter than we are.' He rubbed the side of his broken nose with a callused forefinger. 'I've talked to the young man's mother and grandfather and though they swear he would never have harmed a hair of his fiancée's head, many people saw her flirting with some Bohemian fellow – Horacek is his name – and saw Marek's rage at her. So Marek could have set up this 'vampire' story to keep people from pointing at him. I don't know the man, so I don't know if it's the sort of thing he would do. But somehow, I don't think that's the case.'

'It's certainly one of the stupider alibis I've ever heard.'

Heller smiled again, grimly. 'Exactly. Again our thoughts are alike, Frau Doktor. So what *is* going on?'

Lydia shivered. *What indeed?*

But having Heller's assistance made a search of the hold much quicker and – Lydia had to admit – much less fright-ening, given the possibility that Don Simon might be down there and insane (*and will the poison cause him to be awake in daylight hours*?), or that Cochran's thugs might be searching for him. They found no blood on the floor. Any of the tall luggage racks could have served as an improvised bleeding hook, but neither of them could discover any sign that one had been so used. Nor was anything untoward found among the trunks: no hair ribbon, no kicked-off shoe, no slip of paper with *Meet me in the baggage-hold at midnight* scribbled on it in Polish. At the end of forty minutes Heller said, 'I think it is best that we cease our investigation for now, Frau Doktor. It will be the dinner hour soon –' he meant Third Class dinner hour, not First – 'and I think that whoever did this thing – whyever they did it – they will be watching behind them. They must be.'

'I can't imagine anyone so stupid as to believe that people are simply going to accept that a vampire did it . . .'

'Can't you?' Heller's mouth quirked. Lydia guessed his age at forty, but there was a bitter weariness in his eyes that aged him far beyond that. 'Well, you are English,' he added quietly. 'One would have to go deep into the English countryside to find the sort of ignorance one encounters in the forests of East Prussia, or the mining villages far from any town. And I think the English less inclined to simply hate out of ignorance – hate the Catholics or the Orthodox, the gypsies or the Jews.'

'Don't be so sure of that,' murmured Lydia, and Heller's mouth hardened for a moment into something that wasn't quite a smile.

'Maybe. Certainly there are wealthy Americans and wealthy Germans, who believe that country folk are easily frightened by ghost stories. Just as they will believe anything,' he finished bitterly, 'that will justify stealing from the poor.'

'You are right about that.' Lydia shook her head, remembering Cochran's words over dinner last night.

She didn't know whether to be glad or sorry that they had found nothing. Glad or sorry that whatever action must be taken against Don Simon still rested entirely in her own hands.

She looked perplexedly around her at the looming dark. 'But until we know why this thing was done, we don't know how much danger *we'll* be in, if it's seen that we don't believe either the vampire story or the crime-of-passion story. Someone is clearly willing to kill . . .'

'Exactly. And willing to kill, apparently at random, a girl who could do no one any harm.'

'Might we . . .?' Lydia hesitated. 'Might we meet tomorrow, to continue the search? Quietly, at a time when neither of us would be missed?'

The wry smile lightened the German's eyes, and he removed his cap again. 'Who misses a Socialist troublemaker at any time, *gnädige* Frau? The men in my cabin are a posse of idiots, but they know to ask no questions. But a lady such as yourself will be at all times surrounded – and there is your little girl to be thought of as well. You name the time of your convenience.'

'Just after lunch? I'll come down to the ship's forward deck well.'

He inclined his head, and grasped her hand as he'd have done, Lydia guessed, the hand of a fellow worker in some Brandenburg factory. 'I am glad for the help, Comrade.'

He listened at the hold door for a moment, very much as Ellen had, then opened it quickly and signed her to leave first.

NINE

Only a trifle late – and resplendent in diaphanous plum-colored silk with an aigrette of mint-green feathers – Lydia followed her Aunt Louise into the First Class dining room, identifying already the voices of her fellow passengers as much as the manner in which they stood and walked.

'I looked for you at lunch,' said Mr Tilcott, springing to his feet with an agility Lydia would scarcely have credited to a man of his girth, and guiding her to the vacant chair beside his. 'I trust you were not indisposed? I positively could not eat a mouthful, worrying that you might be laid low by *mal de mer.*'

Lydia would not have bet the hole out of a donut that anything could have reduced Mr Tilcott to self-starvation, but she smiled at him and said, 'Thank you, Mr Tilcott. No, I spent most of the day exploring the ship.' Which was true, in its way.

Mr Cochran, Lydia noticed immediately as she sat, had managed to injure his left arm, and bore it now in a black silk sling, but Tilcott's determination to monopolize her attention – and Cochran's conversation with Dr Barvell on his other side – prevented her, for the moment, from asking what had happened. Though the sky remained gray and a sharp wind keened over the nearly empty decks, the sea hadn't been sufficiently rough, in Lydia's opinion, to make the stairways a hazard, and the millionaire, though in his sixties, impressed her as a fit and active man. Dr Yakunin was absent, and his place, beside the princess, was occupied by Madame Zafferine Izora: gazelle-boned, dark-eyed, and glittering like the night in a beaded gown of ebony fringe.

Even without her glasses and across the distance of the table, Lydia suspected Ellen had been correct about the provenance of her hair.

Izora's voice, though deep, was pleasant, and she had an inexhaustible wellspring of conversation about everything, it seemed, except the War. 'Quite the *toast* of Broadway, but since his wife divorced him he's been involved with some outré suffragist poet or other . . . Oh, I understand Poiret's on the verge of bankruptcy, and can you wonder? When you think of his designs beside those beautiful little gems Chanel is putting out; no one wears hobble skirts anymore! No, spaniels are *completely* out these days, M'am! The truly *chic* companion now is an Alsatian, or a chow-chow.'

She added, lowering her mascaro'd lids as if gazing through the mists of time, 'Cleopatra, you know, owned a black puppy named Amonophis.' She passed the backs of her jeweled fingers across her forehead. 'The dearest little thing. She'd trained him to take sugared wafers from her lips. It used to make Mark Antony almost weep with laughter.' Then her eyes returned to the present and she smiled benignly, as – unsurprisingly – Mrs Cochran and Princess Gromyko begged her for further details about her visit ('I was borne there in a state of trance . . .') to the court of the Egyptian queen.

Yet another belief, reflected Lydia, *like religious prejudice, which didn't seem to be restricted to Third Class.*

'Sounds like Madame Izora might be of use to you, Mr Cochran,' declared Tilcott, signing the waiter to replenish his *laitance de poisson* on toast-points for the third time. 'She'd surely be able to tell who it was who tried to sandbag you.'

Lydia exclaimed, '*Sandbag?*' startled, and the millionaire waved the remark away impatiently with his uninjured hand.

'I don't need spirits to tell me that,' he said.

'The most frightful thing.' Aunt Louise laid down her silver fork – she was keeping up with Mr Tilcott on the fish course toast-point for toast-point. 'One of those dreadful anarchists dropped a net full of sandbags from the boat deck down onto him as he descended from the promenade deck! His shoulder was nearly dislocated—'

'He could easily have been *killed!*' declared Mrs Tilcott, in tones which sounded less concerned for a man's safety than indignant that such things could happen in First Class.

Lydia's eyes flared with shock and – her mind still on Don Simon (would *he risk capture in order to take revenge?*) – she asked, 'What time was this?'

'Just about two hours ago,' responded the millionaire's wife. She was wearing a tiara this evening, emeralds and diamonds so large that Lydia wouldn't have believed they were real had the piece been on anyone else. 'Of course we were all dressing for dinner, so nobody was around.'

'Oh, it was cleverly done,' growled her husband. 'I'll give the man that. I was lured there, M'am.' He turned those sharp black eyes on Lydia. '"Meet me at six at the bottom of the promenade stair. Come alone." And I fell for it, like a sap. If Kimball – one of my boys –' Lydia had seen two of Cochran's 'boys', loitering outside the dining-room door as she'd followed her aunt into the room – 'hadn't followed me and yelled, I might have been brained.'

Six. Light still in the sky . . .

'When I was a girl –' the princess leaned forward like a crimson-enameled serpent – 'my uncle Illya was killed by anarchists. Blown up by a bomb hurled in a train station at a train that was carrying Count Tolstoy – not the writer, I don't mean, but the Minister of Finance . . .'

Mrs Cochran exclaimed shrilly, and her husband jabbed with the fragment of artichoke he'd been eating. '*That's* the kind of thing we'll be having in America next, if these socialist labor bastards aren't stopped.'

His wife frowned at the word *bastard* – which Lydia, after thirty months at the Front, scarcely noticed – and in an effort to smooth things over, the princess continued, 'They never caught the man who did it.'

'Well, they caught this one,' declared Captain Winstanley, a note of pride in his mellow voice. He stroked his silver mustaches. 'A German Communist on the run from his own government; one of those labor agitators. He came aboard with Danish papers, under the name of Paulsen, but his real name's Georg Heller. Mr Kimball got a look at him as he fled, and identified him—'

'But I was with Mr – er – Paulsen,' protested Lydia.

That silenced the table. Aunt Louise regarded her as if she'd announced she'd been engaged in a spitting contest with the engineers.

'*Really*, my dear—'

'It's true.' Lydia glanced from Cochran to Captain Winstanley. 'I saw . . . it sounds so silly,' she added apologetically. 'I saw what I thought was one of Her Highness's little dogs, just vanishing down the stair to D Deck, and I ran down after it. I was afraid it would come to harm down there, or get itself lost. Mr Paulsen was kind enough to help me look for it, until we found it and saw it was really one of the kitchen cats. The big, fat, black one that hangs round the Third Class galley. We parted at six-fifteen. I know, because I didn't want to be late to take a stroll with my daughter.'

'There could be more than one Paulsen,' declared Cochran truculently.

'Oh, I'll come down and identify him,' returned Lydia with an earnest smile. 'And even if he is a runaway German, I don't really see there is anything wrong with a German, of military age, not wanting to go back to the Front and shoot at our men. If they'd all desert and go to America there wouldn't be any more problem, would there?' She widened her nearsighted eyes, as she had learned was most effective when dealing with her father's curmudgeonly uncles when they'd come to call. 'If there's any question, I mean.'

Captain Winstanley cleared his throat, and turned inquiringly to Cochran. 'You did say Kimball was down at the far end of the boat deck . . .'

'The man Heller's a labor agitator,' snapped the millionaire, as if that accusation were sufficient. 'And I know for a fact this Paulsen is him! You can bet he's bound for the States to cause trouble there. Stands to reason they'd try to put me out of the way. They all know me for a man who'll give 'em trouble. A man who's not afraid to take on them and the pasty cowards in the government too—'

'Yes, but it's scarcely a reason for locking him up for something he didn't do. Is it?' Lydia turned her gaze from the captain – who didn't seem to be entirely certain whether to disagree openly with a First Class passenger – to Mrs Cochran, Her Highness, and finally Mrs Tilcott.

'Well,' said Tilcott, 'not *as such*, no. Mrs Asher does have a point.'

'The man should be locked up in any case,' put in Mrs Cochran self-righteously.

'That's hardly the American Way,' responded Lydia, 'is it, Mrs Tilcott?'

Cochran grumbled something and shot her an angry look, but Mrs Tilcott launched into a recital of why the heritage of Philadelphia was superior to such less-American venues as (for instance) Chicago or the South, and under cover of this, Princess Natalia leaned a little across the table to say to Lydia, 'That was most kind of you, darling, to go seeking what you thought was poor Monsieur. He is, alas, addicted to low company, as all men are, though I assure you, my dearest Ossolinska would never be so careless as to let him slip away from her on shipboard! Dearest Zafferine –' she turned to the psychic – 'could you – might you – speak to my Uncle Illya tonight? Bring him, or my poor Aunt Katerina, to speak to me? Will you come?'

She smiled warmly upon Lydia, then turned her great dark eyes to the captain beside her, and to the Cochrans, the moment Mrs Tilcott paused for breath. 'Perhaps the spirits will have seen with greater accuracy than did your good Kimball, M'sieu

Cochran, the face of the man who dropped those sandbags on
you this afternoon? For the spirits see.'

Her smile faded, and the glow of faith illumined her dark
eyes. 'The spirits see everything. Evil most of all.'

'*Nonsense*,' declared Mrs Tilcott. 'Superstitious fol-de-rol. I
must say I'm *surprised* at you, Mr Cochran.'

'Well,' modified her son, 'my man of business tells me that
all those old documents you were telling us about over lunch
make a fine investment, Mr Cochran! No doubt about *that*!
Thank you,' he added to the waiter, who brought in the *boeuf
marchand de vin* and squabs, and helped himself to ample
portions of both. 'But actually going to sit in a darkened room
hoping you'll get to chat with George Washington . . . Not –'
he added quickly, with a glance across at Madame Izora – 'that
under the right circumstances the Father of Our Country
wouldn't be delighted to attend . . .'

Mrs Cochran turned bleak eyes upon him and said, 'You
would think differently, sir, had you ever hungered for the sight
of one lost to this world before their time.'

And Madame Izora laughed gently. 'My dear Mrs Cochran,
pray don't concern yourself with my feelings! A man doesn't
believe until the light comes into his heart. Pity, rather, any who
keep their minds shut, and trust that they will come to understand in time!'

Mrs Tilcott and her son traded speaking glances. Turning her
head, Lydia caught the narrowed, querying look the handsome
Dr Barvell directed at Mr Cochran, while Mrs Cochran
commenced to tell Captain Winstanley all about the spiritualist
she habitually consulted in Lake Forest, and Madame Izora detailed,
to the princess and Aunt Louise, the occasion upon which she
had had tea with St. Francis of Assisi. As they all rose from
their chairs following the last creamy fragments of *mignardises*,
Princess Natalia laid a bejeweled hand on Lydia's arm and
urged, 'We will see you at the séance, no? It will begin at eleven
– there will surely be those there who long to see you!'

'I'll come as soon as I can,' Lydia excused herself quietly.
'I'm afraid Miranda isn't taking this journey as well as I'd
hoped, and sometimes she wakes in the night crying.' This was
a complete lie – between the princess's dogs, the salt wind, and

being with her mother, Miranda's only complaint so far was that she couldn't go down and play Blind Bock with all the little Russian and Slovenian urchins in the aft deck well. 'If that happens, I'll be a bit late.'

And she hurried to catch up with Captain Winstanley, to make sure that he did, in fact, order the release of Georg Heller from the ship's brig.

No light shone at the Hotel de Montadour. No one opened the door when Asher rapped its heavy bronze knocker; nor yet again, when he'd made his cautious way into the next street, where its graceful mansard roofs were visible from the back, and then returned to knock once more. It was past ten, and the Rue de Passy pitch-dark and silent as the grave.

Even had there been sufficient electricity to keep the street lamps burning through the night, Paris, the City of Lights, lay too near the German lines to be safe from air raids. Heart hammering, Asher walked for a distance up the street and down it again, 'promenading himself', as the vampires said.

Tomorrow, then, she had smiled. But when he knocked again, the house remained silent and dark. Asher had gained the impression that in life, Elysée de Montadour had been a flighty piece, as apt to forget appointments as she was to mislay her keys. He had learned that death – or at least Un-death – didn't change people.

Better you go home now. An attempt to enter the house – Asher's picklocks jingled faintly in his pocket – might bring some of the fledglings of the Paris nest, if they were in Paris and not gorging themselves at the Front. Those beautiful young men whom Elysée made vampires – made her servants – for their good looks, Augustin and Serge and Evrard.

Or did she make fledglings anymore? Did she dare? She had never been – Asher recalled Don Simon Ysidro saying – a particularly strong master vampire, and the frightful events during the first month of the war[1] had robbed her of much of the power over them that she'd had. And if she didn't make them, could she now control the ones she *had* made?

[1] See *Darkness on his Bones*

Asher didn't know. But he guessed, as he made his way back
towards his hotel – three long and bitterly cold miles, for the
Metro had ceased to run hours ago – if Elysée had gotten
distracted by some promising hunt, and any of her fledglings
were about, they would kill him out of hand if they found him
waiting. All the way along the river, unseen in the overcast
darkness, he listened behind him, and through what remained
of the night in his hotel room he woke in sickened panic half
a dozen times, dreaming of cold eyes that gleamed like the cats
in Cyril Britten's attic office, of cold hands stronger than the
grip of devils. Lay listening, knowing that even if they were
there, he wouldn't hear.

Knowing he'd have to go back.

He had four days, before he'd have to start for the Eastern
Front again.

Emerging from the dining room, Lydia tracked down Captain
Palfrey in the First Class lounge, where the *City of Gold's* dance
band was just beginning its evening ration of foxtrots and
decorous versions of the waltz from amid a forest of potted
palms. 'It's infamous of me to send you about like an errand
boy,' she whispered, under cover of the music. 'But I need you
to locate all five of Mr Cochran's private detectives, and let me
know where they are. Now, tonight – at once.'

The young man nodded earnestly, and when Lydia continued,
'I can't – I daren't – tell you the why and wherefore . . .' He
raised a hand to cut off her words.

'You don't need to. You don't think Mr *Cochran* . . .?' He
sounded shocked.

'I don't know,' said Lydia, and again he nodded his understanding, and put a finger to his lips. Lydia had early found it
unnecessary to explain anything to Palfrey. Having accepted
that 'Colonel Simon' was engaged in counter-espionage so deep
that even the Foreign Office didn't know about it, the young
officer was perfectly willing to do anything he was told, either
by Don Simon or by Lydia. At times in the past this purblind
acceptance had maddened Lydia, but she completely understood
why Simon had picked on Captain Palfrey as his servant.

He was a perfect dupe.

She gave him the Second Class cabin numbers of the 'boys' – acquired by Ellen in the servants' dining room – and within thirty minutes Palfrey had returned with the assurance that Mssrs Kimball, Boland, Sweetser, Rand, and Jukes were all playing poker in the Second Class smoking room. Moreover, Cochran's manservant (Mr Oakley, whom Mrs Cochran referred to as a 'boy' or a 'houseboy', despite the fact that he was Jamie's age) was in his own cramped 'servants' quarters' room on C Deck, confirming Lydia's suspicion that, if indeed Mr Cochran had Don Simon imprisoned in one of the tiny, windowless servants' quarters rooms within the Promenade Suite itself, no one but Dr Barvell shared the suite with him.

'Captain Palfrey, you're a marvel,' she whispered, clasping his hands, and then hastened back to a shadowed corner of the Private Promenade, to watch the door of the Princess Gromyko's suite as her séance guests arrived.

'I have no idea where the girl can have gotten to,' complained Aunt Louise as she emerged from her own suite. 'Given the opportunity to actually experience the nearness of the astral plane . . .'

'Beyond a doubt, M'am,' said Mr Mortling's voice. 'I shall send her along when she arrives.'

'See that you do.' The dowager walked the thirty-some feet down the covered way to the princess's door, to be greeted by the soft voice of the Persian butler. Lydia withdrew a little further into the shadows of the stanchions which, in fairer weather, held canvas sunshades over the stairs which led down to C Deck. Mrs Cochran, ascending a few moments later in another expensive but obviously American ensemble and far too many diamonds, passed within a few feet of her without seeing her. Even so, Lydia withdrew down the stairway when she heard Mr Cochran's voice around the corner of the promenade.

She watched him pass, gesticulating savagely (he had dispensed with the sling and his left arm seemed entirely recovered) as he spoke with Dr Barvell. Heard the door of the princess's suite open again, and the murmured words of greeting from the princess's butler. Then, swiftly, she tiptoed up the steps, around the corner, and along the promenade to Cochran's door.

Its locks and those on Aunt Louise's suite were identical. Lydia made short work of them, having practiced several times that afternoon. She lit the candle-stub from her pocket by the light of the promenade lamps and slipped inside. The furnishings were identical as well: sleek American-style chairs and sofa of black enamel and glistening chromium. She dared not switch on the lights, though black linen curtains blocked the glow of the windows. The place was spotlessly – almost forbiddingly – neat in the dim candle-gleam, even the newspapers re-folded to their pristine state, telegrams tucked back in their envelopes. (All concerned the activities of the New York and London stockmarkets. Lydia looked.)

The two bedrooms were similarly immaculate: men's pajamas laid out across the feet of both beds, nary a book or a magazine in sight. The contrast with Aunt Louise's jumble of extra cushions, magazines, photographs and Dresden figurines to the décor of the suite was startling. The only way she could guess which bedroom belonged to the millionaire, and which to his physician, was that the pajamas in his room were silk and the hairbrushes on the bureau solid silver. In that room, also, an almost staggering array of vegetable pills, cathartic mixtures, laxatives ('Epsonade – tastes like lemonade!'), butterfat bath salts, and phials of extracts of monkey glands and rhinoceros horn ranged before the mirror.

Both small, windowless 'servants' chambers' were locked.

One contained what appeared to be a small chemical laboratory: beakers, a Bunsen burner, a glass retort, a small rack of flasks. Lydia wondered whether Dr Barvell was employed to produce rejuvenative potions for Mr Cochran, as well as to tame vampires, and if so, how much he was paid. None of this looked cheap.

The second room held a large black trunk, laid on one of the chamber's narrow beds.

It was what Lydia had hoped to see, but at the sight of it pain gripped her heart. The smallness of it – it looked scarcely large enough to contain the body of a man – brought back to her the memory of the vampire's slight frame, barely her own five-foot-seven-inch height, and narrow-built, like a very old cat. *I should go back to my room and get my satchel*, she thought.

If there's silver mesh inside the coffin he may be helpless. I can do it now . . .

If he's there at all, and not moving somewhere around E Deck looking for some other poor Slovene or Russian girl . . .

Deliberately, her hands shaking, she removed the chains of silver from around her throat and wrists and set them aside. The soft scratching, the faint stirring, within the coffin nearly brought her heart up into her throat. In her mind – she was certain the word was not actually whispered aloud – she heard a murmured voice.

Mistress . . .

The whisper of a dying man.

There were four locks, all plated with silver. It took her only minutes to pick them all, and raise the heavy lid.

A white hand like a skeleton's reached up from within, and caught her wrist in a grip like steel.

TEN

Just as if he hadn't killed thousands of people over the course of three centuries – just as if she hadn't looked on the torn throat and bloodless body of a nineteen-year-old Slovenian girl not quite ten hours before – Lydia helped him sit up. He felt light as a half-grown boy – she had long suspected that human tissue itself underwent some kind of transformation in its change to the vampire state. As she'd suspected, the inside of the coffin was lined with a basket-weave mesh of flat slips of silver, a quarter-inch wide and roughly an inch apart. She winced to think how much that quantity of metal would have cost, even as she observed the places where contact with the metal had burned the vampire's wrists, hands, and face.

But as she thought all this, she wrapped an arm around Don Simon's ribcage, drew him up out of that toxic casket, and helped him sit on the end of the opposite bed. He shivered violently, and his hands, clawed like a demon's and cold as death, clung to her, as if to hope of salvation.

'Thank you,' he whispered, his face pressed to her shoulder. 'I never thought you would come.'

His clothing was crumpled and dirty, the ivory gossamer of his long hair in tangles around a face ghastly, naked of the illusion that conceals the nature of the Undead. Dark bruising marked his sunken eyes and the scars he'd taken, years ago, in Constantinople, defending her, stood out like sword cuts in wax.

She knew then she couldn't kill him. She wrapped both arms around him, held him tight. His own crushed her against the bones that were all that she could feel within his clothes.

'I have to get you out of here,' said Lydia. 'It's eleven thirty, there'll be no one on the promenade deck. They're all at the séance—'

'No good, Lady.' He released his hold on her at last, raised his head to look her in the face. He really did look as if he'd been dead for three hundred years. 'They've injected me with something – I don't know what. Barvell gives me antivenin, in the daytime, when I sleep.' He pushed up the unbuttoned sleeve of his pale linen shirt. The silk-white flesh of his arm bore a line of colorless little puncture marks, tracking the vein. 'I feel it in me, death like smoke in the wind, then turned back for a time. 'Tis worse than the silver, as if ants crawled and bit within the tunnel of the vein, eating as they crawl. *Séance*, you say?'

His eyebrows went up, his yellow eyes nearly transparent in the candle-gleam.

Lydia nodded. 'His detectives are all down in the Second Class smoking room, waiting for him to ring for them when he's done. Did he—' She hesitated, studying that impassive face. 'Has he brought you . . . prey?' She almost couldn't speak the word, and saw his pale brows pinch, very slightly, above the aquiline of his nose. 'Or have you gotten out, at any time?'

'Prey?' he repeated. '*Here*? On a ship, where every passenger must be accounted for? The man's a lunatic but he's not stupid. And no,' he added, the absolute abyss of his despair like a whispered echo of brimstone in his voice. 'No, I have not gotten free.' The quirk of his brows deepened as he sought an answer in her eyes.

'There's a vampire on the ship,' said Lydia. 'Not you – another one. A girl was killed last night.'

'*Dios.*' He was silent then, turning the implications over in his mind. 'Are you sure of this, Mistress? For a vampire to kill here, on shipboard, 'twere madness.'

'Heller – one of the Third Class passengers – is convinced it's someone counterfeiting a vampire kill, but that's lunacy also. Most of Third Class is in an uproar. They're ignorant people, country folk, Italians or Russians or Slovenes. The Captain is putting it about that the girl was killed by her fiancé, but I saw her body. Two gashes, small but very deep, like some of the shrapnel wounds I'd see at the clearing station.' She touched the flesh of her throat. 'She was nearly drained of blood, and . . . and there was no sign of struggle.'

She turned her face aside, wanting to weep – as she had wanted to weep hundreds of times, in the moribund ward or the clearing station for the men dying under her hands. Men killed, not by pale monsters like this blood-drinking ghost beside her, but by other men. *But he* is *a monster*, she thought. *And I cannot let him go free.*

'We need to get you out of here,' she said, looking around her quickly. 'We can go into all this later . . .'

''Twere no good, Lady, if we cannot lay hands on the anti-venin. Within hours I will be incapacitated by pain. How long 'twould take me to die, an I did not have the next injection, I know not. Days, the good Dr Barvell –' his voice slipped with chilly hatred over the name – 'hath assured me.' Rising, he took her hand, led her into the narrow interior passage which separated the servants' rooms from the elegant portion of the suite, and so through to the physician's workroom again.

'*Cagafuego,*' he added, as Lydia switched on the electric light. The harsh illumination shone on laboratory flasks and fittings, on locked cabinets which, when opened, proved to contain phials of assorted sizes, only two of which – silver nitrate and pyrrol-idine – were labeled. 'And no notes, either.' His long, thin fingers flicked open drawers, sorted through the several small boxes and cases as swiftly as Lydia unlocked them.

'He can probably tell which is what by their smell,' Lydia guessed, checking the two other cases. 'Or by the shape of the bottles. Drat the man, there's no way of telling whether these things are the antivenin or the poison, or ingredients of one or the other . . . phew,' she added, stoppering a large bottle. 'And *that* one is liquor. So much for his pontifications on pure bodies and pure health. Captain Calvert at the clearing station used to hide cognac in his laboratory things . . .'

'He was not the only one.' And, when Lydia turned to him in surprise, Don Simon added, 'Think you that I was not ever somewhere near, when you were at the Front, Lady? I know the men of your clearing station well.'

Killing men in the moribund ward . . .

Her eyes met his, and blurred with tears.

Men who would die anyway. She had known their condition, and had never had the smallest doubt. She felt that there was something she must say to him, but words wouldn't come. It was she who turned away first, and went back to picking the simple locks on satchels and chests. Most of these had been silver-plated. Don Simon moved behind her, checking through their contents.

'The lining hath not the feel of having been tampered with. He will have notes – if he hath such things at all – upon his person.' He lifted out a small box containing a hypodermic syringe and held it up, glinting evilly in the reflected light. 'Myself, I would not trust this Cochran no matter how much he paid me. And here are ampoules for the drug. *Hijo de puta,*' he added. 'Only one is full. The others, empty.'

'And they'll know,' said Lydia quietly, 'if that one has been tampered with, and will change all their precautions. Until we have some plan, some next step, we can't let that happen.' She looked across into the vampire's sulfur-yellow eyes. 'These empty ones have been used . . . Ah.' She withdrew another box, still in the wrapping of a medical supply house.

'And here are new ones, not yet filled. He'll be putting up a new batch, now that he's settled in.'

'And mayhap he fears that once he hath mixed sufficient quantity to keep me obedient, Cochran will dispense with him, and find another alchemist to do his bidding when we reach New York. Could a good chemist, given this –' his clawed forefinger made the tiniest *tick* on the glass of the single filled phial – 'and quantities of each element, come on the right mixture?'

'I doubt it.' Lydia replaced the box of new phials, arranged the luggage in the cupboard exactly as it had been. 'Not without Barvell's notes as to temperature and timing of the reaction. We'll have to check again, later – so he mustn't even suspect I've been in here. We have five days,' she added. 'Can you – do you have any power at all within the coffin?'

Don Simon held up his hand, the silk-white flesh on his wrist seared – literally blackened with second- and third-degree burning. 'Within that coffin, nothing,' he said, in his expressionless whisper. 'Even here outside, the mental glamour – the influence on the minds of the living – is impossible on so vast a world of moving water. Yet I can hear as I do upon dry land, and see, as always, in darkness. Only for perhaps ten minutes on either side of midnight – true astronomical midnight, when this ship, this tiny world, stands exactly opposite to the power and pull of the sun – do our full powers return, if we be free to use them. Know you when this girl was killed?'

She shook her head. 'Her body wasn't found until around three in the morning, in a place public enough that it could not have been done there. Do you know –' she took his cold fingers in hers – 'why it is that you only regain power at midnight? Jamie told me about that – that a vampire is helpless on running water, except at the very hour of midnight, or at the turning of the tide . . .'

'I know not, Mistress. Believe me, I have studied the vampire condition for centuries, e'en as my masters did, Rhys the White of London, and Constantine Angelus in Paris. I know – they knew – that our flesh itself alters, cell by cell, into something which is not human flesh; something which will take unquenchable fire in the sun; something lighter and stronger than the flesh of men. Whatever it is, 'twill not bear the touch of things which living men find harmless: silver, garlic, the petals of the Christmas rose. My masters knew, as I know, that our minds alter as well, and we acquire the capacity to deceive the minds of the living. They knew, as I know, that this capacity waxes as we age, until we can walk in the dreams of the living, or command them from within their minds. But what it is in the deaths of our victims which feeds our powers; why our powers slack and wither without such feeding; why we cannot deceive

our own eyes in a mirror, or use these powers upon water save
at certain brief seasons – this we do not know. Nor do I know
– nor did they know – why any of this came to be.'

He was silent for a time, looking down at the hypodermic
which he still held in his burned fingers.

'Nor do I know whether they knew – as I have observed –
that many of the vampires I have met over four centuries of
age go mad.' He turned his head sharply, as if at some noise,
then said, 'Best we go outside, Lady, where you at least will
be able to flee.' He set the hypodermic back into its box, pinched
out the candle, switched off the light. Then he took her hand,
his own cold as a dead man's. His right hand touched her back,
guiding her across the little corridor again and then out through
the dark parlor.

'Are they coming—?'

'Not yet. And from what you have told me, Mistress, I
suspect,' he added, as they slipped from the blackness out into
the harsh chill and electric glare of the promenade deck, 'that
when your aunt and all others leave this magical circle which
they have made, Cochran and Barvell will remain for a time, to
question the seer in private.'

'About what?' asked Lydia, surprised.

He answered as if the reply were self-evident. 'The whereabouts of this vampire.'

'But he's *got* a vampire!'

'An unwilling one, heretofore. One who was taken in a
trap.' He turned his hands over, considering the burns on his
wrists. 'Though now that I know you are indeed on the *City
of Gold* – is my good John here also, by the way? Or our
James?'

'Captain Palfrey is, yes. James – I think –' her voice caught
a little – 'is still in Paris.'

'Forgive me, Lady.' He raised her hand to his lips. 'Forgive
me calling for you as I did. I was . . . in terror and in pain.'
The words came out as if he could barely bring himself to admit
it. ''Twas beyond hope that you would come for me; beyond
expectation that I could avoid the fate of being enslaved by this
American.'

'Is he working for the Germans? Or the Americans?'

'Nothing so noble –' his voice again turned for a moment to cold acid – 'if noble be the word. For himself only. To kill, undetectably, those who would cause trouble for his factories, his railroads, his mines. 'Tis money, not the honor of land or king or God, that moves him. The man has the mind of a tradesman. His own convenience is all he sees.'

In his voice she heard the hidalgo of antique Spain, the nobleman who would suffer the greatest of hardships and danger in the cause of God or his king, but would starve before he earned his own bread.

She remembered, too, the contempt in Georg Heller's voice, when he spoke of the rich who stole from the poor.

'He wants a bravo, like unto his other hired bravos. Now that he has this poison, this weapon, he will scour the world, I daresay, for another of my condition to enslave. The murder of strikers and socialists,' the vampire went on slowly, 'would be only the beginning, I think. In time, I think this Cochran would find other uses for one who can kill with impunity, and I suspect it would come to being lent out like a whore to politicians who have need of their enemies to vanish.

'Now that I know that you are here, Mistress – now that I know that I am not alone –' he shut his eyes for a moment, as if in prayer (*do vampires pray?* she wondered) – 'I think that I will capitulate, and swear my allegiance to him. Know you if he is a Protestant? That doesn't surprise me. The Holy Father long ago absolved us all of any oath made to heretics.' One corner of his mouth moved in an ironic half-grin. 'I don't suppose an oath sworn on the cross, or a testament, would reassure him. Both he and Barvell wear crucifixes the size of frying pans when they speak to me and seem to think that this –' he held up his left arm, displaying, on the back of the wrist, a savage cross-shaped burn – 'was the doing of Our Lord's image rather than the silver content of the talisman. I thank you,' he said again, more quietly. 'Deeply as I value my good John Palfrey's loyalty and strength, he hath not, as my valet would have said long ago, sufficient brain to outweigh a pistol ball. E'en with the sea all round me, 'tis good to stand here in open air. To not be in pain.'

For a time neither spoke, and the voice of the water murmured about them like the heartbeat of the world. Voices drifted to them, formless murmurs, from the public First Class promenade below them on C Deck, and from the Second Class promenade further amidships of that. The hour was late, the North Atlantic night freezing. Beyond the glow of the ship's lights only thin spumes of white flicked along the crests of ebon waves. Lydia guessed that only young (or possibly not-so-young) lovers would be strolling those covered decks in the yellow electric radience, huddled in their greatcoats and warmed by each other's nearness.

She hoped James, wherever he was, was keeping warm. The thought of him went through her palpably: heart, flesh, tears. She made herself ask, 'Is there anything that can be done about the pain? I know – you've told me – that the Undead don't . . . don't process substances the way the living do, not unless they've been mixed with something like silver nitrate. Does that go for anodynes as well?'

'Even so, Lady. Another, I assume, of those little jests God plays upon those of us who would sacrifice the lives of others, that we ourselves might live forever.'

He paused, and glancing sidelong at him, Lydia thought he was – incredibly – about to say something else, something perhaps concerning God and pain and three centuries of preying upon those he had personally considered less worthy of life than himself. But after a moment he only said, 'I think it likely that Cochran, having convinced himself that he hath the means to bring the Undead to heel, will enlist my aid in hunting this vampire aboard ship. He might even bribe me with the promise that, the other's services being secured, he will let me go free. Always supposing there is a vampire.'

Lydia frowned. 'Who would fake such a thing? And *why*?'

'What vampire would be such a fool as to kill under these circumstances?'

'He – or she – could be mad. You've said vampires *do* go mad. I mean, why would a vampire come on board ship at all? I was afraid,' she faltered, 'that it was you. That you had been . . . either deranged, or made so desperate by . . . by hunger. But it is true,' she added thoughtfully, 'that such a killing could be faked. And whoever killed poor Pavlina Jancu – either a vampire or a . . . a hoaxer – they killed her elsewhere and left her body where it would be found, rather than disposing of it. But if it was someone who wanted to cover up his tracks for actually murdering that poor girl, it's an absolutely cork-brained way to go about it.'

'One never—' began the vampire. Then his head snapped around, and his brows twitched down over the bridge of his nose again.

Lydia turned her head also, listening. Was that a noise from the fore deck well of the ship, above the throb of the engines?

'Screaming,' said Don Simon softly. 'Best you lock me up again, Mistress, and go to see what's afoot.'

ELEVEN

Clattering down the gangway into the fore deck well, Lydia was overtaken by the maid Tania. 'What is it?' she gasped, and the young woman stammered, partly in French and mostly in a torrent of Russian, that (as far as Lydia could make it out) Zhenya – the princess's footman – had rushed into her room telling her that a child had been killed by the vampire. The door from the deck well into the Third Class section was jammed with people, pushing in and out and clamoring in a mix of languages. A big fair-haired man in livery caught Tania by the arm and poured out an explanation in Russian, then, with Tania ably assisting (she was nearly as tall as he), began to force a way for Lydia through the press towards the room where the child lay.

'*Ya doktor*,' Lydia gasped, clinging tight to the back of Zhenya's belt. '*Zhdravnik* . . .' She hoped that was Slovenian for doctor, anyway. Or close enough, to what some of the orderlies at the clearing station had called the surgeons. '*Giatrass* . . .'

'*Giatros*,' Tania corrected over her shoulder – either she'd picked up a little Greek from another servant, or knew it from someone at home.

'*Giatros. Doktor*,' Lydia repeated, thrusting her way through the narrow door of the chamber. '*Doktor . . .*'

'I fear –' Old Father Kirn turned from the bunk, on which the body of a dark-haired seven-year-old girl lay – 'that this is not the province of medicine anymore, good Madame.' His deep-scored face was ravaged with horror, grief, and barely-suppressed rage. Beside him, the woman who had been bent over the child's body half raised herself and screamed again, a wailing cry of anguish.

'Luzia! Luzia!'

Tania knelt at once by the woman's side, put an arm around her shaking shoulders. On her other side a girl of fifteen or sixteen knelt with her arm around her waist, dark-haired and swarthy, wearing the gold earrings and tawdry jewelry of a gypsy. Little Luzia's ears, too, had been pierced, and many of the women in the minuscule cabin – crammed to suffocation – looked uncertain whether to hang back, or to offer comfort to one who they'd all, clearly, been taught was a daughter of Ishmael.

Close behind her, Lydia heard the whispered words, *Gypsy trash . . .*

But four or five clustered round, offering what comfort they could, in Czech, in Walloon, in Yiddish or Russian. Mothers who knew what it was, to lose a child.

'Luzia!' the gypsy woman screamed again. '*Copilul meu!*'

'What happened?'

'The little one was not in her bunk this evening,' said Father Kirn in his inaccurate German. 'This was not unusual in the earlier hours after supper.'

'The room is hot,' spoke up the golden-haired Sudetendeutsche girl Ariane, who had defended Valentyn Marek last night. She was on the bed, wedged in beside the distraught mother's family. 'I said I'd take them all up into the deck well. Everybody's cramped and bored down here. It was dark, but there are lights up there. I should have watched better—'

'No, no,' the priest whispered. 'No, this was none of it your fault, Ariane.' To Lydia, he said, 'The little one's sisters could not say exactly when last they saw her. And it is, indeed, dark, with many shadows. I think,' he added, with a crooked attempt at a smile, 'in truth, that is why they consider it such fun.'

'We thought she came back here.' Tears flooded Ariane's eyes. 'Or would soon. It was ten before anyone began to search.'

In the corridor a man was shouting in German, 'It is as I said! There is a vampire on this ship, a devil – *vodolak! Nosferatu*! Undead!' Someone cried out an objection – at least, it sounded like an objection, but Lydia's Russian (if his language *was* Russian) was too fragmentary to be sure.

Ariane flinched, but the old priest only reached for the small wooden box – like a microscope case, thought Lydia – that sat on the floor at his side, and carefully took out a fragile wafer of flour, stamped with part of a design. Ariane crossed herself. Luzia's mother only grasped the priest's arm and wept.

Lydia, kneeling in the narrow space that Father Kirn had made for her at the bunk-side, saw by the makeshift bundles beside the pillow that at least two children were meant to sleep there, possibly more. Tiny Luzia, her tangled black curls still disheveled from the evening's play, looked calm, and Lydia couldn't help noting, when the priest opened her mouth to insert the fragment of Host, that her jaw hadn't yet begun to stiffen.

The big artery of her neck had been slit, two short deep cuts such as Lydia had seen made by vampire claws. The flesh around the wounds looked pinched and bruised, and Lydia mentally cursed herself for not having studied more closely the exact appearance of vampire bites – *heaven knows I've had the opportunity* . . .

The child's hands and face, chalky with dearth of blood, were still faintly warm.

Leaning close, Lydia moved aside the grape-black curls, to look behind the ears. No blood, but the hair itself was slightly damp, and smelled of . . .

Something. Sourish, dirty water . . .

Another smell. Lydia bent to sniff the child's lips.

Chocolate.

There was the tiniest trace of it, still clinging to a corner of the child's mouth.

Turning the little hand over, she sniffed the fingers. The

dirty-water smell lingered there, too, as if someone had mopped at the delicate ivory fingers with a wet rag.

'Is there a chance that I can examine this child?' she whispered to Father Kirn. 'To see if she was hurt in any other fashion?' Something about the smell of the candy revolted her, reminded her that there were monsters very much alive in the world that also killed little girls after giving them sweets. But it would not do to say so, not with the girl's mother sobbing inches from her shoulder. *Don't lay that on her, along with her child's death.*

And indeed, on the ocean, without the use of mental powers of illusion, a vampire would have to hunt with candy, to draw his prey.

'In what other fashion do you need, good Madame?' Gently, the priest removed the short prayer rope from his own belt, tied it to a piece of string from his pocket, and put this like a necklace around the child's neck. 'The poor little mite is dead—'

'*Tata, tata!*' The mother shook the priest with a convulsive strength. 'Tell me her soul not forfeit! Tell me my little one not walk as living damned!'

Out in the corridor, the man Vodusek sniffed, 'Damned indeed! I swear the gypsy brat wasn't baptized . . .'

'Be at peace.' The old man made the sign of the cross on the woman's forehead, then from the pyx beside him took a little vial of holy oil, and with it, repeated the sign on Luzia's forehead as well. 'Jesus the Christ said, "Suffer the little children to come unto me". Your daughter is safe in God's arms.'

'It's true, Frau Pescariu,' urged Ariane, putting her arm around the mother again. 'You know it's true. The Cross, and the Host, they will keep her safe. The vampire can endure none of these things.'

Lydia could have disagreed, but didn't. Someone standing deeper in the room made the sign of the cross and Lydia recognized old Grandpa Marek, tears of agony running down his face. She couldn't keep herself from wondering, *How* would *one go about staking someone through the heart on shipboard? Much less cutting off their head and burying them at the crossroad?*

'Let us through! Let us through!' Voices in the corridor.

'*Proydem cherez*,' they added, fumbling at the pronunciation. '*Lasciaci passare . . .*'

Dr Liggatt squeezed and thrust his angular way through the door, with the vessel's bantam-weight First Officer, Mr Theale, a couple of burly deck stewards and a translator. The translator was repeating, in Russian, Italian, and laborious German, 'Please to clear cabin. Everyone, please to clear corridor. Admit these people out. Everything be take care of – please to clear cabin.'

Pani Marek, holding the hand of the weeping young sister and speaking to her quietly, whirled upon the officers with a perfect storm of Slovene. Tania and three other women in the room added their voices to the din, while the girl Ariane held the grieving mother tight.

'For love of God, sir,' said Father Kirn to Liggatt in German, 'this woman is the child's mother!'

The men hesitated, then Mr Theale said, 'Stand over there for a moment, if you would, Father, with her. Does she have a husband? A relative? They may remain, but we must have room. Yes,' he added, as Lydia rose and approached Dr Liggatt, 'Mrs Asher may remain as well. The rest of you, please clear out and give us room.'

Ariane, edging out into the corridor, gently took charge of the two young girls who'd been crowded into the cabin's farthest corner: dark and tangle-haired and dressed in gaudy cast-offs, aged – Lydia guessed – twelve and ten. They looked enough like the mother to be the dead child's sisters. They clung to the older girl, their faces soaked with tears: guilt as well as grief. They were the ones who'd been playing with her, dodging about the decks in the chilly evening before another night – Lydia looked around her in pity and distaste – of the suffocating closeness of a cabin overheated by at least ten other sleeping bodies.

Stepping back beside Father Kirn, Lydia whispered, 'Where was she found? And when?'

'Just after midnight,' said the old priest. 'When Luzia was found not to be in her bed, we began to search. Even those who believed that poor Pavlina Jancu had been killed by Valentyn Marek, thought themselves again of the *upír*. I was one of those who found her –' he averted his face quickly, wrinkled eyelids shutting as if to close out the sight of the crumpled little body in her mended hand-me-downs – 'at the foot of the stairway, in the – what is it called? The gangway well.' He pronounced these last words carefully, in English. 'Not a hundred feet from this place. This thing, this devil, it is merciless—'

'Had you been up and down that stairway before? During the search? Had anyone?'

The old man shook his head, tears tracking down through the wrinkles of his face. 'How could they have, and not have seen her? The crew uses that stair, but mostly here, we go up and down the larger stair near the dining room. Does that matter? The child is dead, she is dead, even the least of these, the children of Ishmael, is a soul in the eyes of Christ.'

Lydia bit back the comment that she had seen Father Kirn stop two of the little Greek children from playing with the three gypsy sisters only that afternoon.

'And the thing that killed her – the thing that drank her blood – it is still somewhere on this ship. In the darkness, in the thousand corners where no one goes. But we will find it.'

He turned to look at Dr Liggatt, kneeling with thermometer and probes beside the cot, and his dark eyes gleamed with sudden, somber fury. 'There is great evil in this world, Madame. And not all of it concerns guns, and aeroplanes, and the shouting of the War. Some of it is deeper, and older, and more terrible. But it is given to each man, that he has the power at least to stop that evil. And that we will do, Madame. That we will do.'

Gathering up his small supply of the wafer in its box, he crossed himself again, and edged his way to the little gypsy's mother and sisters, to offer them what comfort he could.

All Friday morning, Asher spent at the embassy, alternately drinking tea with Cyril Britten and thumbing through reports on various persons with whom Spenser Cochran was connected. He was easily able to work in quiet, for the old head clerk was in and out of the room: word had just reached the ambassador that the Tsar of Russia had abdicated, not only for himself but also on behalf of his fragile son. As the next-in-line – the Tsar's scapegrace younger brother – was refusing the title (and the responsibility for a rapidly-destabilizing government in the midst of a horrifying war – Asher was fairly certain that in his place, he'd turn it down as well) until elections could be held, the embassy was in an uproar. Whenever the head clerk was called away, Asher took advantage of his absence by asking the assistant that Britten had assigned him – another man in his eighties who, like Britten, knew every file and dossier in the place, but had to be reminded of who the ambassador was and who the Allies were fighting – for documents pertaining to many subjects that had nothing to do with Spenser Cochran, but which he suspected might come in useful later.

He helped himself to some embassy stationery and a copy of the ambassador's signature on his way out.

In the afternoon, armed with credentials and letters of introduction as questionable as the major's uniform that he wore when on his own side of the lines, he made his way to the Quai des Orfèvres and found out everything that the Paris Sûreté knew about Dr Louis Barvell. Which, it turned out, was quite a bit.

'He's a Belgian,' said the one-armed clerk who showed Asher into the department library. 'Studied in Louvain, though his name was Hendrick Doumont at the time. He seems to have specialized in occult lore and chemistry. Though he never obtained a medical license, he set himself up in Paris as a "nerve doctor" and did a fair business among wealthy women: I don't believe there's ever been a record of him paying his own rent.' He limped to a cabinet and brought back a folder of newspaper cuttings, which included a photograph that seemed to have been taken on the front steps of the Hotel de Crillon. Barvell, a tall, broad-shouldered man of dark good looks and natty tailoring, had evidently realized he was being photographed and was half-turned away from the camera. The middle-aged woman clinging to his arm wore an expression of shocked dismay.

'He's a good-looking fellow,' the clerk went on, an ironic sparkle in his dark Gascon eyes. 'Seems also to have a talent for getting people to hand him money. He's well-known these days in what they call "occult circles", both here and in America.' He fetched another photograph – equally blurred – with the clumsiness of one still learning to maneuver with a missing limb and what was clearly a shattered pelvis. 'America's where he went – in a hurry – in . . . Let's see . . . 1909.'

'Fraud?' inquired Asher. 'Or women?'

'Accusations –' the clerk put a world of implication in the cock of his brow – 'which were later dropped. When he returned to Paris in 1913 – which is when he started calling himself Barvell – he touted himself as a mentalist healer, and it was thought prudent to keep an eye on him, though nothing was ever proven about the client of his who disappeared. But it was noted that from that point the rent on his apartment was paid by an American who had controlling interests in German manufacturing and mines.' The man shrugged, and made that characteristically French back-and-forth waggle with his remaining hand. '*En effet*, many Americans had – and indeed, have – investments in Germany.'

'I understand,' said Asher, 'that Dr Barvell – and his employer – took ship for New York only Wednesday. Would you happen to know if his apartment is for rent again?'

'It is not. The rent has been paid up for six months.' He handed Asher another file. 'You have perhaps information which can be added to our store, on the subject either of Dr Barvell or M'sieu Cochran?'

'At the moment, no,' lied Asher blandly. 'But I will certainly communicate with you with whatever I might learn.'

The ambassador's signature – and a few carefully chosen hints about Spenser Cochran's German investments – served to get Asher into Louis Barvell's apartment on the Rue Monceau, in company with a small white-haired gentleman named Lepic who had, like Asher and (Asher guessed) nearly everyone else he'd encountered at the Sûreté, retired from the service and been re-called to duty when every available man under the age of forty-five was drawn to the Front. He didn't expect to find much, and wasn't disappointed. The apartment was one of the thousands constructed during the Second Empire, four spacious rooms on the 'premier étage' overlooking the building's courtyard with wide windows, electricity laid on (wartime shortages permitting), and its own kitchen. One of the rooms, though stripped of all books, papers, and references, had clearly been used as a laboratory.

A few chemicals remained, in bottles in the cabinet: silver nitrate, silver chloride, and distilled extracts of things like garlic and aconite. Though not a chemist himself, Asher had been tasked to pilfer many chemical formulae in his time and recognized the names of the powders and salts. He recognized also a number of botanicals, from his folkloric researches. Everything was neatly labeled, and he copied the information. The equipment on a lower shelf was mostly standard, familiar to him from Lydia's laboratory at the end of their garden on Holywell Street. He listed those, too.

In the unswept corners of the room he encountered shavings of silver mixed with the dust, and shavings of sawdust.

Trestles in a corner stood precisely as they would stand, to support a coffin.

He turned back to the door, where his white-haired Sûreté guide and the landlady stood with the keys. 'Who lives in the apartment above this?'

The landlady's tone was flat. 'The gentleman who rents this apartment also rents the one above. No one lives there.' And, as Asher's eyebrows went up, she continued, 'It is not my affair, so long as they pay on time.'

Asher responded, 'No, indeed, Madame.'

Smaller and lower-ceilinged, those rooms contained nothing, not even furniture. The uncurtained windows were shuttered, and cobwebs stitched those shutters together. Fragments of web likewise stirred in the corners, like the ghosts of fairies slain by the sound of siege guns and falling bombs.

'Whatever it is he's doing,' said Asher, as he and his quiet guide descended to the street once more, 'he – or Cochran – doesn't want the neighbors to overhear. And given the crowding in Paris, and the demands for apartments, to keep such a place empty for four years argues a positive mania for privacy.'

'*En effet*,' replied Lepic. 'So much so, that when Barvell's flat was burglarized a few years ago – in May of 1913, it was – no report of it was made, though our sources tell us that Barvell was most exercised over the disappearance of several of his notebooks. Is this not true, Madame?' He glanced back at the landlady, standing in the doorway behind them.

'What my tenants choose to do and not to do is none of my concern, M'sieu.' She closed the door.

'Nevertheless,' the policeman continued, 'I trust you have no objection to my reporting our conversation to M'sieu Ladoux?' He named the head of France's counterintelligence division.

'None in the least.'

'And what is it, might I ask –' Lepic offered him a cigarette, at which Asher shook his head – 'which has prompted your interest in this American and his tame professor?'

Asher shrugged. 'They give me names, and ask for "anything you can find". Sometimes I learn what it's all about, sometimes I don't.' He glanced down at the shorter man, who was regarding him with evident disbelief in his light-green eyes. 'But this should interest them.'

TWELVE

'There are storerooms –' Lydia consulted her printed plan of the *City of Gold* – 'at the farthest extent of the bow, on Decks D, E, F –' she paused, propped her spectacles, and looked around at the place by the hard glare of the electrical fixtures which drowned whatever morning light might have come down from three decks above – 'and down below here on G.' The *City*'s crew had already been through that morning. Any traces of blood – or footprints – had been swabbed away. 'That stairway goes right down through the ship.'

Not, she reflected, that many clues would have survived the comprehensive trampling of every Third Class passenger who'd swarmed this portion of Deck F throughout last night, either searching for Luzia Pescariu or clamoring for news after her body had been found.

Georg Heller touched her elbow, guided her down the low-ceilinged passageway away from the fore gangway well itself, to the door of the storeroom at the end, nearly hidden in shadow. 'Can you pick the locks?'

Lydia glanced over her shoulder, at the long artery that fed not only the Third Class cabins in this bow section of F Deck, but, farther on, the noisy cavern of the engine rooms and coal bunkers that made up the whole center section of the lower decks. Beneath the heavy vibration of the machinery surged the mutter of talk as the 'black gang' – as the stokers were called – came and went from their quarters on the deck above: as many white men as blacks, but everybody – by this hour of their shift – universally grimed in coal dust and grease.

'I shouldn't care to try it at this hour.'

A cabin door on the other side of the open well of the gangway creaked; the one-eyed man Vodusek slipped out, crossed quickly to a locker in the shadows under the stairs, and brought something out of his trouser pocket – a picklock or a key, thought Lydia. A noise down the main corridor made him turn his head, however, and he startled at the sight of Lydia and Heller. Touching his cap, he said casually, '*G'n morgen*,' and strolled away in the direction of the engines, slipping whatever it was – key or picklock – back into his pocket. Turning a corner, he disappeared into the tangle of side-halls and Third Class cabins.

Heller raised his eyebrows and Lydia said, 'It's none of our business . . .'

'One never knows,' returned the German, 'what may turn out to be one's business.'

With the guilty sensation of a schoolgirl in mischief, Lydia crossed to the locker and made short work of its Chubb cylinder lock. The electric ceiling-fixture nearby showed them only shelves containing bottles of ammonia, Jeyes Fluid, a number of folded canvas tarpaulins, bleach and sponges. There was no sign of blood, but, tucked behind the sponges, was half a bottle of Glenlivet (of the sort Lydia had glimpsed behind the bar in the First Class lounge the previous evening) and two packets of Turkish cigarettes.

She made a noise of distaste, and Heller calmly extracted a cigarette from each packet. 'Even if he notices, he can't very well report the loss. Like as not he'll just think he miscounted. Would you like one?' He held it out.

Smiling a little, Lydia shook her head.

Voices in the stairwell high above made him close the locker door quickly, and steer Lydia away in the direction Vodusek had gone, tucking one of the cigarettes into the pocket of his tattered jacket and putting the other in his mouth.

'Are keys that easy to steal?'

'I expect he borrowed one.' The German shrugged. 'He could get into the ship's machine shop easily enough: he was a machinist at the Vulcan shipyard in Hamburg, before they started transferring men to the Front. No blood, at any rate,' he added, grimly, and fished forth a steel lighter, such as the men had carried in their pockets at the Front. 'Or candy.'

Lydia said, very quietly, 'No.' She wondered if, when they found the hiding place of the vampire, there would be a box of chocolates tucked in whatever he – or she – was using for a protective coffin.

As if he sensed her thoughts, Heller said, 'What you have told me, of the smell of sweets on the little gypsy's lips – and of wash-water on her fingers . . .' He grimaced. 'To a poor child, and that young, a friendly man's whisper that he will give her chocolate, that is enough to make her hide from her sisters, sneak away to meet him. They starve for sweets, these little ones here.'

Lydia remembered how the children had greeted Tania with joy, as the dispenser of treats. Evidently sweets weren't difficult to acquire, if one scraped acquaintance with the kitchen staff, who seemed to have their own ideas about what First Class amenities could be quietly peddled to whom.

A little hesitantly, she said, 'She wasn't . . . harmed . . . in any other way.' She wondered at her own delicacy. A man like Heller would certainly have heard the word *rape* before. And would know about men who preferred their victims young. 'I asked Dr Liggatt – both about her, and about Pavlina Jancu. That is . . . curious. If we're dealing with a madman.'

'If we're dealing with a very cunning madman . . .' Heller frowned, and did not finish his thought. At the foot of a smaller stairway – the ship was pierced everywhere with them, tying the upper reaches to the lower – he paused, and took the cigarette from his mouth. 'I have not thanked you, Frau Doktor, for speaking out for me to the captain yesterday evening. Myself, I do not believe that anyone made an attempt on Cochran's life.

And I do not think that this will be the last attempt the man makes on mine.'

And, when Lydia opened her mouth protestingly, Heller went on, 'I will not conceal from you that I am a Socialist, Madame. In my own country, before the war, I led workmen's strikes, first in the mines of Saxony where I was born, then at factories in Hamburg and Berlin. We shut down Cochran's steel mill at Rotenberg for nearly three months. I felt that the war was an abomination and a cheat – a betrayal of workingmen on both sides. Yet I volunteered and fought for my country, until I could endure no more. My country – and yours – is being betrayed by the pride and idiocy of those who govern it. I know that this makes me reprehensible in the eyes of everyone I meet – yourself, probably, included. I am sorry for this.'

He looked seriously into her face, giving her the chance to speak. Behind them, the fragile-looking little Jewish boy that Lydia remembered from that first night outside the Third Class passenger shed darted past them and up the stairway, followed by a slightly older girl, dark braids bouncing, who called out, 'Yakov! Yakov!' amid gales of giggles. A moment after they disappeared the tall, elderly Jew she'd seen with the children came striding down the main corridor, scowling and grumbling horribly and carrying a belt looped up in his hand, as if ready with it to whack some juvenile bottoms.

He paused by the foot of the stair, looking around him – a narrow corridor crossed at that point leading to Third Class cabins on either side – and, diffidently, he approached Heller and Lydia. 'I beg pardon, good sir, good madame . . .' He bowed with the obsequiousness of one who all his life, thought Lydia, had been thrashed, and worse, for being disrespectful to his Christian betters. On either side of a monumental beak of nose, his dark eyes were wise and bright behind the gold pince-nez. 'But did you see two children run past here? A little lad, a little girl . . .'

Lydia glanced at the belt and said nothing. Heller replied, 'They went up the stair.'

'Ach,' grumbled the old man, climbing laboriously. 'Little monkeys.'

To Lydia, after he had gone, Heller said, 'Goldhirsch makes

great threats, and it is true that he's merciless to those who owe
him money. Yet these two days I have never seen him strike his
grandchildren. Nor are they afraid of him, as children are with
those who beat them. The other children throw things at Yakov
– and at his grandfather – because they are Jews.' His mouth
twisted, as at the sour taste of lemon. 'Myself, I think it is well,
that children are kept a little closer now, as this killer seems to
have a taste for the young and the helpless.'

Lydia thought of Miranda, safely watched over by the grim-
faced Mrs Frush, by the cowed little nursery-maid Prebble,
and by the faithful Ellen.

She shivered, and said, 'I'm sorry.'

Heller shook his head. Below-decks the air was close and
frowsty, but chill draughts flowed down the gangway from
above, where rain had fallen, on and off, all morning. Like the
distant tinkle of windchimes, she heard the voices of the children
from the deck above.

'You are of a different world, Frau Doktor,' Heller said.
'Yes, you've been to the Front. You've seen men die. But you've
not lived in these little villages, these little towns, where every
pfennig and every mouthful of bread must be counted. Where
you cannot even give the milk you take from your own cow,
and the eggs from your own chickens, to your children, because
such things must be sold that you may pay the rent on your
cottage, while your children exist on water and bread. I can tell
you that being shot at every day is not so bad as that.'

Lydia recalled some of the letters she'd read to the men in
the moribund ward, too weak to hold up the ill-spelled notes
sent by mothers and wives, or blinded by gas or shrapnel.
Matter-of-fact accounts of the endless, grinding shifts to afford
a few scraps of bacon, or to come up with the interest on what
they owed the local money-lender, or the weekly rent due the
owner of the rooms they shared with another family. Even at
her worst, sharing an attic with two other young women at
Oxford, tucking newspapers inside her shirtwaist for extra
warmth and having to make the nightly decision between
supper and heating-fuel, Lydia had known she had hope. That
she would eventually become a doctor one day, and be out of
all that.

Quietly, she asked, 'That's what you're fighting to save them from, isn't it? That world. That life.'

'It is, *gnä'* Frau. For that, too, is a form of death. Not only in Saxony or Germany, but everywhere there are rich people who own mines and factories, and poor people who accept a few *pfennigs* a day because they have no other choice. Cochran knows this,' he finished with a sigh. 'It is why he seeks to keep me out of the United States. Since the crimes, as they call them, which I have committed were in Germany, they may have trouble at that. And my Danish papers are quite good.'

'Do you speak Danish?' asked Lydia, amused.

'*Som en infødt.*' Heller bowed with a flourish. 'Probably better than whoever the authorities will produce to question me in it. My captain – in my brief career in the Kaiserliche Marine – was a Schleswiger; half the crew of our U-boat spoke Danish better than they spoke German. I will probably "jump ship", as they say, rather than present my papers to the authorities . . . if this Cochran doesn't come up with some means of getting rid of me before we land.'

As she climbed the stairway to First Class to meet Captain Palfrey for luncheon, Lydia shivered again, guessing what that means might be.

After luncheon, rather to Lydia's surprise, she found herself being recruited as a vampire hunter by Mr Cochran himself.

When she'd finally returned to her stateroom the night before – and she had not come up from Third Class until nearly two thirty in the morning – she had lain awake for nearly an hour, wondering what she was going to tell Palfrey: about Don Simon, about Spenser Cochran, about the killings deep in the hold of the ship. He would almost certainly not believe her if she told him the truth: that Don Simon Ysidro, his 'Colonel Simon', was in fact a vampire, one of the night-walking Undead who survived by drinking the life-energies of those he killed. Certainly not that Don Simon had deceived him, had skillfully planted scenes and pseudo-memories in his dreams, to convince him that he, John Palfrey, was in fact working for and with a member of a British Intelligence branch so secret that even the rest of the government wasn't aware of its existence.

That the vampire was simply using him as he'd have used
any cab driver in London, as a means to get himself safely
home.

To begin with, Lydia wasn't completely certain that this was
true. She knew that even without recourse to illusion, Don
Simon could be extremely charming. But she also knew that
he could be loyal to his 'servants', as he called them, and had,
upon one occasion, risked his life to retrieve Captain Palfrey
from danger when there was little likelihood that the young
man would ever be of any use to him again.

And, reflected Lydia – not without exasperated misgivings
– she found herself deeply unwilling to betray the vampire. *Let
alone kill him*, she added. *Which is what I should do.*

She pushed the thought away.

I have five days yet, to make up my mind what to do.

In any case, she found herself, over a veal and ham pie and
an apple meringue in the Willow Grove (she didn't feel up to
dealing with either Aunt Louise or Mr Tilcott), explaining, to
the worried young officer, that Colonel Simon had indeed been
in touch with her. 'He leaves notes, in the farthest book to the
right on the top shelf of the right-hand bookcase, in the Second
Class library,' she said. 'Last night it was *The Pickwick Papers*,
which I can't imagine anyone taking down on purpose to read.
He's in hiding, he said, somewhere on the ship – "hiding" is
what he said, so I don't know if that means disguise or actually
concealing himself in a baggage-hold or a coal-bunker or
somewhere.'

'Did he say what danger he was in?' Palfrey leaned forward,
heaven-blue eyes dark with concern. 'Is there anything we can
do?'

Lydia shook her head. 'But the mark he made on the edge
of the paper – a star in a circle – is the one that means, *the
danger is very great*. All we can do is stand by and await
instructions.'

The young man nodded, accepting. Not even asking – and,
Lydia suspected, not even asking himself – how Colonel Simon
was able to come and go in the Second Class library, much less
how he'd informed Lydia where the drop box was. Simon – or
Simon's long-dead valet – had been perfectly right when he'd

compared the weight of Palfrey's brains unfavorably to that of a pistol-ball. Lydia had devised an elaborate series of back-up explanations, in case it did occur to him to ask, but Palfrey never even blinked.

But an hour later, as she was taking Miranda (and Mrs Marigold) for a tour of the Second Class promenade deck ('Mrs Marigold wants to watch out for German submarines, Mummy.'), Lydia was accosted by the Princess Gromyko and, of all people, Mr Cochran, trailed at a respectful distance by the footman Zhenya, Ossolinska, and the burly detective Mr Kimball resplendent in the most American suit Lydia had ever seen.

'My darling, I've been looking for you all over the ship!' Her Highness thrust her leashes – Monsieur and Madame were also part of the entourage – into Ossolinska's grip and seized Lydia by the hands. 'Tania told me this creature, this thing, struck again last night, even as we sat in our circle of light around Madame Izora's cabinet. Even as dear Spenser here –' she laid an impulsive hand on the millionaire's shoulder (Lydia saw him flinch as if threatened with a rotting fish) – 'had written already, upon his secret card, asking the spirits about the Undead.'

'It was all about a – a dream I'd had.' The hawk-faced millionaire brought the words out clumsily. Lydia was fairly certain by this time that he usually had his secretary, the sleek young Mr Oliver Cochran, tell his lies for him. 'The first night on board ship, it was, and it isn't like me to dream. Almost never do. Shook me up, I can tell you.'

'Spenser dreamed of the vampire.' The princess lowered her voice, drew Lydia closer, dark eyes burning. 'He dreamed of that poor girl Pavlina, following a whispering voice down into a corridor in dead of night. Dreamed of a dark figure enfolding her in a dark cloak . . .'

Cochran nodded vigorously. Lydia had seen more convincing performances in her young nieces' Christmas pantomimes. 'That kind of nonsense isn't like me, M'am. Don't even read novels. But this dream – this thing I saw in my dream – looked to me like something out of one. And all yesterday I had this . . . this *feeling* that what I'd seen was true. I've been to séances, M'am – hundreds of 'em – and I never felt about 'em what I felt waking from that dream. I knew that banana-oil Winstanley was spreading around about a crime of passion, and "we've got the guy and it's all safe now", was bunkum.'

He fixed Lydia with those sharp black eyes, as if gauging how much of his story she believed. 'Don't know how I knew it. But there's something down there. And Her Majesty tells me you've gone down and talked to the people involved.'

This was a man, Lydia thought, whose business was to judge character; to read when someone was bluffing, to sense evasions or lies. Millions of dollars worth of accumulated factories, mines, railroads and banks couldn't be controlled, much less added to, by someone who didn't have a ruthless instinct about people and – she suspected – a fairly good information system of his own.

Who has he *talked to? How much does he guess about why I'm on this ship?*

Is this a trap?

Jamie had told her of the times when he'd allowed himself to be recruited by German or Ottoman Intelligence, turning their own game against them. *There's nothing in the world more terrifying*, he had said, *than working as a double. You never quite get over it.*

Her glance flickered momentarily to Mr Kimball, six feet three inches of solid muscle wrapped in that appalling mustard-brown check, his neck bigger around than his head and eyes like two pale-blue china beads. Remembered what Heller had said, about it being easy to account for a passenger's disappearance.

Did I leave some sign – a dropped handkerchief or a foot-print – in his suite last night? Good Heavens, can they take fingerprints?

If he'd kidnap a vampire – pay and support Dr Barvell in his quest for whatever awful poison they've come up with – in order to kill off strikers and troublemakers, what else would he do to protect his tame assassin?

But Lydia had worked her own years of meticulously schooling herself to show not one needle-weight of guilt or dread when her father or stepmother (or her formidable Nanna) got close to the subject of the books she had hidden in the attic;

not one flicker of an eyelid when plans were discussed that might interfere with her exams to get into Somerville College. She'd long ago learned how to brace herself for a good, big lie without the smallest twitch of hand or lip.

She turned her face a little aside, in a way that had always worked for sneaky, stuck-up Arabella Howard at Madame Chappedelaine's Select Academy for Young Ladies, and said in a low voice, 'It sounds mad to me, too, sir. When Tania, and Princess Gromyko, told me about it, I . . .' She looked back at him, her eyes wide. 'There was a girl at my school, you see. A girl – Mollie, her name was – who . . . died . . .'

She shook her head with a sort of quick violence, as if the recollection were too much to face, even now. 'It's true. And when I went down with Tania, and heard the girls' mothers – Pavlina's, and poor little Luzia's – and the men from the villages all talking about . . . about other things they'd seen, and heard . . .'

'Here.' The American looked for a moment as if he would have grasped her elbow peremptorily, then seemed to remember his lessons in deportment and offered his arm instead. 'Please join me and Her Majesty for a cup of coffee. Would you like to come with us and have a chocolate ice, little girl?' He bared his big yellow teeth at Miranda in what he obviously thought was an encouraging smile.

Miranda cast a hasty glance at her mother – clearly aghast at the prospect – and Lydia put a hand on the child's thin shoulder and stooped down to her. 'Would Mrs Marigold mind if Mademoiselle Ossolinska continued our tour of the deck with you? I'm certain Her Highness would let Monsieur and Madame continue with you . . .'

She glanced back at the princess, who nodded at once.

'I have secrets to talk with Mr Cochran. Deep, dark secrets.'

Miranda tiptoed, and when Lydia drew closer yet, whispered, 'Will you tell me later?'

Lydia met her daughter's eyes – coffee-brown, like Jamie's – and nodded.

THIRTEEN

'What are they saying below decks?' Cochran leaned across the delicate wicker table in the Willow Grove Café and grasped Lydia's hand. 'Does anyone down there have any ideas of where this thing might be hiding? We cannot risk such a monster coming ashore,' he added sententiously. 'This may be our only chance to destroy this thing before we reach New York. If it gets ashore the consequences to America will be unthinkable! There are no such evil beings in the United States.'

Lydia put on a terrified expression, and raised a hand to her lips as though to stifle a gasp.

Princess Natalia Nikolaievna asked, with great interest, 'Truly? No vampires in America?'

'None I've been able to hear of.' Cochran shook his head and started to say something (Lydia guessed) in proof of this statistic, then seemed to remember that his belief in the Undead was supposed only to date from the beginning of this voyage. 'I make it my business to – um – inform myself about peoples' beliefs.' Personally, Lydia suspected that he'd searched very carefully for vampires in his own country before taking steps to import the commodity from Europe.

'And of course, Mrs Cochran, growing up as she did in the country outside of Charleston, has heard every Negro superstition and folk tale in the countryside.'

The waiter appeared with tea and coffee, petits fours, biscuits, and a small dish of poached pears for Cochran. He remembered all their names – his, Lydia recalled, was William – and even asked after the health of Monsieur le Duc and Madame la Duchesse. Cochran wiped the spoon with his handkerchief, tasted a mouthful of the pears, and snapped, 'You call these poached?' William took them back to the kitchen, with apologies.

Lydia recalled her own investigations of property, interlocking

bank accounts, curiously linked wills, which had led her to
vampires and vampire nests. The Undead obsession with
owning multiple refuges – with the power that money can
supply – made them relatively easy to trace, if one knew what
one was looking for.

If one believed they existed in the first place.

*You took that much trouble and expense, all so that you could
kill the people who* dare *to question your treatment of your
workers.*

'So far,' she answered slowly, 'I think the Italians and the
Slovenes and the Russians – the ones who already believe in
. . . in vampires –' (*Remember you're only just coming to this
belief yourself.*) – 'are still so shocked that all they're thinking
of is protecting themselves. When I was down there this
morning, they were all wearing rosaries around their necks –
except the Belgians and some of the Sudeten Germans – and I
saw most of the cabin doors had crosses marked on them.'

Cochran grimaced a little at that – Lydia recalled his remarks
about peasant superstitions from their first dinner on the *City
of Gold*, and the cross-shaped silver burn on Don Simon's wrist.

'Some people,' she went on, '—there's a Sudeten Slovene
named Vodusek, and a man named Marek, the grandfather of
the young man who's accused of the first murder – are pretty
vocal about there being a vampire, and more people are starting
to listen to them. Old Father Kirn – and . . . and I, too – fear
that people are going to panic, and start turning on each other.
Though aren't vampires only supposed to come out at night?
So it couldn't be anyone down there—'

'No!' protested Natalia, setting down her coffee cup. 'The
upír walk about in the daylight, of course they do—'

The American half-opened his mouth to tell her they did
nothing of the kind, then shut it again. He prodded the pears
that William brought back for him from the kitchen, and sent
them away again. 'What the hell is wrong with those nigs they
got working in the kitchen? They never seen a pear before?
And that dish was filthy.'

'Daylight robs the Undead of their powers,' continued the
princess, delicately squeezing a netting-wrapped lemon slice
into her teacup. 'As does the sea. Only at the hour of noon, or

of midnight, or at the turning of the tide, does their strength return for a little time. In the daylight hours they are as mortal men, save for the coldness of their flesh, and the stench of decay that lingers in their flesh and on their breath. That is the great fear.'

She lowered her voice, and leaned close. 'That is the great danger. That any one of those people – or any one in Second Class, or in First – might be *vampir, nosferatu.*'

Lydia made herself glance around in affright and forced herself not to say, *Nonsense!*

She supposed it was a more rational belief than the truth: that when the disease of vampirism (which Lydia suspected was what the Dutch microbiologist Beijerinck called a *virus* in plants) took hold, it transmuted the very nature of human flesh. As Don Simon had said, cell by cell, it became something other than it had been. *Really, to those unfamiliar with the chemical processes of decay it would make more sense, that the Undead are simply walking corpses.*

'I hope – I trust,' the princess went on earnestly, 'that Father Kirn has taken what steps are necessary, to guarantee that this poor child, this poor girl, do not themselves become *nosferatu—*'

'Is that true?'

Lydia could almost hear the clicking of wheels as the millionaire turned his intent gaze on her again.

'That those the vampire bites, become vampires in their turn?'

She bit back, *Of course not! There's more to it than that*! but realized that was something else that she herself wouldn't know.

Natalia nodded vigorously. 'Unless they are staked through the heart, and their heads cut off; their mouths stuffed with garlic or with the earth from a graveyard—'

Where in Heaven's name would you get that *on shipboard*?

'Father Kirn seemed to think,' Lydia interposed diffidently, 'that putting a rosary around their necks, and a piece of the Host in their mouths, would have the same effect . . .'

She paused, as William returned once more, with new pears, a clean spoon, and – obviously having waited on Mr Cochran before – a fresh napkin.

'In any case,' she added, remembering some of the more

melodramatic incidents of *Dracula* – and the burn on Don Simon's narrow wrist – 'I should think if the victims had been . . . been *transformed* . . .' She just stopped herself from saying *infected*, 'the Host and the Cross would have burned them, and it didn't.'

The princess nodded, much struck by this argument, and Cochran couldn't hide his look of discontent. Whether this was because he suspected he wasn't getting accurate information, or at learning that vampires couldn't be propagated like sweet potatoes – or because the pears still weren't to his liking – Lydia couldn't determine. *Dear Heavens, I hope he doesn't take it into his head to see if that business of walking about in the daylight is true!*

'Will you help me?' The millionaire looked from Lydia's face to that of the princess, almost straining with the effort of making a request instead of either a demand, a threat, or an offer of money. 'It is imperative that we – as educated believers in these terrible fiends – find this thing before these ignorant peasants do. Why, if these things do multiply just by a bite – if this priest of yours can't get to them in time – the consequences would be terrible!'

You mean, thought Lydia, *the consequences would be terrible if Gospod Vodusek and his mates do manage to get up a mob and find the vampire before you can bring it under your control as you've brought poor Simon.*

'We know it must be hiding somewhere on the lower decks.' The princess stirred her tea, tasted it, and grimaced. William materialized like a genie at her shoulder, murmuring how it must be cold and could he get Madame a fresh cup? When he'd gone, she went on, 'Tania has made many friends among the children, and their parents as well. The girl Ariane Zirdar, seems to have taken it upon herself to organize them – the children, I mean – to keep together, and she and Tania speak when Tania goes down to F Deck. Tania can tell me all of what is being said.'

'Good!' Cochran turned his attention on Lydia. 'You said you were down there this morning, that you spoke to the girl's mother, and the parents of this boy who's supposed to have killed the bohunk girl. And this Father What's-His-Name . . .?'

'Father Kirn.'

'Do you speak their lingo? Enough to overhear what they say to each other?'

'Only French, and a little German.'

The man grunted, and sipped his mineral water. 'You know, Mrs Asher,' he said slowly, 'it was foolish of you to speak to that man Heller. And it *is* Heller, I know it is, and to hell with what his papers say. He's lying to you. He's wanted in Germany for robbery, rape and murder. While I doubt he'd be so stupid as to commit one of his crimes on-board ship, myself, I don't trust any man who's too lazy to work for his living – much less one who goes around blaming everybody else for how tough his life is. You want to be careful how you deal with him.'

Lydia widened her eyes. 'How dreadful!' she gasped. 'And he was so good about translating what the others said! Perhaps, after all, I'd best not go down there . . .'

'No, no,' Cochran reassured her hastily. 'I'm sure you'll be perfectly all right dealing with him. It's perfectly safe to *use* him, to get on with our greater cause. Just – um – be careful around him. And don't believe a word he says.'

'Oh.' Lydia nodded with an expression of relief. 'Oh, I see.'

Natalia looked as if she would have protested at that. *And no wonder*! reflected Lydia indignantly. Not the coarsest of the soldiers she'd known at the Front would have urged her to associate with a man known to be a rapist and a killer, not if there were a hundred vampires breeding like rabbits in the coal-bunkers. For as long as it took Lydia to drink another cup of tea and Cochran to snap his fingers for William and order another portion of pears, she listened to the American's further animadversions on Socialists: their ruthlessness, their treasonous alliance with Germany, their attempts to cripple America's industries and sabotage its railroads and mines.

After ten minutes, Aunt Louise entered the Willow Grove and made her way purposefully towards their table. 'Good grief, look at the time!' Cochran jumped to his feet. 'Your Majesty –' he turned to the princess – 'would your good Mrs Izora be available this evening, for a consultation about this? We shouldn't neglect even the irrational, in search of this abomination. You'll both remember what I said?'

He divided his glance between the princess, Lydia, and the speediest route away from Aunt Louise. 'We must find this thing – and we must find it before those dago ignoramuses in Third Class do. It'd probably be best if neither of you breathed a word to them about what we're doing – hunting for this thing.'

Lydia said, 'Of course!' and Natalia Nikolaievna nodded decisively.

'*Bien sûr*! The Slavic soul has great intuition, and mystical powers of perception, but it is undisciplined. As we have seen in my poor country, their hearts are pure, but one cannot always count on the actions of the ignorant among them. Not a word!'

Aunt Louise was getting close and Mr Cochran strode off on a course that would keep at least a couple of tables between her and himself. He left no tip.

'*Irrational* indeed!' The princess scowled after that well-tailored back. '*So* American! And those teeth! *Barbare*! Yet it is good to have an ally in our search for this monster. We will find it,' she added. 'We must find it, while it is still here, in this small space. While the magnetism of the ocean still binds its powers and renders it helpless.'

'We will,' agreed Lydia softly, and looked out through the long windows at the ocean; sapphire-black and endless under a chilly, endless sky.

If we're not torpedoed first.

FOURTEEN

Lydia spent the remainder of the daylight hours giving her daughter's doll a guided tour of the ship, while Miranda herself provided Mrs Marigold with instructive but odd glosses upon Lydia's statements: 'They braid hair from unicorns' tails into the ropes,' she informed the doll, after Lydia had pointed out the locker where the cables were kept (*could a vampire hide in there?*). 'Unicorn hair can't be broken.'

Lydia wondered where on earth her daughter had acquired

this piece of lore – *is love of folk tales hereditary?* 'Then how do they cut the cables to the length they need?' she inquired.

Miranda regarded her with slight surprise and an unspoken, anybody *knows* that. 'They burn them, with a candle.'

'It is very wrong of you to encourage her,' Aunt Louise informed her, when she came into Lydia's stateroom (without knocking) later, as Lydia was changing for dinner. 'Superstition makes children light-minded and impairs their ability to concentrate. I daresay she'll become addicted to novels, like Lavinnia's girls. I instructed Mrs Frush to break the child of the habit and she has reported considerable progress even in the past two days.'

Lydia had heard all about Mrs Frush from Miranda, who said the nanny would tell only one bedtime story per night and those, the dullest the child had ever heard. 'All about little girls who got to go to parties because they didn't get their dresses dirty. I'm glad she only tells me one.' Lydia and Miranda had had story time already that afternoon, sitting in a nook behind the lifeboats.

'It wouldn't be nice to ask her for another one,' Lydia had pointed out. 'She may only know just enough for one a night all the way across the ocean.' Miranda had nodded, understanding. Story time – since Lydia had never seen the point of bedtime stories and didn't know even enough for one a night – had always consisted of Miranda telling her mother stories, about princesses who ran away to live with bears, and fish who blew bubbles to help bees collect honey from underwater flowers. ('The bees had to pay them in honey, but you get better honey from underwater flowers than you do from the ones that grow in gardens.')

But Lydia had discovered that, dearly as she loved her child – or perhaps as a result of the afternoon's intimacy – even Miranda's company had not served to distract her mind, the way vampire hunting had done, from the danger of submarines. From nearly any point on the promenade deck, she'd been able to see the lookouts in their tall crow's-nests ('They're watching for submarines,' Miranda had confided to Mrs Marigold. 'They're going to torpedo us, because of the war.'). She had been frightened, poking around in the deeps of the hold, even with Heller at her side: she knew how quickly vampires could strike. The thought of Miranda drowning in those freezing sapphire-black depths visible beyond the deck-railings made her sick with terror, and sometimes almost blotted all other thought.

Not Miranda . . .

Maybe it's because I've dealt *with vampires,* she thought, as Ellen gently worked the skin-tight lilac kid of her glove over her powdered fingers and Aunt Louise continued her monologue about the proper way to raise children. The Undead were terrifying, swift and pitiless and almost unstoppable, but she knew them.

Submarines were like the guns at the Front.

One moment you were talking to a man in the sandbagged deeps of a trench, and the next you were trying to stop the bleeding of torn arteries on his screaming, half-dismembered torso for the two minutes and forty-seven seconds (she'd clocked it even while applying tourniquets) that it took him to die.

First Class dinner was at eight. The First Class passengers began to gather in the glass-domed foyer at about seven thirty, to chat – chat being the chief occupation of an ocean voyage, Lydia was finding out. Near the frosted-glass doors she glimpsed Captain Palfrey, enmeshed in conversation with a young couple named Allen ('The trick, you see, is to put your money into a holding company to get around all those regulations . . .'), whom she'd seen on the promenade. Closeby, Aunt Louise was discoursing to the fascinated-looking Dr Barvell about the countries and races which existed on the inside of the Earth, which was hollow, with secret entrances at the poles. Dr Barvell always appeared fascinated when any woman of sufficient wealth spoke to him – Lydia had seen him hang breathlessly on every word while Mrs Cochran described a bridge hand.

Mr Tilcott fetched her a glass of very excellent sherry, and proceeded to enlighten her on his family's contributions to American higher culture, and the precise sources of his family's income. ('Papa would never *touch* the kind of shady holding companies that Cochran hides behind.') The moment he turned his head to answer young Mr Oliver Cochran's greeting, Lydia excused herself and darted through the double doors and out into the cold darkness of the deck.

As she walked quickly along the promenade she donned her glasses, and pulled tight around her arms the beaded silk wrap which had been warm enough to get from the Promenade Suites to the foyer. Through breaks in the cloud-cover crystal-cold stars were visible, arching down to an ink-black horizon; the wind was bitter. *Anything*, she thought, gazing at the shifting blackness, *could be out there.*

The vampire – the other vampire – can't get up onto First Class . . . can it?

Not if it's been hiding down in the grease and soot of the lower decks. Stewards were posted – discreetly – near every gangway that led to Decks D, E, F, and lower, and at ten, Lydia knew, the wire grilles at the tops of these gangways would be locked.

It's nowhere near midnight.

The thought brought no reassurance. Even without illusion, the Undead could move unnoticed as cats in shadows. The still face of the girl on the refrigerated slab returned to her; the child on the bunk in that crowded cabin. The bruised, pinched look of the torn flesh of their throats . . .

'Mistress.'

And there he was. Don Simon Ysidro, his white shirt front like a shred of ectoplasm in the shadows of the furled sunshades.

His hands were icy when she gripped them, even through his gloves and hers.

'Did he let you out?'

'You had been proud of me, Lady –' the scarred side of his face pulled askew with a momentary, bitter smile – 'to witness how I abased myself to his will.' In his expressionless tone she caught the bitterness of a man who has bowed to no one in his life.

'He believed you, then?'

'I have seen men enough, when the Inquisition broke their wills, to know what to say, and how to say it convincingly. Proud men, until they were shown the instruments.' The shrug was barely a flex of his lips. Vagrant breeze stirred his long hair. 'And indeed, where on this ship can I go? I must needs return to Barvell for antidote, ere many hours pass.'

Lydia studied his face in silence. His true face, she reflected. The one he needed the vampire 'glamour' to conceal. A skull barely masked by the stretched white skin, eyes sunken and fangs visible with each word that he spoke. She barely noticed it now, save to remark whether he was using his skills to conceal his true nature or not. Undead face or the features of the man he had been, he was what he was.

Vampire. The terrified passengers in Third Class would need no urging from the likes of Vodusek and Father Kirn to tear him to pieces and drive a stake through his heart.

No wonder vampires avoid mirrors.

'Did he command that you find this other vampire?'

'E'en so. As it is impossible for me to walk among the living passengers – being unable to mask myself from their eyes, save for the minutes on either side of midnight – I shall engage myself thus through the deep of the night. I would take it as a kindness – nay, as a help nigh indispensable – if you would join me.'

'Of course.'

'Know you where the two victims lie? The young girl and the child?'

'They've put aside one of the pantry's refrigerator compartments for them. Father Kirn went in this afternoon, I understand, and – I suppose one could say he vampire proofed poor Pavlina's body, with holy oil and a cross and a piece of the Host in her mouth. It's all . . . It *is* all bosh, isn't it? The whole idea of someone turning into a vampire just because they've been bitten? You've told me vampires are made by master vampires, and that they must consent . . .'

''Tis, as you say, Mistress, *bosh*, though I daresay the families of the girl and the child – not to speak of all the other passengers of Third Class – will sleep sounder because of it. If any can sleep sound,' he added quietly, 'who have lost one so beloved. Know you if they keep vigil? Good.'

She had shaken her head. But something in his expression – in the pinch of pain in his brows – made her ask, 'What is it?' It was the first time she had heard him speak of the parents, the friends, of the victims of the Undead, save as potential avengers. As possible threats.

'Naught.' One finger moved dismissively. 'Can we get into the cold chamber, once the kitchen staff finish their work? Excellent. When midnight nears –' he took her hand, as the faint, mellow note of the dinner-gong sounded in the distance – 'bring John Palfrey to me, here, that I may reassure him and devise some means of communication that will not entail his seeing me thus.'

'I've set up a letterbox, as Jamie would call it. Far right end of the second shelf on the right-hand side, in the Second Class library.'

'Excellent woman!' He brought her hand to his lips. 'Bring him to this place at a quarter of midnight – 'twill give you ample time to attend this séance of theirs – and afterwards, you and I can search the lower decks, when all sleep. We shall find this creature yet.'

'That's what Cochran said to me this afternoon. Simon—'

Her hand tightened on his, when he would have withdrawn it and vanished. Only he could not, she realized, simply vanish, the way he usually did, masking himself from her eyes or making her think she'd only seen a dissolving shred of mist. He was, like herself, a prisoner of his flesh, closer to his days of living manhood than he had been in three centuries.

'Lady?'

She had meant to ask him, what that flinch of pain had been a few moments before, when he'd spoken of those who had lost one they loved, to the need – or the greed – of the Undead. But she found she could not.

'What would a vampire be doing here?' she asked instead. 'On a ship, where it's all but helpless, even without submarines and torpedoes thrown in? Why leave Europe, when it could simply go to the Front and . . . and *revel* in death.'

Don Simon, looking quietly into her eyes, shook his head. 'This is another of the many things I find most odd about this situation.'

'I can't even see that it has a servant on board – the way you've always gotten someone to travel with you, to deal with problems during the daytime. It's powerless, the same way you are, save for those minutes just around midnight, which must be when it makes its kills. If the ship is torpedoed, even by night it could only survive in a lifeboat until first light. By day, if the ship gets sent to the bottom, it will have to go with it, entombed and conscious . . .'

She shook her head, cold with horror at the thought. *Entombed and conscious* forever . . .

'I thought it might be one of the Russian vampires,' she went on. 'But even with the rioting in St Petersburg, that's no reason to have to flee Europe. And vampires aren't – *you* aren't – political, so far as I know.'

'We are not.' His yellow eyes narrowed. 'E'en had the rioting in Petersburg progressed beyond what the newspapers said last week, the vampires of that city, and of Moscow, all have country places in which to hide – if, indeed, any remain in Russia at all. But this traveler . . . Having killed once, why would he kill *twice*? *Is* there only one?' And he shook his head at the startled horror in her eyes. 'I shall be much interested in what this Izora woman has to say. Listen for those things which she cannot have learned from the gossip of the maids – if anything. For there is something happening which I do not understand, and that,' he concluded quietly, 'is never a good thing.'

FIFTEEN

Asher returned to the Rue de Passy that same night. The Hotel Montadour was still dark.

The wind had started up, turning the day's thin rain to driving needles of ice. The *City of Gold* would be plowing heavy seas under starlight while the U-boats that almost certainly followed her could glide in still darkness below. He wondered if Lydia were asleep. Or did she lie awake amid a strew of books and magazines over the counterpane, wrapped in her green satin dressing gown, coppery hair lying half-uncoiled over her shoulders and spectacles perched on the end of her nose?

Has she found Ysidro?

Has she killed him?

Will *she kill him?*

He knocked on the door of the porter's lodge, the blows echoing like a bronze hammer in the silence beyond. A wet gust tore at the skirts of his trench coat, rain spattering off his pulled-down hat.

The thought crossed his mind, as he moved off down the empty blackness of the street, that if U-boats torpedoed the American liner tonight, he himself wouldn't hear of it for days.

They could be already dead, and all of this – all of everything, all of life – *for nothing.*

He'd been in the Secret Service – he'd associated with the London vampires – far too long to think that any despairing cry of his heart – *no!!!* – wouldn't be whipped away by darkness long before it reached the ear of God. And God probably had a great deal else to do tonight. It would be blowing sleet in that wretched camp in the black Silesian forests, where the men thought he was Major von Rabewasser, where poor little Dissel, his batman, huddled beside the smoky fire in their tent praying he wouldn't freeze by morning.

The man's a German, my enemy. I shouldn't care.

I should be prepared to shoot him as promptly and discreetly as I shot my young friend Jan van der Platz, behind the barn of his family's farmstead near Johannesburg, when he began – only began – to suspect me . . .

Hands like the steel rings of a vise closed on his arms and he was shoved into a doorway; cold-clawed fingers caught at his throat and jerked back from the silver he wore. Reflective eyes flashed in the distant glow of a window down the street.

He hadn't even seen them surround him.

His mind had been somewhere else.

He tried to wrench free as one of them caught the front of his coat, jerked him forward so as to smash his skull against the brick of the wall behind him . . .

'It's Madame's *Anglais*,' said someone.

He grabbed the wrist of the man who gripped his coat, steeled against the blow if it was coming. 'I need to see Madame.' He knew he'd stand a better chance of surviving the next five seconds if he caught their interest.

They were around him, like sharks in the water, gripping his arms again. Still he felt the whisper that went among them – they were entertained. He knew they could hear the hammering of his heart. The terror of the living always amused them. They loved it when someone sobbed despairingly, *No!*

They pushed him back against the panels of a door, deep-set in a soot-grimed wall. Three of them, all young men, though they'd probably been born before his grandfather. All in evening dress: he could see them silhouetted dimly against the reflection of windows across the street. Smelled Parma violet in their clothing, and stale blood.

'Madame has left Paris.' A trace of Norman dialect, stronger than he'd heard those few hours crossing through Rennes on his way to Brest. There was an archaic inflection, such as one sometimes heard on the Channel Islands. The speaker – no more than a dark shape – was as tall as himself, and wider-shouldered. Asher could hear the smile of cruel amusement in his tone. *You think you can distract us, talk your way out of death. But we will kill you and you know it . . .*

Keeping his voice matter-of-fact, Asher said, 'Then perhaps one of you gentleman can help me. There was a man named Barvell in Paris, a chemist who claimed to be a nerve doctor as well. I have reason to believe he was studying the Undead.'

'Never heard of him.' There was an almost childlike glee in the voice. *See, there's nothing you can say . . .*

'He was working on coming up with a way to enslave and control vampires. He has experimented on at least one, maybe more.'

It was a bow drawn at a venture but beside him, he felt the slightest perceptible twitch in the grip on his right arm. The vampire holding him on that side said, in the light voice of a youth, 'So that's what—'

The tall vampire moved his head, slightly, and the youth beside Asher fell silent.

'He had an apartment on the Rue Monceau.'

'No one controls us.' The tall vampire released his grip on Asher's coat-front. Cold hands framed his face. 'No one enslaves us. Not Madame, for all her airs and graces. And only a fool believes the rumors of wartime. He is an even bigger fool, who goes seeking the Undead in their lairs.'

'Serge!' The voice of Elysée de Montadour, coming from the street behind them, was like the chop of a silver knife. In the same instant Asher kicked Serge, knowing the blow would do absolutely nothing but knowing also that he had nothing to lose. He heard Elysée's voice as Serge twisted his head, trying to break his neck. The kick at least knocked the vampire's balance and timing askew and the next second Serge was torn away from him and slammed against the corner of the doorway in which they stood. Asher twisted free, leaving his trench coat in the hands of the vampires on either side of him and lunged past Serge, stumbling, his senses swimming. At this hour of the night, in the blackness of the sleet-wet street, he guessed he'd make it about three steps before they'd be on him.

He fell, but heard Elysée curse like a sailor, standing above him, and her three fledglings – despite Serge's earlier assertion – evidently didn't want to challenge the master vampire who had made them. When Asher turned painfully over and sat up, only Elysée was there beside him.

'*Connards.*' She pulled him to his feet with the frightening strength of the Undead. 'I will have to deal with that conceited whoreson one day. Why I ever loved him I'm sure I don't know.'

'Did you love him?' Asher turned his head, very carefully, and felt blood in his hair where the vampire's claws had gouged. 'Do you love them?'

Elysée widened her great green eyes at him. 'But of course! Why would one make a vampire of a man that one did not love passionately? That one did not wish to keep at one's side forever? But what a block-head!' She touched his bleeding scalp, licked the blood from her fingers and then smelled them, as if savoring the residue of perfume. Asher backed away from her second touch, took a handkerchief from his pocket and dabbed at the cuts, then knelt to daub the cloth in the puddles underfoot, and wiped the blood more thoroughly away. When he went into the doorway to retrieve his trench coat, he dropped the handkerchief there; she'd smell it in his pocket and it would distract her.

He was aware that she glanced towards it, still drawn to the blood-smell, before she returned her attention politely to him. He was reminded of a child eyeing the last cookie on the luncheon plate.

'I am desolated that I was not here last night. Did you come, you silly man?' She put her arm through his, drew him in the direction of her own door. 'I asked Serge, and Louis-Claud – and I'm very much afraid that Louis-Claud suggested the most diverting hunt yesterday evening, for some drunken Australians who had lost their way down by the river. Was I very naughty?' She leaned against him, and Asher fought the impulse to thrust her away.

As if she felt his disgust at her she smiled at him, and in the same fashion that inattention and thoughts of his responsibilities had, ten minutes ago, swept all watchfulness from his mind, he felt the warm wave of her sexuality surge around him, as it had two nights before: the nearly-uncontrollable impulse to pull her to him, to kiss those blood-red lips. To push up her skirts and have her in the nearest doorway.

With careful calm he said, 'It was vexing. I learned some facts Thursday, and traveled to Brest, to send a wireless message to Lydia on board the ship where, I'm nearly certain, Ysidro is being held captive.'

'Captive?' The dreamy urgency of lust snapped off as if with the turning of an electric switch. 'It is true, what you said?' She straightened up in the doorway of the lodge. 'That this what's-his-name you spoke of, this Barvell, has found a way to *enslave* us?'

'I think so, yes.' Asher scratched a corner of his mustache. 'Or at least that's what he has to be seeking. And if he's been in Paris since 1913, I think he must have used at least one vampire as a subject to experiment on. You say –' he spoke carefully, knowing the Master of Paris was extremely touchy about any slurs on her absolute command of her territory and fledglings – 'that you know every vampire in Paris. Yet in the past I know that there have been some who were not your get—'

'Pah! Insects. I have driven them out.' Her eyes glinted dangerously.

'Are you sure? Because—'

She looked sharply past his shoulder, and, following her gaze (with an agonizing cramp in the bruised muscles of his neck), Asher saw, in the dim reflection of the hooded lamp that now burned over the lodge door, that they had been joined by another. Dark eyes caught the feeble lamp glow like mirrors, and his hair, slick with brilliantine, was fair. The high cheekbones and cupid-bow lips, the delicate Grecian nose and well-shaped chin, were all very much the 'type' that Elysée de Montadour favored, and like the others of her fledglings that he'd seen, this one seemed to be wearing evening dress under his greatcoat.

'He gets them at the Front,' said the young man, in the youthful voice, and slight Provençal trill, that Asher had heard minutes before.

His eyebrows went up.

Elysée snapped, 'Who does?'

'This man – Barvell?' The fledgling took a step forward, and looked hesitantly from Elysée to Asher. 'Augustin – Augustin Malette – I swear to you, Madame,' he added, to Elysée, whose eyes had flared wide at the mention of her 'tricky' fledgling. 'Augustin has no thought of disrespect to you, no thought of challenging you for control of Paris. But he has made fledglings – four that I know of – at the Front. He says that when the fighting is over, he will take them to some other city—'

'Lying *canaille*!' Elysée moved with the terrifying speed of the vampire, so that Asher didn't see her strike, but the fair vampire staggered and put a hand to his bleeding cheek.

'—Bordeaux or Brussels or Marseilles,' he continued, 'and set himself up there. Not that he does not have the deepest respect and love for you, Madame.' Hand still to his face, he executed a profound and wary bow. 'Please do not doubt that.'

'Species of toad!' By the look on her ghost-pale face, Elysée clearly did doubt it, and was just as clearly going to have some words with Augustin on the subject.

But Asher only said, 'And does Augustin, or one of his fledglings, know of vampires . . . disappearing?'

'Two of Augustin's fledglings, M'sieu. One was a nurse at one of the clearing stations, a most beautiful young lady, the other a young captain of the Signal Corps. Augustin . . .' The fledgling hesitated, trying to find a tactful phrase. 'Augustin has not the care – the experience – to advise his fledglings, to guide them as you do, Madame.' He bowed again, and took Elysée's hand, to bring it to his lips. 'This young captain, this young nurse, they were very inexperienced. They had only been numbered among the Undead for a week, perhaps ten days.

Augustin told me – some months ago it was, now – that they had been kidnapped, disappeared.'

His sharp, youthful face twitched in a look of concern, almost fear. 'He said – this was just after Christmas, Madame – he said they were still alive. Alive and in terrible pain. He spoke of going to Paris to seek them, but he – he feared you would be angry if he confessed to you that he made fledglings of his own.'

'And well he should be afraid!' Elysée's hand flicked out and slapped him again, hard. The young man only turned his face meekly aside. 'Pig!'

'I have only seen him once since then, Madame, and I did not ask what had come of it.'

'And you told me nothing of this?'

'Madame,' Asher broke in quietly, as the enraged vampire showed signs of striking her fledgling again and, possibly, driving him away. 'This is a serious matter. I don't know the capabilities or the exact intentions of this Dr Barvell – though I have some guesses about the latter. But I do know he's being financed by an American industrialist, and I need to learn of him what I can. Not only to what extent he is able to control the Undead, but how many of the Undead he *does* control. Don Simon may not be the only one. And Dr Barvell may not have kept his findings to himself.'

Elysée's eyes flared with horror. She hadn't thought of that.

'As Augustin's master, would you be able to find him at the Front?'

'Of course!' She spoke so quickly that he guessed she had no idea whether she'd be able to locate her erring fledgling or not. 'Joël?' She turned to the fair young vampire. 'Whereabouts is Augustin, at the Front?'

'Near Nesle,' Joël replied.

Asher did some rapid mental calculation. 'Can you meet me there tomorrow night?' he asked. 'I can get authorization to travel, and quite possibly a motorcar.'

'Don't be silly,' retorted Elysée. She tilted her head a little, listening to the clock on Notre Dame d'Auteuil striking the half-hour. 'It is not yet two o'clock. We can be there long before the sun rises.'

*   *   *

'Darling!' The princess kissed Lydia on both cheeks, and slipped an arm around her waist as one of her footmen – an American ex-boxer named Samson Jones, according to Ellen's gossip – resplendent in blue velvet livery laced with gold, shut the suite door behind Lydia, bowed, and helped her off with her shawl. 'I am so glad you could come. How is the little one? Well asleep? I thought that aunt of yours would never cease her chatter, and her without the slightest knowledge of what it is to be a mother.'

Her voice dropped to a whisper as she led Lydia across the parlor. As in the parlor of Aunt Louise's suite next-door, Her Illustrious Highness had added her own touches to the hyper-modern American furniture: a discordant assortment of purple velvet cushions, peacock feathers in brass Chinese vases (Lydia could almost hear Ellen's cries of horror at the bad luck evoked by this, particularly in the middle of the Atlantic with all the U-boats of the Kaiserliche Marine on their trail), sinuous sculptures of ebony and alabaster, assorted photographs and four icons in silver frames. The largest of the photographs, set prominently on the piano, was of the princess with two children, a tow-headed boy and a slightly older girl whose dark ringlets and heart-shaped face marked her almost definitively as Natalia Nikolaievna's daughter.

By the style of clothing, the photograph had been taken just before the War began. Lydia had never heard the princess so much as mention the children, and wondered where they were now. In a couple of Select Academies in Switzerland? Or had she, like her maid, lost them? Was that what had drawn her to Madame Izora and conversations with the dead?

Beside that likeness, nearly as large and in a frame of unmistakable Fabergé work, was a photograph of Monsieur and Madame, the two French bulldogs. There was also a solid silver icon of the Virgin of Kazan.

'Of course,' Aunt Louise proclaimed from the inner room into which Natalia led Lydia, 'it isn't the same thing as superstition at all. Lydia, take those ridiculous glasses off! They make you look like an insect! Communication with spirits on the Astral Plane,' she resumed, turning back to Mrs Cochran, 'has been scientifically proven, incontrovertibly, time and time again.'

'Incontrovertibly,' echoed Mrs Cochran, moving up beside her at the round pedestal table – its glass and chrome surface, Lydia noted, suitably covered in black velvet. The handsome Dr Barvell helped her into her chair, with considerably greater attention than Cochran demonstrated. The room – the equivalent of Lydia's own chamber in the next-door suite – was a large one, its windows heavily curtained in black velvet which had clearly been added to the suite's existing draperies. *Not a shred of light can enter* . . .

Of course, she recalled. Spirit contact was supposed to be impossible in daylight.

Lest accident disrupt the etheric vibrations, the bulbs had been removed from the electrical fixtures and two oil lamps substituted (*did she bring those, too?*), glowing with a soft golden light. Between the windows the mysterious box that had drawn Lydia's attention on the gangway Wednesday loomed like a peak in the Grampians: she couldn't imagine how it had been brought into the stateroom. Closer to, she recognized it as a structure similar to the one she'd seen at the séance which her cousins had held at Peasehall Manor last summer, when she'd been home, briefly, from France. Mediums (*media?*), her cousin Maria had informed her, called them 'spirit cabinets'; their function was to 'focus astral energies' or 'act as a spiritual battery'. As far as Lydia could tell, their actual function was to conceal behind their black velvet curtains the fact that the medium him-or-herself could easily slip out of the ropes that bound him hand and foot, and so produce all sorts of sounds and effects while supposedly tied up.

It resembled a large armoire, some seven feet tall and mounted on trestles which raised it another twelve inches from the floor. Black velvet curtains hung over its open door. (*Heaven only knows what's inside it.*) Though the stateroom was generously proportioned, the cabinet took up a great deal of it. Additionally and disconcertingly, along the wall at right angles to it there was a sort of platform which could have been two trunks placed end-to-end, or one trunk easily large enough to contain a human body. It was difficult to tell, because yet another black velvet pall covered the whole.

Her earlier conversation with Don Simon returned to her. *Surely not . . .?*

Lydia cast a startled glance at the princess, who was directing the footman Zhenya in shifting the eight chromium chairs around the central table. Everyone was bumping elbows and tripping. Six bells rested on its top of the draped platform, each covered with a glass dome, and, also covered in glass, a slate. Lydia, when she made the excuse of stepping out of Mr Cochran's way and put her hand on top of the almost-six-foot platform, didn't feel a break in the surface beneath the cloth.

It could almost have been a coffin.

Good Heavens, is Madame Izora *the servant of this other vampire? With the princess as her dupe?*

She removed her glasses again before Aunt Louise – expounding on the nature of the Superior Race to Dr Yakunin – could get to her feet to take them forcibly from her face, and glanced quickly at Mr Cochran, who also appeared to be studying the platform or whatever it was under those draperies. With the lamps so low it was impossible to tell, and she couldn't think of a convincing reason to look under the drape herself.

Good Heavens, is he going to send Mr Kimball and his thugs to burglarize the room?

But just then Monsieur le Duc, escaping from Mademoiselle Ossolinska in the outer parlor, slipped through the door and jumped nimbly up onto the platform, the better to lick his mistress' face.

Hmmn . . . well, another theory gone west. In any novel the dog would have taken one sniff of a vampire's coffin and run yelping from the room.

It probably only holds more equipment of Madame's or the works for ringing those bells under the glass domes. But still . . .

Madame Izora, sylph-like in a clinging gown of iridescent black silk (*Vionnet*, Lydia guessed), lit a single candle in the center of the table. Zhenya blew out the lamps, tucked Monsieur le Duc under one arm, and stepping outside, closed the door. 'Please,' said the seer, 'look into the cabinet, all of you.'

Both the Cochrans demurred, insisting that they trusted Madame Izora implicitly, and that to peek behind the curtains was an insult. But at the Princess Gromyko's urging they did so at last. More bumping and blundering among the chairs. Lydia put on her glasses again, despite furious disapproving signals from Aunt Louise, and looked also. She guessed there would be comment if she took out her pocket measuring tape and checked the inner against the outer dimensions.

It reminded her forcibly of the narrow locker of cleaning supplies where Gospod Vodusek was hiding his pilfered liquor. A few shelves contained, among other things, a small brass bowl of what smelled like some kind of herb seeds – Lydia later learned these were lavender buds – a branch of fern lying on an intricately folded piece of white silk, and a 'talking board' or 'ouija board' of the sort that Lydia's cousins had used at the Peasehall Manor séance last summer.

When everyone was seated – Lydia still bespectacled – Madame brought out the fern and the lavender buds and performed what looked like a ritual aspersion (James had told her all about such folkloric practices in their various local guises). Replacing these (and presumably hooking up whatever equipment in the cabinet was necessary to ring the bells), the seer brought out the ouija board and its little wheeled planchette, and took her own place with her back so close to the cabinet, owing to the crowding of the room, that the velvet curtains which draped its opening actually swagged over the back of her chair.

At last summer's séance, Lydia's cousins had informed her – with a good deal of reproach – that the reason their attempts to communicate with spirits had come to nothing was because of Lydia's unbelief. 'The spirits do not deign to convince unbelievers,' had declared Cousin Maria, while Cousin Tilda, fourteen and passionate about nearly everything, had begged Lydia to 'open her heart to the forces beyond our comprehension'. Clare, still adrift in her personal darkness after the death of her husband in the Ypres Salient, had silenced the other girls with a quiet, 'It isn't anybody's fault'. But the way she'd glanced at Lydia had given the lie to her words.

And much as she sympathized with Clare's desperation to have some word from George, Lydia could not help reflecting on how convenient it was that no 'spirits' would manifest themselves in the presence of those who were not ready and willing to unquestioningly believe.

In any case, whatever spirits floated above the heaving Atlantic outside, they seemed to have no qualms whatsoever about presenting themselves in the company of a skeptic. They obligingly chimed the bells within their domes of glass, and played the piano in the parlor. Muffled by the closed door of the séance room, Lydia thought there was something strange about its tone and wondered if in fact there was a gramophone somewhere out there. In the dense gloom it was difficult to tell. ('The harsh rays of ordinary light are inimical to the spirits,' had said Cousin Maria. Another convenient circumstance, had reflected Lydia – despite the fact that she was, perforce, a firm believer in the Undead and was in fact wearing a pearl-and-emerald Tiffany necklace given to her by a man who'd been dead for 362 years.)

Aunt Louise received a brief message from her deceased school friend Martha Barnes (full of generalities, Lydia thought – and in any case it was difficult to picture Aunt Louise at boarding school) and she herself one from her mother. *Safe*, the planchette laboriously spelled out, sliding across the polished ouija board under the skilled hand of Madame Izora. *Child safe upon the waters. No enemy here.*

Lydia guessed the seer had been chatting with Aunt Louise. It was all window dressing, but she still felt the sting of anger at seeing her mother's name.

They joined hands. Madame Izora closed her eyes. In time, when the bells chimed again within their glass prisons and then fell still, Madame whispered, 'She is here. Phyleia . . .'

Phyleia, the princess had earlier informed Lydia, was the name of Madame's spirit control, formerly a hetaera in fifth-century Athens. Had Jamie been present, Lydia would have whispered to him to address the spirit in Classical Greek.

And Jamie, Lydia was sure, would have whispered back that to do so would only distract the medium when there was information that she might, possibly, be able to sense.

'The Undead,' whispered Princess Gromyko. 'The drinkers of death. The drinkers of souls. Are they on this vessel?'

In a curiously flat, harsh voice, the seer replied, 'Yes.'

'This thing that killed the child Luzia,' urged the princess. 'That killed the girl Pavlina . . .'

Madame Izora's dark brows knit below the edge of her black-and-gold headband. She flinched, and turned her face aside, like a woman who is being shouted at and fears violence. Glancing beside her in the candlelight, Lydia saw Cochran leaning forward across the table, his eyes fixed on the woman and glittering with a kind of starved eagerness.

'Killed them.' The word came out a flat croak. 'Not . . . Spanish . . .'

The others looked baffled, but Lydia had to pinch her own hand, hard, to keep from exclaiming aloud.

'Where is the one who killed them?' demanded Cochran. 'Are there two on this ship?'

The princess gasped, '*Two?*' and Mrs Cochran looked as if she would have brought her fingers to her lips, had not her husband on the one side and Aunt Louise on the other gripped them hard.

'Two . . .' Madame Izora's face convulsed. 'Two of them. One who killed. One who . . . One who . . .'

'Where is the other?' Cochran looked as if he were about to grab her by the arms and shake the answer out of her. 'The one who killed?'

'Darkness . . .' The slender little woman began to tremble convulsively. Then she sobbed, 'Oh, dear God! Somebody stop him! The little boy – he's got a little boy! Darkness – chains – oh, dear God, somebody help him!'

'Where?' shouted Cochran.

Lydia, leaning forward, asked, 'What do you hear? What do you smell?'

'Where is it hiding?' Cochran leaped to his feet and let go of the hands of both Lydia and his wife, to grab Izora by the arms.

With a cry the little woman tried to twist free of him, then crumpled forward in a storm of weeping.

SIXTEEN

The dead travel fast, Bürger says in 'Lenore', and after an hour in the rear seat of a big Peugeot touring car with Joël at the wheel, Asher wanted to ask the author of the ballad if this was what he'd meant. 'You know if he runs us off the road,' he remarked in what he hoped was a conversational tone to Elysée beside him, 'it won't kill him, or you, but it may very well strand you in the open at sunrise.'

She leaned against his chest – warily, because he still wore chains of silver around his neck and wrists – and tweaked his mustache. '*Eh bien*, Professor, we all of us, who hunt the night, have learned how to find shelter. And all the more so now, when so many have fled their homes before the guns.'

It was true, Asher observed, as they drove north and west through Compiègne and Noyon and on into the darkness, that no lights glowed in the abysses of what had once been populous and pleasant countryside. War had advanced, and retreated, and advanced again – the Germans had swept through here nearly to the suburbs of Paris in August of 1914. Though Joël persisted in driving at a speed suitable for the roads of what felt now like a distant past – almost another planet – the pavement was broken and torn by the passage of heavy vehicles, and the motorcar swerved wildly and repeatedly to avoid shell holes half-filled, by the smell of them, with stagnant water and dead things.

Not a place to be stranded afoot, Asher reflected grimly, even without a broken leg or a broken shoulder, if the Undead driver happened to demolish the car and then flitted off to seek shelter from the day's accusing light.

At a little after three, by his watch, still the dead of the early-spring night, the flicker of what he would have taken for heat lightning – had it been summer – began to show in the north-east. With it, the far-off rumble of the guns.

He'd spent nearly a year on the Western Front, mostly dressed in a German uniform sitting on benches in prisoner depots. He'd listened to the captured men around him, chatted occasionally with them of where they'd been stationed and where they'd come from, and what conditions were like back home ('I've been here so long it seems like some other world to me,' he'd say to them. 'Like something I dreamed . . .'). His German was flawless and he knew the boffins back at Whitehall could discover all kinds of information from the bits he collected, fragments that could be fed back to agents more deeply buried in German itself, or tiny wedges that could be leveraged in the event of negotiations, once Germany became sufficiently desperate.

Later, he had hated the dark forests of Silesia, the dank sour wetness of those endless half-frozen marshlands – the months of inactivity, starvation, and despair. But living as a lost soul in a regiment of lost souls was still better, he felt to the marrow of his bones, than living with the constant hammering of the guns.

Joël hadn't switched on the Peugeot's headlamps, so Asher could see nothing of the land around them as they neared the lines. But the smell of them intensified, even in the cold. The smell of the trenches, faint at first, grew stronger: the stink of latrines, or of corners of the maze of those interconnected ditches where men relieved themselves rather than bother to walk the distance to the rat-swarming privies. The stench of corpses, dead in the wires and shell holes of No Man's Land, that the medical orderlies hadn't been able to retrieve. The reek of cordite that overhung the trenches like a fog; of woodsmoke where the men burned whatever deadfalls or bits of shoring – or the ruins of smashed farmhouses – they could find, against the bone-eating cold; of the churned-up earth itself. As all these grew stronger, he caught now and then in the blackness the flickering whiff of cigarette smoke, where a sentry sucked on a Woodbine to keep himself awake or to stave off hunger.

The guns got louder. As the flare of an explosion lighted the distant sky, they passed a makeshift signpost that marked the way to Chauny and Amiens, and as if through the wrong end of a telescope, tiny and very far away, Asher saw the countryside as he had seen it first in his teens. Hedgerows white with blossom, farm tracks shaded by oak and beech. The smell of hay. It pierced the very core of his heart.

He had walked this very road, half a dozen times. Could remember the name of the farmer half a mile east of this cross-road, who would give him lunch and ask him about England, and boast about his own son who worked in Arras.

Asher wondered if that farmer – or his son – were still alive.

Did the vampires ever feel like this? he wondered, looking at the dark curls lying against his shoulder, clustered beneath Elysée's fashionable velvet hat. See a place, changed and chewed and unrecognizable with time, and remember?

Was that why some of them went mad as they aged?

Or did people to whom such thoughts were likely to occur, not become vampires?

The car slowed, as the potholes grew thicker and the road surface vanished in a morass of chopped-up pavement, earth, and mud. Joël swore, and Elysée said, 'Never mind, my beautiful one, we're only a short walk from the hospital.' Asher guessed she meant the clearing station, a mile or so back from the lines. And indeed, the reek in the darkness had become worse, not only of No Man's Land itself, but of gangrene and rotting tissue, and the horrible greasiness of human flesh consumed by incinerators. They abandoned the car and walked, the lights of the clearing station appearing dimly through the ruins of what had been – Asher guessed from the ground under-foot and the regularity of the trees – an orchard.

Tents surrounded what had been a sizeable farm. One, set a little apart from the others, was, he guessed, the Moribund Ward, where men too badly hurt to live were made comfortable in the few hours or days left them. Among the black trees of that black orchard he smelled more cigarette smoke. In another place, vomit. Once he saw the glimmer of a bullseye lantern, shaded down to a slit, and beside it, heard a woman crying as if her heart would break.

He knew there were vampires in the orchard but knew that the woman – a nurse, or an ambulance volunteer – was perfectly safe. A crumb on the floor of a banqueting hall. He was so tired he barely felt anger, though he knew he would do so later.

Closer to the tents, he could hear the vampires. See them,

sometimes, or at least see their eyes, when they caught the light of the lanterns. Much of his adult life he'd studied the legends of the Undead – much of his adult life, not believing in them – and nothing had prepared him for this. Glimpses of pale faces, pale hands. The flicker of movement out of the corner of his eye. Voices below the lowest whisper, yet audible, 'Darling, absolutely the most delicious little whore . . . pursued her for *hours* through the warehouses . . . Well, one has to keep one's skills sharp . . .'

'Going to be a push on, up at Arras . . .' This last in French. 'The shooting should be over by Wednesday.' And in Italian: 'The miserable little catamite had cards stuck under the bottom of the table! If he hadn't been Graf Szgedny's I'd have broken his skinny neck . . .'

Graf Szgedny, Asher knew, was the master vampire of Prague. He held sway, with an enclave of his fledglings, over this area of the Front. Or he had, a year ago, before Asher had been transferred east. It sounded like he still did. Beside him, Asher heard Elysée whisper, 'Augustin . . .' A moment later she, and Joël, were gone, leaving him alone in the haunted darkness.

He stood still, knowing – or at least hoping – that she would return.

Hoping – and there was no guarantee that this wouldn't actually be the case – that all of this journey hadn't been an elaborate game, of the kind that vampires liked to play. To sweeten the taste of another's death with the fragrances of despair and trust betrayed.

He certainly wouldn't put it past her.

He felt them behind him, around him, whispering in the dark. They knew he'd come here with one of their own. They passed the word along.

Without even the challenge of a hunt anymore, they would be more nosy than ever – and cruel with the cruelty of the bored.

He asked aloud, in French, 'Is the Graf here this evening, then?'

After a long stillness, a woman asked, also in French, 'Who is it who would know?'

'My name is Professor Asher,' he responded politely, and removed his peaked uniform cap. 'I'm here with Madame

Elysée. We seek Augustin Malette of Paris, or any of his fledglings. I was under the protection of the Graf Szgedny in Amiens,
two years ago,' he added, vampires no less than motor pool
clerks being susceptible to name-dropping. 'I would like to pay
him my respects.'

He felt rather than heard them whisper. Then a woman –
maybe the same one, maybe another – said, 'Elysée will kill
Augustin, for going and making fledglings. He'll be halfway
to England before morning. For certain she'll kill his fledglings.'

'I can take you to him,' said another woman, and Asher felt
his hair prickle, guessing she would not. Being sated with deaths
would not lessen, for them, the entertainment of a long chase
through the horror of abandoned trenches. 'He's not far.'

She stepped from the darkness then, a pale glimmering shape
in the far-off gleam of the lanterns in the clearing station.
Vampires at the Front often wore officers' uniforms. This girl
had chosen to clothe herself as a dream dreamed by dying
men, or men in terror that each quarter-hour would be their
last. Thin white lawn moved like a shroud with the motion of
her narrow flanks. Her arms were bare, and much of her throat.
The warmth, Asher knew, of the deaths she had absorbed kept
that milk-white flesh warmer than the heart which had once
beat in it. Blonde hair hung past her waist. Her face was the
face of a trusting child.

When she reached to take his hand he stepped back a pace,
and she regarded him with pity in her dark eyes.

'There's nothing to fear. If it's something so important that
you come here, come with Elysée, come among us, can you
not trust, even for a little while?'

She probably wasn't very old in her Undead state – the exag-
gerated rush of desire for her was heavy-handed and obvious. If
she survived, Asher guessed she'd be very good at it in time.
When he shook his head her eyes seemed about to fill with tears.

Then she retreated, seeming to be re-absorbed into the
darkness.

'Where is it?' Cochran jerked Madame Izora upright in her
chair. She stared at him, with the blank, utterly baffled face of
one pulled suddenly from deep sleep.

'What?' She wiped at her cheeks, looked in frightened astonishment at her wet fingers and then up at the others now crowding
around her.

'Where—'

Princess Natalia thrust him aside to catch the seer's hands.
'What did you see, *chère p'tite?*' Her voice was gentle.

Izora shook her head, clearly – and as far as Lydia could
tell, genuinely – ignorant. 'What did I see?' she repeated.

'The Undead,' snapped Cochran. 'The vampire. You said it
was someplace, that it had killed a boy—' When Izora shook
her head again, he looked ready to slap her.

'We'd better get down there.' Lydia started to rise.

'No!' Cochran clapped a hand on her shoulder, almost thrust
her back into her seat. 'That is – I'll go. Louis, get your gear
– and make sure the suite's locked tight. Kimball!'

Scuffing in the other room of the suite. Angry voices. Then
the door opened to admit the detective and the princess's two
protesting footmen. 'Get the boys and come with me. There's
been another murder down in Third Class.'

Mr Kimball's glance, where it touched the pale and shaken
seer with the princess and Mrs Cochran bending close around
her, was eloquent with disgust and disbelief. But he took the
cigar out of his mouth and said, 'Sure, boss,' and stepped aside
to let the 'nerve doctor' pass.

'And don't ask questions! M'am.' Cochran turned to jab a
finger at the Princess Gromyko. 'Don't you – Princess,' he
corrected himself, at a savage stare from his wife. He fumbled
his watch from his pocket, checked the time. 'It's after midnight,
M'a— Your Majesty. It probably isn't safe for you to go down
to Third now. You stay here. All of you stay here,' he added,
sweeping the little group with his sharp black gaze. 'I'll get
my boys together . . .'

'Should we not notify the captain?' The princess straightened,
her hand still protectively on Izora's shoulder. 'If this thing is
hunting, moving about in the darkness—'

'I can surely be of assistance.' Dr Yakunin, visibly pale
with shock and fear, fumbled with his silver pince-nez. (Lydia
couldn't imagine how anyone could balance the things even
to read, much less chase children up and down F Deck as

old Herr Goldhirsch had done.) 'I have knowledge of these things.'

'No!' snapped Cochran again. 'I'll take care of all that. For right now, don't anyone leave this suite and don't anyone talk to anyone about what was said here. There's no sense starting a panic,' he added, as Aunt Louise opened her lips to declare, probably, that she would do nothing of the kind and he had no right to order her around. 'And that's what we'll have if word of this gets out before we've trapped the thing.'

He glanced over his shoulder, making sure that Kimball was out of the room. Then he lowered his voice still further. 'It's dangerous. Deadly. And though its powers are halved by the power of the ocean, it can still cause terrible harm if it thinks it's been found out. M'am – Princess – why don't all you ladies stay here and look after Mrs Izora? Get her some smelling salts or something. See if you can find out anything else from her.'

His eyes darted to Lydia, and he bent closer to her, to whisper. 'You're a doctor. You know anything about hypnosis? Maybe that would—'

Izora looked frightened (*as well she might!* thought Lydia), and Princess Gromyko said, 'She remembers nothing, Mr Cochran. She never does. Remember, it was not she who saw this thing, but the spirit Phyleia.'

He opened his mouth to suggest something else – or possibly to damn Phyleia as superstitious nonsense – then closed it. 'See what you can find out,' he ordered after a moment, then turned and strode from the room. Lydia heard the outer door of the suite open, and close.

'*Well*,' said Aunt Louise. 'I think we would all be better for a cup of tea.'

'I'll see if Ossolinska is about,' said Lydia quickly, and hurried after Cochran and into the parlor.

The over-decorated room was empty – she wondered if Cochran would have the presence of mind to know he'd better take a translator with him below decks – and she crossed it, quickly, to the outer door. This she opened the barest crack, and peered out.

And, yes, Cochran was outside, a dozen feet down the promenade, holding Don Simon Ysidro roughly by the arm. '—made a kill,' the millionaire was saying in his sharp, harsh voice. 'The crystal gazer said "darkness" and "chains". We need to get down there fast and catch it before the kid's body is found. She said it was a "little boy" this time. I hope to God the thing hid the body better this time than those other two. The whole place'll be in hysterics and we'll never find where it's hiding.'

Don Simon inclined his head. 'It shall be as you command, lord.' He moved as if to withdraw, but Cochran's hand tightened hard around that thin bicep, jerking him back.

'And I better not find you teaming up with that thing to double-cross me. You're on parole, Ysidro. It won't take me and Louis any trouble at all to pick you up and stow you back in the box when you double up screaming – except maybe to get you away from the mob that's gonna tear you to pieces because they think it was you that killed those girls. And they *will* think it's you, the minute they get a look at your face. So don't you try any funny business.'

In a tone that held as much shock as disgust, Don Simon said, 'Ally myself with a *peasant*? What will you think of next?'

Cochran laughed, and let him go. Don Simon brushed his sleeve, as if to straighten wrinkles or dust away filth. The millionaire looked at his watch again, and said, 'Looks like you got four hours, before the antidote starts to wear off. I'll see you back at the cabin at four thirty.'

'It shall be as you command,' the vampire murmured again. And, stepping back into the shadows, he was gone.

SEVENTEEN

Lydia darted to the electric bell the moment Cochran was out of sight in the opposite direction, gave the order to Bahadir, the princess's butler, to have cocoa and tea brought to the séance room (presumably Her Illustrious Highness' cook was still awake also). Though she was overwhelmed by the desire to remain and listen to what Madame Izora had to say about her vision – or whatever it was – she hurried back into the chamber and said, 'I'm terribly sorry, but . . . I'm going to go back to our suite, Aunt. I can't – after what Madame said – I don't want Miranda to be alone.'

'Nonsense,' snapped Aunt Louise, who had pre-empted the seat beside the still-shaken Madame Izora the better to solicitously coax from her whatever revelations might be pending. 'For Heaven's sake, Lydia, this maniac that's prowling the ship – and I *refuse* to believe it's some sort of vampire or werewolf! – isn't going to come up to First Class.'

Had she been confronting her aunt alone, Lydia knew that tears would have been useless. But with Her Highness and Mrs Cochran present, she let her face crumple a little – she'd prudently removed her glasses on her way back across the parlor – and said, in her most quavery voice, 'I . . . I just don't want her to be alone.' And threw in the tiniest sniffle, for effect.

Aunt Louise looked as if she were about to tell her not to be silly – she didn't disbelieve the tears, simply regarded them as a sign of weakness. But the other two women crossed swiftly to her in tenderest sympathy. 'Of course, sugar,' said Mrs Cochran, and the princess put her arm around Lydia's shoulders in a warm hug.

'*Bien sûr*, you must go, dearest,' murmured Natalia Nikolaievna. 'We shall be here until Monsieur Cochran returns, which I think must not be until nearly daylight. Otherwise, send me word the moment – the very moment – you wake, and I will tell you everything. Though in truth –' she sank her voice to a whisper, and glanced back at the very pale woman beside Aunt Louise – 'my dear Izora never remembers what Phyleia speaks through her mouth. And if that weasel Barvell comes near her – I would not put it beyond Cochran to try to give poor Izora hyoscine or paregoric! – I shall have Samson and Zhenya throw him overboard. *Alors*, my little ones,' she added, as the anxious Monsieur and Madame pattered into the room and crowded to her ankles. 'All is well, *mes enfants*! All is well!'

'*Dear* Dr Barvell *always* prescribes morphia for my nerves . . .' Mrs Cochran was hinting to Dr Yakunin.

'There is something fanatic – did you not think? – in the man's pursuit of the *vampir*,' the princess went on in a hushed voice, picking up Madame la Duchesse in her arms. 'The way he insists that it be *he*, and no other, who finds this terrible thing. Like a trophy hunter, who will let a lion go on killing villagers rather than see another man slay it. Did he not seem so to you?'

'He did indeed.' Lydia gave the princess a quick kiss on the cheek. 'But please don't tell him I said so. We may need him.' She put on her glasses, and slipped out into the night.

Don Simon fell into step with her, halfway down the promenade. He murmured, '*Dios*,' when Lydia described Madame Izora's vision, and waited while Lydia slipped into her stateroom and fetched the long, drab garment that she thought of as her 'vampire hunting coat' and a woolen cap, for the night was now bitterly cold. She also snatched up her satchel, which Don Simon regarded with raised brows when she emerged onto the promenade again. *Can he sense the silver, the garlic, the Christmas rose inside?* She had removed the necklace and wrist-chains of silver that she habitually wore after dark – Cochran would almost certainly have noted them – but carried them, too, in the bag.

But he only said, 'What think you, Mistress?' as he guided her to one of the many narrow gangways that led down to the bowels of the ship.

'Do you mean, do I believe a child really was killed tonight?' She shivered as she said it. *Someone's child. Someone's little boy . . .*

He shook his head. 'I am certain that one was. What think you of this vampire?'

'She said,' recalled Lydia quietly, 'there are two. I thought she meant you were one of them, but . . . What you said about there being more than one. You've often told me that the Undead can go many days, sometimes weeks, between kills—'

'Heaven knows,' agreed the vampire quietly, 'there are places enough on this ship for a dozen to hide.'

Lydia wondered if the princess might be prevailed upon to volunteer her dogs.

'If it were someone who has been on the Front,' she said. 'Who has been killing – as I know most of you have been – two and three times a night . . . Does it become habit-forming, like a drug? Having . . . having gotten used to that level of

feeding . . .?' (*I can't* believe *I'm talking of this, of the murders
of three people, two of them children, so calmly . . . Though I
can't imagine that me having hysterics would help matters.*)

'There could be that, also.' Don Simon paused at the foot
of the stair, where it opened into the corridor communicating
with the lesser First Class suites, and consulted the map of the
ship which he'd taken from his pocket. He wore, over his rather
frayed evening clothes, the officer's coat that was part of his
persona as 'Colonel Simon' at the Front. It was the first time
Lydia had seen him less than completely assured of where he
was going. But after a moment's study, he led the way a few
yards down the corridor to another gangway, this one leading
straight down what looked like a shaft of sixty or seventy feet.
Even with electric bulbs burning, in the silence there was an
eerie horribleness to it, like a place visited in a dream.

'They are people of no account, these victims,' he said. 'A
woman with no family of her own; a gypsy's child. Even as
I, for many years, killed only Protestants, knowing their
souls to be damned in any case.' He looked around him. The
corridor was silent, save for the distant heartbeat of the ship's
engines. John Palfrey, Lydia knew, had a room halfway along
this corridor; she shivered at the thought of encountering him.
Madame Izora's suite lay only a few doors from where they
stood. 'It may be their only sin was that they were weak, and
poor.'

Lydia wondered if the stylish Mr and Mrs Allen, or the
overbearing Mr Bowdoin of Massachusetts – another casual
Promenade acquaintance – or his gentle little wife, who'd
admired Miranda's prettiness yesterday – did they sleep the
sleep of the just and wealthy? Were they secure in the knowledge that, as Aunt Louise said, *this maniac that's prowling the
ship isn't going to come up to First Class*!

The reflection made her deeply grateful, and profoundly
ashamed.

'*Does* it become habit forming?' she repeated, as they
descended again.

'I know not, Mistress. In the days of Napoleon's wars in
Spain, I was in London, or in Paris for a little time. As at the
Front today, those who hunted the night upon the peninsula

killed with absolute impunity, and the Peace of Paris did not bring peace to Spain. 'Tis difficult to know whether the Undead who had followed the battles left off indiscriminate killing, in the years when the liberals and the Carlists fought one another all over the countryside. The vampires of England – of all Europe – visited the place. Myself, I think not. One heard rumors . . .'

She remembered the last glimpse of the green coast of England, as it vanished into the silvery haze. 'Have you never been back to Spain, then?'

She had traveled a good deal in the past nine years – to Constantinople, to Russia, to China. But on every journey, on every day that she'd watched the desert on the banks of the Suez Canal or marveled at the low-built grubby labyrinths of the Peking streets, there had been in her mind, in the very marrow of her bones, the green quiet of England. The smell of rain in her garden on Holywell Street. The knowledge that she had only to get onto a train, to return to Willoughby Close where she had been born.

He said, in that soft uninflected voice, 'Never. And the vampires of Spain – if any survived those years of war – do not cross the Pyrenees. Perhaps for that reason.'

He was silent for a time, and around them – save for the throb of the engines, and the muted clank of their footfalls on the metal stair – the *City of Gold* was quiet, too. 'Yet there were some in France, and in the German lands, in the wake of the Wars of Religion, who did indeed go mad in those years of horror. They became so used to killing when and how they pleased that they did not or could not leave it off. There were at least two such in Paris, and Constantine – the Master of Paris – spoke of them to me. One, he said, called such attention to herself with the number and indiscretion of her kills that the men of the St-Antoine quarter banded together to hunt her systematically, under the command of a cattle drover.'

In the open doorway at the stair's foot they stopped again, the shadowy space before them throbbing louder, smelling of coal and oil and steam. Metal walls crossed between boiler rooms. Steam pipes hissed softly in the darkness overhead.

'They killed three people, I was told, ere they located the vampire. One man they burned for a sorcerer, and a woman

they drowned because her husband and children had all died
of the smallpox that had left her unscarred. They killed also a
moneylender – though not, I think, because anyone actually
thought him Undead. Constantine commanded this woman to
leave Paris, for the hunters were coming too close to others of
the Paris nest. He said she did so, but killed with such frequency
in the countryside that she was obliged to return to the city,
and so was found at last and dragged from her coffin, to burn
like a torch in the light of day.'

'Because she could not stop killing?'

'That also I know not. She *did* not stop, when 'twas clear to
her that her life was at stake for it. Not long after that another
came into Paris from the battlefields of Germany, where he had
followed in the wake of the Protestant armies and slew three
and four victims a night among the villages and in the woods, and
none noticed nor cared. This man also Constantine warned, and,
Constantine told me, the man begged him, weeping, for mercy,
saying that he could not help what he had become. A sort of
frenzy seized him, he said, and he could not go a night – nay,
not half a night – without the ecstasy of a kill. The vampires
of Paris themselves killed this man, lest there be another hunt.
Yet others, Constantine said, had also followed the armies
through Thuringia and Bohemia, and had suffered no such
madness.'

'*A sort of frenzy*,' echoed Lydia softly, and followed Don
Simon into the shuddering gloom. 'I suppose,' she added, almost
shouting as they neared the huge turbine room, 'that if a vampire
traveled to the United States, he – or she – could find places
where he could kill like that. From what Mr Cochran has told
me, there are strikes and lockouts in factories and mines all
over the country. People being killed every day. Heaven knows,
in the South, if one moved about enough, one could feed off
the poor Negro children every night and no white sheriff would
turn a hair.'

'The difficulty being,' said Don Simon, 'moving about. What
you describe is in essence what Cochran has offered me.' The
vampire paused before the metal doors of a coal bunker, spread
his long fingers and held his palm an inch from the door, yellow
eyes half-shut. Then he moved along to the next. Lydia saw the

fine-cut nostrils flare, and knew that though Don Simon did not breathe, his sense of smell was acute.

Can he smell the child's blood?

'If the vampire is killing down here,' she ventured, 'why not leave the corpse hidden in one of the bunkers? One from which the coal has already been taken? It wouldn't be found, probably, until we reached New York. Or why not throw it overboard? Although I suppose since it's four decks up to the outside air . . .'

Somewhere in the maze of metal-walled corridors large and small, Lydia heard light footfalls running, and a girl's voice called out, 'Kemal? Kemal, where are you? Can you hear me?' The sound was swiftly lost in the noise of the engines, but as they moved on other sounds whispered to them, other voices. Women's voices, mostly, though Lydia thought she heard the man Vodusek shouting. Then, like a flurry of bird-cries, from another direction, those of children again: 'Kemal? Kemal?'

Don Simon said softly, 'Even so.'

Together they hunted through the lower holds until shortly before daylight. Don Simon would sometimes pass his hands across the doors of the coal bunkers, or along the walls of the vast, dark, crowded baggage holds, but frustration and discontent flickered in his eyes, and Lydia recalled what he had said about the effects of the living magnetism of the sea. Other times he would stop, as if listening, or his nostrils would widen, like a dog's trying to scent the elusive trace of prey. But the lower holds of the *City of Gold* held in them all the clammy dankness of air that has been years away from sunlight or wind. *Does he smell all those years?* wondered Lydia. The exhalations of thousands of crewmen, the sweat of their pores mixed with the stink of the bilges, the dry foetor of coal and the oily reek of the steam?

How could you tease out even the coppery trace of blood from all of that?

We are as other men, he had said, saving – Lydia guessed – that he had the hyper-acute perceptions of the Undead state. In the lightless cavern of the deepest baggage hold he had moved about, his hands on her waist and on one of her hands, as if they were ice-skating, picking his way unerringly among trunks and crates and (Lydia presumed – such was the darkness that she was literally and absolutely blind) mail sacks. Only once or twice did her shoulder brush the edge of something, or her foot briefly touch a corner, to tell her that this hold contained the same jumble of objects she'd already encountered by Georg Heller's lantern-light in the First Class Baggage Store on the deck above. Twice, moving silently among the cacophony of metal walls that enclosed the engines and boilers, the vampire stopped, and drew her aside into the darkness, half a minute before her own less powerful hearing detected the footfalls of a crewman.

Once she heard a man – in a party of clattering feet – grumble, 'Mohammedan brat . . . all a prank . . .' and deduced that the missing boy was one of the little group of Bosniak Muslims, shunned by Catholics and Orthodox alike.

He had her wait in the darkness in the very stern, while he slipped down a final ladder into the deepest belly of the ship, the bilges beneath the orlop where, Lydia knew, the rats bred in the blackness and the great black beetles and roaches hid – creatures she'd already glimpsed among the engines, bunkers, and lockers of the orlop deck. In the few minutes that he was gone she shuddered at the nearness of the abyss – *we must be thirty feet beneath the surface already!* – and of its black depths falling away below her. Though neither fanciful nor timid, Lydia found herself wondering how thick the hull plates were: just under two inches, she read later, but layered and re-enforced so that the actual hull was nearly two feet. Even that information didn't remove the terrible sensation that she had, of being inside a bubble, deep and inescapably far down in the world of airless, deadly water, a curtain's breadth from death. *If something happens I can never get out . . .*

Nothing's going to happen, she told herself firmly. *And you've had casualty clearing stations shelled over your head and you came through that just fine. And anyway the* City of Gold *has been crossing back and forth for six years without mishap.*

Movement in the corridor. Close to the floor, the pin-light flicker of reflective eyes. Lydia was able to tell herself, *I've seen bigger rats at the Front*, but she was still revolted. Even the trenches hadn't served to eradicate her horror of the vermin.

Don Simon emerged from the ladder, and stood for a moment, leaning one hand against the wall. In the dim light he looked ghastly, half stooped-over, his face set against a wave of agony.

'What is it?' asked Lydia, shocked, and the vampire shook his head.

'Serum,' he whispered. 'Poison. Takes hold . . . thus . . .'

He was shaking all over, unable even to draw away from her, when she put her hand on his arm. He managed to say, 'Cold . . .' and then set his jaw hard, until the trembling ceased.

''Twill come on worse,' he said after a time. 'Best we return to the regions above, Lady. First light will stain the sky in less than two hours. They inject me with antidote once I sleep, with daylight – I think they fear I will somehow learn where they keep it, rather than fearing me. They know that unless I have that physic, I will quickly be rendered helpless. They have but to stand back, and watch me scream. For as long as they find it amusing.' So bitter was his voice that she guessed this was precisely what Cochran, and the smooth-mannered Dr Barvell, had done, at least once, to convince him of the poison's efficacy.

She felt her ears get hot with rage.

'Curious,' he went on, as he took her hand and guided her toward one of the inconspicuous gangways, 'that we have found nothing so far. Not coffins, or travel trunks, or places secured as hideouts. Myself, I should not care to travel so.' He looked around him at the great greasy cylinders of the steam pipes overhead, the huge steel turbines and gears. 'One could never get the coal smell out of one's clothing. Yet did I so, I should at least take pains to make for myself a sleeping place secured alike from rats and from chance discovery by stokers and mechanics going about in pursuit of their duties.'

'Not to mention,' commented Lydia, 'thieves looking for places to cache their goods.' Their search had revealed half a dozen bottles of the American Line's best liquor, cigars, and tins of caviar and foie gras, tucked in corners of lockers and storerooms. Lydia wondered if these were all Vodusek's gleanings, or if there were several petty thieves at work.

'I have seen a dozen likely places, on which no mortal

eyes have looked I daresay since these walls were riveted in place.' He frowned, following her up the metal steps to the quieter regions above. 'Yet I see nothing that would offer protection from rats, during the hours when we sleep perforce, and cannot wake.'

'I suppose one *could* travel First Class – the cabins in Second are all shared – and hunt in Third.'

'Too many servants in First.' His slight gesture dismissed the whole of non-Promenade First. 'If there is one thing I have learned in three-hundred-and-sixty years of being dead, Lady, 'tis to beware of servants. Bribe them as you will, threaten them as you might, yet they will talk, and for us, a whisper can mean death. Here upon the ocean, I have not the whole of a night in which to mold their dreams. Only for those few minutes before and after the hour of midnight can I whisper to them the impression that they saw me walking on the Promenade Deck in the full of the day. Can I make them think they did not truly see what they saw. Some might attempt it.' He shrugged. 'I would not.'

'It's true,' agreed Lydia slowly, 'that Ellen, or Tania – the Princess Gromyko's maid – the one who *hasn't* been laid up from the start of the voyage with sea-sickness – would have heard, had one of the First Class passengers been locking his cabin during the daytimes. I understand that it's general knowledge in the servants' dining hall that Mr Cochran locks up one room of his suite.'

'Did I travel upon the ocean –' Don Simon stepped past her at the top of the flight, to open the door that led onto F Deck – 'for no consideration would I hunt, nor yet permit others to hunt for me. Six days is—'

'*Vampír!*' shrieked a voice in the corridor. '*Vrkolak!*'

Don Simon moved back immediately into the shelter of the doorway, but Lydia, stepping forward, saw in the hallway no one near them, only a scrimmage of men and women with their backs to them. Others were emerging from the cabins that lined the corridor, women with their long hair plaited down the backs of patched and shabby nightgowns, men in undershirts and pants with braces dangling.

'They've found him,' breathed Lydia.

EIGHTEEN

'**G**o.' She caught Don Simon's hand. 'I'll see what's happening.'

Without a word he touched her fingers to his lips, and was gone, even on the metal stair his swift ascent soundless. Lydia shivered at the thought of his being taken by another convulsion, being trapped, unable to flee, by those who would see him as he was.

But even as the thoughts went through her mind she was running along the corridor, hearing before her the jumble of shouting. Meaningless words, mostly, but charged with the hysterical venom of hatred. Now and then a Belgian or a German would shout to some compatriot words that Lydia understood.

'Bosniak boy—'

'Deck well—'

'Mohammedan—'

'Bled dry—'

'Blood on her dress—'

'Whore—'

And a woman screaming.

Lydia dashed along the corridor as hard as she could pelt, following the mob and joined on all sides by hard-faced, old farmers, half-crippled soldiers, carrying hammers and wrenches from toolkits, knives and screwdrivers which they held like stilettos – a couple of genuine stilettos as well, and a couple of guns. The women who surged among them bore ropes, or clutched the crucifixes that dangled from their necks.

The mob bunched up suddenly, jammed tight in the narrow space in front of the doors of the Third Class dining saloon. Lydia could hear a man shouting in German and then in French, and recognized Heller's voice. Others yelled to drown him out, '*Vrkolak. Upír.* Vampire.'

Lydia pushed and wriggled through the press, slithering along the wall until she reached the front. A woman crouched in a corner of the hallway near the doors of the Third Class dining room. Heller stood in front of her, a huge pipe wrench in his hand, facing outward to the mob. One of the older men – a farmer with muscles like an ox – had fallen back before him with blood streaming down his face and another sat slumped against the wall holding his head, ghastly pale and sweating.

Oh, dear, I hope his skull isn't fractured . . .

Heller shouted at the crowd, 'Who is this woman? What language does she speak?'

'She's a whore!' yelled a woman in German, and someone else howled something that ended in *'vampira'*.

The woman crumpled to the floor, hiding her face in her long black hair. Her nightgown had been torn nearly off her – it was close to two in the morning. Lydia could see scratches and bruises on her arms, and blood on the front of the tattered linen garment.

Father Kirn pushed his way to the front, demanded something sternly of the woman in what Lydia thought might be Czech, then in halting Greek.

One of the Slovene women yelled in bad German, 'She kill little boy! Drink blood, leave body in stairs place—'

'Nikogda,' sobbed the woman. *'Ya nikogda—'*

'She is a whore who sleeps with good men and makes them bad!' another woman yelled. 'And now she murders this little boy!'

Heller knelt beside the woman, turned her face to him and looked at her for a moment, then stood again. 'You're idiots,' he said to the crowd. 'You say she's a vampire, no? I have seen her walking about the deck well in the daylight.'

There was a pause, and an angry ripple of translation. Then Vodusek said, his voice pitched to carry, 'Everybody knows vampire can walk about in daytime. Just they have no power in sunlight, being children of Satan. There was man in my village, in Malareka, that was vampire. Everybody see him walk about by daylight. Then in night, he turn himself into wolf, into bat. Slavik here saw him do this—'

'With my own eyes, myself!' One of Vodusek's friends stepped forward, pockmarked and limping a little on a wooden leg, but muscled with a lifetime of farm work.

Heller turned to Father Kirn. 'They found the child, then? The boy who was missing?'

The old priest nodded, and his lined face was harsh. 'Kemal Adamic. He was in the deck well—'

'Where everybody had been running about since the boy was found gone?' demanded Heller.

'She stand by his body—'

'That blood on her hand—'

'She is a whore,' repeated the German woman. 'A witch, Satan's servant—'

'Somebody,' shouted Heller over the din. 'Someone Russian. You say she's a vampire, eh? Can a vampire speak the scripture? You . . .'

A golden-haired boy had emerged from the crowd. Twelve or thirteen, thought Lydia. Just too young to be conscripted. In German he said, 'I Russian.'

'You want to see justice done?' Heller laid his hand on the boy's shoulder, looked gravely down into his eyes.

'*Da, Gospodin.*'

'Good. Good man. You ask her, speak Lord's Prayer. Can vampire do that?' This last he addressed to the mob, his pale blue eyes singling out first Vodusek, then the German woman. Then he turned to the priest. 'Can vampire do that? Say prayer?'

Somebody in the mob shouted, 'What you know about prayer, you Communist?' Heller ignored her.

'No,' said Father Kirn. 'Walk about in daylight – so I have sometimes heard. But never can the Devil speak the words of Our Lord.'

'You tell me.' Heller looked back at the Russian boy. 'Tell me true, does she speak the words of the prayer.'

The boy knelt beside the woman, asked her something in her own tongue. After a moment, the woman stammered, so faintly that she could barely be heard, '*Otche nash, suschiy nah nebesakh* . . .'

When she had finished, the boy stood up, nodded, and said, 'She say it all, every word.' He glanced from Heller to the mob, and looked scared – understandably, Lydia thought. They were ready to turn on anyone who kept them from ending what they saw as the cause of their fear.

Father Kirn took the Russian woman's hand, helped her to her feet. The mob growled, and shifted about, reminding Lydia of the horses penned for transport to the Front. Terrified of new sounds, new smells, of a threat they couldn't define. The man sitting beside the wall had slipped over and lay on the floor, breathing stertorously. No one gave him a glance. From around his own neck the priest removed his crucifix, and holding up the woman's hand, pressed the silver cross first against her palm, then against her forehead.

'That's Eastern Church!' yelled someone within the mob. 'Eastern heretics, like her! Not real Christian!'

And a woman shrilled furiously, 'And she's still a whore!'

'Oh, put a sock in it, Gertrude!' retorted Heller. 'Whose fault is it if your husband wants to stay out of your bed? It's no reason to kill someone.'

The man Vodusek stepped forward, heavy eyebrows bristling, and looked from Father Kirn to the dark-haired woman. Then he turned back to the crowd. He called out something in his booming voice, spreading his arms as if making a speech, making a point. He held up the woman's hand, to show it unmarked by the touch of the Cross. Lydia heard him say something and recognized the word *vrkolak*. Then he said it again, declaiming, his single dark eye blazing with anger. Heller stepped forward and grabbed him by the arm with an impatient word, and Vodusek shook him off.

The mob began to disperse. The pockmarked Slavik said to someone beside him, 'Well, the brat's only a heathen.' Father Kirn led the woman away, murmuring something to her. Probably, reflected Lydia, *Go thou and sin no more*. Somewhere, far off in the corridors, she could hear a woman wailing, 'Kemal! Kemal!'

She went to kneel beside the injured man, but Vodusek and Slavik thrust Lydia aside and gathered the man up, and helped him away.

Lydia stood up again, in her battered overcoat and the green silk dinner frock she'd worn to Madame Izora's séance, her red hair coming undone from its pins and trailing down over her shoulders. She felt suddenly exhausted, and wanted only to go into some dark corner and not see or speak to anyone and particularly not Aunt Louise. She wanted the voyage to be done.

She wanted Jamie.

'He should see a doctor,' she said, as Heller came to her, his wrench still in his hand. Like the other men, he was clothed only in his undershirt and in trousers hastily donned, the braces dangling about his thighs. His feet were bare. She saw two scars where bullets had torn into his collarbone and shoulder, not more than a few years ago. There was a much older knife-scar on his chest.

'They'll make up some muck of duck-shit and herbs,' he said. 'They don't trust doctors. They – Slavik and those others – don't trust anyone that's not from Malareka. Don't trust Catholics, don't trust Jews. They are villagers, ignorant – frightened. Don't even trust those from the next village. It isn't their fault but it's maddening to deal with. They've got one of them who was a doctor back in Malareka; there's about six of them, all from the same village. Vodusek and Slavik served together on the Eastern Front.'

He shook his head. 'Did you come down here hunting for the little Bosniak boy, Madame? That was good of you. It is a maniac, a madman, that we deal with here, but sometimes I wonder if that gang from Malareka aren't just as mad. Why make it into a monster? People are frightened enough, waiting every day to be torpedoed, not knowing if each hour – each minute – is going to be your last.'

'What did he say, there at the end?' asked Lydia. 'Oh, drat, here come the stewards . . .'

The clatter of feet echoed in the corridor, men's voices asking in hesitant Italian what was going on. Heller padded swiftly to the one open door left on the hallway – his own cabin, Lydia guessed. Someone called out a question to him in German from within, and she had a vague impression of movement, and of the smell of male sweat. He called out over his shoulder, '*Bulles* on the way. You heard nothing, saw nothing.' Then he dropped the wrench inconspicuously around behind the door jamb and said to Lydia, 'You must go . . . Vodusek said, *There is a servant of Satan on this ship, and we shall find him.* Heaven help the man they pick on, when they do. Because they are ready to kill.'

* * *

The guns went quiet around five. Only the splat of rifle-fire echoed across the desolate wet acres of blood-soaked ground, where sentries shot at wire-cutting parties or at the orderlies who'd sneaked out in the hopes of rescuing the wounded. Sometimes the hard rattle of machine-gun fire swept the ground where a bored gunner wanted to make sure of a prey he couldn't quite see. At about that time, Asher sensed that the vampires vanished, either to seek their holes – in dugouts or abandoned farm cellars, or the vaults of ruined churches or chateaux – or to have one last kill, out on No Man's Land itself, while the sentries drowsed.

Night's swift dragons cut the clouds full fast, Puck warns Oberon – words that even before he had known their truth, had always stirred Asher's heart.

> *At whose approach ghosts, wandering here and there,*
> *Troop home to churchyards: damned spirits all,*
> *That in cross-ways and floods have burial,*
> *Already to their wormy beds are gone,*
> *For fear lest day should look their shames upon*

Or for fear, reflected Asher, lest day should ignite their transmuted flesh to unquenchable flame . . .

He continued to pace the orchard, not daring to sit down between fear of falling asleep and awareness of the constant, stealthy scurry of rats in the dead leaves underfoot.

By six thirty, he guessed that Elysée had gotten distracted by either a kill or a chat, and would not be returning for him.

Annoyed, weary, and chilled to the bone, he turned his steps towards where he guessed the road lay – yes, this was old Vouliers's farm, all right. He recognized the line of the smashed hedges and the shape of the square-built roof. Quietly, from the bottom of his heart, he damned the war and the men who made it. The orderlies moving about among the rough shelters and tents emerged when they saw him come up the road, but didn't raise the fuss they would have, had he approached through the orchard. He asked where he was, was taken to the camp commander, presented his credentials, and explained that he had become lost and that the engine of his car had failed.

'Didn't sound like fuel lines or the carburetor, but there was no sense in trying to sort it out in the dark.'

Given the iffy state of most motor-pool engines at the Front, not to speak of the quality of the available petrol, Asher doubted that anyone would find it odd that the Peugeot would start up just fine for whoever Major Briscoe sent out to fetch it in. And at a guess, the commander had other things to think about than telegraphing wherever the hell Joël had stolen the Peugeot from, or checking Asher's bona fides.

Major Briscoe sympathized, offered him breakfast and a drink of far-from-contemptible Scotch, and assigned him a cot in the tent reserved for visiting officers. 'We'll have you on your way in no time, sir.'

NINETEEN

'The freighter *Cumberland* was torpedoed last night,' Ellen whispered to Lydia, as she tiptoed into the stateroom at what Lydia – normally an early riser – felt to be an embarrassingly late hour Saturday morning: *Ten thirty! Poor Miranda, to have breakfast only with that horrid Mrs Frush.*

She put on her glasses, and sat up in bed. Rain had been falling by the time she'd climbed to B Deck after leaving Heller, and only grayness showed through the porthole when Ellen put back the curtains. Lydia was conscious of the heavier chop of the sea, and of the wind screaming along the half-deserted promenades.

Through the connecting door came the welcome odors of bath soap and the faint, dry-leaves scent of clean towels heating on an electric rack.

'Two-hundred-fifty miles south of here,' the maid continued. 'A hundred men lost. The E.C. *Baldwin* picked up the survivors an hour ago, and Mr Travis – our cabin steward – says Captain Winstanley refused to change course to help, even though we were closer. He says the sub that did it will still be in the area, waiting for just that. Mr Travis says in the crew lounge the bets are four to one against the *Baldwin* making it a hundred miles before they're torpedoed, too.'

She fetched Lydia's robe, and gathered up the shabby coat that Lydia had left draped over the back of the chair, and brushed lightly at the coal dust on its skirts. In a voice more quiet still, she added, 'Mr Travis tells me there was a riot below decks last night, over a little Arab boy being found dead. They're keeping it quiet, he says, but he says the immigrants are in an uproar over it, and no surprise, I say.'

And she looked inquiringly from the black smudges on the coat, to Lydia, who murmured, 'Another time.' She didn't feel up to explaining that the Bosniak Muslims were no more Arabic than Aunt Louise was.

Above the racing of her heart, she thought, *Two more days. Tuesday at the latest, we'll be safe.*

'Well, it's no more than is to be expected,' Aunt Louise declared an hour later when Lydia – bathed, powdered, creamed, coiffed, manicured, clothed in tobacco-colored Vionnet and embellished with delicately undetectable whispers of rouge and *mascaro* – finally emerged into the parlor. 'Peasants straight out of the Middle Ages, as Her Highness said at dinner Wednesday night. Of course they'll turn a perfectly straightforward case of lunacy into a vampire tale. And it does cause me to wonder whether Mr Cochran actually believes it's a vampire doing this, or whether he's just using that term because it's what Madame Izora believes is happening. It's shocking,' she added, her plucked gray brows clouding with self-righteous disapproval, 'that a woman of her spiritual insight doesn't have the judgment to realize the difference between genuine communication from the Astral Plane, and these silly fairy tales that the ignorant make up.' She placidly turned a page of *The Passing of the Great Race.*

'I suppose,' said Lydia, her voice held steady with an effort, 'the danger of being torpedoed magnifies—'

'Nonsense.' Aunt Louise folded up her book. 'We're in no more danger of torpedoes than we would be lunching at the Café Metropole. I'm surprised at you, Lydia. That freighter, whatever it was called, that Malkin was blithering about this morning – it's astonishing how the lower orders can work themselves into a panic over nothing! – was simply asking for what it got. They were taking munitions to a belligerent country in wartime: what on earth did they expect? Take those *frightful* spectacles off, child, if we're going to luncheon! Honestly, your husband should *never* have permitted you to go to the Front, if it's caused you to forget . . . I suppose the crew of the *Cumberland* were being paid by the British Crown. All those American freighters are, these days. Of course one cannot countenance blowhard bullies like the Germans, but they aren't stupid, you know.'

At luncheon, this opinion was heartily seconded by Mr Cochran, to a degree that would have gotten him called out – in Lydia's opinion – had not Captain Winstanley absented himself from the meal. 'Cowardice!' stormed the millionaire. 'Submarines – bunk! Like any German captain in his right mind is going to run the risk of sinking an American boat! Why, the Huns are shaking in their boots at the thought that Wilson's going to join the Allies! They wouldn't blow a spitball at us for fear we'll come over there and slap them into submission.'

'Do you think they will?' Dr Yakunin cocked his head, fish fork poised delicately above an artistically-curled pair of shrimp. 'Enter the war?'

'Wilson'll be a fool if he does.' Tilcott mopped with a roll at the hollandaise that was all that was left of his second helping of deviled lobster. 'Americans'll never stand for it, after all that campaign ballyhoo last year: "America First" and "He kept us out of War". He'll look a damn fool if he turns around and gets us *into* a war. Let the kings and the kaisers and the emperors and the sultans fight it out among themselves, that's what *I* say. It's no affair of ours.'

'It'll be our affair if we get torpedoed on account of it,' ventured Lydia, and Mrs Cochran patted her hand.

'That's simply not going to happen, sugar.' She was wearing pink diamonds this morning, to match her frock, and by the look of her pupils had clearly gotten Dr Barvell to administer an injection 'for her nerves'.

'Damn right it's not going to happen,' sniffed Cochran. 'But it'll damn well be our affair if the kaiser starves Britain into submission and takes it over, given all the money we've lent the Brits. You can bet we'll never see a dime of it if they lose.'

'My dear Mr Cochran.' Aunt Louise looked down her nose at him. 'What *have* you been reading? The Germans are no closer to starving Britain into submission than they are to flying to the Moon. It is *we* who control the seas.'

'Just what I'm saying.' He stabbed at her with his fish fork. 'Only Winstanley's an old woman who's so afraid of his own shadow that he'll let people freeze out on the open ocean, rather than turn aside to go get 'em. But people are in such a frenzy to make it to New York the day after tomorrow he'll let ordinary folks go hang.'

'Well, really, Mr Cochran,' his wife said with a frown. 'Common humanity is one thing, but as you yourself said Wednesday night, the American Line *does* have a responsibility to the business community, to provide the swiftest transportation. We need to get to New York, and have a right—'

'I said nothing of the kind,' snapped Cochran, from which Lydia deduced that his burst of common humanity probably stemmed less from concern about the *Cumberland's* passengers than fear that he wasn't going to find the *City of Gold's* vampire in time to work out a strategy of entrapment before the ship docked.

Once in New York, he was well aware – and Lydia was even more conscious – the unknown vampire would vanish for good.

At eight hundred feet by ninety, the *City of Gold* was one of the largest ships afloat: ten decks deep, mazes within mazes of corridors, staterooms, coal bunkers, storage holds, refrigerated lockers, smoking rooms and squash courts (*squash courts?*), but that still only came to five hundred thousand or so cubic yards. As Lydia excused herself from her un-eaten lunch and made her way across the dining room to the table where she recognized Dr Liggatt, a part of her mind was tortuously aware that the moment the liner drew up at the New York docks, her own options as to what she could do and what she should do would change, irrevocably.

I can't let a vampire go ashore in America.

And her heart pounded at the knowledge that it wasn't the

second unknown vampire that she meant. Or that she should mean, anyway.

I have to kill him. I have to kill them both.

I can't let a man like Cochran have one – let alone two *– vampire slaves.*

Freeing Don Simon from his coffin was not a solution to either problem.

There was only one solution.

The ship's surgeon, Mr Allen and Mr Bowdoin (to whose opinions about bi-metallism Dr Liggatt had been politely listening), rose from their places and bowed as Lydia approached. 'Please,' she smiled, the portion of her mind not taken with grief and anxiety grateful that at least Dr Liggatt, with his flax-pale hair and sunburned complexion, was readily identifiable at a distance without glasses.

When the other men sat, the surgeon retreated with her to the side of the room. 'You'll be wanting to have a look at the little Adamic boy? It was all I could do, to get him away from his mother.' He shook his head, face tightening with concern and dread. 'Just like the others. Two short incisions in the throat, most of the blood drained from the body. No blood on the clothing or in the hair. Poor tyke. He couldn't have been eight years old.'

Later, reading to Miranda in the shelter of the Promenade while gray rain sluiced into the gray sea, Lydia couldn't erase from her mind the mother's despairing screams: *Kemal! Kemal!* She remembered Aunt Louise's casual remark, *I'll wager she can't remember all their names*, while looking down at the children crossing the gangplank, and tears blurred the print before her. Kemal had been his mother's eighth child. The despair in her voice had been no less.

Dr Liggatt had been perfectly correct in his report. There had been no blood on the wax-white little face, under the cold electric lights in the meat room; none in the rumpled black hair. The cupid-bow mouth had been slightly ajar. The child's mother had placed a rolled-up fragment of writing – presumably Koranic scripture – on the boy's tongue, and a string of prayer beads encircled his chubby neck.

A boy who would never see America. Brothers and sisters who would one day say, *We had a little brother but he died on the voyage over.*

His short, stubby fingers had been sticky. The smell of peppermint lingered, very faintly, on his lips.

Lydia's rendition of the account of the intrepid Dorothy's conversation with the King of the Winged Monkeys faltered, and Miranda's small hand closed around her thumb.

'Mummy, don't be afraid.'

She set the book quickly on the deck beside her, and dug in her pocket for a handkerchief. Miranda, on the child-sized chair beside her, set Mrs Marigold aside and leaned closer to Lydia, and whispered, 'Mrs Marigold is scared, too. But I told her it's all right.'

'Of course it's all right.' Lydia deftly dabbed away the incipient tears – from long practice managing not to disarray her *mascaro* – and smiled.

'The mermaids got to the submarines,' explained Miranda. 'They rub them all over with blue lotus, while the crew are sleeping, so sea monsters will come and swallow them whole. Sea monsters love blue lotus.' She looked up into her mother's face, serenely certain and at the same time concerned for Lydia's distress. 'They like the blue best, but they'll eat the yellow, too, if they can't get blue.'

'That makes sense,' Lydia agreed. 'I'd never heard that.'

Miranda explained in detail about mermaids and the blue lotus that grew in Atlantis (*where on* earth *did she get that?*) then listened to the remainder of the chapter fourteen, sufficiently distracting Lydia's thoughts from her sense of oncoming despair. But when she saw the Princess Gromyko at the far end of the Promenade with her dogs, she thought long and hard before tucking the book beneath her arm, removing her glasses, and following Miranda to greet them.

I can't let him go ashore. Not as Cochran's slave – and not as a free man.

'Darling . . .' The princess greeted her with a kiss, and, with a glance before her at Miranda, handed the leashes to Mademoiselle Ossolinska and lowered her voice. 'Tania says they know who the vampire is.'

Lydia stared.

'I think it's nonsense, myself,' the older woman continued. 'Peasant rumor—'

'*Who?*' asked Lydia. 'Not, *where?*'

'In plain sight, under their very noses.' Natalia Nikolaievna shook her head, a look of consideration on her exquisite face. 'Which I suppose would make sense, if one were a vampire seeking to emigrate. Myself, my old nurse always said that the vampire cannot go about in the daylight, but Tania says no, that is not the case—'

'They can't,' said Lydia. 'I know this,' she added, as her companion opened her mouth to argue. '*Who* is saying—?'

'Everyone, evidently. Men from the villages of the Sudeten say they have seen them. And it is a fact, that the Jew can give no good account of himself at the time those poor children were killed.'

'What Jew? Old Mr Goldhirsch?'

The princess shrugged. 'I don't know what Jew. There's a wicked old Jew in Third Class, Tania says, and she says that word is going about that he is the vampire . . . which I must say doesn't surprise me. There is something . . . *sinister* . . . about the Jewish race, isn't there? Something accursed. One hears frightful things . . .'

'That's nonsense.' Lydia was almost too startled, for the moment, even to feel angry. 'One hears frightful things about fortune tellers also, but that doesn't mean that Madame Izora is a madwoman or a confidence trickster.'

'That's not the same thing at all!'

Lydia opened her mouth to snap back that first, it was a good deal more likely that madame was a confidence trickster than that Mr Goldhirsch – however hard-fisted and unsympathetic he might be – was a vampire and second, there was no way of knowing whether the old man could give a good account of his movements at the times of the murders or not because nobody knew what those times were. Then in the back of her mind she heard Jamie saying – following one of Aunt Isobel's diatribes against the Irish – *There isn't much likelihood that anything I say is going to change her mind . . . and we need to pick our battles.* (That was, Lydia recalled, on an occasion on which

they needed Aunt Isobel to introduce them to a Member of
Parliament regarding a right-of-way near Oxford.)

In any case, between her stepmother and her Nanna, Lydia
had grown up picking her battles.

So she took a deep breath and said, 'No, of course it isn't
– forgive me. That was a bad simile. One has only to look at
Madame to see her honesty.' Lowering her voice and laying a
hand on her companion's arm, she went on, 'The thing is,
Natalia Nikolaievna, I've come across something entirely
different. And if it's true, I don't see how poor Mr Goldhirsch
could have anything to do with anything. I've come across—'

They'd reached the corner of the Promenade and she glanced
around her, though in fact the covered way that fronted the
Tilcott and Cochran suites was completely vacant.

Almost in a whisper, she said, 'I've come across evidence
that Mr Cochran knows more about this vampire than he's let
on. Shh—' she added, putting a quick finger to her lips.

The princess, dark eyes wide, nodded her understanding,
and steered the party back along the way they had come.
Behind them, Lydia heard a door open, and a moment later
the bulky Mr Kimball and another 'detective' – lanky and
sallow, and clutching a Gladstone bag – passed them, muttering
discontentedly.

'The thing is,' continued Lydia in a hushed undervoice,
'Mr Cochran has had his men searching the ship – quietly,
secretly – since the start of the voyage, even before the first
killing. I heard him the first night giving them instructions:
The silver crucifix should keep you safe, he said. *Bring him
to me, I need him.* Then later he said, *Remember, this is a
business deal.* I didn't know what he meant, until last night.
Mr Cochran knows he's on board, and is trying to keep
everyone else from finding him, until he's met with him – and
not to destroy him, as he'd have us believe. He's protecting
him. He wants to make a deal with him.'

The princess's breath left her in a little gasp. '*Infamous*—'

'I wouldn't be surprised,' added Lydia darkly, seeing she had
her full attention and belief, 'if it was Mr Cochran who is
putting it about that Mr Goldhirsch is the vampire, as a way of
deflecting the search from wherever the *real* vampire is hiding.'

That made sense even to her, and the Princess Natalia, much struck, whispered, 'You're right!' She did not, Lydia noticed, even question whether the American millionaire would do such a thing.

'Don't tell Tania.' Lydia glanced around her again, trying to sound like someone in a blood-and-thunder novel. 'Whatever you do. Don't tell *anyone*. You know how these things get about. But I need to get in and search Mr Cochran's suite.'

'Ah! So!' Illumination brightened the princess's face. 'And if our good Madame Izora has a . . . a revelation, a vision, a dream—'

'Exactly!' Lydia marveled again at her friend's combination of cleverness and absolute credulity. 'And if Madame says she sees or smells a . . . an unknown substance, a jar or bottle clutched in the vampire's hand, Cochran will bring Barvell with him, to ask questions about it. Barvell is a chemist, you know. It will have to be tonight,' she added quietly. 'We cannot risk even the slightest chance, that this . . . this *monster* . . . will reach America. Certainly not if it's allied itself with Cochran. If one of his detectives is in the suite I'll have to come up with some way to—'

'They won't be.' The princess shooed the problem aside like a mosquito. 'Samson – my footman, you know – says that none of them have been about the suite all day. Only Barvell. See—' she pointed back along the Promenade toward Cochran's suite – 'they've put extra locks on the outer doors. A padlock – Heaven knows what they paid Captain Winstanley to let them do it!' She put a hand on Lydia's elbow, when Lydia would have taken her at her word and gone to look. 'And it makes sense, you know. Samson told me yesterday that M'sieu Cochran's valet, even, shares a second-class stateroom – the smallest of that class, down on F Deck! – with Oliver – the nephew, you know, the secretary. Oakley – the valet – is obliged to go up *five flights* at a set time each morning, to shave M'sieu Cochran and help him dress, and does everything by time schedule, and now I see why! The American does not want him – or anyone! – in the suite, except that poisonous creature Barvell. You don't think he is hiding this vampire, this creature, in the suite, do you? Like mine, it must have an inner room which can be kept lightless . . .'

Lydia shook her head quickly. 'If he were, he wouldn't be searching for him, which he obviously is.' And, because the princess was coming uncomfortably close to the truth, she added, 'Monsieur seems to have made a friend,' nodding along the Promenade toward the little group of Ossolinska, Miranda, and the two dogs. They had been joined by the Allens, Mr Allen holding a well wrapped-up infant in his arms while his slender, stylish wife stooped to caress the little dog's head.

'Dreadful people.' The princess raised her lorgnette momentarily, as if peering through opera glasses at a distant stage. 'If Allen is their real name. Tania tells me that it was originally *Altmann*; Jew bankers from Holland.' Disdain curled the edges of her voice. 'M'sieu is constantly up and down to the wireless room, trying to get news of the New York stock market. He must be, as Madame Cochran says, like a rooster in an empty henhouse, with the wireless out this afternoon. It's all Jews think about, you know.'

She paused to bestow a warm smile in passing upon a Mr Tyler, wealthy – according to Ellen – from the proceeds of a string of factories in Pittsburgh in which immigrant girls worked sixteen hours a day. The industrialist beamed and tipped his hat.

'Is the wireless out?' Lydia glanced up automatically in the direction of the Marconi room, though it was hidden by the roof of the promenade.

'So they say. Though myself, I say, one of the great joys of travel is to be adrift from the cares of the world one has left behind. To be one with the sea and the sky. To come to know one's fellow passengers –' she smiled, and tightened her elbow over Lydia's hand – 'without all that pestering about how many men were killed last week in Flanders, and what those imbeciles in Petersburg are doing now. I can read about it all when we reach New York.'

Lydia could not stop herself from thinking, *If we reach New York.*

The two women rejoined Miranda and the dogs and Ossolinska (Miranda was explaining to the fragile-looking Mrs Allen about mermaids and blue lotus), and the little girl's words turned Lydia's eyes towards the gray surge of the sea.

She shouldn't have to be making up stories about why we aren't really in danger from submarines.

At the far end of the promenade, Lydia could see the ship's lookout mast, a thin spike of wood with the round white crow's nest halfway up it, rather like a Sterno tin impaled on a kitchen spit. The pale gray daylight glinted on binoculars: two men searching the ocean's surface.

Searching for something they probably wouldn't even see until it was too late.

They're out there, thought Lydia. Under the water. Sniffing, like wolves on a blood trail, for prey. She wondered if the crew of the E.C. *Baldwin* had yet paid for their Good Samaritan impulse. Aunt Louise had remarked, when Lydia had spoken of it on the way to lunch, that she was entirely sick of hearing about submarines and that she heartily agreed with the Royal Navy's orders that no vessel was to go to the aid of a torpedoed ship for fear that the attacker might still be in the neighborhood.

Is it worse, Lydia wondered, *to be trapped on a ship with a vampire (well,* two *vampires), or surrounded by enemy submarines?*

Or to know that before the end of the voyage, you're going to have to kill someone you love?

'Personally,' said the princess, moving on along the promenade and obliging the rest of her party – companion, dogs, Miranda, Lydia – to abandon the unworthy Allens, 'I shall be glad when this voyage is done.'

A gust of wind flung spray and rain on Lydia's face.

It was four o'clock.

TWENTY

'I'm to wait for him at half past eleven.' Captain Palfrey, his face aglow with relief, checked his wristwatch, as if to make sure he'd reset it earlier that day when the *City of Gold* had crossed through into yet another time zone. Lydia tried to mentally calculate what time it actually was, in relation to where the sun would be (*on the other side of the world*) when it was midnight here, and failed (*drat it, I forgot to pack a sextant. I wonder if Captain Winstanley would lend me one?*).

(*Probably the reason Don Simon set their rendezvous for eleven thirty. He'll be as late as he needs to be to bring the illusion into play.*)

A Willow Grove waiter – Roger – brought their pot of tea and plate of sweet biscuits. Across the café, she could see Miranda sitting, very lady-like in her pale-green, ruffled frock, with the princess and Madame Ossolinska, drinking 'cambric' tea heavily laced with milk from the demi-tasse cup that William presented to her with a smile. Aunt Louise could say what she liked about Aunt Lavinnia as a preceptress, but Lydia could see no fault in her daughter's beautiful manners.

Probably better than had I had charge of her, she thought sadly, *for the past two and a half years . . .*

But her grief at having left her child, at the age of two and a half, to volunteer her skills at the Front was still a dagger in her heart.

'Do you know,' went on Palfrey eagerly, 'I saw Colonel Simon yesterday, on the Second Class promenade? I passed on my way to the barber shop, and saw him standing by the forward deck well, chatting with Mrs Bowdoin. He caught my eye, raised a finger to his lips –' the young man demonstrated – 'when I looked again, he was gone. He's a deep one,' he added, pleased and proud.

'He is indeed.' As Lydia had spoken to Palfrey on Friday afternoon, she knew that, had he actually seen Don Simon a few hours before that – in the morning on his way to the barber's to be shaved – there was no way he would have neglected to mention it to her. *Simon must have put a dream into his mind last night, at midnight of local time – a dream that he'd seen him that morning.*

A dream so real that poor Captain Palfrey now thinks it actually happened.

No wonder Mr Cochran wants someone who can do that, to be his slave.

She sipped her tea. It was five. The rain had ceased, though the sky remained gray as iron.

I can't let it happen. The thought turned again and again on itself in her mind, as she returned to her room to change into her Third Class togs, after arranging with Palfrey to stand watch on the promenade that night. Nor, she reflected, would Don Simon want it to happen. There were things about him that she knew she would never understand, but she knew his pride, the cold haughtiness of a sixteenth-century Spanish nobleman. To be ordered about like a hired assassin by a cold-blooded money-grubber like Cochran . . .

To be brought to his knees, helpless in the kind of pain she had felt through dreams last week . . .

To be passed along, to whoever Cochran needed political favors from . . .

He would rather die.

She thought about that, slipping quietly from her stateroom when Ellen gestured to her that the coast was clear.

Would *he rather die*?

She had seen him double over, for a moment speechless with agony, as the poison first bit. Had heard, on other occasions, the screams of vampires as their flesh ignited with the sun's first touch.

Had seen men die . . .

The girls in the Swiss boarding school she'd gone to, the young ladies who had come 'out' with her, in the Season of 1899. They were always saying, *I'd rather die* . . .

At the prospect of wearing last year's hat to the Royal Horticultural Society Flower Show, or being seen taken into dinner with poor stammering Hugh Wigram. At the mere thought of staying – and being *seen* to be staying – at an inexpensive boarding house rather than one of the grand seaside villas in Deauville . . .

I'd rather die.

Lydia wondered if they said things like that still.

In the fore deck well, older brothers and mothers grouped in the corners, watching the few children who still played games of bounce ball and hopscotch in the gray chill of the wet decks. Their movements were hesitant, as if they feared to get too far from their friends. They missed easy shots because they were looking over their shoulders. In the shelter of the crane mechanism,

Ariane Zirdar was telling a little cluster of the smaller ones a story, with elaborate pantomime because several of them spoke no German. But when Lydia went through the door into E Deck, she saw many more of them, either playing in the cramped cabins, the doors propped open for air circulation, or sitting just outside cabin doors under the watchful eyes of their elders.

More were in the dining room, fretful and crying, while the men smoked and muttered in corners.

'I'm ready to settle that imbecile Vodusek with a wrench,' growled Heller, fetching two cups of execrable tea from the samovar at the side of the dayroom. The coffee was exhausted already, and unwashed cups again piled the long sideboard. 'After they nearly killed that poor Russian woman last night, he's still insisting to everyone who'll listen that it's a vampire who's doing these things. Shouting that we need to find the abomination, not that it's a madman and that we need to get police to take fingerprints and measurements. Listen to me,' he added, with a bitter chuckle. 'My old comrades would laugh their heads off to hear me say we *need* the pigs. But I think this is a case where we do. We need their resources. This will end—'

He shook his head. 'Did you see the child's body?'

'Yes. I think he was lured with candy, like the other.' She gave a detailed account of her examination of Kemal Adamic's little corpse, ending with, 'Are the men still searching?'

'Some of them. Enough of the black gang, and the engine crew, have come to believe the talk, that they let searchers into the engine rooms and the coal bunkers. Though if the killings were done in a coal bunker there'd be signs of it on the victims' clothing.' He grimaced. By the soot smudges on his unshaven face, Lydia guessed he'd been one of those patient, tireless searchers. It crossed her mind to wonder if the sneak thieves of liquor and cigarettes had steered the searchers away from their personal hidey-holes.

She certainly wouldn't put it past Vodusek to do so.

'And some of the black gang are as superstitious as the farmers and miners. I tried to talk some sense into that old God-peddler Kirn, but all he had to say to me was "*Get thee behind me, Satan"*, and quote me some Biblical swill about the Jews being an accursed race of Christ-killers.'

'They're saying,' said Lydia, 'that the vampire is old Goldhirsch.'

'*Quatsch!*' He made a face of disgust.

'And a woman in First Class,' went on Lydia carefully, 'who claims to be psychic, says that the boy was killed in a place with chains. *A dark place with chains*, she said . . .'

Heller had lifted his hand as if about to beg to be spared any more claptrap, but paused in the gesture. 'Chain locker,' he said. And seeing her blank look, explained, 'The space in the nose of the ship, where they stow the anchor chain while we're at sea. It's right above the ballast tank. Now that you speak of it, were I to murder someone aboard-ship,' he added thoughtfully, 'that would be a good place to do it. Nobody goes there. It's full of rats, and so close to the bilges, it's foul as any slum outhouse.'

His eyes narrowed as he turned the matter over in his mind. Near the depleted coffee urns, Vodusek and his sour-looking friend Slavik harangued a knot of uneasy women in Slovene, amid a cloud of cigarette smoke.

'If I wanted to hang and bleed someone,' the German went on, 'I could do it from the upper portion of the chain itself, where it rises through the ceiling to the anchor. The bottom of the locker's always a couple of feet deep in water, just from what drips in when the chain's pulled up. You can't even see it, because of the chain piled in it. With a funnel you could just drain the blood straight down into the bilge and nobody would notice anything until we docked. Probably not then. With the other stinks in there, I doubt you could smell even a couple of gallons of blood mixed with the water at the bottom.'

'Could someone get to it? The chain locker? Dragging or carrying a body, I mean?'

'Oh, yes. There are always emergency doors into it, in case the chain itself kinks or hangs itself up. On this ship, it's probably from one of the dormitories where the stokers and greasers sleep. Maybe another from the bulk cargo hold one deck below. You could go in when the men in that room are all on-shift. Nobody would see you, if you're careful.'

And if you timed your kill, thought Lydia, *for those ten or fifteen minutes on either side of midnight, when the vampire mind regained its full powers, to turn the perceptions of the living aside . . .*

'Can we . . .?' she began, but voices interrupted her, shouting in the corridor outside. A child's frantic wail of fear. Another child, shouting something . . . Lydia sprang to her feet and strode to the door, followed by every person in the room.

But in a weird parody of last night's riot, a crowd of the children that Lydia had seen so recently in the deck well were pushing, shoving, throwing bits of chalk and trash at the two children – Yakov and his sister – that she and Heller had seen yesterday while searching the rear portions of the ship. They'd cornered them in a turning of the corridor and Yakov was crying. He tugged at his sister's skirt and sobbed, 'Rivkah! Rivkah!' and the girl Rivkah pushed him behind her, stamped her foot and shouted something at the juvenile mob. Lydia heard them yell back, '*Zid! Iudey! Jüden!*' and knew what the trouble was.

Before she could step forward, the girl Ariane, gold braids swinging, shoved her way through the pack and grabbed the dark girl's hand. Her face convulsed with anger, Ariane turned and shouted at the mob, evidently words to the effect that they were cowards and (probably, Lydia guessed) no great advertisement for Christianity themselves. They protested, but backed off a few paces – at fifteen Ariane was halfway to adult authority, and larger than most of them. Frau Zirdar strode from the group around Vodusek, shouldered past Lydia in the doorway and called out to her daughter, gesturing for her to come away and not interfere. Lydia caught the word for *Jew.*

Ariane drew herself up and retorted.

Frau Zirdar gestured more firmly, and her voice hardened.

Threat of a thrashing, guessed Lydia, seeing the girl's face. Tears flooded Ariane's eyes but she didn't give ground. Yakov and Rivkah, meanwhile, bolted away down the corridor to the WC at the end, evidently the only goal that could have gotten them out of their grandfather's cabin. Frau Zirdar strode forward, grabbed her daughter by the wrist, and at the same time shouted something at the other children that made them scatter. Then she hauled her daughter away down the corridor for the promised punishment, whatever it was. Ariane followed meekly, her one attempt to explain being silenced with a harsh, '*Utihnil!*'

'Little bastards,' said Heller quietly. 'There will be trouble indeed, if we don't find this madman, and soon.' He glanced sidelong at Lydia. 'Some of the stokers were saying this morning that an American freighter was torpedoed, a few hours south of us. Have you heard further of this?'

Lydia shook her head. 'The ship's wireless is out,' she said. 'They've got extra men up on the lookout, but I'm not sure how much good that will do, against a submarine. Particularly not once it gets dark. I did hear that at least some of the freighter's crew – and passengers, if there were any – were picked up by another freighter.'

'The captain of that ship is a courageous man,' said Heller. 'I've never really blamed the priest and the Levite, you know, for hastening away from the stricken traveler in the tale of the Good Samaritan. That's the oldest trick in the book. Leave a dying man by the roadside as bait, and rob those who stop to help. That Samaritan was lucky he got away with his own life.'

'It's what most of the people in the First Class dining hall were saying this morning,' said Lydia. 'They're probably right. And I'd probably tell them that the priest and the Levite went to Hell anyway, if my own daughter weren't on board. Do you have children, Herr Heller?'

'I did,' said Heller. 'He was killed in a mineshaft cave-in, because the company had skimped on the shoring in the tunnels. He was eight years old. That was when I became a Socialist.'

Movement in the darkness.

Asher checked his watch. It was eight o'clock, well after full dark. The barrage, which had begun late in the afternoon away to the northeast, seemed to be moving closer. Far off he could see activity around the casualty clearing station, lanterns barely visible through the tangle of orchard trees. He wondered if they were getting ready to clear out.

Older vampires – Elysée, Asher knew, had become vampire

around the year 1800 – were able to move about at the end of twilight: he hoped that pale flicker he had glimpsed was she. In the open motorcar, drawn up a few hundred yards from the clearing station among the tangle of disused trenches, he felt hopelessly exposed.

He pulled the blanket around him, and waited.

He'd left the clearing station while it was still light, to avoid suspicion, not to speak of the possibility that the commandant would get a reply to questions – if he'd wired them to Paris – that the Peugeot had been stolen. After jolting away on the shell-holed road he'd doubled back at Nesle, and pulled up to his present position at shortly before seven, where the ruins of one of old M'sieu Vouliers's barns concealed the dim beam of his bullseye lantern from view.

It would be safer, of course, to wait in the empty trenches that slashed the landscape to the west. The vampires would find him easily enough in either place, and if the enemy chose to shell the clearing station he would be far safer. But aside from the fact that the men in the front-line trenches were clearly using these secondary ones as latrines (rather than take a longer hike to the designated areas), the thought of the rats that swarmed the ditches and dugouts filled him with loathing. Even in the front-line trenches they were everywhere, barely bothering to get out of the way of the men who were forced to sleep, eat, and wait in those half-flooded muddy hell-pits for six weeks at a time. Last year – during his stint as a 'listener' – Asher had sometimes gone with bored soldiers on shooting expeditions to the less inhabited portions of the foul labyrinth. The thought of sitting down there in the darkness tonight was more than he cared to deal with.

At least, he thought, this early in spring one didn't have to deal with maggots wriggling on every surface as well.

He tried not to think about the fact that he wasn't going to have access to a newspaper until sometime tomorrow. *Even if the ship was torpedoed the news wouldn't be printed.*

Stop that. It was, as he'd seen in Paris, another way in which vampires hunted. The older ones could get your mind to drift, so you didn't see them until it was too late.

She's fine. She's safe . . .

He shivered in the damp wind. Like a thousand other rendez-vous. How many hundred nights spent waiting, for somebody to show up with information: a word, a name, a packet of letters or maps. Prague, Vienna, Constantinople, Tsingtao. The sour darkness of the marshland below the ruins of Nineveh. Wondering if he'd be quietly on a train the following morning with his information tucked into a hollowed walking stick or the lining of his luggage, or if something was going to go wrong, that would result in his death.

Seventeen years of it, before he'd had enough.

Before Africa . . .

There. Movement again.

He flexed his hand, which he had wrapped with the silver chains from his wrists. The silver would badly burn a younger vampire. Even Elysée, seasoned by the kills of a century, would be scorched and seared, forced to flee and seek healing in the energy released by a kill. He wondered if killing three and four times a night rendered even the young vampires, the fledglings, tougher than those he'd encountered in the days and the times of peace.

It was the kind of question Lydia would have asked Ysidro, he thought.

Don't think about them . . .

He snapped his mind back to full concentration in time to see two vampires about a yard from the car, visible in the sudden glare of an exploding shell a half-mile to the east.

He switched on the car's headlamps and brought up his silver-wrapped hand, but he'd already recognized Elysée's fledgling Joël, fair-haired and pretty as a girl in the evening clothes he'd worn last night. The other, dressed in the uniform of a French colonel, was also fair – Elysée liked blonde men – but of a heroic handsomeness, as tall as Asher and broad of shoulder. Asher wondered if he'd stolen the uniform from one of his victims, or had purchased it from some venal stores clerk. It was clean, smart, and fitted him as if tailored.

Asher saluted him, letting him see the coils of chain that gleamed around his hand.

'Keep watch, Joël,' the pseudo-colonel said, and the smaller vampire faded into the darkness.

The 'colonel' regarded him in silence for a moment, and another explosion flashed sudden and sinister, reflected in his eyes.

'You've spoken with Elysée?' asked Asher politely, but did not offer his hand.

The officer took a step nearer, wary. 'Do you know where she is?'

Asher shook his head. 'Looking for you, I presume. She wasn't pleased when she heard you'd made fledglings of your own – if you are indeed Augustin Malette.'

'I am.'

'And if what Joël says is true – that you're planning to set yourself up as master of some other city – I assume you've been recruiting helpers to do it with.'

The gold head nodded again in assent. 'Paris has changed,' said the vampire, in a hoarse baritone and an inflection Asher recognized as belonging to the lower-class neighborhoods of that city's Right Bank. 'Between the Boche and that swine Bonaparte gutting half the districts' – by which Asher guessed he meant the third Napoleon, not the first – 'there's not a lot left of the city where I grew up. I should be just as happy to leave it.'

'I know the feeling.' Asher thought of the bombed-out ruin of the countryside around them. 'Joël said that two of your fledglings had vanished?'

Augustin Malette glanced over his shoulder, as if fearing to be overheard. 'Yves and Miriyam,' he said. 'Captain Yves Galerien, *pied-noir* from Algeria. Miriyam was an ambulance driver, an Algerian Jewess. I took them both, in 1915, near Soissons. One of the Prague vampires, Petrus, told me – showed me – how one . . . what one does, to create a fledgling. To . . . to take, to hold, the soul of a victim in one's own mind.'

For an instant, his face convulsed with distaste.

'And I take it Elysée never told you what happens when one of your fledglings dies?'

'No. Miriyam . . . when she was . . . was killed, I felt it. Not what had happened to her, but the pain. Days of it. I knew it was she, but I couldn't ask Elysée. The Graf – Graf Szgedny – said that not all masters feel it to that degree. Some feel nothing at all. But I'd seen . . .'

He hesitated, looked around him again, searching the darkness.

Quietly, Asher said, 'Had you seen a man named Barvell, here among the trenches?'

'Faugh.' Then, after a long moment's stillness, added, 'What do you know about Barvell?'

'What do *you* know?'

Another silence. Augustin was still listening all around him, though Asher heard little beyond the distant pounding of the guns. Behind the arrogance in the vampire's eyes, Asher read fear. He knew that Elysée de Montadour herself was ignorant of the deeper lore of the Undead state – and jealously guarded those elements of it that she did know. Keeping her fledglings ignorant in their turn was part of her control over them, and he guessed that this heroic-looking figure in the pale-blue uniform was seriously inexperienced in the simple logistics of being Undead.

Of knowing what situations were perilous, and what were not.

At length Augustin said, 'He met me in the Boul' Mich', before the War. He knew who and what I was. Offered to buy me a drink, damn his cheek.'

'And did he?'

The man's fangs gleamed in his ironic laugh. 'An eleven-year-old whore, jaggered to the eyebrows. And you'll laugh, *Anglais* – like that brainless witch Elysée laughed – when I tell you, I bunked it. I didn't touch the little bint. He'd shot something in her arm – I saw the mark – but how was I to know it wasn't silver nitrate? Or one of those other things everybody always whispers about, that'll paralyze us, turn the blood in our veins to poison?'

His mouth twitched at the recollection. 'Serge called me coward, to turn down a kill, and a sweet little tasty kill like that one. *You should have took the child and the man, too, while he was getting himself happy at the sight of her death. That's all he wanted*, he said. But it wasn't.'

'You know that?'

'I know.' He turned his head sharply at some noise below the range of Asher's hearing. Then he stepped close, eyes like fire in the headlamps' reflected glare. Asher raised his silver-wrapped hand warningly, but the vampire came within arms' length of the car, his face suddenly like a demon's. 'If you're working for her, *Anglais*—'

Asher shook his head. 'She deserted me here last night, after coming out with me from Paris. I think she thought she could follow Joël to you. You know what Barvell was looking for, when he spoke to you in Paris? Why he captured, and killed, two of your fledglings, the two least experienced and weakest vampires in this section of the Front? *Has* anyone else along the Front made fledglings?'

Augustin shook his head. 'The masters keep a tight rein on things,' he said. 'Damn them. Damn Szgedny, and that spidery old spook Hieronymus of Venice. They've warned us all – as if there wasn't enough and to spare for everyone and a thousand more. Bastards, every one of them, and Elysée the Queen Witch and stupid as a cobblestone to boot.'

'Did you tell her about Barvell?'

'No.'

'Did Barvell offer to help you against her?'

The gleaming eyes narrowed, suspicion in every line of that godlike face. 'What do you know of it? Who've you been talking to?'

'No one,' said Asher. 'It sticks out a mile. What do you offer a whore, or a beggar, to walk down a dark alleyway with you? Money. What do you offer a drunkard? A bottle. He offered you what he guessed you'd follow: freedom from your master. He knows enough about vampires, to promise that.'

A fang glinted, with the lifting of the vampire's lip.

'Did he speak to you again?'

'He wrote me twice. Second time, I had to give up a perfectly good 'commodation address, for fear he'd be watching the place and follow me. God only knows how he found out where I got my letters. I didn't know what he wanted, but he wanted something . . . And it was pretty clear he knew about us. *Merde*,' he added, turning his glance to the east. 'Here they come.'

TWENTY-ONE

The roar of the guns suddenly redoubled to the east, and the open car shuddered with the shaking of the ground. Beneath the artillery chattered the staccato of defenders' machine guns; the Germans, presumably, had crept close to the British lines and were now readying a charge. Asher reached for the Peugeot's self-starter and flinched as a shell screamed overhead and struck to the west of them. Before Asher could breathe or blink Augustin sprang to the car's running board, grabbed Asher's coat, and dragged him out.

'Don't be a fool,' he added, as Asher brought up his silver-wrapped hand. 'Get under cover!'

The vampire thrust him in the direction of the nearest trench.

As he did so another shell landed to the west of the car, closer than the one before. The next second a hit obliterated the Vouliers' barn – in which Asher had napped one hot August afternoon thirty years previously – and Asher plunged, slithering, down the mucky side of one of the caved-in trenches, in which Joël had already taken refuge. When another explosion bleached the sky above them he saw rats streaming along the bottom of the trench on either side of the wide band of muddy water that flooded it. Clods and filth rained down, and the three men – living and undead – huddled into what had been a sleeping dugout for shelter.

'This way.' Augustin took his upper arm, dragged him toward a zigzagged, narrow communications trench that had at one time led back toward the rear. Asher stumbled after him, flattening against the wall every time a shell struck near. The vampire's keener hearing seemed able to distinguish between the genuinely dangerous trajectories, and the simple near-misses, so they made good time. At length they ducked into another dugout, this one almost a proper room (*and we'd better not take a hit above us*), flooded ankle-deep, shored up with the broken beams of some farmhouse or shed, and still containing the tattered, rat-stinking remains of a couple of mattresses and a broken Louis XVI chair.

Between flashes of the explosions above them, the room was pitch black.

After a time, Augustin whispered, 'What is it that he wants? This Barvell . . .'

'You didn't try to find that out?' inquired Asher softly. 'In May of 1913?'

The vampire cursed, unimaginatively. 'Some muck. I couldn't make heads or tails of it.'

'He's come up with a way to subdue vampires to his will,' said Asher quietly. 'Did he tell you that? Something chemical, I'm guessing, from what's left in his laboratory. Some way to make them his slaves. And I'm guessing that he knew that every vampire in Europe would be here, at the Front, and that it was here that he could find subjects to try it out on. When did your fledglings disappear? Yves, and Miriyam?'

'November,' said the vampire. 'And yes, I thought I saw him – glimpsed him – in a convoy, a week after Miriyam's death. I knew he was back in Paris, but I didn't think—'

'Why else would he have returned? He already knew about the Paris nest, probably more than any of you realized.' Asher shrugged. 'He'd have guessed you'd be somewhere in this area of the Front, close to Paris, to territory you know. He'd have guessed you'd have made fledglings.'

'And he was telling the truth?' Augustin's voice sounded suddenly thoughtful in the darkness, and his hand tightened on Asher's arm. 'He can enslave the Undead. *Any* undead? You know this of him?'

'I know this. He's in the pay of an American, a millionaire. I don't know if the man's an agent of someone else, or working on his own.'

'Where is he now?' asked the vampire. 'This Barvell?'

'On his way to America. And I don't think there'd be much chance of making a deal with him. More likely you'd be enslaved yourself. He—'

'You let me be the judge of that.' Another shell struck outside, farther off this time, and in the brief gleam Asher saw the calculating look in Augustin's narrowed eyes. 'This method of his, of enslaving vampires to his will – it is . . . science, you say? It can be used by anyone?'

Because Augustin was young and ignorant in his powers, Asher felt the vampire's clumsy attempt to turn his thoughts aside before he struck. He dodged, shucked himself out of his greatcoat, and even as the claws raked at the side of his neck, slapped with the silver wrapped around his hand. He felt it connect with flesh and heard Augustin scream. Joël, he recalled, was near the dugout's entry: he flattened back against the earth wall behind him, hand raised, ready for a second attack – *if it's both of them I may be able to slip past . . .*

A whisper of sound – clothing. He swung in that direction with his hand, then flung himself back into a corner of the cramped earthen room. A hand caught his neck in the darkness and released him at once – he was still wearing treble chains of silver around his throat – and he heard a hoarse, sobbing scream of rage.

Then silence, for what felt like ten minutes but was actually, he thought later, about ninety seconds.

The dugout shook under the force of another explosion and harsh light flared outside.

The room before him was empty.

It was ten o'clock before Lydia could escape from the protracted ritual of First Class dinner. Nearly everyone at the table – and the other tables as well, so far as Lydia could overhear – was still preoccupied with the ship's malfunctioning wireless. Indeed, most seemed considerably more indignant about the absence of stock market news than about the possibility of a torpedo attack. Certainly no one seemed concerned with the fate of the crews of the *Cumberland* or the *Baldwin*.

Don Simon, impeccable in evening dress, was waiting for her on the private promenade outside Aunt Louise's suite.

'Is it possible for you to listen for submarines,' Lydia asked him, 'the way I've seen you listen for peoples' dreams? Trace the crew somehow by their dreams? Or does the sea deaden your perception the way earth does?'

'At midnight.' The vampire considered, his eyes on the inky blackness that lay beyond the promenade's lights. His skeletal face was haggard, as if even with Barvell's periodic treatments some deep pain threatened to consume him.

'T'would be at the expense of missing speech with our good Captain Palfrey, and I mislike letting him go so long without actual converse with me. 'Tis true I chose the young man for his stupidity – aye –' he raised a gloved hand against Lydia's indignation – ''twas the act of a cynic and an evildoer, and an insult to a good and well-meaning young man. Yet a man of such mental acuity as yourself, or our James, would long ere this have spotted the discrepancies in my story. Few on board,' he added softly, 'will not at least know that there was a riot below-decks last night, sparked by rumor of a vampire on the ship.'

Lydia reflected on the lines of communication – cabin stewards, barbers, dining-room staff . . . and thence to the valets and maids. They all ate together, and passed gossip from one to another, and thence, back to their employers. 'Captain Palfrey might not be . . . well, there might not be a great deal of furniture in his attic,' she admitted. 'But he has the kindness, and the simple decency, to refuse to serve you, if he knew what you were.'

''Tis more than that, Lady.' Don Simon's fingers were cold within the pearl-colored kid of his glove as he took her hand. 'He is a soldier, and, I think, hath the soul of a hero. 'Twere not beyond possible that, in the anger of disillusion and the outrage at these killings – for how would anyone believe that there are two vampires aboard one vessel? – he would turn upon me and kill me. And he might well think it appropriate to kill you as well.'

She hadn't thought of that, and after the first shocked, *he wouldn't*! anger flashed through her. Though his expression didn't change she knew he saw it: anger at him, for putting her in the position of being accomplice – accessory after the fact – to his murders. And to murders that weren't his.

'I need a henchman, Mistress,' he finished quietly. 'You – and Miss Miranda – need a protector. And will the more so, should this vampire – or vampires – get ashore in New York, and oblige us to track him there.'

He was right, of course. He must have seen the indignation

in her eyes, for he went on, with the faint flicker of a human smile, 'Fear not, Lady. There is too much in this that we cannot know or control, for me to refuse my help on shipboard simply to stay you from killing me. The situation on this vessel grows hourly more volatile, to say nothing of the danger that lies –' his gesture took in the blackness of the invisible sea – 'separated from us by no more than a curtain, perhaps. I will do what I can. But to touch the dreams of those to whom I have never spoken – those whose eyes I have not met – takes time. I need a door, an entry of some kind, into the deep realm of dreams. With time, at the hour of midnight, I can—'

He broke off, turning his head, then touched Lydia's elbow and led her down the flight of steps toward the fore deck well, out of sight of the promenade above.

A moment later Lydia heard Princess Gromyko's honey-dark voice: 'And, Lady Mountjoy, I swear my poor Izora was white as a ghost when she told me this! She dreads this evening's revelations, she says, but because of what the shining figure told her, she knows she must find out! She says, only in the company of the true believers, and protected by the strength of their inner light—'

'I knew it!' boomed Aunt Louise's voice. 'What time will the séance begin?'

'Your idea?' murmured Don Simon's voice in Lydia's ear, as the two women went into Aunt Louise's suite. 'Very good!'

'I've managed to get two hypodermic syringes from the infirmary,' said Lydia. 'I told Dr Liggatt that the ones I use for injections of vitamins, and for a paregoric solution for neuralgia, were broken. Dr Barvell should have brewed enough antivenin by this time, to take you through to New York, and a day or two beyond until he can get his laboratory set up there. Depending on how much he's made, I hope to be able to take enough from each ampoule for a few injections for you, without the loss being obvious.'

Rather like Georg Heller, she thought, stealing one cigarette from each of Vodusek's stolen packets, lest the thief realize his hiding place had been rumbled.

'It will buy us time, should we need it. If I can, I'll take small amounts of the chemicals he has as well, to make more . . .'

She bit off the words, *once we get to New York.*
Do *I let him go ashore? Knowing what he is?*
Do I help *him? Knowing what he is?*

She didn't know, so she only went on, 'I've already told Ellen
– who thinks we're hunting German spies – to gather up as
many small jars as she can, for whatever I can pinch. And if I
have time I'll search Mr Cochran's stateroom and luggage again,
now that I have a better idea what I'm looking for. If you'll
stand watch on the promenade . . .'

'I shall, Lady.' The vampire listened for a moment, then led
her up the steps to the sheltered walkway again. 'I misdoubt
that time shall vex you tonight. Cochran gave orders this morning
– and sleep though we might in our coffins, we the Undead can
hear what goes on near us – to Kimball and his attendant lubbers,
that they should sufficiently impair the engines of this craft, so
as to slow its progress toward America and permit him more
time for his search.

''Twill come to nothing,' he added, as Lydia's eyes flared in
alarm. 'He catechized the five of them on the best way to set
about it. As the owner of steamships and railroads himself, he
has a nice understanding of the workings of such machines,
and I doubt not that 'twas he who had the Marconi room disabled. But from their conversation as his Merrie Men departed
'twas clear they have no more notion of what he meant than
they have of how to make pastry crust. Nor, I think, will they
find it possible to even get at the ship's engines unobserved.
Yet they will be all the night in trying.'

He stopped with her, just outside the door of Aunt Louise's
suite. 'Thank you, Mistress.' The voices of the princess and
Lydia's aunt came clearly through the panels; they sounded
occupied for a good while yet. 'I know you would kill me, ere
you let me be carried ashore as Cochran's slave. I daresay, ere
you would let me go ashore in America at all.'

In the cool electric light his yellow eyes seemed nearly
colorless, gazing into hers.

Helplessly, she said, 'Yes. Yes, I would.' She thought that
saying the words would hurt, but it didn't, and afterwards, she
felt a kind of peace. She knew he'd guessed, of course, but felt
glad in a way that it was in the open between them.

'I should rather that power lay in your hand, Lady, than in his.' He took her hand in both of his, and kissed her palm.

'And I shall protect you, and your child, through the remainder of the voyage,' he went on, 'and as far beyond it as may be needful. We know not yet what this American will do to protect my . . . *counterpart* . . . here on board, nor what steps he will consider appropriate once we reach land.'

And seeing, perhaps, the tears in her eyes, as much of exhaustion and uncertainty as grief, he added gently, 'Where there is life, there is hope, Mistress. And though my life is done, yet the gates of Hell have not yet clanged shut behind me.'

Then he was gone.

TWENTY-TWO

Hands unsteady with shock, Asher dug in his pockets for the matches and candle-ends he always carried. The flash outside seemed to have been the last hurrah for the barrage. By the noise of the Vickers guns, and the shouting of the men, the Germans were trying to rush the trench, perhaps a hundred yards to the east.

Had the Peugeot survived, he wondered? And if so, would he be able to retrieve it before Augustin and Joël commandeered it to head back to Paris?

Damn Augustin, he thought. *He's a fool if he thinks he can make a deal with Barvell without being enslaved himself, so it's just as well Barvell's out of the country.*

He wondered if the man had a confederate in Paris.

The candle flare showed Asher his coat floating in the three inches of water that flooded the dugout floor. A rat had scrambled up onto it, that bared its teeth at him and fled when Asher poked the flame at it. He was freezing cold, but the heavy wool was soaked, and even trying to carry it, he guessed, would soak the rest of him and chill him still more.

Reluctantly, he sloshed toward the dugout entrance.

Eyes flashed in the blackness outside.

They could see in darkness and they knew he was there. He took two strides back to the corner, knowing it would do him little good. *Three of them . . .*

Then Augustin cannoned into the dugout as if shot from a catapult, nearly falling over the broken-down chair. He was clutching the side of his face, welted and burned from the silver on Asher's hand, and with the poison of the metal, and the stress of pain, he had lost his powers of illusion. His face was the face of a demon, skin stretched thin across bone. His eyes, when he saw Asher, flashed with animal hatred and he strode toward him, fangs gleaming.

'Be still.'

The voice from the entryway stopped Augustin in his tracks. Still holding his cheek, he stood hunched, trembling with agony, as a tall old man ducked his way in. Joël trailed meekly behind.

Vampires, Asher knew, look as they wish to look, save when they were hurt, as Augustin was hurt. Vampires taken into the world of the Undead in their prime, continued to look – as Augustin had looked – like young men and women, heedless of the centuries that might well have passed over their heads. They looked, Asher sometimes thought, the way they looked to themselves in their own dreams. The way they existed in their own minds: beautiful, strong, and young.

He had only encountered two vampires whose illusory image was that of age: faces seamed and wrinkled, hair gray, hands spotted.

One of these had been the Master of Peking, the ancient lord of the Chinese vampires.

The other stood in the flooded dugout before him, from whom even the rats fled in terror.

The Graf Szgedny Aloyïs Corvinus, the Master of Prague. Silver eyes, silver hair, and a face like a thousand-year-old Nordic god.

'*Anglus.*' He made no move. Like Ysidro, he had settled into the stillness that lies beyond life. But about him hung an atmosphere of animal brutality, cold, calculating, and absolutely unconcerned with the living or the dead. A brain that lived on after the soul was gone.

'I hoped to find you, ere you fell victim to the intrigues of

the Paris nest. What is this rumor I hear, of a man in Paris who
has a means to bend the Undead to his will?'

'The man's name is Barvell.' Asher replied in the old-fashioned
High German in which he had been addressed. 'He's a fake
nerve doctor, or at least he was before the War. A student, as
I understand, of occult lore. He's come up with some method
– chemical, I think – to incapacitate and enslave vampires. I
have reason to believe he's done so with Don Simon Ysidro,
and is taking him to America in the service of an American
millionaire named Cochran.'

Something altered in the dead eyes, a far-off steely glint.
'Cochran,' said the Graf. 'The owner of the Roterberg Steel mills.
The Berlin vampires would go there during strikes, knowing they
could kill workers without anyone asking questions.'

'That's him.' Asher had the sensation of talking to a sentient
cobra.

'And this Barvell is his servant?'

'Barvell may have presented the scheme to Cochran, and
asked for financial backing. Or Cochran may have heard of his
work, and sought him out. Either way, it's Cochran who pays
the bills and calls the tune now.'

The cold eyes went to Augustin, and he switched to an
archaic, eighteenth-century French. 'I heard you say that you
were acquainted with this Barvell?'

'We . . . We had met, my lord.' Augustin's reply came out
as a stammer. Elysée had made Augustin vampire, and supposedly held command over her fledgling's will and mind – though
Asher wondered what the outcome of a contest of wills would
be, between them. But few vampires in Europe would go up
against the Graf.

'And *did* he,' inquired Asher quietly, 'offer to give you the
means to dispose of Elysée de Montadour, if you would meet
him in some quiet place?'

The wounded vampire looked sulkily around his fingers at
Asher. 'When he came back in 1913, he said he would make
me Master of Paris. I didn't go,' he added. 'The man's offer
smelled, a mile away. I'm not an idiot.'

Szgedny neither moved nor spoke, but something in his
silence implied that he disbelieved this last assertion.

'And was it at that point,' pursued Asher quietly, 'that you burgled his flat?'

The Graf tilted his head a little in Augustin's direction. The golden vampire answered that movement rather than Asher's question. 'Only to see if the man bore watching. There was a laboratory there, blood and bones and the skulls of children and animals. Clothing, in a box in a cupboard, the sort of thing you see poor children wear, the ones who sleep in doorways and in the Metro stations. A pile of newspapers, like a newsboy would have been selling. A box of cheap candy, like you'd use to lure a kid.' He shrugged. 'Nasty.'

The Graf said nothing.

'You didn't happen to steal his notes, did you?'

Augustin's head snapped around at Asher's question, and his fang glinted in a snarl. 'Why would I do that? I told you they were just chemical muck.'

'Did you?' inquired the Graf.

'Course not.' Augustin's eyes shifted.

Asher didn't even see the Graf move. Neither, apparently, did Augustin, because even with a vampire's preternatural senses, with the uncanny speed of the Undead, the golden vampire was still standing there, mouth open in shock, when the Master of Prague was beside him, one huge hand gripping his neck. With the other hand Szgedny had Asher's right arm in an unbreakable grip, drawing him forward bodily, his silver-wrapped hand extended like a weapon: like a burning poker, aimed at Augustin's eyes.

Augustin screamed, twisted, tried once to strike at the Graf and then shrieked louder and buckled at the knees as the older vampire's single-handed grip on his spine tightened. 'I did! I did! I have them!'

The Graf released Augustin's neck, and tossed Asher aside like a discarded stick. 'At your flat?'

Asher, guessing what would happen next, caught the Graf's sleeve – with his left hand, his right being numb from the force of the grip that had crushed his arm. '*Dominus*,' he said quickly.

Eyes like gray ball bearings met his.

'Let me see the notes.'

The eyes shifted, dismissing the request. A wave of sleepiness crushed Asher's mind like the onset of poison gas.

'My lord, you will be in danger as well.' The unbearable weight lifted, as if it had never been. Breathless, Asher went on, 'Don Simon is already his slave. Do you think a man like Cochran will stop there? Do you think Barvell – or Cochran himself – would stop at selling this method, whatever it is, if the price is right?'

Szgedny made no reply, but Asher thought the shadow at the corner of those immobile lips darkened, just slightly, as a vicious dog's lip will move before it lunges.

'My wife is on the ship that is carrying them to America. I have, literally, no idea what conditions she faces there or what she can do to help him, if anything. But there's a good chance that she will be able to interpret Barvell's notes – extrapolate from them – even if they are from an earlier stage of his research. Don Simon will work with her, if he can be freed, if this process can be stayed or reversed. Will you let me wire a copy of these notes to her in America, to be there for her when she arrives?'

'This from a man who has sworn to kill vampires, whenever their paths might cross?' The Graf had taken his hand from Augustin's neck, but the younger vampire lay face down in the filthy water on the dugout floor, like a drowned man, unmoving and unregarded. In the flicker of the candle flame, which Asher had dropped on one of the dugout's shelves, the elder vampire's gaze seemed fixed and unmoving as that of a statue.

'The man who four years ago killed all the vampires of the London nest as they lay in their sleep? Who, I am told, killed half a dozen maiden vampires in St Petersburg, new-fledged younglings who had drunk no human blood – dragged them forth into sunlight and watched their bodies burn? What will this wife of yours do with this grimoire when she gets it? Enslave Simon in her turn? What will *you* do with these spells, once you have read them, and sent them across the sea?'

'That I do not know,' returned Asher. 'I know not what they are, nor what can be done with them. They won't be in finished form. You have commanded men.' It was a guess, but something in the way the old man held himself told Asher that this was true. 'You know that more information is always better than less information. My wife may not be able to even reach Don Simon until they are ashore in America. Cochran almost certainly has men at arms aboard ship. I hear her voice in the darkness,' he said, desperate that the vampire should understand. 'If I can throw her a weapon across the chasm which separates us, this is what I want to do. I have no idea how to use this weapon myself.'

'Do you not?'

The words seemed to come to Asher from a great distance away. He wasn't even sure they'd been spoken aloud. For an instant a part of his mind wondered if – as he had feared Szgedny would – the old vampire had covered his perceptions with a mist of sleepiness and had departed, unseen. Yet he was cloudily aware, through dreamlike haze, that the Graf stood directly before him, clawed hands framing Asher's face – as those of Serge had two nights ago – as he looked into his eyes.

And as the very old vampires could do, Asher was aware that the Graf was looking through his thought, through his recollections and memories, and on into Lydia's mind, Lydia's thought. Aware of her and her surroundings, though she was yet waking. Far off, Asher thought he could glimpse her, at a dressing table in a luxurious room squinting short-sightedly at her reflection in a mirror as she applied *mascaro* and kohl to her eyes without the aid of her glasses, red hair shining from brushing in the cheerful glow of electric lights. But aware of her thoughts and memories and fears as well . . .

She looked around her quickly, then passed a hand over her brow. *I'm just tired . . .* He could almost hear her saying it. Knowing something, not knowing what.

For a moment Asher struggled against suffocation, as if he were drowning in deep water. Voices seemed to come to the edges of his hearing, crying far-off. A taste of something, intense heat like a drink of brandy, deep in his heart.

He understood, with a fathom's-deep grief, that the Graf's power to do this – to see into Lydia's mind through Asher's – drank like a root from the lives he'd taken. The voices he heard were theirs. Hundreds – thousands – killed across the years.

Then the grief was gone and even the memory of it evaporated, leaving – as the old wizard says in *The Tempest*, – not a wrack behind.

But Asher didn't fully regain consciousness until he was in the motorcar, wrapped in a decrepit German greatcoat and aching with cold, with the Graf beside him and Augustin at the wheel, roaring through utter darkness towards Paris.

TWENTY-THREE

Returning to their suite, Lydia paused in the doorway to assure her aunt that she had no desire to learn what Madame Izora's 'terrible revelation' had been, and that she would far rather simply go to bed.

'I should think that, placed as we are, in peril of German submarines, you should be desperate to know the truth, for your daughter's sake.'

Lydia blinked at her, wide-eyed through her thick glasses. 'I thought there was no danger of submarines, Aunt!'

'There isn't,' retorted the older lady, with the flat firmness of one who has only held up the danger as a bugbear to thrust her niece into joining the group – not that Lydia had needed any proof of this. 'Yet as a mother, my dear, I find you sadly wanting in concern for how these terrible events may affect your child!'

'Now, Lady Mountjoy, I will not have my poor Lydia chided.' Princess Natalia rustled back from her own door to put an arm around Lydia's waist. Her gentle purr banished any hint of admonition from her words. 'Poor child, she does not look well at all. Do you not see how pale she is? Like my poor Evgenia, who after four days is *still* seasick. And she touched nothing of her dinner.'

In fact, Lydia had made her usual sparing forays into the fantasias of veal croquettes, poached salmon, Cincinnati ham and banana fritters, but Aunt Louise – who had had no attention for anything but her own plate and Mrs Cochran's philippics

on the subject of the still-silent wireless – easily believed her
to have consumed nothing, and declared heartily, 'Nonsense!
Mal de mer is no more than an illusion of the mind, and can
easily be overcome with the proper mental attitude. Your maid
is malingering . . .'

With real heroism Natalia professed a willingness to hear
more, engaging the dowager's attention while Lydia slipped
into the suite, and across the parlor to her own room. There she
changed quickly into her simple skirt and shirtwaist, and
opened her dressing-table drawer. Ellen had outdone herself.
Caviar jars filched from the kitchen, a container which had once
held face cream, another bearing the remains of the label
'Restorative Pectoral Drops', had all been thoroughly rinsed
with boiling water. Strips of adhesive tape had even been
helpfully stuck onto the lids, for labeling purposes.

I shouldn't be doing this. Lydia swiftly transferred these
objects to the small leather satchel she'd carried at the Front.
But there was no question, now, about whether she should
turn all her efforts to breaking the millionaire's hold on Simon
– or at least transferring that power to herself.

And then what?

First things first, she told herself desperately. *One thing at
a time. You don't know what's going to happen, or what
you'll need.*

She heard Natalia and her aunt leave the suite, discoursing
with great intensity on the location of the entrance to the realms
and cities which exist within the hollow earth: 'If there is in
fact a cavern at the North Pole, how does one account for the
teaching of Lady Paget's spirit guide, that the people of Atlantis
journeyed there?'

Slinging the satchel round her shoulder, Lydia ghosted
back across the parlor, and out onto the Promenade. She
glanced at her aunt's gilt camelback clock as she passed the
piano. Ten thirty.

'Time enow,' Don Simon murmured, from the shadows at
the corner of the Promenade. 'Cochran and Barvell have
passed here and gone on into the princess's suite minutes ago.
They have, as you see, locked the door behind them.'

'Good heavens!' exclaimed Lydia in a whisper, as they

rounded the corner of the private Promenade and she saw the huge silver padlock glistening on Cochran's door. 'Where on earth did they find such a thing? Silver hasps, too . . .'

'I suspect 'twas furbished up in my honor,' returned the vampire. ''Tis not a new model of lock.'

This was true. Lydia turned it over in her fingers, identifying it as an old-style railroad padlock which had been electro-plated. 'I wonder what the deck stewards – not to speak of Mr Cochran's nephew and servants – think of it?'

'Like all of my own servants over the years – and every tradesman and tailor and bootmaker with whom I have met in the hours of night to get properly fitting coats – what they think is that money is a very good thing to have in this un-sympathetic world. And like my tailor and bootmaker,' added the vampire thoughtfully, 'I daresay the deck stewards and the servants – and perhaps Mr Cochran's nephew as well – have seen stranger things.'

He stepped back, as Lydia's picklocks made short work of the simple innards of the elderly Yale – which had probably been selected for the job, Lydia reflected, because its size made it simpler to plate.

'I must say,' Don Simon went on as she worked, 'that I feel myself insulted, if they counted beforehand upon breaking my will ere the voyage was over.'

'If they counted on it,' said Lydia thoughtfully, 'they clearly didn't trust you. You didn't happen to overhear how they plan to damage the engines, did you?'

'I did, but I am no mechanic, Lady. 'Twas a long explanation involving bribery and reciprocating turbine housings, and I made no more of it than the dogsbodies did. Cochran cursed them roundly for imbeciles, until at length they said they understood, in tones which sounded to me as if they did no such thing. Myself, I doubt of their being even able to get near the machines, yet I daresay 'twould do no harm to inform Captain Winstanley that German spies may be trying to sabotage the engines.'

'He'll believe that sooner than he'd believe such a thing of Mr Cochran.' Lydia pushed the door open cautiously, and ducked inside, Don Simon retreating to the end of the Promenade to keep watch.

In Barvell's silver-locked case, the ampoules of antivenin serum had, as Lydia had suspected, been neatly re-filled. Only one flask in the lower section of the case showed a significant reduction of its contents – constant theft at the casualty clearing station's pharmacy had given her a very exact eye as to the levels of any substance in containers. She took as much from each ampoule as she dared, but altogether this didn't even fill one of the little phials that she'd begged from Dr Liggatt – *how much is the least amount needed to keep the poison at bay? How long can he survive on a half-dose, or a quarter-dose? And in how much pain?*

She likewise took a small quantity from the flask (*which might be* anything, *even the poison itself*), and tiny amounts of the contents of all other jars, carefully copying the meaningless symbols on their labels. *If Jamie can decode these later . . .*

But that brought up again the subject of allowing Don Simon to go ashore in New York, and again she turned her mind from it.

The symbols looked arbitrary to her – an insect, a cow, a frog, the moon – but once in New York, she reflected, she'd at least be able to figure out what they were. The moon was, by the smell of it, and the way it stained her fingertip, almost certainly silver nitrate.

After that, with heart pounding and ear cocked for the scratch of Don Simon's claws on the outer door, she combed first Barvell's room, then Cochran's, the parlor, and the dressing room, searching for anything that resembled notes or information on how much of what to mix, and whether to heat it or dilute it or distill it or what. Anything that she might have missed or overlooked before. *And what am I going to do with all this?* she asked herself, as she moved methodically through the drawers and closets. *Mix up more to give to Simon so he can go on killing people in New York?*

She blinked back tears of frustration and anger. What was it her Nanna – and Jamie – always said? *Better to have it and not need it – or never dare use it – than to really, really need it and not have it . . .*

And they *would* need it, if the second vampire got ashore.

In any case, the wretched Mr Barvell seemed to be like Jamie, carrying everything in his head. Or, like Jamie, he'd done something clever, like mailing all his notes to himself at General Delivery in New York, *Left Til Called For.*

'Something's amiss.' Don Simon was listening, head cocked, when Lydia came quickly up the Promenade. ''Tis difficult to discern at this distance, and with water all about us, but there is uneasiness in the deeps of the ship. Too many people hurrying about for this hour of the night.'

'Someone's disappeared.' Her stomach seemed to turn over with dread. 'Another child . . .'

''Tis not yet midnight.' A pin scratch frown appeared between the vampire's brows. 'How could a vampire lure any child now? Three people have died, and every child on the ship must be seeing *El Cuco* in every shadow. Only at midnight could a vampire work upon a child's mind.'

Lydia couldn't keep herself from thinking, *As you're going to work on poor Captain Palfrey's in three-quarters of an hour . . .*

'Two of the children were lured with candy—'

'They are *niños*,' retorted the vampire, 'they're not stupid. With things as they are, would your daughter go with a stranger who offered her candy? I didn't think so . . .'

He turned his head again, and seemed to fade into the shadow as stealthy feet mounted the stair from the Second Class promenade below. 'Is it you, Comrade Doctor?' breathed Heller.

'Madame, Madame,' whispered a young girl's voice in halting German, 'please you must help—'

Stepping forward to meet them, Lydia saw under the electric gleam of a lamp the dark-haired girl Rivkah Goldhirsch.

'What is it?' She looked quickly at Heller. 'And how on earth did you get past the gates? If anyone catches you up here you'll probably be locked up as a thief.'

'I will beg you then to speak for me,' said the German. 'I only hope the gates will yet be open, when we return.'

'Who's missing?'

'Ariane Zirdar. I've been to the chain locker, there's no one there, no sign.'

'Please,' said the girl again. 'My grandpa.' She said something else in Slovenian.

Heller translated, 'She says, He is mean and he says bad

things but we must help him. She means that there is enough
anger now below decks, that she fears – as I fear – that if this
girl turns up dead, as the others turned up, they may well mob
old Goldhirsch before the quartermasters can muster enough
stewards and porters to keep him from being lynched.'

He turned back, listening, as Rivkah pleaded.

'She says you have showed yourself kind, Comrade. She
asks, would you hide him, for tonight, somewhere up here? Or
speak to the captain . . .' He paused again, the girl turning to
Lydia, dark eyes wide with desperation. 'He has money, she
says, in his bag. He can pay. He gathered in all his debts
before leaving their village. She says once before, they had to
hide him, when the Christians back in their village said he
kidnapped babies and the Jews drank their blood in the
synagogue, only because they all owed him money. But it was
his money that got the village seed wheat when—'

Lydia held up her hand as her ear snagged a familiar word.
'Did she say *Malareka*?'

Heller nodded, with a slight frown. 'Malareka, yes. It is the
name of her village.'

'That's the village Vodusek comes from. And his friend
Slavik. I've heard them a dozen times, saying Herr Goldhirsch
is the vampire. Do they owe him money?' She turned directly
to the girl. 'Vodusek, Slavik – do they owe your grandfather
money?'

She knew the answer before the girl nodded, before Rivkah
poured out another stream of Slovenian and before Heller
translated: 'She says, yes. Her grandfather got all that he could
from Vodusek before leaving their village. Gospod Vodusek
claimed it was all that he had, but it wasn't true if he could get
his ticket. Herr Goldhirsch had to pay half of it to the Russian
commandant of the village to collect it, and then, she says,
Vodusek tried to rob them of it at an inn on the way.'

Lydia felt, in that first instant, merely stunned, as if she'd
walked into a shut door in the dark. Then heat swept her, blazing,
burning fury.

Heretic . . .

Gypsy trash . . .

Mohammedan brat . . .

He was a shipyard mechanic . . .

'He has her in the locker beside the stairs next to his cabin,' she said quietly. 'Where we found the liquor. It's not . . . It's not a real vampire at all. That's where he keeps them . . .'

The German stared at her for a moment, blankly, not understanding. Then his eyes widened as he understood. He whispered, 'Motherless sons of a whore—'

He caught her wrist, started toward the gangway back down to C Deck, and Lydia braced her feet. 'Tell Rivkah to go along to that cabin, there –' she drew them along the Promenade to the starboard corner, pointed to the door of the princess's suite – 'tell her to ask for Tania. Tell her to tell them all there that I sent her, that I'll explain later—'

And, as Heller explained, in his rough Slovenian, to the girl, Lydia whispered, 'Simon, I have to go with him. The man has the girl in a locker, beside the stairway on F Deck, near the forward hatch. It has to be there, it's near where the gypsy girl was found.'

Heller caught her wrist and they ran for the gangway. She glanced behind her at the Promenade, but saw no one in the shadows. She knew he'd heard her; *he'll have to get through his interview with Palfrey without me to keep watch.*

But for the most part her mind was a clinical swordblade of icy rage.

On F Deck, people were just starting to panic. They were still looking for Ariane, still asking one another, *Who saw her last? Where was that? Maybe she went . . .?*

Lydia could almost read their words in their gestures, in their faces as they spoke. It was quarter to midnight. Early, still . . . *The others were found between two and three,* she thought. *Little Luzia within a few yards of the locker.* When the search had widened, away from the sleeping quarters? When the rhythms of the vessel's work shifts left gaps of time in which it was safe to smuggle the victim down to the chain locker, and then, later, up to some public place where late-roaming searchers would find the body?

Gypsy brat . . . Who do you call heretic . . .?

Bastard, she thought. *Bastard.*

In her mind she heard Don Simon's soft voice: *For years I only killed Protestants, because they were already damned.*

In the corridor she saw the man Slavik at the head of a sizeable gang of men and boys, leading them in the direction of one of the gangways to the coal bunkers. Heard him shout something back to them and recognized again the word for Jew.

'Slavik's told people that bag Goldhirsch brought on board was full of gold,' said Heller, striding along ahead of her. 'Somebody – I forget who – said that's why he stays in his cabin all the time. And I've heard that he transferred all of it to a money belt around his body.'

'If he stays locked in his cabin all the time,' returned Lydia grimly, 'I expect it's because – whatever his other sins – he's afraid for his life. He'd know it the minute he saw Vodusek and Slavik in the passenger list. But of course it also means nobody will be able to say they'd seen him, when somebody is killed. And when that poor girl's body is finally found I can just bet you there'll be something of Goldhirsch's nearby, or clutched in her hand, or something . . . Vodusek will yell something about this being proof, they'll break down the cabin door, and one of his friends will "find" something of the girl's in the cabin itself.'

'And it'll be all over,' concluded Heller, 'before the master-at-arms can get down here with a couple of stewards – if he can find any stewards, at this point, who'll want to risk going up against a mob. Wait—'

He opened the door of his own cabin, ducked inside, and came out again with a pry bar in one hand, and his German Army pistol in the other. It flashed through Lydia's mind, as they clattered along the corridor that ran past the engines amidships, that somebody had probably better tell Mr Cochran that there wasn't a second vampire aboard the *City of Gold*, so he'd call off his men from their silly attempt to sabotage the ship's engines.

And this, she realized – this attempt to commit murder by pogrom – was being done tonight for the precise reason that Cochran had given instruction to his myrmidons about the engines: because they were approaching New York. In two days, the enclosed circle of the ship's world would split wide open. The vampire, if there had been one, would have gone ashore and vanished into the nameless masses of the city's poor. The moneylender, another drinker of blood, presenting his proofs of solvency, would slip beyond Vodusek's reach upon landing, with all the huge country to hide in.

There was no one in the well of the crew gangway on F Deck. Voices echoed down the corridors in the direction of the boiler rooms. The bulb of the electric light immediately beside the stair was out. Searchers, Lydia guessed, could easily miss the locker entirely. Keeping his body carefully to one side of the door itself, Heller shoved the pry bar into the crack and heaved on it—

—and nearly fell over as the door was flung open from within and Vodusek sprang through it like a tiger.

Heller swung at him with the pry bar, but he was off balance and far too late. Vodusek had a knife in his hand and only the German's reflexes saved him from being disemboweled. Lydia slithered past them and ducked into the locker, trying to identify which of the shapeless tangles of rope, tarpaulin, canisters and canvas would be the bound and muffled form of a girl.

Before she could reach for the closest (and most promising) bundle, she heard a body fall behind her. A hard arm grabbed her around the waist while a hand clapped over her mouth, dirty and reeking of tobacco. *He has a knife . . .*

She stomped hard on where his foot probably was – she was right – and dropped her weight down, the way Jamie had showed her. Felt the blade slash her shoulder as she twisted loose, turned as the man cursed . . .

And found herself standing free in the doorway of the locker, facing Don Simon over the collapsing body of the Slovene.

The vampire stepped past her without a word. The canvas bundle for which Lydia had been reaching flinched from Don Simon's touch with a cry.

'It's all right,' whispered Lydia. '*Dir wird es . . . es . . .*'

Don Simon pulled the canvas aside and the girl Ariane stared up at him, face streaked with tears of terror. The vampire put a hand on her shoulder and said something; Lydia didn't hear what it was. But the tension vanished immediately from Ariane's body, and she began to weep. 'Get the knife,' said Simon, and Lydia, looking around on the floor near Vodusek's unmoving – but still breathing – body, found the bloodstained weapon.

'Heller . . .' she gasped, and Simon slid past her with the bony agility of a ghost. Lydia cut away the cords that bound Ariane's wrists, and the girl sat up, tears streaming down her face, and grabbed Lydia in a desperate clutch.

Behind her, Lydia heard Heller say, 'Who are you?'

And in German, Don Simon replied, 'A friend of Mistress Asher's.'

Turning her head, Lydia saw Heller in the light of the gangway well, face bruised and blood trickling from his slashed side. Don Simon was helping him to his feet, calm, aloof, and absolutely human-looking, as he had planned to face Captain Palfrey. *It must be midnight . . .*

Shouting in the hall. Slavik's nasal voice, and Father Kirn's. Others, baying like wolves – Heller turned and yelled over his shoulder, 'She's here!' Or at least, Lydia guessed that's what he yelled, in Slovenian, because in the confusion of shouts that followed, as the information was relayed, she caught '*Sie ist da!*' and '*Lei è li!*' and people came cramming and shoving into the space around the stairs.

Ariane scrambled to her feet, flew toward them, some men grabbing her in a desperate embrace and others gripping Vodusek, who had staggered up and attempted to flee. Ariane was sobbing, pointing . . .

Heller cried out something and dove into the locker past Lydia, snatching from one of the shelves a pair of gold pince-nez – Goldhirsch's, Lydia realized. He held them up and shouted, and Vodusek, catching a knife from one of the men holding him, slashed at that man – even in the heat of the moment Lydia wasn't sure what he thought he could accomplish by flight. She and Heller were thrust deeper into the locker by the sheer weight of bodies pressing into the gangway well, shouting, furious as Ariane pointed at Vodusek, while her weeping mother held her tight.

'*Assassino!*' screamed a woman – poor little Luzia's mother – and threw herself at Vodusek, clawing his face as if she'd have torn out his remaining eye. '*Assassino—!*'

Then the deck beneath Lydia's feet lurched, the walls shuddered like shaken tin, and far off a heavy, splintering *boom* rocked the ship to its bones.

TWENTY-FOUR

O
h, dear God, we've been hit!
Screaming, shoving, swaying.
Heller thrust Lydia deeper into the locker and pushed himself into the doorway, yelling at the same time – first in German and then in Slovenian – 'Stand still! *Stand still!*'

The noise outside in the metal-walled gangway well was deafening. People pushing, thrusting, trampling . . .

Lydia's mind was blank with horror. *Torpedo – I have to get to Miranda!*

Oh please God don't let the lights go out . . .

She was suddenly aware of Don Simon in the locker beside her, miraculously unruffled. *Dear God, if it passes midnight and everyone here sees him as he is . . .*

Then, louder than the clamor of terror and panic, she heard a man scream in the midst of the crowd, and as people started to pour up the stairs, and away in the direction of the deck well and the wider stair beyond, she saw the trampled bodies, not only of Vodusek, but of Slavik as well, crumpled on the floor in a widening pool of blood.

She'd seen worse at the Front. The knowledge of what Vodusek had considered he was entitled to do, in order to recover his money from a Jew, killed whatever sympathy or shock she might have felt. Nevertheless, the sight made her ill. She had no idea whether Slavik had known anything about his friend's scheme or not.

There are two of them, Izora had said.

Had she meant Don Simon and Vodusek? Or Vodusek and Slavik?

Light-headedness made her suddenly breathless and looking at Don Simon beside her, she saw that his right hand was covered with blood where it pressed her shoulder.

Vodusek. Vodusek stabbed me . . .

We've been hit . . .

She looked up and met the vampire's eyes, over his dripping hand. With quiet deliberation, he took a rag from the shelf behind him, and wiped the blood away. With another – clean and rough and smelling sourly of disinfectant – he made a pad which he bound over the wound, his face expressionless.

'The ship isn't listing,' he pointed out in his soft voice as he worked. His glance went to Heller. 'How long does it take, once a ship has been hit?'

'Minutes,' said the German, and put his hand on the knot of bandage so the vampire could double it. 'Less.' Heller was looking at Don Simon, squinting as if he struggled to see something that he couldn't quite make out. He put out a hand, touched the wall. 'The engines have stopped . . .'

'Miranda.' Lydia was astonished at how calm she sounded. 'I need to get to Miranda.'

'I'll take her,' said Simon. 'Find out what you can, if you would, Herr Heller. Myself, I think it sabotage, not enemy attack.'

Heller hesitated, straining to listen – but, Lydia reflected, probably feeling, with the trained senses of a sailor, whether the deck beneath their feet was still level (and it certainly felt level to her).

'Why do you think that?'

'Rumor. I was telling Madame of it, when *la niña* came up to us. Will you do that?'

'He was,' affirmed Lydia. 'And I was telling him it was a ridiculous idea, because who aboard would be that . . . that *silly* . . .'

'You have been at the Front, Comrade.' Heller turned from his watchful perusal of the now-empty gangway well to meet her gaze, and saluted her ironically. 'I should think that any doubts you ever had about the depth of human stupidity should by this time have been resolved.' His eyes returned to Don Simon, and Lydia saw them widen with shock.

Midnight must be past . . .

Don Simon asked softly, 'Will you bring us word?'

Suddenly white under his tan, Heller replied, 'I shall.'

First things first, reflected Lydia, but she saw the German look over his shoulder twice, as he strode away across the gangway well toward the engine room, his boots tracking in Vodusek's blood.

Lydia and Don Simon joined the streams of Third Class passengers pouring up the gangways, women and children too frightened to notice anyone around them, even a woman with blood on her dress and a vampire with a face like a scarred skull. The corridors picked up shouting, furious now, the howling of a mob in full cry – *Don't tell me that wretch Vodusek has managed to convince them poor Mr Goldhirsch caused* this. The echoes went right through her head.

'I thought you said Kimball and his idiots were told to . . . to cripple the engines, not blow up the ship!'

'Of a certainty they were, Mistress,' returned the vampire. By the tilt of his head, she could see he was listening to the distant uproar. 'And I am as certain that when they could make nothing of the instructions they were given, one or the other of them manufactured a simple pipe bomb. Such things are easy enough to make, and God knows they were carrying sufficient ammunition in their luggage. They could have sneaked it into some corner of the engine room while the engineers were, perhaps, helping in the hunt for the missing *señorita*. Successfully,' he added, as they approached the gateway that led to the upper decks. 'There is no list to the boat.'

They were densely mashed into the moving stream of emigrants, as it paused, then proceeded, then paused on its way to the open gateway.

Dizziness swamped her again. *We'll never be able to get clear if something happens . . .*

'Neither do I hear nor feel the change in the air that speaks of water rushing in.'

His soft voice calmed her, and to the eternal credit of Captain Winstanley, the grilles that were ordinarily locked across the gangways to Second Class stood open. Stewards had been posted beside them, reassuring those who passed through that: 'We have no reason to think we have been hit' in an assortment of mispronounced European languages, and directing people to the Boat Deck just in case. Over the heads of the crowd, Lydia could see the tall, stooped form of Mr Goldhirsch, holding his grandson in his arms and clutching a heavy portmanteau.

Lydia gritted through her teeth, 'I should think Mr Cochran's going to *kill* them—'

But she was wrong about that.

Barely had she and her companion reached the private Promenade, when a thunderous roar of voices burst from the deck well over which it looked. Turning back, Lydia saw a man thrust his way past the grille, and run, stumbling, toward the gangway, the stewards half-heartedly trying to catch him, then making a futile attempt to stop the mob that spurted like poisoned lava from the gateway and poured at his heels. She recognized Mr Kimball as he scrambled, slipping and stumbling, up the gangway toward the Promenade. His jacket had been torn off him and there was blood and engine grease on his face and shirt. She was too far to see his eyes, or hear his breath, but it was as if she were next to him: she knew his eyes were blank with terror for his life, knew his breath was a hoarse gasp of despair.

He was fast for so big a man, but the mob was faster. He hurled aside the steward who'd been assigned to keep unauthorized people off the private Promenade, and if the man had had any notion of trying to stop the pursuers, he gave it up at once. Simon drew Lydia back out of the way as Kimball bolted up onto the Promenade. The American's screams of: 'Boss! Boss!' were drowned by the howling of the mob: *Swabo! Shpion! Saboter!*

Austrian! Spy! Saboteur . . .

The corner of the Promenade hid Cochran's door from Lydia, but she heard Kimball pounding on it, then as the mob surged nearer jerking the handle and kicking the panels, screaming Cochran's name.

Then just screaming.

After they killed him, and broke down the door, Lydia heard shots fired, so she knew Cochran had been in his suite. 'They'll find your coffin in there,' she said softly.

Don Simon murmured, 'Yes.'

She could imagine what they'd make of *that*. She slipped the satchel from her shoulder, handed Don Simon the syringe, and the ampoule of antivenin. 'I'll see what I can salvage, later.'

With lips like iced marble he kissed her hand, and faded into the darkness.

By the time the quartermasters came up to the Promenade – with rifles – the mob had scattered and gone.

Somewhere in the Stygian bowels of the old gypsum mines that lay beneath Paris, there was a cell whose bars were plated with silver. Asher recognized it, from the days he had spent there after being almost killed by the Paris nest. He assumed it lay somewhere near the Hotel Montadour, and guessed it had been installed by one of the earlier Masters of Paris – the Masters of Paris, he had gathered, had for three hundred years had trouble controlling their fledglings.

'I regret –' Szgedny dumped Augustin's limp body inside and locked the door, carefully wrapping his hands in a mangy carriage rug – brought from the Peugeot – against the touch of the bars – 'that there are not two such cages. You should be safe enough. Few of Elysée's get remain in the city.'

The cell was indeed a sort of cage, set within a larger cavern: cold, damp, pitch-black and smelling of the sewers and the river. They had left the Peugeot in the Place Denfert-Rochereau and descended through the Catacombs, turning aside from those endless tunnels walled in bones into one of the side corridors nominally blocked off with sawhorses. The walls, as Asher had observed on previous occasions, were marked with chalk signs of various ages. Communards had hidden in these tunnels, in the days of the siege of '71; quite possibly refugees from the Terror eighty years before that. The Master of Prague had brought a bullseye lantern from the motorcar as well as the carriage rug. Even with the bloodstained German greatcoat, Asher knew he was in for a miserably cold day.

'Sleep if thou canst, *Anglus.*' The Graf set down the lantern. 'I do not know this city well enough, to send someone here to you with water and food. Don't try to search for a way out yourself.'

He straightened, and with a fragment of chalk from his pocket made a sign on the wet stone of the wall. 'There are three hundred miles of tunnels, perhaps more, and I have no desire to spend the first three-quarters of the night searching them for you.'

Asher said, 'I'm grateful,' though he wondered how many

of Elysée's beautiful fledglings actually were hiding down there, and whether they were earlier risers than the Graf. He also wondered where the nobleman meant to sleep. When Augustin had stopped, halfway along the narrow seam in the rock, leaned against the wall and then suddenly collapsed into the unwakeable sleep to which the Undead were prey in daytime, he had feared that Szgedny would likewise drop unconscious. He knew it must be almost light, above ground.

But the Graf had lifted the younger vampire with effortless strength onto his shoulder, and continued to this place deep in the belly of the darkness. In addition to the mines, and the vast silent boneyard of the Catacombs themselves, Asher knew that there were a hundred hidden doorways where cellars, church crypts, forgotten vaults and communication tunnels from the sewers gave ingress to the black rock seams. Though the Graf might not have living servants in Paris, three hundred years was presumably plenty of time even for a stranger to the city to learn the maze well. A similar network of underground passage-ways and rooms – though not nearly so extensive – existed in Prague, though the Prague vampires avoided such places because of the other things which haunted them.

As he lay down, Asher wondered whether Joël had followed them back. Or had the little fledgling found refuge somewhere near the Front, in a caved-in wine-cellar or the sub-crypt of some old monastery, before going out again tonight when it grew dark, to feast on men dying in shell holes. Men slain not by the Undead, but by their living brothers.

He felt little fear of Joël, even if he had returned to Paris. As to what else might be down here . . .

Elysée had said nothing of such matters. But then, the Master of Paris herself might not know.

Asher slept lightly, exhausted though he was. His memories of Paris underground were foul, and he woke, half a dozen times, always in total darkness, dreaming sometimes that he was back in one of the dugouts on the Western Front – terrified that the trench had been undermined by enemy sappers, or that there had been a near-direct hit by a shell, and that he'd been buried alive, with the maggots and the rats. Sometimes he dreamed that he was on board the *City of Gold*, that she'd been torpedoed. The electrical plant had flooded as she began to go down and he was slipping, fighting for balance on slanted decks through utter darkness, searching for Lydia. Feeling the ice-cold water around his knees and knowing that in minutes the ship was going to begin its long fall to the bottom, carrying him trapped in darkness with it.

Once he jerked from sleep convinced there was someone – something – in the dank rock-cut room with him. He had dreamed of her – he knew it was a *her* . . . *Elysée*? Someone who stood beside him for a long time, looking down at him. When he woke and groped for the lantern he found that it had been moved, and it seemed to him that in the darkness he could smell, faint and elusive, the whiff of expensive perfume mixed with blood.

It was a long time before he dared grope about him for the lantern – it was not, in fact, very far off. Longer still, before he lay down again.

TWENTY-FIVE

'How *dare* Captain Winstanley confine us to our cabins?' demanded Aunt Louise, her face blotched red with outrage at the steward who had been stationed on the Promenade and who had firmly escorted her back when she'd attempted to 'learn what on earth was going on.' 'How *dare* he?'

Lydia, emerging from her bedroom where Miranda lay sleeping – finally – crossed to the table where Mrs Flasket had laid out tea. The level of the amber liquid, when she poured it out steaming, was perfectly aligned with the rim of the Wedgwood cup – the same cup that Aunt Louise had served her from less than a week previously at Mountjoy House in London. Dimly, from the Promenade outside, she heard the steward posted there – ostensibly to keep intruders from the elite suites – saying, 'I've seen Lady Mountjoy and Mrs Asher myself, Your Majesty, and they're fine. But please, the captain has asked that everyone stay indoors until we've secured the ship.'

'We could be sinking for all he knows!' declared Aunt Louise. 'We might all be in danger of our lives!'

Lydia walked to the window, looked out at the black sea horizon outlined by the silver line of the westering moon. 'We don't seem to be any lower in the water than we were twenty minutes ago,' she pointed out. That was the first thing she'd showed Miranda, when Mrs Frush had carried the child down from the boat deck and Lydia, who'd been watching the gangway, had intercepted them and brought them to the suite: 'See, darling,' she had said, 'the horizon is just the same place – right below the deck-rail – that it was a few minutes ago. That means we're not going down.'

'We didn't get torpedoed?' had asked the little girl in visible disappointment.

'It doesn't look like it,' she had replied, at which Mrs Frush had pronounced a little homily about their escape from danger.

Not, reflected Lydia, that they were out of danger yet, or anywhere near it.

They have to know we're here. They have to be on their way.

Mrs Frush, Honoria Flasket, Ellen, Malkin, old Mr Mortling and even little Miss Prebble, were in the suite's kitchen now, drinking their own cups of tea (second-class American Line's china, not Wedgwood) and speculating about what could have caused first the explosion below decks, and then the irruption of a shouting, cursing mob into the most elite portion of the ship. When Lydia had passed the door of the kitchen she had heard Mrs Frush's deep Scots voice predicting that they would all be murdered in their beds, and that she would never travel on an American vessel again.

While in the bedroom with Miranda, Lydia had discreetly re-bandaged her shoulder, with the little girl's awed assistance ('I won't tell, cross my heart an' hope to die an' stick a needle in my eye. Did you get stabbed by a German *spy*, Mummy?'). Miranda was clearly and utterly thrilled.

She had also changed into a tobacco-colored Worth walking suit – again with her daughter's help – and demonstrated to the little girl how to wash bloodstains out of a cotton shirtwaist (*honestly, what kind of an upbringing is the poor child getting?*). As she put on the jewelry which she customarily wore with the Worth ensemble, she paused, fingering the sautoir necklace of pearls and raw emeralds with a pendant of an enameled mermaid.

Simon had given it to her.

Even had she believed in prayer, she was fairly certain that one wasn't supposed to pray for the safety of people who'd killed approximately 27,600 people (she had once calculated, at the rate of two per week over the course of 362 years) in order to prolong his own existence.

It would be dawn in an hour. She hoped he'd found somewhere safe to sleep.

She hoped there had been enough serum in the hypodermic to allay the growing fire of the poison in his veins.

She hoped Aunt Louise would put her tears down to exhaustion and worry about Miranda.

Shortly after first light Mr Travis, their cabin steward, rapped gently at the door of the suite, with the information that order had been restored to the ship. 'As far as we can tell, M'am,' the young man said, bowing a little warily to the still-fuming Aunt Louise, 'the men who were killed were German saboteurs. Some of the emigrants saw them running from the engine rooms after the explosion. Seems that three of them were working for Mr Cochran as detectives. One fellow ran all the way up here, hoping, I think, Cochran would protect him, though of course poor Mr Cochran had nothing whatever to do with any of it. Like his nephew says, even if he *wasn't* a loyal American, why would a man that rich want to take money from the Germans?'

'I trust that the men who perpetrated that *dreadful* outrage,' proclaimed Louise, 'have been placed under lock and key?' She looked at the stout, freckled young man as if he were personally responsible for seeing this done.

Mr Travis looked evasive. 'They will be, of course, M'am.'

Meaning, Lydia guessed, as she followed her aunt from the suite, that there was absolutely no way of telling which members of the mob had actually beaten Mr Kimball unconscious and thrown him from the rail of the Promenade, into the freezing black ocean eighty feet below. Or which men had clubbed Cochran and Barvell to death.

She had wondered how she was to slip away from Aunt
Louise to have a look at Cochran's suite. She was well aware
that the redoubtable dowager had eyes in the back of her head
and would seize her before she had stepped back two feet. But
in the event, it was Aunt Louise who led the way, not to the
gangway down to the dining room and an unwontedly early
breakfast, but around the corner to the Promenade onto which
the rooms of the two American parties opened, only to find
another steward posted outside the Cochran suite's door.

'Well, *really*!' Aunt Louise sounded as indignant as if she'd
had some legitimate business there. With the haughty air of one
who has been insulted by the merest suspicion that she'd try to
view the scene of last night's violence, she turned on her heel
– 'Come along, Lydia . . . and take those *frightful* spectacles
off your face!' and stalked to the stairway. Lydia trailed meekly
at her heels.

Though breakfast service began in First Class at seven, the
white-and-gold dining room was generally deserted until
almost nine. Not this morning, however. Nobody in First Class
had slept anyway – Lydia noted several people clothed in their
dinner costumes of last night – and at the first moment of their
liberation from their staterooms, they had swarmed to the source
of coffee, muffins, and minced chicken on toast.

And not, Lydia reflected uneasily, simply to discuss the murder
of two First Class passengers and three of Cochran's detectives
(whom nobody in First Class had liked). Though there was far
more conversation going on than she had ever heard in that room
on the voyage, it was hushed, like the growling of the sea on
rocks. 'Subs,' she heard as she passed among the tables in Louise's
wake. 'Spies . . . dead in the water . . .'

Dead indeed . . .

She waited for the inevitable moment when Aunt Louise
was stopped by Mrs Tilcott, murmured, 'Excuse me a moment'
and was gone before her aunt could turn around and tell her
not to be ridiculous. She put on her glasses as she went.

'Mrs Asher!' John Palfrey sprang to his feet as she approached
his table. His face was pale and haggard, his eyes wide as he
caught her hands. 'Thank God you're well! You didn't get caught
up in any of that ruckus last night, did you?'

Lydia shook her head, not feeling up to the invention of a story she would, she suspected, be hard put to remember once she'd had some sleep. 'But I saw Colonel Simon on the boat deck,' she fibbed, and the young man's wide shoulders relaxed.

'Thank goodness.' He drew her down to a vacant seat at his table, gripped her hand and lowered his voice. 'I was afraid – I don't know what I feared. When he didn't show up . . . And then there was that explosion, and the riot below decks. What happened? I can't believe Mr Cochran was mixed up in sabotage for the Germans!'

'Do you know—' Lydia began, and her words were cut off by the silvery chime of a water glass being tapped at the captain's table. Turning, she saw first, to her astonishment, Mrs Cochran, clothed in black and veiled as became a widow (*she must have gotten the weeds from Mrs Tilcott or one of the other widows in First*), sitting at the captain's side (with young Mr Oliver Cochran on her other side, holding her hand). Second, she noticed Aunt Louise looking sharply all around for her; and third, Captain Winstanley standing up at his place and signaling for attention. He looked absolutely exhausted but his smile was as charming, and his voice as firm, as ever. *Part of the qualifications for Captain, I suppose . . .*

'Ladies and gentlemen,' he said. 'First and foremost, I want to thank you all for your patience, good sense, and cooperation in the events of last night.'

According to Ellen, Mr Bowdoin and a number of other First Class passengers had shown none of these attributes, but Lydia forbore to say so.

'As I suppose all of you know, there was an act of sabotage perpetrated on board last night. A small bomb was set off by German agents in the shaft tunnel aft of the ship's engine room at shortly after midnight. The hull was not damaged – I repeat, there was *no* damage to the hull of the ship. We are in *no* danger of sinking.'

'Unless the Jerries come along and torpedo us,' muttered the industrialist, Tyler, on Palfrey's other side. 'We're sitting ducks . . .'

'The rioting below decks,' the captain continued, 'was triggered by the saboteurs being sighted fleeing from the scene of the crime. Three of these men were killed—'

'Serve 'em right,' said Mr Allen, across the table, and Mrs Allen nudged him sharply.

'—but tragically, one of them – whose "cover" was being in the employ of Mr Spenser Cochran, of Chicago – fled back to Mr Cochran's suite, hoping to hide there. The rioters pursued him, killed him, and in an act of outrage and hysteria, also, tragically, killed both Mr Cochran and his personal physician, Dr Louis Barvell.'

'What the hell did he expect,' groused Mr Tyler, momentarily drowning out the captain's graceful words to Mrs Cochran, 'if he goes around hiring kraut spies?'

Someone at one of the tables closer to the captain asked him a question, and Captain Winstanley said, as if the matter were well in hand, 'Every effort is being made to repair the ship's wireless and to summon assistance as quickly as possible. The S.S. *Northumbria* and the HMS *Ruritania* were last recorded as being only a few days behind us. Flares will be launched beginning at dusk this evening—'

'What, so the Jerry subs can find us quicker?' called out someone, and a female voice chimed sharply, 'Carlton, *hush!*'

Someone had asked another question: 'So far as we know, the failure of the ship's wireless was entirely coincidental and had nothing to do with the sabotage, though that, too, is under investigation. And to address the concerns that I'm sure all of you are feeling—'

The captain raised his voice slightly, and the growling murmur of every sentiment from 'letting murderers get away' to 'what if there's more of 'em?' simmered to stillness again.

'Watchers are on duty fore and aft,' Winstanley continued, 'with the best visual equipment on board the ship. Lifeboats are prepared and ready, and though the danger is slim, you are all urged to keep your life jackets on hand. Should an emergency occur in the next forty-eight hours – before relief ships can arrive – obey all orders given you by officers and crew, immediately and without question. They are given for your protection. If an incident does occur' – he couldn't seem to bring himself to say, *If we get torpedoed* – 'report to the boat deck at once.

Do not attempt to return to your cabins for any reason. The officers and crew are trained professionals. If everyone keeps their heads and does as they're told, all should be well no matter what happens.'

Nor, apparently, could he say in so many words, *We should all survive*. Or, *Most of us should survive*. Or, *Very few of you will drown* . . .

'I won't be quiet,' sobbed Mrs Bowdoin at the next table, echoing everyone's thoughts. 'All well for him to go on about all being well, but a torpedo could be heading for us, *right this very second* . . .'

Miranda. Lydia's stomach lurched at the thought of the child she'd left sleeping – deeply content – on her bed, small hands curled possessively around Mrs Marigold's stout silk waist.

Am I really going to go to the bottom without ever seeing Jamie again?

She realized she was trembling all over, but shook her head at Captain Palfrey's offers of coffee or tea. 'Take me back to my stateroom, if you would,' she said, tightening her hand over his. She really should, she knew, go speak to Mrs Cochran (*and say what? Can I go in and search your husband's effects?*), or try to sort out the chemicals she'd pinched from Barvell, or go below decks in search of Mr Heller . . .

But all she wanted, now, was to be beside her daughter. Because, as Mrs Bowdoin had said, a torpedo could be heading for them, *right that very second* . . .

She knew she was so tired that things seemed distorted, and that she was incapable of thinking clearly. But as Palfrey led her up the steps of the gangway to the private Promenade, she could see the watchmen standing, back to back, in the little white crow's-nest, and she shuddered at the thoughts their vigil brought to her. The sea lay vast all around them, under a sky now roofed with gray cloud. Nothing – no land – not the slightest possibility that anyone would know what happened to them.

She couldn't imagine how so slender a thing as a periscope would be visible in it, even from up there.

One of the men moved, scanning the surface of the churning ocean, and the daylight winked palely in the lenses of his glass.

TWENTY-SIX

L ydia dreamed, and dreaming, with Miranda in her arms, it was as if she sat in some dark place that stank of rats and wet filth. A place that shivered, rhythmically, with the soft repeated clinking of monstrous chains. Water lapped below, and she could see Simon, lying incongruously in a hammock, slung a few feet above the unseen surface of black deeps, profoundly asleep.

He looked like a dying man, a man long dead; a scarred skull face half concealed by the spiderweb tangle of his colorless hair. He shuddered in his sleep, and cried out, as the poison ate his bones. Once she thought he said her name.

In her dream she saw the ship's makeshift morgue, bodies laid out now not only on the tables, but on the floor between them, their faces covered with a rime of frost. Lovely Pavlina Jancu. Little Luzia Pescariu. Sturdy dark-haired Kemal Adamic, with a folded packet of Koranic verse lying on his breast. Pilgrims who would never reach the promised land. They'd all been moved to the same table, so that Mr Cochran and Mr Barvell could each have a private resting place. *I should go in and search their pockets,* she thought in her dream, *in case Barvell carried his notes around with him.*

If the ship is torpedoed, none of this will matter at all.

Vodusek, Slavik, and two of Mr Cochran's detectives lay on the floor along one wall. Even in the absolute darkness of the refrigerator room, she could see the horrible wounds on their bodies, faces, heads. Vodusek's throat had been cut and his skull crushed. She wondered if *Pan* Marek had done that.

For a fleeting moment, she found herself in a tiny stateroom, stuffy and eerily silent with the stillness of the engines. Mr Goldhirsch lay on his bunk, Yakov, Rivkah, and his portmanteau full of gold and credit papers all wrapped in his long arms. His face was absolutely expressionless but his lips moved in his long gray beard, repeating the name of God, over and over, while tears streamed from his open eyes. Weirdly, Lydia had a blinking glimpse of the boy – nineteen years old and almost his grandfather's tall, gawky double, but with a gentler mouth – climbing the front steps of an ivy-covered college building somewhere in America. *Somewhere in the future.* Then a lovely, bespectacled young woman who had to be Rivkah, studying something – a chemistry text? – in some well-furnished library. The sight of them, safe and protected in that new land, that new time, made her want to cry.

She saw Jamie, unshaven, shockingly thin, haggard with fatigue and sleeplessness, lying on the floor in some dark place. He was in uniform, covered with a coarse blanket and a German officer's coat. A quenched lantern stood close to his hand, his hand wrapped, round and round, with silver chain; she wondered where he was. She tried to call out to him, to tell him she was all right, Miranda was all right – to tell him that she loved him – but could not wake herself to do so.

I'm sorry. Jamie, I'm sorry . . .

But he had wired her. *There is nothing to forgive.*

Then she was below the sea. Like a mermaid in green-gray dimness she could see the submarine, the froth of bubbles around its lean flanks and streaming back where its periscope cleaved the surface over her head.

The water carried the voices of the men to her, muffled but strangely clear. She could smell the stale, filthy air inside the vessel, exactly as Heller had described it to her. Dirty clothes, piss in the bilges, the stink of men's unwashed bodies. Like the Front. *For them – as it had been for Heller – that* is *the Front. The place where the War is fought.* For a moment, too, she smelled – felt through her skin, itched in her bones – the other things Heller had told her, about being underwater, all those weeks. Living on top of one another like pigs in a sty. Constant fear. Mental cloudiness, when the fumes that leaked from the engines grew too thick. Hatred and disgust with the tiniest mannerisms of one's shipmates, and the vigilance that ground one to exhaustion. Dreams of home shredded away by the relentless demands of simply getting through each day.

She heard the captain's voice saying something about tonnage. About Americans.

About *Stadt aus Gold.*
Heute Abend.
Tonight.

The voices of Ellen, Mrs Frush, and Aunt Louise arguing woke her. 'The child needs to go out onto the deck for some fresh air, and then back down to her nursery for some lunch. This is no place for a little girl.'

Miranda, rumpled and still in her nightdress, looked up warily from her paper dolls, spread out over the foot of the bed. Lydia sat up and said, 'You're quite right, Mrs Frush.' She groped for her glasses on the small table beside her. 'Would you please go down to the nursery and fetch up clean clothes for Miranda? And Ellen, could you draw her a bath up here? In view of the . . . *situation* . . . I think I'd rather have my daughter up here, closer to the boat deck, until we're rescued.'

'If by *situation* you mean torpedoes,' declared Aunt Louise – Miranda turned her head sharply at the word – 'it's a ridiculous notion, and Captain Winstanley is an idiot for getting the passengers riled up with his *constant* harping on the subject. I shouldn't wonder if the hysteria among the peasants in Third Class could be traced back to *his* unfounded terrors.'

'Be that as it may –' Lydia suspected that what her aunt really wanted was an argument, and kept her voice cheerfully level, pretending she was addressing some infuriated supply sergeant on the subject of bandages – 'I should like to keep Miranda up here until we're relieved.' She repeated this statement twice more, in the identical words, in reply to her aunt's contention that Miranda would actually be much happier in her nursery on C Deck with Mrs Frush, and that the Promenade Suite was no place for a child.

Not trusting her aunt as far as she could throw the parlor piano, Lydia then assisted Ellen to bathe Miranda and dress her in the neat white frock Mrs Frush fetched up, and took her along – with Ellen in tow – to the infirmary, to call on Dr Liggatt.

'Lord God, woman, what happened down there?' The Virginian turned haggard eyes on Lydia as she slipped to the front of the line outside the infirmary door and peeked around the door frame. 'And what in God's name were you doing down on F Deck in the first place – which is where at least three of the people I've seen this morning say you were. Thank you, Mrs Roberts,' he added, to a stout young woman with an apron pinned over her fashionable pink walking suit, 'if you could put a dressing on this one –' he'd just finished stitching up a swarthy little man's split forehead – 'and— Lordy!' This when Lydia slipped her blouse down from her shoulder to show the makeshift dressing. 'You been to the wars, M'am, and no mistake! You should have come in earlier with that! Let me have a look . . .

'They're saying –' he went on as hc threaded up a needle, once he'd made certain the wound was clean – 'near as I can make out, that one of the Third Class casualties was the murderer all along.'

'He was,' affirmed Lydia. She had turned down the surgeon's offer of morphine ('I appreciate that, M'am, if it's really all right with you. We're short on it now and God knows how much we may need of it later') but had accepted a few swallows of brandy, and as she spoke, kept her eyes resolutely on the corner of the wall just beyond his shoulder.

'That's what I was doing down there. I'd found out that one of the men had been stealing candy, and remembered the smell of chocolate on Luzia Pescariu's hands, and of peppermint on Kemal Adamic's lips. I told Mr Heller this and he and I rushed to the man's room, and found a girl tied up in a locker nearby it, where we'd seen him Friday. It's a long story. I promise I'll tell you all about it—'

'You better report it to the captain, if you haven't, M'am.' He applied a fresh dressing, and rubbed his eyes. He had, Lydia guessed, not been to bed at all. The men and women still waiting to be seen were the cuts-and-bruises end of the night's casualties. Everybody really badly hurt would have been seen to while she herself had been trapped in Aunt Louise's suite in the small hours.

'I'll do that.' Lydia was aware that she should already have done so. 'Were many badly hurt?'

'How badly is badly? Seven men dead . . . four concussions, eight broken arms and two broken collarbones – not to speak of yourself. No, you sit back for a minute . . .' He pressed another small glass of watered brandy – part of his private stock – into her hand. 'Though what any of it had to do with those men planting a pipe bomb in the shaft tunnel—'

'Nothing, I shouldn't think.' Lydia sipped cautiously. 'Did anyone go through their pockets? The . . . the dead men, I mean. Or through the quarters of Mr Kimball and the other detectives? What happened to the other detectives, by the way? Mr Cochran had five . . .'

'Boland and Jukes are locked in the ship's brig.' Liggatt turned away, and rinsed his hands in a small basin of permanganate of potash. 'Captain Winstanley's going to turn them over to the authorities the minute we reach port. The captain inventoried the possessions of the deceased – Mrs Cochran and that secretary of Cochran's are threatening a lawsuit against the American Line, for not handing Cochran's watch and hankie over to them – and secured them in the safe in his own quarters.'

Drat it! 'Nothing connected with sabotage or Germans, I trust?' She made her voice dry and a little exasperated at the turn of events, and hoped it didn't sound flippant.

To her relief, Liggatt grinned tiredly and shook his head. 'String and matches and about twenty-five cents – which I'll swear was change he found lying on the deck! Not to speak ill of the dead, you understand. Barvell had a flask of whiskey, and some suitcase keys. But it was strange: both of them wore crucifixes around their necks – Catholic rosaries.'

Lydia murmured, 'How very strange.'

'I reckon you've heard – we all have! – Cochran go on about papists, as if they were South Sea cannibals or something. And Cochran was transporting *something* in this huge trunk – it had triple locks on it, and they'd put another padlock on the suite door. But the trunk itself was empty, as far as we can tell – the mob literally tore it to bits. It was too big to account for that laboratory set-up Barvell had in his stateroom, and besides, *that* trunk was also in Barvell's room. It's a fishy set-up,' he concluded, helping Lydia to her feet. 'A fishy set-up whichever way you look at it. *Something* was sure going on, but I'm blessed if I can think of what. You sure you're all right?'

Lydia nodded, and stepped aside as the stout Mrs Roberts escorted a half-grown boy in, gingerly clutching a swollen hand.

'And of course poor Mrs Cochran knows nothing about it. I gather she and her husband hadn't lived as man and wife in years, for all those diamonds he gave her. There'll be an inquest when we reach port. *If* we reach port.'

If indeed, thought Lydia, returning to the corridor where Ellen waited with Miranda (and Mrs Marigold – 'Mrs Marigold wanted to come because she's afraid Mrs Frush is going to take and lock her up in the nursery.').

On their way back to the Promenade deck they encountered, to Lydia's surprise, Heller, discreetly escorted by young Mr Travis. 'They've had everybody on board who knows anything about wireless up into the Marconi room this morning,' the German explained, when Lydia fell into step with them. 'I was assistant to the wireless man, on the . . .' He visibly bit back the word, 'submarine'. 'Once the regular Marconi operator tried to repair the apparatus, it became clear that not only had the wires been disconnected, the equipment itself had been damaged, and the store of spare parts rifled. The Marconi room itself is not constantly manned, you know – a stupid thing, in time of war. Anyone could have broken in, if they had a decent set of picklocks. In view of the sabotage to the propeller shafts—'

'Have they searched Mr Cochran's rooms?'

Heller's pale brows dove down. 'Cochran?'

Mr Travis gasped – he evidently knew enough German to follow the conversation. 'Mrs Asher, surely you aren't suggesting—'

'I'm suggesting,' said Lydia slowly, 'that if Mr Kimball was being paid to sabotage the engines –' *and we're not going to go into* who *was paying him* – 'he may well have hidden the spare parts somewhere in Mr Cochran's suite, while his employer was at dinner some evening. I mean –' she widened her eyes innocently – 'who would *dare* search Mr Cochran's suite?'

Heller shot her a sidelong look, but the steward appeared thunderstruck. In English, he exclaimed, 'By God, Mrs Asher, you may be right! M. Heller –' switching to German – 'if I can trust you to get yourself back to Third Class . . . The captain needs to be told this right away. Mrs Asher—'

Heller bowed to the steward. 'You can indeed trust me,' he said, a little sardonically, 'to retire to Third Class where I belong.'

'Er – thank you.' The steward looked awkward, as if aware of how gauche that had sounded. Lydia didn't blame him – he didn't look as if he'd had any sleep either, and dealing with Aunt Louise certainly couldn't have helped. 'Your help has been enormously appreciated. Mrs Asher, if you'll come with me . . .'

Captain Winstanley – who didn't look as if he'd had any sleep either – sent at once for the chief radioman and the quartermaster. Lydia accompanied them to Cochran's suite. But even as the captain unlocked the door, Oliver Cochran – who had been next door in conference with Mr Tilcott – strode up and demanded to know a) who had made such an accusation against his uncle and b) why he, or his aunt, as his uncle's co-heirs, had not been consulted.

'I wasn't aware that passengers had anything to say concerning the scene of a crime on board a vessel in international waters,' said the captain drily. Despite the bruises of sleeplessness under his eyes, he had changed into a fresh uniform (*how many of them does he have? When did he take the time to do that?*) and had trimmed and laundered his snowy beard. (*Does he have a valet?*)

Young Mr Cochran, as if aware of the moral advantage of looking completely *point-de-vice,* had clearly done the same: clean shirt, tie tied, and not an atom of stubble on his freshly-barbered chin. 'As my uncle's heir I have the right to make sure that his name isn't slandered by accusations of complicity in treason—'

How did you know there was a question about his complicity in Kimball's sabotage? Lydia had the good sense not to say – there being no point in throwing oil on what promised to be a roaring blaze. The captain having already unlocked the door (the silver padlock and its hasps had all disappeared), she slipped inside even as Oliver Cochran dispatched Tilcott's butler to search for Mr Hipray, the Cochran lawyer.

She might, Lydia reflected bitterly as she flicked on the lights of the inner rooms, have saved herself the trouble. Barvell's laboratory had been well and truly sacked. Not only had Don Simon's coffin been reduced to matchwood, but every phial and beaker in the laboratory had been smashed, the hypodermic case and all its ampoules trampled deliberately under heavy boots. The stink of blood and spilled chemicals took her by the throat, and the fouled carpet crunched underfoot with broken glass as she searched every drawer and cabinet for notes, formulae, anything that might help her. With a glance over her shoulder at the door, she produced a folding penknife from her pocket and quickly slit the lining of the luggage in the closet. (*Who'll notice, at this point?*) Nothing. Nothing under the mattresses, or inside the pillowslips, of the bed.

('—require you to sign an affidavit to that effect,' she heard a man's voice saying outside, and Winstanley's deeper tones retorting, 'You can go to hell! As captain of this vessel I have absolute authority—')

Nothing in Cochran's room – or luggage – or the pockets of any of his clothing – or under the carpet. As she searched she remembered the old man's seamed, foxy face, and recalled what Heller had told her about the men he'd casually ordered shot by his strike breakers.

Yet she found herself wondering which of those splotches of blood on the carpet were his, and how long it had taken for the enraged men of Third Class to club him to death. There was blood spattered on the walls, too, and something white stuck in the blood on the floor that turned out to be two broken teeth.

He would have enslaved Simon and used him as a supernatural assassin.

She still couldn't look at the teeth.

His sabotage – purely to give himself time to find another vampire to enslave – has immobilized every person on this ship directly in the path of a German submarine.

Her dream returned to her, the gray-green dimness underwater, the way the bubbles curled along the submarine's sides. The voices of the captain and his officers, the stink of the air within . . .

Heute Abend. Tonight.

Where did that vision come from?

Heller told me . . .

When she slipped out of the suite again, the group on the Promenade had been augmented by Mr Hipray, stout and slightly greasy-looking with hair that curled thickly around a bald spot the size of a pancake, and two deck stewards. '—putting yourself and your company severely in the wrong,' young Mr Cochran was saying. 'I assure you, I will have no hesitation in bringing suit against both the American Shipping Line and against you, personally, for wrongful sequestration of a passenger's goods—'

'There is no proof as yet that those *are* your goods,' Winstanley retorted, 'unless you have a copy of your uncle's will and proof that it was in fact his most recent testament. Until the reading, and probate, of such a will, you are putting *your*self in danger of prosecution for impeding the conduct of a murder investigation, and, depending on what we find, as accessory after the fact to sabotage and quite possibly to treason as well—'

Quietly, Lydia crossed the Promenade to where Ellen and Miranda (and Mrs Marigold) waited for her at the head of the steps. She took her daughter's hand, said quietly, 'Thank you, Ellen. I'll let you go now – would you like to go down to the lower promenade, sweetheart? Where it's a little quieter?'

Miranda nodded. She looked pale and a bit overwhelmed. Together they descended the steps. As they did so, Miranda glanced back and above them, to where two watchers still stood on the lookout, scanning the uneasy sea.

Lydia's heart pounded hard. Those first seconds after the explosion returned to her, her own sickened terror at being caught five decks down and knowing there was no way she could have made it to a gangway, had water begun to pour in through a torpedo hole in the hull.

Tonight, she thought.

She knew the dream hadn't been a dream.

'Will Simon be all right?' Miranda asked.

Lydia stopped in her tracks. Around them on the silent – but oddly crowded – First Class Promenade, men and women were looking out to sea, or sitting, some of them wearing cork-and-canvas lifejackets, bundled in blankets or fur coats, on their deckchairs, unwilling to be caught indoors even in these upper cabins that had easy access to the boat deck. A few children played, and their mothers watched them anxiously. She heard Mrs Bowdoin call out, 'No, sugar, stay here where Mama can see you . . .'

Carefully, Lydia asked, 'Where have you met Simon?'
Miranda thought about it. Then she said, 'He's your friend.'
'Yes,' said Lydia. 'Yes, he is.' She felt a curious stillness
inside, hearing her daughter speak his name. The man who had
saved her life, the man she had always hoped she could keep
away from her. *How can I tell her what he is? What he does?*
How can I make her understand how I can care for such a man?

The little girl's frown deepened. 'I met him in the garden,'
she said slowly. 'But I knew who he was.'

She'd only been two and a half when Simon had gotten her
away from the vampire Damien Zahorec.[2] *Surely she doesn't*
remember. Yet she knew, too, how the very old vampires could
reach into the minds of those whose eyes they met. Could, in
many cases, whisper to their dreams, as she had seen Simon
feed and manipulate the dreams of those he wished to dominate
– sometimes, apparently, without even meeting them.

Only from knowing something about them. From having
some link.

Jamie's face came back to her, visible even in the pitch-black
of . . . *of where? Prison? Hideout? Tomb?*

Was the garden Miranda spoke of really the garden behind
the house on Holywell Street? Or some bower in her dreams,
where bees made bargains with snails about which flowers
belonged to whom, and mice learned French from moles?

'Did he speak to you?' asked Lydia.

'One time. When you went away to be in the war, he came
and told me he'd take care of you and make sure you didn't
get hurt.'

Lydia's throat closed and she had to look away. The wind
had picked up, throwing cold white spume from the crests of
the waves.

Beside her, Miranda went on, 'I told him you could take
care of yourself, and he said, even the Queen of the Amazons
needed somebody to guard her back. Ellen read me about the
Queen of the Amazons,' she added. 'Mrs Marigold was scared,
but I wasn't.'

And then, more quietly, 'Is Simon sick?'

[2] See *The Kindred of Darkness*

'He is,' said Lydia. She wondered where he was now. A
hammock in the chain locker? A corner of a coal bunker?
What happens when they torpedo the ship?

She could feel they were coming. Plowing through the gray
water, long curls of bubbles streaming back from those lean
gray steel sides.

'Is he going to die?'

He is dead already, she thought, her eyes still on the freezing
blue-black ocean. *He has been dead for three hundred years.
And if the ship is torpedoed and goes down, he will be trapped
in her bowels, conscious, freezing, and in agony at the bottom
of the sea, until the poison destroys him . . .*

Heller, she thought. *He looked into Heller's eyes last night,
in the locker. What I saw beneath the sea was part of Heller's
thoughts. The smell, the voices, the fear . . .*

Simon knows what Heller knows . . .

Her eyes widened, shocked, shaken to her marrow, and she
stepped to the rail, to look at the gray churning of the sky.

Impatient at the uncommunicative clouds, she consulted her
watch.

Four o'clock. *No wonder I have a headache, I didn't have
breakfast or lunch.*

She looked out at the sea again.

Three hours til darkness. Eight until midnight. If we live til then.

TWENTY-SEVEN

'**W**ait here for me.' Lydia glanced up the fore gangway,
where the grilled doors had been closed with the
approach of twilight. A deck steward had been
assigned to stand watch, given the imminent peril of torpedoing
– more terrible, with the coming of darkness. Down here in the
Third Class areas, the silence was even more eerie than it had
been up on the First Class Promenade, for in her comings and
goings in these lower quarters Lydia had grown used to the
throb of the engines, the vibration of the decking underfoot.

Without the ship's heartbeat, it became hideously obvious what the *City of Gold* had become.

A metal coffin, dangling above an abyss.

Four hours . . .

'I don't know how long I'll be. I – I have to find someone, someone you need to speak to . . .'

Heller frowned into her eyes, his own pale in the electric gloom. She'd found him – after a hasty meal of tea and biscuits in the Willow Grove, since she suspected she might not get any dinner either – in the midst of a meeting in the Third Class dining room, a frightened conference among the emigrants as to what could be expected of the police when – if – they reached New York.

The German had been preoccupied, patient as he'd helped organize and frame everybody's stories to make the riot appear as if it had entirely concerned outrage at an act of sabotage. Mention of a vampire was to be entirely avoided. One might perhaps obtain clemency – or at least a degree of sympathy – for killing saboteurs in German pay. 'If any man says "vampire",' he had said – and had waited for this to be translated into six different languages, 'the pigs will say, "Hah! Superstitious immigrants who do murder from stupidity! Send them back where they come from!"'

But alone now in the frightful silence near the stairway, Lydia saw his eyes shift.

'Is it the man who was with you last night?' he asked quietly. 'The man in evening dress?'

She said, 'Yes.'

He took a deep breath. 'Who is he? *What* is he?'

And, when Lydia did not answer, he went on, almost desperately, 'There is no such thing as a vampire. You know this, Comrade. Only those human ghouls who do not care about the men who die of black lung in their mines, the children who lose their fingers and hands in their factory machines. The women who burn up in their sweatshop fires because they lock all the doors to prevent them from sneaking out for some air. *Those* are the vampires. *Those* are the blood drinkers.'

Lydia said softly, 'Yes.'

'Those who declare war because they want each other's colonies, each other's oil wells, each other's coal mines and farmland and trade. Those who lie to poor men, untaught men, and tell them the poor and untaught men on the other side are the true enemy and must be killed. Those who hold up pictures of saints, or pictures of monsters, to keep the poor and the untaught from looking about the world for themselves.'

She said again, 'Yes.'

Heller was still looking at her. Trying to convince himself, she knew, that he had not seen what he saw.

She said, 'You were in the German navy. On a submarine.'

'I was, yes.'

'He's going to ask you about it,' she went on, hesitant. 'He is a . . . a mesmerist. A hypnotist. He has psychical powers—'

His face flinched and waved the idea away like a cobweb. 'What, like that imbecile Russian woman keeps talking about? Do you actually believe that, Comrade?'

'I've seen him do things,' said Lydia, 'that can be explained in no other fashion. I have known him for years—'

Heller shook his head, as if trying to recover from a blow. 'This I did not expect of you, Comrade. You are a scientist, you are a woman of strength and sense. Leave that kind of drivel to idiots like Tania – yes, she's a good, kind woman but soaked in superstition as a sponge in brandy. She says precisely that, about that charlatan Izora – because it's what she's been taught to believe. That's how she's been taught the world works. But *you* . . .'

'Then if you don't believe,' said Lydia, 'why are you afraid of him?'

'I'm not afraid of him.' She saw the lie in his eyes. Heard it in the pause – too long – before he came out with the words.

'If you're not afraid of him,' said Lydia, 'will you at least wait here? And speak with him, answer whatever he asks, when I bring him?'

Another pause, also slightly too long. 'I don't like to see him make a fool of you.'

In his voice she heard that it wasn't that.

'As a free woman, Comrade,' smiled Lydia, 'it is I who have the right to make a fool of myself. Will you wait here?'

He folded his arms, and turned grudgingly away. 'Yes.'

Asher heard Augustin stir in the darkness. The whisper of his clothing, the faint squeak of the leather of his boots. Another indication, he reflected, of the man's youth among the Undead. As they aged, they learned silence, or else how to turn the minds of the living away from whatever sound they might make: he was sometimes not entirely sure. He heard the faint, thin clatter of the silver cell's barred door (*he must have pushed at it with his foot*), and then, sullenly, 'Come and let me out, *Anglais*, or it will be the worse for you.'

'I don't have the key,' said Asher.

The young vampire muttered an obscenity. Asher had observed, in the entire long day of dozing in the blackness, that there had never been so much as the whisper of rats.

He knew the vampires feared them. But even the rats, it appeared, feared the mark Szgedny had made on the wall.

'I hope the bitch drinks your blood for a week before she kills you. She'll be here, you know,' Augustin added. 'She'll have guessed we met somehow, or those idiots Roger and Baptiste will blab it all to her when she catches them . . . and fat lot of good it will do them. She'll break their necks and leave them lying in a shell hole for the sunlight to find. Bitch. A whore made for the devil.'

'I can see why the thought of getting a few fledglings of your own and emigrating to Bordeaux sounded like a good plan.'

Augustin cursed at him.

'Or breaking into Barvell's apartment and getting whatever notes he had, on how to subdue even a master vampire to one's will. How was it done, by the way? Drugs? Something that weakens the powers of the mind?'

'If only. *Tchah*! It is pain,' said Augustin. 'Simple pain. That's what I would have loved to see – that whore Elysée spasming and screaming on the floor in front of me, while I held the syrette of antidote in my hand.'

Asher lit the lantern, flashed it briefly around the chamber, wondering if this was, in fact, the same place to which Ysidro had brought him to keep him safe from the Paris nest. Or were there more than one such cell, hidden in the tunnels of the ancient mines? Augustin sat in the very center of the silver cage – which indeed had a cot in it, as Asher remembered – and the vampire kept shifting about, as if even the closeness of the silver bars itched his skin and made his muscles twitch.

'Some of the others – Serge, and Hyacinthe, and later a couple of the Venice vampires I met at the Front – talked about books they'd heard of. Books that told of potions, philtres, that vampires can use, to do things like keep awake into the daylight hours. Abraham – one of the Venice vampires – told me recently, these things all work because they use things we can't touch, things that eat at our flesh, silver or garlic or aconite. Without those things, no medicine or chemical or whatever can harm us.'

The vampire shrugged. 'It all made no sense to me. A gentleman studies literature and the arts, not chemistry like an apothecary. I cleared out Barvell's notes but like I said, I couldn't make heads or tails of them. Then the fighting started, and I had other things to think about. I wasn't going to put my life into the hands of any chemist or doctor, who could use the stuff against *me* . . .'

He stood up, and rubbed his hands, like a man who's had some caustic solution sprayed on his skin, some trace of which remains even after washing. The whole left side of his face was a mass of blisters, puffed and swollen. The rest, the tight-stretched skin of a corpse.

'He's going to kill you, you know,' he added. And he smiled, pleased at the thought.

She walked in the corridors along the coal bunkers, and through the silent dimness of the untenanted engine rooms. With the long propeller shafts bent – and according to Dr Liggatt, they hadn't been bent very much by Kimball's pipe bomb – there was no question of running the engines. Only a few of the furnaces were in operation, powering the generators to keep the ship's lights on. The 'black gang' took turns doing the work, and she had seen them, loitering among the Third Class passengers, in the Third Class dining room or the deck wells, as high up in the ship as they were permitted to go.

Nobody, Lydia suspected, was going to sleep below decks tonight.

Simon, she thought, crushed by the stillness, by the waiting for the torpedo to hit. *Oh, Simon, please come* . . .

Please be well enough to come.

Will he die? Miranda had asked.

When he said, 'Mistress,' behind her, in the shadows of the corridor which led to the bulk cargo hold, she turned, and for a moment had the sensation of seeing him in some terrible dream. He looked not only emaciated; pain was stamped on every line of his face, ageing those terrible yellow eyes, drawing at the scars that crossed his cheek and throat. He had acquired from somewhere the clothing of an emigrant, a coarse tweed jacket and patched corduroy trousers, and they hung on his bones like rags on a picket fence. Over these he'd draped a plaid shawl, and in spite of that, and the gloves that covered his hands – and his claws – he shivered, like a man dying of cold.

She took his hands, icy within the gloves, and then put her arms around him.

Are you all right? would have been stupid.

Where have you been hiding? Irrelevant.

I've been worried sick, obvious.

'Have they repaired the wireless?' he asked in his whispery voice, and Lydia shook her head.

'Cochran – and I'm certain it was Cochran who disabled it, or had it disabled – damaged or stole all the spare parts necessary for its repair. Tossed them overside, I should think, lest they be traced back to him. It's what I'd have done. Jamie, too, probably. I had a look through his rooms, while the captain was arguing with Oliver Cochran's lawyers. Captain Winstanley's having distress flares fired off, though half the passengers are saying they'll bring suit against the American Shipping Line for showing a submarine exactly where we are.'

'I can scarce,' remarked the vampire, 'argue with them on that head. And I trust you found nothing of use?'

She shook her head. 'Barvell's room was smashed to atoms.' She thought a corner of his mouth moved at that. Only pain, she reflected, would have wrung any expression of anything, from his habitually expressionless, devastated face.

'I trust also,' he went on, 'that there is no need for me to tell you that when we *are* torpedoed – as I think we must be, and soon – you are to take your daughter and get onto the first lifeboat that offers, without the waste of so much as one moment hunting for me? If it happens in darkness, daylight is bound to come ere a rescuing vessel does, and I must perforce slip off the lifeboat and into the lightless deep. I cannot drown,' he added, seeing the tears that filled her eyes. 'And I expect the poison will kill me in fairly short order. 'Twill be welcome,' he added quietly, 'to end the dreams.'

His hand trembled, very slightly, in hers, a sort of steady vibration that belied the calm of his voice.

'Dreams?'

'Of every soul,' he said, 'that I have killed. All of them. Each of them. Of every life taken, over the years. Every day, since the poison has been in me. Those energies that I absorbed, to feed my own powers of illusion and mastery – each of those lives comes back to me, individually and whole. Names, memories, the faces of those they loved or hated, and what made the love or the hate. Wives, children, sweethearts. Whores they killed, for most of my victims were human swine who well deserved their deaths. Children, sometimes, they raped and then hanged from the rafters of their dead parents' houses in the wars. All those memories. All those deeds. An army of the dead.'

He held out his hand, turning it as if he saw it once more clotted with blood. 'Each by each. As if each life were my life. Each deed the work of my hand. As if I journeyed through Hell kissing the lips of every soul I met.'

Lydia's eyes met his, sickened with pity and stabbed by the involuntary thought, *It is no more than what you deserve*. And she knew that he knew that, too.

She wondered if her own activities, her own love for him, would get her condemned on Judgment Day as Accessory After the Fact. There didn't seem to be anything to say.

'Listen,' she whispered at last. 'At midnight – always supposing we aren't torpedoed before then – will you have your powers of thought again? Of illusion?'

He put the recollection of the dreams aside, with a slight movement of his fingers, and thought for a moment. 'I think so,' he replied after a time. 'If I were to take the whole of the antivenin – about three-quarters of a single dose remains – I think so. I injected myself with about a drachm of the stuff last night, ere I hid, and I feel the pain returning, even now. I know not how long I will last, when 'tis gone.'

When she did not speak he stood for a time, looking across into her eyes. 'Why do you ask me this, Mistress?'

'If you took a full dose, or nearly a full dose,' said Lydia, stumbling a little in her words, 'as much as you have, when midnight comes, could you see – could you feel – the approach of a submarine?'

'I think I scarce need to do so.' His hands tightened slightly over hers. 'We all of us know they are on their way.'

'Could you enter the dreams of its crew?'

He started to reply, then stopped. Something flickered behind the despair in those bruise-circled yellow eyes. Something likc life.

He almost smiled.

'If you . . . if you were able to look into the mind, look into the thoughts, of a man who has been on such a vessel,' she said. 'It's what you did, after all, with poor Captain Palfrey – who is frantic with worry about you, by the way. But you've convinced him that he's been places, and received orders, and seen things, and talked to people that in fact didn't take place at all. And you've done it with others – I've seen you. Others whom you'd never met, never seen, whose dreams you've read at a distance, whose eyes and steps you've turned aside. Whom you were able to call to you, deceive, and use, through their dreams.'

Still he said nothing, but she saw in his face the run of his thought.

'If you knew about what's on a submarine – what it looked like – could you tell these men, these submariners,' she went on, 'while they're sleeping – in their dreams – to rise from their bunks, and smash up their own engines? Or fire off their own torpedoes at nothing?

'I don't think,' she continued, 'that it would take much. The men are exhausted.' Her voice sank. 'You've seen the men at the Front. Even those who aren't wounded, after six weeks in the trenches they'll fall asleep standing up on guard duty. And in a submarine it's worse, because of the engine fumes. You've seen their eyes. They can barely tell sleep from waking as it is. They aren't really there at all.'

He said, very softly, 'Ah.'

And again she knew his thought.

That if he succeeded, they were still two days from port.

Would he be dead in two days? Dead in agony, or driven mad by pain to the extent that he would either hunt – and lay himself open to lynching by the passengers – or throw himself out into the sunlight, to end his anguish in cleansing fire.

A prelude – she saw this shadow in his impassive face – to the unending fires of Hell.

She didn't know. She wondered if he knew how long it would take. If even Barvell had known.

Would you die like that, for me and my child?

She couldn't say it.

For everyone on this ship – Aunt Louise and Princess Natalia and Heller and William the waiter and Mr Goldhirsch and Ariane and Yakov and all those grubby men in the engine crew.

'Would you have the strength to do that?'

He closed his eyes. The trembling in his hands had worsened, and she saw the corner of his mouth twitch with the stab of growing pain. Then he looked at her again, and pressed her hand with cold lips. 'God help me,' he said, as if he meant the words. 'I know not, Mistress.'

And he smiled again, the brief, sweet smile of a living man. 'But I shall certainly enjoy trying.'

TWENTY-EIGHT

Bells were ringing evensong all over Paris when Asher, Graf Szgedny, and Augustin Malette emerged from the crypt of what had been a monastery in the Rue St-Jacques, three blocks from Augustin's small townhouse in Montparnasse. Asher bought a newspaper at an *estaminet* on the nearest corner – the woman behind the counter, after one look from the Graf, didn't seem to notice that Asher was wearing a blood-crusted German Army greatcoat.

There was no report of an American liner having been torpedoed.

Yet . . .

If they're printing the truth. In wartime, who could tell?

He folded the slender sheets – with the rationing of paper he was a little surprised he'd been able to find a paper at all – and stowed them in his pocket.

It's Sunday. They should reach New York within hours.

He shut his eyes for a moment, in silent prayer.

Whatever the Master of Prague had said to the golden-haired vampire, Augustin made no attempt to lose himself as they walked the dank and smelly flagway, and with scarcely a word he let them into the tall, narrow, eighteenth-century house, and led them up the stairs.

The furnishings were cheap within those graceful rooms; like sluttish hand-me-downs worn by some aristocrat impoverished by time. The place had clearly been set up – as vampires often set up the living quarters of their houses – simply to allay the suspicions of the living. Asher could see that the few books in the single bookshelf had never been read, the garish chromo-lithographs on the walls chosen at random. The upholstery of the chairs was faded and dusty.

Augustin had stowed Barvell's notes under the tiles of a small hearth in the bedroom. There were two notebooks, and a thick sheaf of purchase orders and invoices from chemical firms in France, Germany, and the United States. It took most of the night for Asher to go through them, sifting out data about quantities, mixtures, processes, distillations: 'Some of this isn't chemistry,' he remarked at one point, and Szgedny came to look over his shoulder in the dim glow of an oil lamp. Augustin had been dismissed, presumably to hunt.

The vampire's long, crooked finger traced the diagrams written in the notebook's margins. 'This is the Seal of Solomon. And there, the Seal of Air. We are beings of Air and Earth, *Anglus*: this man Barvell seems to have taken the matter into account. You will send this to your lady in America?'

Asher was deeply conscious of the Graf's other hand where it rested on the back of his neck. The flesh was warm, heated by the life of some victim he'd encountered on his way to the old mineshafts. In wartime, soldiers came to Paris, and if they never returned to the trenches when their leave was up, no one would ask why. The tunnels in Paris ran deep.

Asher said, 'Yes.'

'Hath she knowledge of the deeper ways?'

'She doesn't believe a word of it, but she will follow what I send her. In truth I know more about alchemy than about chemistry.'

The old vampire's fangs gleamed in a smile. 'Good, then.' There was a mirror tucked inconspicuously in a corner of the room – even in a vampire's sitting room, there had to be some way for Augustin to ascertain that his tie was straight and his hair properly combed. In it, Asher could see himself, and the shadowy figure behind him. The thing's face, within the leonine frame of gray hair, was nothing human.

'*Are* there vampires in the United States?' he asked.

'Pah.' The Graf dismissed the Western hemisphere and all who dwelt therein. 'What will your lady do, when she receives . . . all of this?' His claws brushed the growing stack of pages at Asher's elbow. 'Enslave poor Simon herself?'

'No. That much I do know. It may not even work, you know,' he added. 'These notes were stolen five years ago. Since that time, Barvell killed at least two fledglings that I know about – maybe more – experimenting . . . maybe with dosage, maybe with concentration, maybe with the rates at which the efficacy of the formula decays over time. Augustin said he felt them die, and that it took days. Lydia may kill Ysidro with the first injection she gives him. Or cripple him, or drive him mad.'

'But her goal is to save him?'

'Her goal is to break Cochran's hold on him,' said Asher quietly. 'And his hold on any other vampire he may acquire, through whatever means. I don't know what she'll need this for.' He straightened his aching shoulder, his aching neck. 'But some information is better than no information, when you're dealing with those who place personal power over the rights and lives of the innocent.'

For the first time, the Graf chuckled. 'Ah, *Anglus*, who among us is innocent?'

Asher was silent after that, correlating dates and invoices, quantities used and methods noted. He wondered if the Seal of Earth, the Seal of Air, would be the same in whatever reference book Lydia would be able to find in New York, as the one that Barvell used. In over thirty years of studying the frontiers where folklore touched the fringes of alchemy, he'd encountered at least four different versions of each.

He wondered if it mattered.

Would Lydia have to pursue Cochran from New York back to his home in Chicago?

Once in America, would she be able to keep the unscrupulous millionaire ignorant of her pursuit of him? Always provided he was still ignorant of her aims, after five days on shipboard?

Through the closed shutters, the thick curtains over the bedroom's windows, the chimes of St-Jacques de Haut Pas struck midnight. *Monday morning.*

The *City of Gold* might already be in port.

Before night came again, he would be on a train back to Venice. On his way to slip across the mountains, change his uniform and his identity papers, and start the long trek to the Polish forests. The five days that in some alternate world he would have spent lying in Lydia's arms, memorizing the shape of her body and the sound of her voice and the peaceful delight of her love, were over now. The two worlds merged . . .

He glanced up at the mirror again. At the thing that stood behind him.

If I see morning.

'The telegraphy office at the embassy should be manned.' He riffled the stack of yellow foolscap with one hand. Even drastically condensed, the encoded notes covered twelve closely written pages. 'I could send it from headquarters . . .'

'Those at the Post Office will also be working,' returned the graf. And, when Asher looked across at him, he had gone to the window, peering out through the louvers at the lightless street. 'I prefer whenever possible to be anonymous. Men would remember a message of this length, at the embassy, and – I should hope – at the headquarters of your Army. I have,' he added, letting the curtain fall back over the shutter, 'the money to pay for such a volume. To General Delivery, in New York?'

'She should be there today. Afterwards,' Asher added, 'you can watch me burn it. This –' he laid his hand on the much larger, unruly pile of notebooks and invoices – 'as well.'

'Afterwards,' said the Graf, 'I will take it. All.'

By concentrating, Asher could see him move, crossing from the window to stand behind his chair once more. Asher still wore three chains of silver around his throat and several more around each wrist, but knew they wouldn't do him a particle of good. Not against the Master of Prague.

'You'll need to find a tame chemist or pharmacist, like Barvell,' he pointed out at length, 'or someone who's done research in organic chemistry, to make sense of them. You may not find that easy, these days.'

'*These days*,' repeated the Graf. 'Time is long, *Anglus*. And men forget.'

Heller was still beside the steps when Lydia and Don Simon turned the corner of the corridor. He was talking to old Mr Goldhirsch, the tall Jew nodding. 'And it is true, good sir,' she heard the old man say in his thickly accented German, 'that the men of Malareka, Vodusek and Slavik, were in the German Army. Malareka lies on the German side of the lines. For your help to me, I will be glad to say to the Americans that the Mareks, and the Adamic family, fled with me to Lemberg, to come here. For surely there will be investigation when we land.'

'We'll get through it, sir.' Heller clapped him on the arm. 'The main thing is for everyone to stick together and tell the same tale.'

When the old man had left, Lydia stepped around the corner, and saw Heller's eyes widen with shock, even at that distance, at the sight of Don Simon.

Oh, dear, he must really look pretty bad . . .

She glanced sidelong at him, and had to admit that now, even after he'd given himself an injection of antivenin and stopped shivering, he did not look like a living man.

He looked like something that hadn't been alive for a very long time.

Simon held out his hand to Heller, and said, in slightly old-fashioned German, 'Herr Heller? I am Don Simon Ysidro.

Madame—' he nodded infinitesimally towards Lydia – 'tells me that you are willing to be of help.' His eyes, like abysses of sulfur and salt, met the German's blue ones, and Heller – suddenly pale under his tan – did not speak.

Could not say, Lydia guessed, *It's ridiculous.*

Or ask, *What are you?*

Only after Don Simon had gone – by then it was nearly ten o'clock – did Heller whisper to Lydia, 'He was not one of the emigrants.'

'No.'

'They said—' He stopped, not able to say, *They said there was a vampire, and was it him?* She felt a little sorry for him, understanding – from all she had seen on the ship, of ignorance and prejudice and the twisted lies told by the power hungry – why he insisted with such doctrinaire rigor on the materialistic view of the world. Jamie had never done so. And Jamie, she knew, had had enough trouble, coming to completely believe that the creatures that had existed in the legends he studied were, in fact, real.

She said, gently, 'You were right, Herr Heller. It was Vodusek who invented the vampire kills, to get rid of a man whose demands for the money he owed him had ruined him. Maybe – probably – to get into his cabin and help himself to the money in that suitcase, in all the confusion. Don Simon had nothing to do with that.' She briefly clasped his hand. 'But there are more things in Heaven and Earth than are dreamt of in your philosophy, Comrade. Or mine.'

And quickly she climbed the stair, her shoulder throbbing, her whole frame shivering at the thought of how long she'd been below decks. Waiting every second to feel the jarring explosion of a torpedo gutting the *City of Gold's* bowels, condemning them all to death.

And I have the right to go up to B Deck whenever I want, she reminded herself. *What about all these women down here who have to wait for the impact, before they can flee?*

It felt like the longest night of Lydia's life.

She spent it on the Promenade, dressed in her warmest clothing, with Miranda at her side wrapped up in a blanket. *If we end up in a lifeboat there won't be room for anything.*

Mrs Marigold, clutched in Miranda's arms, was tucked inside a rabbit-fur muff that Mrs Allen had given her 'to keep her warm'. Icy wind lashed across the lightless ocean; clouds hid the smallest glimmer of moon or stars.

They weren't alone. Aunt Louise, firm in her conviction that no German submarine would dare torpedo an American liner, slept – presumably soundly, and in her flannel nightgown – in her stateroom, after giving Lydia a lecture about the dangers of the cold night air on her child (and telling her to take her glasses off). But Mrs Tilcott was there, swaddled in sable and frothing with indignation at President Wilson for permitting Americans to find themselves in such a predicament. Likewise swathed in fur, her son poodled back and forth between his mother and Lydia with offers of hot cocoa (provided gratis by the Willow Grove) and extra blankets.

Princess Gromyko appeared, bundled in chinchilla and equipped with a deck of cards. 'There is absolutely no reason not to amuse ourselves while waiting for Armageddon, darling.' Her entire suite accompanied her, Ossolinska carrying Monsieur and Madame snugly arrayed in warm little knitted coats. At least five people – with varying degrees of subtlety and discretion – came up from C Deck to Princess Gromyko's card party to ask Madame Izora if they would, in fact, be torpedoed in the night. Lydia, watching over the rail as the distress flares burst in long trails of red or green in the sullen darkness, was never close enough to hear what the seer replied.

Other First Class passengers came up from the lower tier of the Promenade also, including poor Mr Hipray, who spent an uncomfortable night standing guard over the locked and sealed door of his deceased employer's suite. When Lydia took him a cup of cocoa, he unbent enough to tell her that young Mr Cochran was staying with his widowed aunt in her stateroom on the deck below, playing two-handed pinochle and discussing the provisions of her husband's will.

Sometime after midnight, Lydia rendered Miranda over into Ellen's care (Mrs Frush and Prebble were down on the lower First Class Promenade) and went into her stateroom. Deliberately closing her mind to what she was doing, she unlocked her big steamer trunk and removed everything from it, distributing dresses, nightgowns, toiletries, medical journals, gloves, coats, and stockings among her other luggage, and concealing what couldn't be crammed into the other bags, under the bed and in the cupboard. The phials she'd taken from Barvell's workroom she wrapped in a shawl and tucked in one corner of the trunk, and left the trunk itself standing half-open, its key on the nearby nightstand.

Returning to the Promenade, she left not only the door of her bedroom, but the door of the suite unlocked. *Every soul I have killed*, Simon had said, *each life taken, over the years . . .*

How many others will he kill in America?

If he makes it to America.

If any of us make it . . .

When the British liner *Freedonia* appeared on the horizon shortly after nine the following morning, Lydia returned to her stateroom and found the trunk closed and locked. She secured its two outside locks, and pocketed the key. As she had suspected would be the case, First Class passengers were permitted to bring one trunk aboard the *Freedonia*. Relief vessels – Captain Winstanley reassured the assembled First Class passengers in the dining room as the *Freedonia* neared them – would be dispatched from New York the moment First Officer Theale stepped aboard the rescuing vessel and could wireless the American Shipping Line's offices. They should all have the remainder of their luggage (and their servants) within the week.

Monsieur and Madame were included in the rescues taken aboard the *Freedonia*.

The *Freedonia,* it transpired, had been delayed for several hours in her mission of assistance to the stranded *City of Gold* by a detour, to rescue the crew of a surfaced and disabled German submarine, whose captain, second officer, and three able seamen had inexplicably taken a fire axe to their vessel's generator.

Forty-eight hours later, the overcrowded liner put in at New York.

TWENTY-NINE

I t took Lydia most of Wednesday night, the twenty-first of March, to decode Jamie's three long telegrams, after a day of arguments with Aunt Louise that left her exhausted and close to tears of nervous dread. From the *Freedonia* she had exchanged wireless messages with the house agent recommended to her by Mr Tilcott, and Barclay's Bank in New York. With Tilcott's help she had made arrangements to lease – and occupy immediately – a slightly rundown town house on Charles Street in the Greenwich Village district of the city, and had wired instructions back to Mr Mortling on the *City of Gold* that her luggage be sent directly there when the great liner finally landed.

Aunt Louise, who had taken an apartment at the Osborne (furnished) before leaving England, was both scandalized and furious at being deserted. It was all Lydia could do to get free of her, and take a cab – accompanied by Captain Palfrey, Miranda, Ellen, and her trunk – first to General Delivery, then to 13 Charles Street. During the first night she'd spent on the *Freedonia* – at the cost of a hundred-dollar go-away bribe to the two friendly young ladies in Second Class who'd agreed to share their stateroom with her and Miranda – she had obtained from Don Simon the name of a lawyer in New York who could be trusted to hire reliable servants.

The sight of him, when she'd helped him sit up in her trunk, nearly made her weep, from grief and shock and anguish. It was he who brought up the name of the lawyer, in a voice nearly inaudible with exhaustion and pain.

'This isn't the time to be talking of hiring servants!' she'd exclaimed, and he'd made a small gesture with fingers like a dead bird's claws.

'You will need them, Lady.' He could barely get the words out. 'I doubt I shall last until then—'

He was dying, she thought, and then, *he died long ago*. She could only grip his hand. 'Of course you'll last . . .'

He shook his head, and she thought, *he chose this. With small doses of antivenin, he might have made it.*

She made herself sound cheerful. 'You don't mean there *are* vampires in New York?' which brought the smallest touch of a smile to his mouth. She had long suspected that a network existed of living men and women willing to hire out their services – no questions asked – to those who hunted the night.

'I know not.' His scars stood out livid on a face ghastly with agony. Where the sleeves of his shabby shirt were pushed back, she saw that his hands and wrists were bleeding where his claws had torn at his own flesh. 'This Madame Quarterpace . . . recommended to me . . . Master of Venice. We spoke . . . upon a time . . . of America.'

Another wave of agony made him shudder, clinging to her hands.

'. . . made arrangements,' he whispered, in a voice barely louder than the scratch of mice feet on tile, '. . . transfer funds . . . to you.' And his fingers fumbled with the signet ring that lay loose, now, around the bone.

This was the first Lydia had heard, that Don Simon's intricate net of financial trusts and corporations extended to the New World.

'I'll take care of it,' she promised, and gripped his hands. He returned her clasp, and she had to wear gloves the following day, to hide the finger marks where his clutch nearly broke her bones.

When, on the night of the twenty-second, she descended to the dark sub-cellar of the Charles Street house, she felt nearly ill with dread that she would open the trunk to find only dust and bones.

And would that be more merciful? She unlocked the doorway of the crypt (*what on earth did* anyone *store down here?*) and stood for a time, looking at the locked trunk in its center, and fingering the signet ring on her hand.

It was, in fact, what she knew she should do. Every way – *any* way – that she looked at it, Don Simon was a vampire. He had not hunted on the *City of Gold*, not only because he could not conceal how he looked, but because he was well aware that even Third Class passengers were tallied and accounted for. On the *Freedonia*, he had been too far gone even to get about.

Here on land, in a city of three million people – many of them so poor that nobody would bother to investigate their deaths – to restore him to health would be as irresponsible, as reprehensible, as to turn loose a pack of rabid dogs in the streets.

Why do I even think of it? Pani Marek's tears seemed to stain the shoulder of her dress. The cries of poor Mrs Adamic, and Mrs Pescariu, to ring in her ears.

I can't do it. I shouldn't want to.

The fact that he was charming – the fact that she loved him – did not change what he was. Nor what he would do, when he was able once again to deceive the eyes and the minds of his victims.

In her hand she held the hypodermic syringe of the fluid on whose manufacture she had worked throughout the afternoon.

It had taken her all the morning, to visit chemical supply houses and purveyors of scientific instruments, and to look up alchemical symbols in the New York Public Library. Her head buzzed from lack of sleep and from a dozen cups of café noir; every bone in her body seemed to hurt. She felt like Henry Jekyll, like Dr Moreau or Victor Frankenstein, pottering over secret formulae with the certain knowledge that her work would bring evil to the world.

If it works, she thought, with a queer sense of detachment from her true self. *It might not.* She didn't know whether she would be glad, or sorry, if it didn't. The serum had been perfectly straightforward – given the requirements of the alchemical vessels and formulae – but in his very brief note, Jamie had warned her that the notes had been sourced from an early phase of Dr Barvell's work.

And this cold little cylinder of steel and glass, that seemed so heavy in her hand, contained only her first attempt at the serum.

It's been four days since his last dose of the antivenin.

Since he saved the lives of everyone on that ship . . . over three thousand people.

Even if – as she suspected *– he only did it to save Miranda's life, and mine . . .*

I should go back upstairs. She pressed the worn gold of Don Simon's signet ring to her lips. Her shadow, by the wavery glow of the gas light in the stair, stretched into the little crypt and lay over the trunk, then disappeared beyond into the blackness. *Lock this door, have one of the servants* – Mrs Quarterpace had provided butler, housekeeper, cook and maid – *make me some supper, go to bed in that lovely room on the second floor.*

Arrange to have this door, this room, bricked shut tomorrow.

And after another day or two, get Miranda from Princess Gromyko – she had not dared consign her daughter to Aunt Louise's care, knowing how determined her aunt was to bring her, Lydia, to heel – and . . .

And what?

Forget?

Upon the arrival of the *Freedonia*, word had swept the vessel that the Tsar had abdicated, that Russia had become a republic. The Princess Natalia Nikolaievna had shaken her head, as if in exasperation; Lydia had asked her, 'Will you go back?'

'Back?' Her Illustrious Highness had seemed startled at the thought. 'To what? To be ruled by those peasants in the Duma?' And for the first time, true sadness had filled her eyes.

'War or no war, republic or no republic,' she said softly, 'it is gone. The Russia I grew up in. The world that I knew. That my husband knew, and my children – that my mother knew. Things as they were – things as I knew them – loved them . . . they will never be the same. They will never come back. The only way for me to walk is forward.'

Stroll in the park with the princess? Accept invitations from Mrs Tilcott? Help poor Captain Palfrey search New York for Colonel Simon?

Wait to hear from Jamie.

If I ever hear.

She closed her eyes, remembering his voice, the touch of his hand. The first time their eyes had met, and he'd smiled at her. The last time they'd kissed. The man she had loved since her girlhood, the man whose love for her was steady as rock. Not a pale elusive chimera with one foot already in Hell.

At the conclusion of the long transcripts of notes had been a single final communication:

Leaving today. Will see you next year. Forever – J.

Destroy the laboratory upstairs, she thought. *Burn the notes.* Along with the antidote had been what was supposed to be the formula for the poison Barvell and Cochran had given Don Simon after trapping him – given its percentage of silver chloride and aconite, it probably *would* kill a vampire (*or pretty much anyone else,* she reflected) – and the temporary antivenin, the chemical leash that had made him Cochran's slave.

But what, she thought, was the use of that? *To keep him as my slave?*

No. Just . . . *No.*

She closed the door, locked it – double locked it – and went back up the stair.

Halfway up it she turned around, unlocked the door, and entered the vault.

He should have been awake when she opened the trunk, but the wax-white, twisted body didn't move. Only, when she touched his arm, she could feel his muscles rigid and shuddering, as if he were being eaten up from the inside, nerve-thread by nerve-thread, cell by cell. As he had been transformed, she thought, three and a half centuries ago, by the initial contamination which had altered him – nerve-thread by nerve-thread, cell by cell – into vampire flesh to begin with.

Had it hurt like this, then?

There was no real need to seek a vein, since his heart did not beat, but she nevertheless injected the fluid into the carotid artery in his throat.

She sat beside him for nearly an hour, during which even his eyelids did not move. Then, slowly, he went limp, his trembling stopped.

After another hour she got up from the damp stone of the floor, left the vault, and locked the door behind her.

She gave him another injection on the second night. By the hardness of the flesh around the first puncture mark, she could tell that the serum hadn't even dispersed into the tissue. What that meant, she had no idea.

She barely knew how she'd spent the day. She had slept like a dead woman, eaten a little lunch (Mrs Quarterpace had found her an excellent cook – *if the woman works for vampires, why do* they *care what food tastes like?*), and went uptown to the Belcourt, to take Miranda to play in the park. 'Darling, what are you *doing* to yourself?' demanded the princess, when the little girl dashed away to explore the cast-iron bandstand at the end of the Mall. 'You look *ghastly* – don't tell me that handsome Captain Palfrey is that *exigeant . . .*'

And Lydia had shaken her head. 'I'll be all right,' she said. 'But if I can trust you to look after Miranda for another day or two . . .'

'It will be my delight, my sweet! We have already been invited to the birthday party of Elenya Trubetskoy – cousins of mine, dearest, and they have taken an apartment at the Apthorp – and that *tedious* M'sieu Tilcott has telephoned I don't know *how* many times, asking how he might reach you.'

He is dead, she thought now, looking down into the vampire's still face. But she gave him the second injection in any case, and sat beside him.

Two hours later his hand stirred, and when she took it – cold as death – he whispered, 'Mistress?'

'I don't know if this will work,' she said.

Under the black-bruised lids, his eyes moved a little. 'I only want it over,' he murmured. 'I am in Hell, and to Hell I will go for my sins. To be thus forever. But thank you.' And then, after a time, 'Leaving you will be hardest of all.'

She had dreamed of him during the morning just passed – dreamed of searching through a hedge maze, hearing him scream in the distance but unable to come to him. When finally she returned to her room and lay down, she did not sleep again until there was light in the sky. That morning she did not dream at all.

On Friday, the damaged *City of Gold* had been towed into New York Harbor, with its cargo of emigrants – Third Class passengers had not rated transport on the *Freedonia*, though Lydia guessed they had at least had the benefit of the elegant rations of salmon, shrimp and lamb that their economic betters had left behind in the pantries. In the morning, Lydia had Captain Palfrey escort her to City Hall, where she gave her own testimony to the police commissioner and the immigration officials regarding the deaths of Pavlina Jancu, Luzia Pescariu, and Kemal Adamic. 'I think,' she explained, 'that the young people involved must have seen something that could have been connected with the German saboteurs who were on board: Third Class passenger Vodusek, and possibly Mr Slavik as well.'

She gave further opinions concerning the connection of the Third Class murderers with Kimball and his men, being careful to exonerate Spenser Cochran from any suspicion of connection with either the murders or the subsequent planting of a pipe bomb in the ship's engines: 'Believe me, your Honor, I dined with Mr Cochran many times on the voyage and the idea that he would have had anything to do with sabotage is absurd!'

Oliver Cochran and his lawyer, also in the commissioner's office with a file of injunctions and affidavits the size of an unabridged dictionary, looked mollified, and agreed, later in the day, to sell Lydia the entire contents of his uncle's – and Louis Barvell's – libraries.

But the whole of the day – for she was also called to give evidence at the Immigration Offices on Ellis Island in the afternoon – Lydia felt as if someone else were talking through her mouth. She was familiar with the feeling. She'd mastered the arts of appearing interested, intelligent, and businesslike while ready to scream or weep during her London season, and even the spectacle of the Princess Gromyko's reunion with Madame Izora – who had refused to abandon her spirit cabinet and had thus remained on the *City of Gold* – did not lighten her mood. 'Andreas Paulsen' – a.k.a. Georg Heller – had simply vanished, the moment the ship had reached its berth.

When Captain Palfrey began to speak of Colonel Simon in the cab, speculating desperately about where his mysterious employer might be hiding, Lydia could only say in a small, calm voice, 'Please. Can we talk about this tomorrow?'

He'd taken one look at her face, offered to take her for sweets to Delmonico's, and then, at her carefully phrased request, told the motorcab driver to return to Charles Street. 'We'll find him,' he promised, clasping her hand as he guided her to the green-painted door. 'I promise you. You know what he is – he's in hiding, up to something brilliant. He'll get in touch with one or the other of us when he's ready.'

Lydia managed to close the door between them before she wept.

Climbing quickly to her room, she lay down and cried, before falling almost instantly to sleep.

When she descended to the crypt that night, though the door was locked as she had left it, she found the trunk open, and empty.

Don Simon Ysidro was gone.

THIRTY

The troop-train from Lemberg to Brest-Litovsk averaged an hour's travel before it was pulled over, to let trains of supplies or ammunition – or traveling generals – or nothing at all – pass by; sometimes it remained on the siding for three hours or more. Then it chugged on, sometimes for another hour, sometimes for half that time. The cars were unheated and what had been First Class had long ago been taken over by regiments of Ludendorff's Army and the Austrian signal corps, men sleeping in exhaustion on the seats, the floors, in the corridors. There was no coal for the heaters, which, Asher reflected, was just as well. The one in his own compartment was so seriously damaged that he doubted it could be lit without killing everyone in the crammed space from carbon monoxide gas.

But the fug of crowded bodies, of suffocating cigarette smoke and dirty uniforms, did little to pierce the bone-breaking cold and he wondered if this would be his fate: to escape being murdered by a vampire in Paris, only to freeze to death in a train on his way back to the Eastern Front.

He would laugh, he supposed, if he wasn't so tired.

'You are a useful man,' the Graf Szgedny had said to him, on the steps of the Central Telegraph Office at four thirty Monday morning. Cold drizzle soaked through Asher's great-coat – formerly one of Augustin's, since he'd disposed of the German one in the alley behind the golden vampire's apartment block – and chilled him to the marrow. 'One does not waste such servants.'

'I will never be a servant of yours.' Asher was bone-tired, his head aching after hours of writing, concentration, and explanation – again and again – to a succession of telegraphers. Only the fact that it had been the early hours of the morning had prevented him, he was certain, from being lynched by a queue of irate customers, who would have been behind him at any other hour of the day.

At that moment he had scarcely cared whether the Graf killed him or not.

'*Anglus* . . .' The vampire grinned like a wolf. 'I'm certain you swore you would never do Simon's bidding either. Or that of that tedious monster Lionel, who rules London. And you have served both in your turn.'

The soul-stripped eyes held his, like a steel blade cutting into what was left of Asher's own soul. 'You swore no more to be a servant of your king.'

The Graf's hawk-nosed face was shadowed from the electric lights above the telegraph office door by the peaked cap of a French colonel; the dispatch case at his side bulged with Barvell's notes. Asher wondered, tiredly, what use he would or could make of these, in the days after the war ended, if the war ever ended . . .

In the telegraph office he'd glimpsed headlines about the new provisional government in Russia pledging to continue the fight against the Central Powers, and he guessed that both British and American funds were at the back of that decision. At times it seemed to him that all of civilization would be sucked down into the black mud of the Front, to die of typhus, poison gas, and despair.

Szgedny had walked with him to the Gare de l'Est, through the bitter damp of the pre-dawn hours. 'I understand Madame Elysée is back in Paris, and if you're going to be of use to me in the future it won't do to have her find you.' At the station canteen, over watery ersatz coffee and something that was supposed to be soup, Asher had wondered what the war's end would bring to the Undead. Would Szgedny's power extend from Prague over the pulped ruin of Eastern Europe? Would the other vampires – glutted like maggots from years of feeding at the Front – have the power to fight him? Would Augustin indeed take over Bordeaux or find some way to oust Elysée from her rule in Paris?

Would the provisional government of Russia manage to hold itself together in the face of what sounded like some of the most horrendous factional fighting Asher had ever encountered?

Would Germany in fact bring Britain to its knees with starvation? And what would she demand at the peace table?

Or would America come charging in and prolong the fighting, then rule over the blood-soaked shambles that remained?

At quarter past one on Monday afternoon he'd finally gotten on the military train for Venice, and had been traveling – or sitting on sidings – ever since.

At times he pretended to himself – in clouded dreams of exhaustion – that the days in Paris had in fact been spent with Lydia. That they'd eaten at cheap restaurants, drunk bad beer in the cafés of Montparnasse, lain together at the Hotel St-Seurin long into those icy mornings listening to the chimes of Notre Dame. Memories pieced up like a patched garment from other times: that he'd been with her, that he'd waked to see her face, relaxed with sleep, on the pillow beside him. That they'd walked along the Seine, and seen on the barren trees the first dusting of the green of spring.

It made, he reflected – now as he tried to find a more comfortable way to doze sitting up between two smelly, exhausted Austrian privates – absolutely no difference. He was headed back to the black pinewoods of Pripet Marshes, to the men who knew him as Major von Rabewasser. To the men he would betray to their deaths when he received orders to do so.

At least, as far as he could tell, she had arrived in America safe.

Or at least the *City of Gold* hadn't been torpedoed.

That he knew about . . .

He closed his eyes. It would be a year or more before he learned whether she was dead. Whether she'd been able to save

Ysidro. Whether the telegrams had reached her at all, and whether she'd outsmarted Spenser Cochran's scheme.

'James.'

He looked up. Don Simon Ysidro stood in the doorway of the compartment. He was clothed as a railway porter, the compartment was tidy and clean (and empty), and Asher knew this was a dream.

He asked, 'Is Lydia all right?'

The vampire smiled. 'She is well,' he said. He looked as he always did: a young man in his late twenties, long wispy hair, pale as ivory, hanging to his shoulders. Cold yellow eyes like a weary demon's.

He must have survived.

'And yourself?'

'I, also.'

It was Saturday, he recalled. 'Did Lydia get my telegrams?'

'She did. I am more deeply in debt to both of you, than I can ever say.'

'I take it you're free?'

Ysidro inclined his head. 'As you say. Mr Cochran suffered an accident aboardship. Not of my doing,' he added, lifting a white-gloved hand. 'Nor yet of Mistress Asher's. We are safe – all three of us, for her execrable aunt brought Miss Miranda on the voyage as well—'

Asher started up from his seat with such violence that he almost woke himself from his dream.

'All is well.' Ysidro signed him to sit again, and Asher felt his real self, his waking-world self, slide back down into exhausted slumber again. 'We are safe in New York. I know not if I will be able to speak to you like this again.' A slight frown tugged at his brows, and he shook away some thought. 'But since I can still do so tonight, I wished to tell you this.'

He moved as if to step back into the corridor – as if to step back out of the dream – and Asher saw around him a secondary image, of the sleeping soldiers, the filthy compartment, the broken heater, the cold. The future . . .

Asher said, 'Watch over her.'

The vampire inclined his head. 'To the end of my days.'

* * *

Lydia went with the Princess Gromyko to the promised children's party at the Belcourt on Saturday night, and – to Miranda's grateful delight – afterwards brought her daughter home with her to Charles Street. *Home* was how she had already begun to think of the tall, rambling mansion among Greenwich Village's narrow streets. Through the evening, as had also been the case on the day before, the terrible feeling of separateness had persisted, the sense of operating her body, her words, and even her thoughts at a distance, like a puppeteer.

Don Simon is in New York. The thought came back to her, again and again.

He has killed. Probably several times, as ill as he was. As needful of the healing that only another's death can bring a vampire.

I have killed. The blood of those victims is on my hands.

She felt sick with contempt at her own weakness.

I'll need to tell Jamie that. And, one day, Miranda.

When she tucked the little girl into bed – in the night nursery which would, tomorrow, be graced with a young nursemaid from New Orleans whom Mrs Tilcott had recommended in the highest terms – Miranda took her hand and said softly, 'I dreamed about Simon, Mummy.'

Lydia's throat closed. 'Did you?'

'I asked him if he was still sick, and he said, *I will be well.*'

There was a garden behind the house overlooked by a sort of balcony outside the window of Lydia's bedroom. Stepping out onto that balcony, looking down into the well of black fog from which the wet scents of its tangled and overgrown foliage rose like a great, primeval sigh, she heard on that sigh the ghost murmur: *Mistress . . .*

And thought she saw something pale move down below, in the blackness and the fog.

She almost didn't go down. The thought that she had loosed him in New York sickened her. She didn't want to know. But she did, and he was waiting for her at the end of the garden.

He'd acquired evening dress from someplace – which fit him as if it had been tailored for him. His face was as it had been when first she'd seen him, before its flesh had been gashed by the talons of the Master of Constantinople in protecting her life. Before he had been shredded with pain. Before he had whispered to her, *I only want it over . . .*

Remote, and beautiful, and young.

He removed his glove, and held out his hand. Lydia shook her head, closed her fist, knowing that his touch would be warm, as vampires' are, when they have fed. Knowing the warmth had been taken from some other person's life.

Some person of little worth – like Pavlina Jancu, or Kemal Adamic, or all those Protestants he'd killed in his early days. Somebody that no one would trace or avenge. *Knowing their souls to be damned in any case . . .*

Is that part of the illusion that vampires cast, that keeps me from hating him outright for what he is? For what he does?

But when her hand drew away he reached deliberately and clasped her fingers, and his – long and thin and clawed like the Devil's – were cold as ice, as the Devil's are said to be.

Startled, she looked across into his eyes, and his yellow gaze reflected the lights of the house next door. 'I have not fed,' he said quietly, and for a moment he let her see him as he was, scarred and skeletal within the long frame of mist-pale hair.

Then the illusion was back, elegant as a single white orchid.

'In Fourth Street just now I passed a girl, with a basket of mouse traps that she had been selling. I smiled at her, and she returned the smile, seeing nothing amiss. Last night, when I walked about the city making my arrangements for a place to stay, none pointed at me or cried out. The hunger remains,' he added. 'But it is remote, and tinged with . . . distaste. I seem to have come through my illness . . . changed.'

Nerve-thread by nerve-thread, she thought. *Cell by cell.*

'And the Army of the Dead?'

'They are with me still. But they no longer torment me as they did – thus providing the definitive answer, as my confessor would have said, to the question of whether God is merciful or just.' His voice was flippant, but there was a somber stillness in his eyes.

She had no answer to that, or to any thing that he had said. 'What . . . are you, then?' she asked in time.

'I know not. Not what I was.' He shook his head. 'Our James

and his colleagues speak of the Undead as blood-drinking ghosts. Without the hunt – without the kill – what *am* I then? Merely a ghost, like the voices that pipe in old houses, until time and the convenience of a changing world sweep those ruins away? I am still flesh.'

With a fingertip he prodded his arm experimentally. 'I can trick the minds – the perceptions – of strangers, as ever I did. My flesh retains its weakness to silver –' he took the glove from his left hand and held up the two smallest fingers, to show where the colorless flesh had been savagely burned – 'as I ascertained just now in your dining room, ere coming out to the garden. I presume to daylight as well.

'Last night I spoke to James in his dreams, but could not do so tonight. Yet I had no trouble entering the mind of our Captain Palfrey, and convincing him that he'd glimpsed me in a crowd on Fifth Avenue. I expect he will come to you tomorrow, effervescing with the news. Whether this is an effect of distance, or of the poison, or of the new moon for that matter, I know not, nor whether this will alter with time. Nor do I know how long this grace – if grace it be – will last, nor what state will follow it. Nearly every other Undead that I have ever encountered older than myself has been mad.'

He turned his hand over slowly, looking at the burned flesh, the demon claws, the unhealed gashes where he had torn at his own wrists in agony. 'In truth I know not what I am now, Mistress, nor what is native to me.'

His voice was expressionless as ever, a whisper like the stirring of the new-leaved branches in the dark garden, like the far-off occasional conversations heard in the foggy dark of the unknown city around them. But Lydia heard in the bare words the note, not of fear, but of loneliness incalculable; the damned soul cut off not only from God, but from the other damned as well. As if, reaching Hell, he had found its endless bolgias empty and dark.

She answered him, 'You are my friend.'

His cold fingers tightened on hers. 'Friend indeed,' he said softly, 'to have led me to this place.'

'Was it the poison that did this?' she asked. 'Or the combination of the poison and the antivenin? Or the length of time

that it was in your system? If it can free the Undead of the
need to hunt . . .'

'I suspect, rather, 'twould kill them in the process. And few
indeed would even desire to be other than what they are, not
were it given them free and without pain or consequence.

'We toughen as we age, Mistress. Had I been younger among
the Undead, I doubt I would have survived these past five days.
Be assured I would never have undertaken such a process, had
I had any choice in the matter.'

'Do you feel all right?' She recalled what he had said to
Miranda: *I will be well.*

He thought about it. 'Oddly, yes. Disconcerted. But much
the same.' He drew on his gloves again. 'Aware of the change,
but not certain what it means. I tread untrodden ground, Lady.
I think I shall miss the . . . the *intensity* of the kill, yet I am
not sure that I would even be capable of feeling such a thing
now. Certainly I have no desire to risk re-awakening the Army
of the Dead. But as to what I am . . .'

'What do you want to be?'

And he raised her hand, with its signet ring of gold, to his
lips. 'Your friend.'

'Have you a house here in the city?'

'I do. I shall show it to you presently, when I have purchased
furbishings for it, and tea to offer you. When chance occurs I
shall send for my books – ghost or vampire, I remain a child
of darkness in this new world, neither living nor dead, and the
nights promise long. Will you remain?'

'I think so. At least until the war is over – and if the United
States plans to join in, the way everyone was saying on the
voyage that they will, it would be even less safe now to try to
cross back. Jamie—'

She broke off.

''Tis a long way to Russia, Lady,' said the vampire. 'God
only knows what is coming to that unhappy land ere the War
is done. Yet I think, were true grief to come to James, I would
know . . . as, I suspect, would you.'

'I'd like to think so.' Lydia heard the shakiness in her voice,
sighed, and straightened her shoulders, as she had when she'd
boarded the *City of Gold*. Like a woman readying herself to

cross a narrow and railless bridge. From the old-fashioned cobblestones of Charles Street a motorcar honked its horn in the fog. A wisp of conversation passed by the rear wall of the garden, Yiddish or Russian, accompanied by the clatter of a pushcart's wheels and the smell of oysters and steam. Down the street at a cellar club, music drifted forth, American jazz, clear and wailing and sad.

Lydia thought, for the first time, *I'm in New York.*

I'm in America.

For the past ten days she had been so preoccupied, so wretched, and so frightened for her child that she had moved from one action to the next almost automatically. Now all the things she had seen and done and said – the pale spring-green in Central Park, the variegated crowds around City Hall, the startling grandeur of that towering dull-green copper statue in the harbor (only *in America*! reflected Lydia, though Miranda had been enchanted at the sight) – all these seemed to fall into place in her mind.

I'm in America.

And this is my new home. With Miranda asleep upstairs. Safe.

She said, 'We both tread untrodden ground, my friend. Jamie—'
She stopped herself again. *I don't know, nobody knows . . .*

'I think Natalia was right,' she went on slowly, 'in that the world we knew – the world we grew up in . . . Whatever happens, in the War, or after . . . It's gone. It will be a new world there, too. Things the way we knew them will never be the same, and I'm . . . I'm no more sure than you are, about what I'll be, or you'll be, or anything will be, in the time that lies ahead.'

'Who among us is?' Again he raised her hand to his lips, pale-yellow eyes gleaming in the darkness. '*Never* is a long time, Mistress. And *ever* stretches ahead for us all. We need see no more before us than what each day – each night – shall bring. Perhaps the time has come, for me to write my memoirs.'

Then he melted into the fog, and was gone.